Praise for
R.C. Ryan and the McCords

"A popular writer of heartwarming, emotionally involving
romances."   —*Library Journal*

Montana Destiny

"Ryan's amazing genius at creating characters with heart-
felt emotions, wit, and passion is awe-inspiring."
—The Romance Readers Connection

"Sure to entertain. Enjoy."   —*Fresh Fiction*

Montana Legacy
A Cosmopolitan *"Red Hot Read"*

"A captivating start to a new series."   —*BookPage*

"Heart-melting sensuality . . . this engaging story skillfully
refreshes a classic trilogy pattern and sets the stage for the
stories to come."   —*Library Journal*

Also by R.C. Ryan

Wranglers of Wyoming

My Kind of Cowboy
This Cowboy of Mine
Meant to Be My Cowboy

Montana Strong

Cowboy on My Mind
The Cowboy Next Door
Born to Be a Cowboy

The Malloys of Montana

Matt
Luke
A Cowboy's Christmas Eve
(available as an e-novella)
Reed

Copper Creek Cowboys

The Maverick of Copper Creek
The Rebel of Copper Creek
The Legacy of Copper Creek

Wyoming Sky

Quinn
Josh
Jake

The McCords

Montana Glory

MONTANA PROUD

2-in-1 Edition with
Montana Legacy *and*
Montana Destiny

R.C. RYAN

FOREVER

NEW YORK BOSTON

Copyright © 2023 by Ruth Ryan Langan
Montana Legacy copyright © 2010 by Ruth Ryan Langan
Montana Destiny copyright © 2010 by Ruth Ryan Langan
Cover design by Daniela Medina. Cover copyright © 2023 by Hachette Book Group, Inc.

Forever
Hachette Book Group
1290 Avenue of the Americas, New York, NY 10104
read-forever.com
twitter.com/readforeverpub

Montana Legacy and *Montana Destiny* originally published in 2010 by Forever.
First 2-in-1 edition: August 2023

Forever is an imprint of Grand Central Publishing. The Forever name and logo are trademarks of Hachette Book Group, Inc.

The publisher is not responsible for websites (or their content) that are not owned by the publisher.

The Hachette Speakers Bureau provides a wide range of authors for speaking events. To find out more, go to www.hachettespeakersbureau.com or call (866) 376-6591.

Forever books may be purchased in bulk for business, educational, or promotional use. For information, please contact your local bookseller or the Hachette Book Group Special Markets Department at special.markets@hbgusa.com.

ISBN: 9781538742495 (mass market 2-in-1)

Printed in the United States of America

OPM

10 9 8 7 6 5 4 3 2 1

MONTANA LEGACY

To Tommy, Bret, Patrick, Johnny Ryan, and
Ryan Paul—the next generation's band of brothers.

And to my darling Tom,
proud patriarch of the clan.

PROLOGUE

❖

Montana—1988

Last one to circle Treasure Chest Butte is a dirty, rotten skunk." Ten-year-old Jesse McCord urged his horse into a gallop, leaving his cousins, nine-year-old Wyatt and seven-year-old Zane, in his dust.

The three cousins lived with their parents and grandparents in a sprawling, three-story house on their grandfather's ranch, Lost Nugget, which covered thousands of acres of rangeland in Montana. Because of the vast size of their families' holdings and the distance to the nearest town of Gold Fever, the three were homeschooled and spent much of their spare time exploring the hills and rich grassland that formed the perfect backdrop for the thousands of head of cattle that were raised here.

The three were alike in coloring, with dark, curly hair, now slick with sweat, and their grandfather's laughing blue eyes. In town they were often mistaken for brothers, which pleased them enormously. They were, in fact, closer than brothers. Not just blood-related, but best friends. Since birth, they'd done everything together.

"Hey, wait for me." As always, Zane, the youngest, had to scramble to catch up.

By the time he and Wyatt slid from their mounts, Jesse was kneeling beside a fallen log, fishing something from the dirt.

"What'd you find, Jesse?" Wyatt looped the reins of his horse around a nearby sapling and crept closer to drop down beside his cousin. Zane mimicked his older cousin's actions.

High above them, the peaks of Treasure Chest Mountain glistened gold in the late summer sunlight.

Jesse held up a dull bronze-veined stone the size of his fist. "Looks like a nugget."

"Gold?" The two boys watched with rapt attention as Jesse turned it this way and that, grinning each time it caught and reflected the sun.

"Could be. Or it could be fool's gold." He rubbed it on his sleeve, hoping to clean away some of the dirt. "Coot's got a shelfful of fool's gold."

"Is it heavy enough to be real gold?" Wyatt held out his hand and Jesse dropped the stone into his palm. After testing it, he grinned. "I don't know what real gold ought to feel like."

Jesse shrugged. "Me neither."

"Let me see." Zane closed his hand around the nugget and felt the heat of the sun-warmed earth radiating from it. He looked up. "You think it's part of the lost treasure Grandpa Coot's been searching for his whole life?"

The three cousins exchanged eager glances.

Everyone in the McCord family knew the story of their

ancestor Jasper McCord, and the sack of gold nuggets he and his son Nathaniel had found at Grasshopper Creek in 1862, which was later stolen by another prospector, Grizzly Markham. Though Markham was found dead scant weeks later, the sack of nuggets was never found, and rumor had it that he'd buried the treasure somewhere nearby after slitting Jasper's throat. That was how Treasure Chest Mountain, the town of Gold Fever, and even the McCord ranch, Lost Nugget, came by their names. Now, following the lead of three generations before them, the McCord family continued the search, much to the scorn of folks around these parts, who believed that the gold carried a curse. Hadn't it consumed the lives of every McCord male?

Jesse broke off a low-hanging tree limb and began pushing it into the dirt. When it was firmly planted he took out a handkerchief and tied it to the top.

Wyatt eyed it. "What's that for?"

"We need to mark the spot so Grandpa Coot knows where to dig if this turns out to be real gold." Jesse pocketed the nugget, then, enjoying the drama of the moment, looked around to make certain no one was nearby. He felt a tingling at the base of his skull. What if it turned out to be part of the lost treasure?

This was, he realized, why his grandfather continued the search, despite all odds.

His voice lowered to a whisper. "We have to keep this a secret. We can't tell a soul except Grandpa Coot. We have to swear an oath."

The two younger boys nodded solemnly, looking to Jesse to show them how.

Jesse spit in his hand, and the other two followed suit.

Then the three rubbed hands, mingling their saliva, while Jesse said, "I swear to God I'll tell nobody except Coot about this gold." He looked properly stern. "Now you have to swear it."

"I swear," Wyatt said.

Zane swallowed, feeling the weight of this momentous occasion weighing heavily on his young shoulders before saying, "I swear."

Jesse pulled himself into the saddle and waited for the other two to mount.

As they started toward the distant ranch house he turned in the saddle. "Remember. Since we all swore, if anybody breaks the vow, something really bad will happen to them."

"Like what?" Zane brought his horse even with Jesse's in order to hear every word.

"I don't know." Jesse shrugged, thinking about all the adventure novels he'd read as part of his homework assignments. "Maybe anybody who breaks the vow will be banished from Lost Nugget ranch forever. Or they'll die or something."

The three boys slowed their mounts and looked properly worried. Not about death, which seemed too improbable for their young minds to conceive. But being banished from the ranch was the worst possible punishment they could ever imagine.

Each boy knew he would take his secret to the grave before he'd risk the loss of this place he loved more than anything in the whole world.

CHAPTER ONE

———◆◆◆———

Montana—Present Day

D amned north pasture's a sea of mud." In the doorway of the barn, Jesse McCord shook rain from his dark hair like a great shaggy dog and shoved past wrangler Rafe Spindler, who happened to step out of a stall in front of him, nearly causing a collision.

With a rough shove he growled, "Get the hell out of my way."

Rafe jumped back before huffing out a laugh at Jesse's mud-spattered jeans and boots and faded denim jacket with a torn pocket. "Looks like you've been wallowing in it."

"Up to my knees. And it's still rising." Jesse's usually infectious smile was gone, replaced by a flinty look that most of the wranglers mistook for impatience. Those closest to him recognized that look as one of pain.

Tall, lean, and muscled from his years of ranch chores, Jesse was, like all the McCords, a handsome devil, with a hint of danger about him that men found daunting and women found irresistible. From the bloodshot eyes it was apparent that he'd been up most of the night.

Jesse turned toward the white-haired man bending over a calf in a stall. "Cal, I'm going to need a crew to get on it right away."

"I'll see to it." Cal Randall, lanky foreman of the Lost Nugget ranch for more than forty years, didn't bother to look up as he continued examining the calf. "I'll see who's left in the bunkhouse before I head on up to the main house."

When Jesse strode away, Rafe ambled over to lean his arms on the wooden rail. "I know we're burying the old man today, but that doesn't give Jesse the right to tear my head off. Like it's my fault it's raining on the day we're going to bury Coot. Damn Jesse. He's just like the old man. Ornery as hell. Hated days like this. Only good for ducks and funerals, Coot used to say."

Grumbling among the cowboys was as natural as breathing. Especially for Rafe Spindler, who grew up not far from here and signed on as a ranchhand after the deaths of his parents while still in his teens. Like so many of the unmarried ranch hands, Rafe was a hardworking, hard-drinking cowboy whose only pleasure was a game of cards and an occasional fling with the local women. Though something of a hothead, Rafe could be counted on to do his share of the toughest, dirtiest ranch chores.

Rafe lowered his voice. "Jesse's been working up a head of steam ever since Miss Cora told him his cousins are coming in for Coot's funeral."

Cal straightened. The ranch might consist of hundreds of wranglers spread out over thousands of acres, but gossip had a way of spreading faster than fire through a bale of hay.

Cal nodded toward the calf. "Keep an eye on him, Rafe. Any change, you can reach me up at the house."

Cal's movements were slow and deliberate as he trudged through puddles. His only concession to the downpour was the wide-brimmed hat pulled low on his head. Autumn had brought more rain than usual to this part of Montana.

After a stop at the bunkhouse, Cal crossed the distance to the sprawling house on the hill. His thoughts were focused on Jesse McCord. He understood the young man's anger and misery. As the only grandson to stay in Montana and share the old man's dream, Jesse was feeling the death of his grandfather, eighty-year-old Coot McCord, more keenly than anyone.

Gabriel McCord had earned a reputation early on as a fool and a dreamer. When he'd begun buying up huge tracts of land around his ranch, folks in the area said he was, like his ancestors, just a crazy old coot, and the nickname stuck. Even his sister, Cora, ten years younger, who some said was just as crazy, had eventually taken to calling him Coot. The old man embraced the name and wore it like a badge of honor.

By the time he died, Coot had bought up over two hundred thousand acres of surrounding land, and he had planned on going over every inch of it with a fine-tooth comb searching for his ancestor's lost fortune. Folks figured if that didn't make a man crazy, nothing did.

Cal didn't share the opinion of the others. There'd been nothing crazy about Coot. Driven, maybe. Determined, definitely. But he was the truest friend a man could want. The old man might not have found his treasure, but it wasn't for lack of trying.

As for Cora, she may have been a bit eccentric, wearing her brother's cast-off clothing while she wandered the countryside alone for weeks at a time, creating paintings of the lush landscapes, which sold for ridiculously huge sums of money in the international art world. But that only added to her charm. She was a true artist. She didn't paint for the money. She painted because she was driven. It was as necessary to her as breathing.

That was another thing she'd shared with her brother. That determination ran like steel girders through all the McCords. That's what made them all so ornery.

Cal stepped into the mudroom, cleaning his boots on a scraper before hanging his hat on a peg. He carefully washed his hands at the big basin before walking into the kitchen where Dandy Davis was flipping hotcakes. As always, Dandy wore a crisp white apron tied over clean denims and a spotless plaid shirt with the sleeves rolled to the elbows.

The wranglers had a bet going that Dandy probably owned more than two dozen shirts in the same plaid, and an equal number of pairs of denim pants and shiny black boots.

Dandy had come to the Lost Nugget looking for work as a wrangler. Instead he'd been pressed into service in the kitchen, and agreed to cook until a replacement could be found. Twenty years later he was still cooking.

He kept his kitchen spotless, spending hours each day polishing everything from pots and pans to countertops. Any cowboy who forgot to scrape his boots or wash his hands before entering Dandy's kitchen did so at the risk of life and limb. His demands were tolerated because he was, quite simply, the best cook in all of Montana. His chili, spicy enough to bring tears to the eyes of old-time cowboys, was his most requested meal on the range. But running a close second was his slow-cooked pot roast, tender enough to fall off the bone, served with chunks of potatoes, carrots, and winter squash. When Dandy was baking bread, the crew found excuses to go up to the house, knowing he was always good for a handout of hot, crusty heels of bread slathered with the honey butter he made from his own secret recipe.

Dandy turned from the stove. "Morning, Cal. Just coffee, or do you have time for pancakes?"

"I'll make time." Cal smiled at the woman in the denim shirt and oversized bib-overalls. Gray hair curled softly around a face too pretty to be improved by makeup. Whenever her hair needed cutting, she simply snipped a curl here and there, and fluffed it with her fingers. She had been, for all her seventy years, completely without artifice. "Morning, Cora."

"Cal." She looked up from the newspaper. "They wrote a nice piece about Coot."

He nodded. "I saw it." He waited until Dandy set a steaming cup in front of him. "Rafe tells me the boys are coming in."

"They are." Cora nodded absently and finished the obituary before setting the paper aside. "Isn't that nice?"

"Yeah." He glanced at the empty chair across the table. "How'd Jess take the news?"

She shrugged. "He's angry, Cal. He said his cousins should have been here all along, instead of waiting until it's too late. I've told him it would please his grandfather to have all his grandsons together, but right now, the only thing Jess knows is that he's lost his best friend, and he doesn't want to share the good-byes with anyone else." She stared down into her coffee. "I know how he feels. I hate the idea of saying good-bye. It makes it all so final. I can't imagine this place without my brother." She sighed. "But I'm glad Wyatt and Zane are coming in for the funeral. It'll be the first time we've all been together since their fathers left years ago."

Cal accepted a plate from Dandy and began pouring syrup over the mound of lighter-than-air flapjacks.

When the back door slammed he looked over to see Jesse McCord hanging his hat on a hook before crossing to the table.

"Morning, Jess."

"Aunt Cora. Sorry I dashed out so early, but I got word that the rain washed out a culvert under the road leading to the north pasture."

"I've got some men on it." Cal sipped his coffee. "Cora tells me that Wyatt and Zane are coming."

"Yeah." Something flickered in the younger man's eyes before he looked away. "Just coffee, Dandy. I'm not hungry this morning."

The cook filled a mug and set it in front of him before returning to the stove.

Cal glanced at Cora. "What time's the service?"

"Noon." She sighed. "Coot told me years ago how he wanted to go out. He always said he'd feel like a hypocrite being buried from a church. It was nice of Reverend Carson to agree to drive out here and say some words. It'll add a nice touch, don't you think, Jess?"

He shrugged. "I doubt Coot cares one way or the other. Just so he's laid to rest on the land he loved."

Cora nodded. "He did love this land, didn't he?" She

closed a hand over her great-nephew's. "It gave him such pleasure to know that you loved it, too, Jess."

He felt his throat closing up and, afraid of embarrassing himself, shoved away from the table. "Think I'll drive up to the pasture and give a hand with that culvert."

"But Jess..." As he stalked out of the room Cora turned to the ranch foreman. "Maybe you should go after him, Cal, and tell him you don't need his help."

Cal gave a slight shake of his head. "He needs to be busy. Work's good for the soul, especially when it's troubled."

"You'll see that he's back in time for..." She fisted her hands in her lap, unable to say the words.

Cal pushed aside his half-eaten breakfast. Funny how quickly an appetite could flee. As he started away from the table he paused to drop a hand on her shoulder and squeeze. "Don't you worry. I'll make sure of it, Cora."

And he would. Even if he had to hog-tie the young hothead and haul his hide home like a sackful of spitting cats.

There was nothing Cal Randall wouldn't do for Cora.

The Harley roared along the open road. Water sprayed up like geysers as the wheels glanced over ruts. As it came up over a hill it slowed, then came to a stop.

Wyatt McCord whipped off his helmet and stood a moment, listening to the incredible silence. Gradually the sounds of the countryside began to seep into his consciousness. The trill of a meadowlark. The distant lowing of cattle. The whisper of the wind through the ponderosa pines.

It was as though the years rolled away. It was all here,

just as he'd pictured it in his mind for the past fifteen
years. It was, he realized with startling clarity, the only
place he'd ever called home. When his parents had taken
their leave of the Lost Nugget, he'd grieved the only
way a sixteen-year-old could. By breaking all the rules.
Dropping out of school. Getting into as much trouble as
he could.

It had taken him years to put his life in order. Long
after his parents had given up on him, he'd returned to
school to earn his degree. But he'd never been able to
put down roots. Instead he searched the world over for
a place that would call to him. He'd meditated in Tibet
and climbed Mount Everest. He'd traveled to India, just
to experience the culture. He'd worked on a luxury yacht
in the South Pacific, and had even wrangled sheep in
Australia. Through it all, he'd made enough money to
live comfortably. Not that he needed much. He'd learned
to travel light. Maybe his mother had been right, all those
years ago, when she'd teasingly suggested that he'd been
dropped on their doorstep by a Gypsy.

He had the look of a Gypsy about him. Thick shaggy
hair the color of coal spilling down the collar of his faded
leather jacket to brush his shoulders. A dark stubble covering his chin and cheeks, giving testimony to the fact
that he'd been on the road for more than a dozen hours.
There was a world-weariness about him, especially in the
set of his jaw and the challenge in those piercing blue
eyes.

He pulled on his helmet and climbed back onto his
Harley before roaring off in a mist of rain.

He'd told himself he was coming home to bury his

grandfather, but it occurred to Wyatt McCord that he'd actually come home to bury his childhood regrets.

Cal stepped out of the barn just as the motorcycle roared to a stop. He hurried over, his weathered face lit with a smile. "Welcome home, Wyatt. It's been a while."

"Yeah." Wyatt set his helmet aside and offered a handshake. "How you been, Cal?"

"I've been better. Your grandfather's death hit us all hard."

"Was he sick?"

"Nope." The older man's eyes watered for a moment before he blinked. "He was climbing around some rock cliffs like always, and took a nasty fall. As soon as he called in his location from his cell phone, I phoned Marilee Trainor and then raced out there with some of the wranglers. Before the medevac could fly in, he was gone."

Wyatt stuck his hands in his back pockets and looked out at the towering buttes in the distance. "Sounds like old Coot, doesn't it? I think that's the way he'd have liked to go."

"Yeah." Cal nodded. "Your great-aunt's inside. You go ahead and I'll get your bag."

"No need." Wyatt reached into his saddlebag. "All I've got is this duffel."

He climbed the steps and let himself into the house, pausing at the mudroom to drop his bag before continuing into the kitchen.

"Aunt Cora."

She was instantly out of her chair and into his arms. "Oh, Wyatt." After a fierce hug she held him a little away.

He took that moment to shake Dandy's hand. "Good to see you again, Dandy."

"And you, Wyatt."

Cora was studying him with a look of disbelief. "Oh, look at you. You're the picture of your daddy."

"Except he wore denim instead of leather." He grinned. "You haven't changed a bit, Aunt Cora. In fact, I think those are the same overalls you were wearing the day I left."

She gave a girlish laugh. Wyatt had always been able to charm her. "They're Coot's. I always liked his clothes better than my own. I think I'll like them even better now."

Wyatt sobered. "I know what you mean." He dug into his pocket and held up a battered watch on a chain. "I've been carrying this ever since the crash. The authorities found it in the wreckage and sent it to me. I like having something of Dad's."

Cora cupped it in her hand and studied it before looking at him. "Coot gave that to your daddy when he graduated high school."

Wyatt nodded. "I know. That makes it twice as special to me."

The old woman wrapped an arm around his waist, loving the big, sturdy feel of him, all muscle and sinew. Like his daddy. "Come on. I'll take you up to your rooms."

He leaned down to kiss her cheek. "Don't bother, Aunt Cora. I remember the way."

As he retrieved his duffel and walked away, she stayed where she was, listening to his footsteps as he climbed the stairs.

Dandy set a fresh cup of coffee on the table. "Here, Miss Cora. You look like you could use this."

"Thanks, Dandy." She sank down onto a chair, wondering why she felt this sudden urge to weep. Instead, she leafed through the paper until she found the obituary, thinking Coot's grandsons might want to have a look at it later.

Wyatt paused in the doorway of the suite of rooms he'd once shared with his parents, memories of his childhood sweeping over him. He'd always loved living in this big, sprawling ranch house, knowing an entire family lived just rooms away. His cousins, Jesse and Zane, had been his best friends and constant companions. If his father was busy, there was always an uncle or his grandfather to talk to. When he needed help with schoolwork, his mother, one of his aunts, or his great-aunt Cora was always available to lend a hand. There had been a strong feeling of camaraderie in this house when he was young.

Gradually, as he grew into his teens, he'd begun to sense the unease. His father and mother yearned to break free of the constraints of ranch life to travel around the world. They resented the treasure hunt that had become Coot's obsession. Angry words triggered endless arguments. As a teen living in his own selfish world, Wyatt seemed barely aware of the tension until his father and mother had ordered him to pack his things. When he realized that there were no plans to return to the only life he'd ever known, he became angry, distant, difficult. While his parents attempted to share their love of world travel with their only son, he repaid them by dropping out of school and out of life. It was only years later that he'd managed to pull himself together and make something of his life. But by then, with his parents gone in an instant, killed in a plane crash, his anger had turned inward, directed at himself.

He'd overcome the anger and guilt. And now, just when he'd accepted a life alone, here he was, back where it had all begun.

He carried his duffel across the polished wood floor of the foyer and paused in the big open parlor, with its massive stone fireplace and familiar overstuffed chairs. Over the mantel was a portrait of his mother and father and the boy he'd been at eight. Dark hair cut razor-short, laughing blue eyes, wide grin with its missing front tooth.

He was smiling as he made his way down the hallway to his old bedroom. Just beyond was the master bedroom and bath, but except for a quick glance, he returned to his old room and tossed the duffel on the twin bed, still covered in the red-plaid comforter he'd chosen for his fourteenth birthday.

He'd slept in youth hostels in Europe, tents in the Andes, and fleabag hotels in plenty of towns he'd rather forget. But in his mind's eye, he'd never forgotten this room.

This was the only place he'd ever thought of as home.

The sleek little sports car, in candy apple red, took every dip and curve with the grace of a dancer. At the top of the rise Zane McCord pulled over just to drink in the view.

Green pastures dotted with cattle. Weathered barns and outbuildings. And that grand sweep of the brick-and-stone house atop the hill where it could be seen for miles in all directions. When he was a kid with a wild imagination, he'd thought it looked like a castle. His own private keep, and he the white knight, saving the kingdom from peril.

Now he saw it as it looked through the lens of his camera. It was all here. The wide-open ranges, with no houses or factories or offices to spoil the view. No people. Just acre after acre of cattle, and the men who tended the herds. There was something mysterious and romantic about this land. This ranch.

He'd been so afraid it wouldn't look the way he'd remembered it. After all, he'd been just a kid when he left. But he'd never forgotten this place. The simple beauty of it. The soaring majesty of the mountain ranges. The icy purity of the streams and rivers.

After years in Southern California he'd really feared that his childhood memories had become fragmented and magnified, taking bits and pieces of the things he'd liked best and making them seem even better than they'd been.

Ignoring the rain, he stepped out of the car and leaned on the hood, breathing deeply. Even the air was different here. It hadn't been just a kid's imagination. It *was* cleaner. Sweeter. Purer.

He relaxed for the first time in hours, softening the sharp angles and planes of his face. A hawkish face that would never be mistaken for movie-star material. His jaw was too square. His steely-eyed look intimidating to most men and intriguing to women. He idly touched a hand to the scar along his jaw. As a kid he'd taken a nasty fall from a horse. Because the Lost Nugget was more than a hundred miles from the town's clinic, most injuries were handled by one of the cowboys. Zane's cut had been treated no differently. Half an hour after being stitched up in a bunkhouse, he'd been back on the same horse, racing to catch up with his cousins. A few years ago a well-known plastic surgeon he'd met at a cocktail party in Malibu had wanted to correct the damage. Zane had refused, considering it his own special medal of honor. Every time he caught sight of it in the mirror it brought back memories of earlier, happier times.

He was smiling as he climbed back into the car. On the oldies station Bob Seger was running against the wind. Zane found himself keeping time to the music as he shifted gears and raced off in a spray of rain and gravel.

Cora looked up at the sound of a vehicle approaching. Setting aside her cup, she hurried through the mudroom to watch as a sleek little sports car came to a smooth stop directly behind the motorcycle. Seconds later a man stepped out and paused to look around.

Cora sucked in a breath, then raced out to greet him. "Zane. Oh, Zane."

"Aunt Cora." He gathered her close and breathed her in, feeling a rush of emotion at the half-forgotten scents of lavender and paint that had always been so much a part of this special woman.

She clung to him for a moment before stepping back and tipping up her head to study him. "Look how tall you've grown. Why, you must be well over six feet."

"And a couple of inches." He chuckled. "Who'd've believed it of that skinny little kid?"

"Skinny and absolutely fearless. As I recall, you did some pretty foolhardy things when you were a boy."

"I'd appreciate it if you wouldn't mention them.

Besides, I had to keep up with my cousins." He glanced around. "Where are Jesse and Wyatt?"

"Jesse's gone to look at a washout up the road, and Wyatt is unpacking in his old room." She nodded toward the car. "Why don't you do the same?"

He retrieved an overnight case and followed her inside where he greeted Dandy with handshake. "I hope those perfect pancakes I remember from my childhood aren't just a fantasy, Dandy."

The cook grinned. "If you haven't had breakfast yet, I'll let you find out for yourself."

Zane shook his head. "I had something at a place called the Grizzly Inn they called a biscuit-sausage-egg combo. I think they make them out of cardboard and use them over and over on every tourist who happens by."

The two men shared a laugh.

Cora looped her arm through his. "Think you can find your way to your old rooms, Zane?"

He nodded. "Yeah, Aunt Cora. It may have been years, but I haven't forgotten the way."

As he started toward the stairway she called, "The service for your grandfather will be at noon."

Zane glanced at his watch, relieved that he had an hour to prepare. "In town? Or here at the ranch?"

"Here. Coot always said he wanted to spend eternity right here on his own land."

Zane nodded. "I'm not surprised."

Zane McCord strode into the section of the house where he'd lived as a boy with his father and mother. Like the Lost Nugget, everything here was bigger than life. The formal parlor, with its Italian marble floor and priceless

Persian rug that his mother had insisted upon, still looked out of place in this homey setting, as did the custom silk draperies and furnishings. But Melissa McCord had been as out of place in Montana as her choice of furnishings. From the time he was a kid she'd made no secret of her distaste for ranch life. There had been endless arguments between Melissa and Wade, and when Zane's father had finally agreed to leave the ranch, it had been a last-ditch effort to save his marriage.

As he walked through the rooms until he came to his parents' bedroom, Zane frowned. The sacrifice his father made had been in vain. The marriage had already been irretrievably broken, and his father had died out in California without even the comfort of his family.

Zane backed away from the ornate master suite and followed the hallway to his old room. He'd rather spend his one night at the Lost Nugget in here. It was as he remembered it, right down to the horse posters on the walls. As a kid he'd been in love with the idea of traveling across the wilderness with a herd of wild mustangs. That was why, when producer Steven Michaelson had offered him the job of assistant on his documentary about the government roundup of wild horses, he'd jumped at the chance.

Zane tossed his overnight bag on a chair and headed toward the bathroom. He was glad he had time for a shower and a change of clothes before his grandfather's funeral.

While Dandy prepared a meal for the mourners, Cora walked to the great room, where a fire blazed on the hearth. If she closed her eyes, she could almost believe

Coot was here with her. Though the paintings on the walls, of wide, sweeping vistas and snow-covered mountains, had all been done by her, the furniture was big and solid, to accommodate her brother and his sons, who had all been big men. It made her smile to remember.

She clutched her arms about herself. "Oh, Coot. It's hard to believe all our boys are so grown up. We've lost too many years."

How ironic, that it took Coot's death to reunite the family. The same family that had been shattered by Coot's obsession with finding his great-grandfather's fortune. He'd been heartbroken when two of his sons, whose wives had grown weary of the search, had left the ranch, and Montana, for good. He'd despaired of ever seeing his family together again. But here was Wyatt, son of Coot's middle son, Ben, back from whatever godforsaken place he called home these days; and Zane, son of Coot's youngest son, Wade, in from California.

Cora turned to look out the window at the mountain peaks, barely visible in the rain. "I know it isn't much. A day or two. But at least for whatever time they can manage, we're all together. And that's a tribute to you, Coot."

CHAPTER TWO

———◆———

"Come on, Jess." Cal slid behind the wheel of the battered old pickup and waited while Jesse stored a shovel in the back before climbing into the passenger side. "Your aunt'll have my hide if I don't get you up to the house in time for the service."

"Doesn't matter." Jesse wiped his muddy hands on his jeans. "Coot won't like it."

"Now what makes you say that?"

The younger man glanced over. "He never liked fuss, Cal. Neither do I."

"This isn't fuss. It's the only way we have of paying our respects. Coot knew that. It's why he told his sister just what to do in the event of his death." Cal's voice lowered. "This is important to Cora. She's hurting as much as you, Jess."

"I know. I wish I could ease her pain." Jesse turned to stare out the side window as the truck rumbled along the rough road. Next to Coot, Cal Randall was the closest thing Jesse McCord had to a father, since his own had died twenty years ago, leaving him lost and bewildered at the tender age of twelve.

Cal wasn't one to give advice, but when he did, Jesse heeded it, however reluctantly. "I suppose I'll have to wear a suit."

Cal nodded. "Me, too. Though I've no use for them."

Jesse looked over. "Didn't know you owned one."

Cal grinned. "Haven't had much need for it, but now and again it comes in handy."

"Especially if you're trying to impress a lady."

"I'll leave that to you, Jess."

The two shared a smile.

As they rolled to a stop by the back door, Jesse caught sight of the unfamiliar vehicles. "Well, well. Looks like the gang's all here." He stepped down from the pickup and turned from the Harley to the sports car. "Let's see. Which one do you think belongs to our free spirit, and which to Hollywood's golden boy?"

Cal shook his head. "Let it be, Jess. They're family."

"Yeah. I keep forgetting." His tone roughened. "Of course, it's hard to remember when you don't see some-one for ten or fifteen years."

"They're here now. Here for their grandfather. That's all that matters."

Jesse nodded. "And by this time tomorrow, they'll be gone."

He stormed up the steps, hoping to escape to his room. Instead, after scraping mud from his boots and washing his hands at the big sink in the mudroom, he stepped into the kitchen and came face-to-face with a roomful.

His great-aunt looked up from the table where his grandfather's lawyer was seated beside the minister. On the other side sat his two cousins.

"Well." If he couldn't manage a smile, at least he didn't groan. "Wyatt. Zane. It's been too long."

"Yeah." Wyatt stepped forward to offer his hand. "The place looks the same as I remember."

"Yeah. Some things never change." But Wyatt had. Even the proper suit and tie couldn't erase the long hair and casual air that gave him the look of an eternal surfer. Maybe, Jesse thought, that's what Wyatt was. Always dashing off to find the next big wave to ride.

When he turned to Zane, Jesse was startled by how much his younger cousin had changed. He'd expected a smoothness to Zane, a polish that could only come from easy living. After all, the suit was custom-made. The shoes Italian. And the watch on his wrist cost more than Jesse's last truck. But there was a toughness in his younger cousin's eyes, a strength in his demeanor that didn't quite fit the image he'd formed in his mind.

"How's Hollywood? I hear you're working with some hotshot director now."

"Steve Michaelson." Zane stuck out his hand. "I assisted on his latest documentary. It'll be on PBS next fall. Good to see you, Jess. I wish it could have been under happier circumstances."

"Yeah, well, too bad you had to wait until Coot was dead to pay a call."

"Jesse." To avoid an all-out war, Cora stepped between them. "I was just about to introduce Vernon to your cousins." She looped an arm through each of theirs. "Boys, this is Vernon McVicker, Coot's lawyer. Vernon, these are my great-nephews, Zane and Wyatt McCord."

The man who pushed away from the table had sad, tired eyes in a long and lean face. Sparse gray hair was combed straight back, adding to his hound-dog expression. As he approached he studied them as he might specimens, with more than casual interest. "You'd be Wade's son," he said to Zane. He turned to Wyatt. "And you'd be Ben's."

They both nodded.

Relieved that she'd managed to smother Jesse's temper for the moment, Cora managed a smile. "Jess, why don't you go ahead upstairs and get dressed while we wait. Reverend Carson is here to begin the service, as soon as we're ready."

Jesse was grateful for the chance to escape. The last thing he wanted to do was stand around making small talk. "I'll just be a few minutes."

As he stalked up the stairs he thought about the two cousins who were no more than strangers now. There'd been a time when the three of them had been inseparable. They'd grown up wild and free on their grandfather's ranch, swimming in the creek, riding bareback across the hills, daring one another to try every dangerous, reckless stunt a young boy's mind could imagine.

They'd all lived here in various wings of the house. One big, noisy family. Even after the death of his father, Jesse had felt safe and protected, because he'd been surrounded by so many family members. But gradually the cracks in the family had begun to show signs of stress. Ben had left first, taking Wyatt away. Later it was Wade, heading off to California with his wife and son.

Jesse undressed and stepped into the shower, letting the hot water beat on the knot of tension at the back of his neck. After toweling himself dry he slipped into a crisp white shirt, tucking it into the waistband of dark pants.

As he ran his fingers through his wet hair he paused. He didn't blame his cousins for leaving. They'd been only kids when their fathers had had enough of old Coot's ravings and had pulled up stakes, in search of a better life. But they'd had plenty of years to come back after they were old enough to be on their own, if that's what they'd wanted. The fact that they'd never returned to the ranch meant one thing to Jesse. They hadn't loved their grandfather enough to spend even a week with him. Not a single week in all these long years.

Jesse slid his arms into the suit jacket, hating the way it felt. Stiff. Phony. That's what this whole fiasco was. A service. For what? So the minister could say a few fancy words about a man who'd never set foot in his church? Coot was gone. Nothing would bring him back.

He took a last glimpse in the mirror, straightening his tie, then slammed out of the room and down the stairs. What he really wanted to do was to get into his truck and drive up to the hills where he and Coot used to spend so much time together. That would mean more to him than any stuffy service. At least then he'd be able to properly grieve.

And he would, he vowed. As soon as the others left, and he had time to himself, he'd bury his grandfather in his own way.

They stood together on a windswept hill. The rain had stopped, leaving the surrounding countryside looking fresh and green, frosted with the pale pink blossoms of bitterroot and waving tassels of golden bear grass.

Jesse looked around at those assembled. It was the first time he'd ever seen so many ranch hands together at one time. Even their roundup barbecue, traditionally held after the cattle had been brought down from the high pastures in late summer, never included all the wranglers, since some were needed to tend the herds. But today, out of respect for the man who had built this amazing spread and had been its heart and soul, every last man was here. Dandy Davis, wearing a spiffy western suit and string tie. Cal Randall, looking as uncomfortable as Jesse felt in his dark suit and cowboy boots. And Cora, in an ankle-skimming dress of black silk with a black fringed shawl tossed about her shoulders. It was the first time Jesse could ever recall seeing his great-aunt in anything but denim.

There were his cousins, tall, handsome, and, like Jesse, refusing to look at the casket standing beside a gaping hole dug in the earth.

"Who are all these people?"

Wyatt's muttered question had Jesse studying the crowd. "Townies."

"So many?" Wyatt exchanged a look with Zane. "When I left, Gold Fever consisted of a gas station, a grocery store, a movie theater showing last year's films, the fairgrounds…"

"That held one of the biggest rodeos in the area," Zane added.

"Yeah. And the Fortune Saloon."

"Just goes to show how long you've been away." Jesse frowned, realizing just how out-of-touch his cousins were. "In recent years they've built a high school and a medical clinic. That brought in teachers, doctors, nurses, who in turn needed new houses, which brought building contractors. There's talk that even more land could be developed to accommodate the number of people moving…"

Jesse's words died in his throat at the shock of recognition he felt when he spied Otis Parrish in the crowd.

Following his direction, Wyatt hissed out a breath at the sight of their nearest neighbor, in fact, their only neighbor. Knowing that Parrish had a long-standing feud with Coot that went back too many years to count, Wyatt whispered, "He's here for only one reason."

"Yeah. To gloat." Jesse continued studying the crowd.

He felt a nudge in his ribs and glanced over at Wyatt.

"Who's that?" Wyatt nodded toward a tall, slender woman whose mass of tangled red curls made her a standout in the crowd.

Jesse followed his direction. "Marilee Trainor."

"Married or single?"

Jesse felt a wave of annoyance. "In case you've forgotten, we're here to bury Coot, not play the dating game."

"Married or single?"

Jesse sighed. "Single. But don't bother. She's a no-nonsense woman who wouldn't be interested in a quick tumble with a rolling stone like you."

"Tell me about her."

"Lee's a medic with the town's emergency services. She was the first one here when she heard about Coot's fall, and she stayed with him until the helicopter arrived." Jesse felt a twinge of remorse when he saw her lift a handkerchief to her eye. "The truth is, she took it personally that she couldn't save him. From the looks of things, she's still beating herself up over it."

On the other side Zane gave him a nudge and nodded toward the old woman pushing her way to the front of the crowd. "Is that Delia Cowling?"

"Yeah."

Zane chuckled. "She was old when I was a kid. Now she must be old as dirt."

Jesse gave a snort. "Yeah. Our town historian."

Delia Cowling called herself that because of her collection of dusty books on the subject of the gold rush at Grasshopper Creek. Folks in town called her the town gossip. There wasn't much that happened in the town of Gold Fever that Delia didn't know about.

"I'm betting she's here to gather any information she can about the personal business of anybody in town."

Ledge Cowling, Delia's brother and owner of the Gold Fever bank, stood beside his sister, whispering behind his hand. Ledge had never married, and most of the folks in town believed it was because the woman hadn't been born that Ledge could love as much as he loved money. Money and his bank were Ledge's only passions. At least the only ones he'd ever admitted to.

Zane and Wyatt continued scanning the faces of so many strangers. There had been a time when they'd known almost everyone in the town of Gold Fever. Now, there were few who appeared familiar to them.

Zane studied a portly man, his gray hair cut close to his scalp, wearing a uniform. "Is that Ernie Wycliff?"

Jesse nodded. "Yeah. Our old football hero is now the sheriff."

"Good for Ernie."

Jesse frowned. "What was Aunt Cora thinking? What did these people care about Coot? Most of 'em are just here to gawk and gossip. Tonight they'll have themselves a good old time back at the Fortune Saloon over a couple of longnecks."

Reverend Carson stepped up beside the casket. His smooth preacher's voice carried out over the crowd. "I'm told this spot has been a burial place for many of the McCord family. Coot's father and mother are here"—He nodded toward the neat row of headstones around which a low, wrought-iron fence stood guard—"along with his baby brother, Edmond, who died in infancy, and Coot's wife, Annie, dead now for over thirty years. Coot's sister, Cora, told me that her brother considered this holy ground. So it seems fitting and proper that old Coot should rest here, now that his labors are over."

He took a paper from his pocket and read the instructions Cora had written, before looking up. "It says here that a couple of folks would like to say a few words." He glanced out over the crowd. "Mayor Stafford?"

Jesse couldn't prevent his eyes from rolling. Rowe Stafford had been the mayor of Gold Fever, Montana, for years, and kept getting reelected to office mainly because nobody else cared to run for the job. Though many enjoyed his speeches, Jesse considered him a windbag who loved the sound of his own voice.

Rowe looked out over the crowd. "Coot and I have been friends for more'n fifty years now. I've spent many a night defending him to those who called him crazy." He gave his famous lopsided grin. "But I'll tell you this. Coot might have gone a little overboard when it came to the search for his lost fortune, but he always said he was doing it for his family." The mayor nodded toward Cora and the three handsome young men standing beside her.

"It's good to see the McCords together again, if only for a day." He started to turn away before adding, "I'll be buying a round of drinks tonight in Coot's name. It's the least I can do for my oldest friend."

The preacher coughed before saying, "And now we'll hear a few words from Cal Randall."

Jesse swiveled his head in surprise and watched as the foreman stepped up beside the casket.

"I just need to say that"—Cal cleared his throat, looking like he'd rather be anywhere than here, baring his soul in front of all these friends and neighbors—"these years with Coot have been the best ever. He was fair and honest. His word was his bond. He was my best friend. I'm surely going to miss him." He jammed his hands in his pockets and walked back to join the others.

Reverend Carson turned to Cora. "Miss McCord?"

Cora stepped away from the others and paused beside the casket, running her hand along the smooth wood. "My brother didn't like fancy words, so I'll keep mine simple. Folks called him crazy for spending a lifetime searching these hills for our great-grandfather's gold. He never cared what others thought." She looked over the crowd, allowing her gaze to settle first on Jesse, then Wyatt, then Zane. "It just runs in the family, I guess. When your name's McCord, you have to do things your own way. I surely hope..." She gave a long, deep sigh. "I hope his dream doesn't die with him."

As she took a halting step away, Jesse hurried forward and offered his arm. She gave him a tearful smile, grateful for his quiet support.

Her voice quavered. "Did you want to say a few words, Jesse?"

He shook his head. "Whatever I've got to say to Coot is between him and me. It's not for here."

"I understand." She patted his hand.

The reverend glanced around. "Are there any others who would care to say a few words, or perhaps share a happy memory or two?"

Some of the wranglers shuffled their feet and coughed in discomfort. As the silence stretched out, Reverend Carson opened a book and began to read the words of a prayer.

As the words drifted over them, Jesse let his attention wander. What would happen to his grandfather's dream? Since Coot had been a young man of eighteen or twenty, he'd been consumed with finding something he wasn't even sure existed. Nuggets as big as a man's thumb. Some as big as a fist. The old man had been the butt of jokes for as long as Jesse could remember.

Maybe it was best if the dream was allowed to die with him. That wasn't the worst thing that could happen. Maybe then they all could have some peace.

There was land here. Rich ranchland. And thousands of head of cattle. Old Coot hadn't cared about the ranch. Had left the running of it to Cal and the ranch hands. And Cal did a fine job. No doubt about it. That old cowboy loved this place as if it were his own. Still, Jesse thought, maybe if he were to keep his attention focused on the ranch now, without the distraction of an imaginary fortune, he and Cal could take the most successful ranch in all of Montana and turn it into the most successful ranch in the world.

He had the prickly feeling that someone was watching him. Lifting his head he studied the crowd and felt his throat go dry when he caught sight of the young woman standing slightly behind Otis Parrish.

"Amy." He wasn't even aware that he'd spoken her name until he saw his cousins turn to glance at him.

He lowered his head and stared hard at the ground. When Amy Parrish had left Montana without a word, a mile-wide chasm had developed between them. And whatever feelings they might have shared had been washed away in a sea of anger and resentment.

Jesse was surprised when he sensed movement beside him and realized Cora was starting forward, taking him along with her. The casket had already been lowered into the ground, and Cora tossed a handful of dirt onto the lid. Jesse followed suit. His cousins, Zane and Wyatt, did the same.

They stepped away and watched as Cal and Dandy and the wranglers took turns tossing dirt and standing with bowed heads, bidding their final farewells.

The crowd had gone eerily silent. Out of respect? Jesse wondered. Or were they waiting for old Coot to rise up out of his casket and hold out a fistful of gold nuggets?

The minister said in his most funereal tone, "That concludes our service. The family asked me to invite all of you back to the house for a meal."

Just then Cora's voice rose with excitement and she pointed to the sky. "Oh, my. Look."

Everyone followed her direction, looking up to see a shimmering rainbow arched across the heavens.

A murmur went up from the crowd.

After watching for several minutes, Cora's voice trembled with excitement. "It's Coot's way of saying good-bye. I just know it." She turned to her nephew. "Don't you agree, Jesse?"

He nodded, too overcome to speak. Everyone in the

family had seen the rainbow keychain his grandfather had always carried in his pocket. When asked about it, old Coot had said it was a symbol of the fortune he intended to find one day. His personal pot of gold. It was now Jesse's good luck charm.

"You aren't just trying to console me, are you?" Cora's eyes glittered with tears. "You do believe, don't you, Jess?"

Jesse swallowed the lump in his throat and squeezed her hand. "I'm telling you straight, Aunt Cora. It's a sign."

CHAPTER THREE

The sweeping front lawn of the ranch house had been transformed. Dozens of picnic tables were spread out beneath shade trees. Sawhorses supported rows of planks covered in white linen and groaning under the weight of enough food to feed the state of Montana.

Dandy Davis moved among the throngs of wranglers that had been pressed into service to slice the side of beef, the suckling pig, the smoked ham, and to serve the amazing array of side dishes he'd managed to prepare for the funeral lunch.

Despite the size of the crowd, it was quiet and orderly. The townspeople and the wranglers mixed easily, since the men who worked on the Lost Nugget ranch spent most of their off-hours in town, either drinking in the Fortune Saloon or eating the rubber that passed for pizza at the Grizzly Inn.

When the mourners caught sight of the car bearing

Cora and her nephews, the conversation faded to a hum. As she stepped out and started toward them, the wranglers whipped their hats from their heads, twisting them around and around in their hands and murmuring awkward words of condolence as she passed by.

Cora paused to speak a word to each person, since she knew them all by name. From the looks on their faces, they appreciated the time she took from her own grief to tend theirs.

The minute she took a seat at one of the picnic tables Dandy was beside her. "I fixed you a plate, Miss Cora. See that you eat something."

She gave him a gentle smile, though she knew she wouldn't be able to manage a bite. "Thank you, Dandy."

"You're welcome, Miss Cora." He turned to Jesse. "If you and your cousins tell me what you'd like, I'll fetch it."

Jesse shook his head. "No need, Dandy. We'll get our own." He walked to the rear of a long line of wranglers, with Wyatt and Zane trailing behind.

At once the wranglers began offering their words of sorrow and regret at Jesse's loss. Though it was painful to endure, Jesse preferred it to attempting to make conversation with his cousins.

He could get through this, he told himself. A few hours more and Wyatt and Zane would be gone. He and Cora could get on with their lives.

Without Coot.

The thought cut like a razor. So sharp and swift, he brought a hand to his stomach and had to suck in a breath on the pain.

"Zane?" One of the wranglers looked beyond Jesse to the young man behind him. "Is it really Zane McCord?"

Zane stepped closer, then gave a whoop as recognition dawned. "Jimmy? Jimmy Eagle?"

The two men clasped shoulders and shared a delighted laugh.

"Last time I saw you, boy, you were too young to shave."

"And you had hair down to your butt."

"Wore it in a braid," the older man said proudly. "Still do." When they stepped apart he turned to the others. "This is Zane, Wade's boy."

As Jimmy Eagle handled the introductions, Zane shook hands and turned to include his cousin. "This is Wyatt. His dad was my uncle Ben."

"You the one been around the world?" one of the men asked.

Wyatt chuckled. "I haven't seen it all yet, but I've been to a few places."

"More'n a few, I've heard."

Soon the men had completely surrounded them, eager to chat up Coot's grandsons, who'd been absent from the ranch for so many years.

"Jimmy taught me to ride," Zane explained to the others. "Dad said I was too young, but Jimmy trusted me enough to just stick me in the saddle and tell me what to do."

"Because you pestered me until I got tired of saying no." The weathered old wrangler shook his head. "You were way too young. Which is why you took that nasty spill that split your jaw. But you were jealous because your cousins were already riding, and you wanted to keep up."

"He was always trying to keep up," Jesse said with a laugh.

"With wild rascals like the two of you, I can't say I blame him. I guess that's why he was so wild and tough." Jimmy Eagle sobered. "Your pa was good to me, Zane. It wasn't easy for a full-blooded Blackfoot to make friends off the reservation, but your pa put me at ease and became a good friend." His voice lowered. "I heard he died in California."

Zane nodded.

"I'm sorry. But I wasn't surprised when he left the ranch. He used to say that one day he'd move to a place where it never snowed."

That had Zane smiling. "He hated snow. He said it was the one thing he never missed about this place." His smile faded a bit as he added, "Of course, he might have said that to appease my mother."

Jimmy ducked his head. "As I recall, she didn't much like it here. What'd she think of California?"

"She settled in." Zane tried to keep the bitterness from his tone. "Made a life for herself there after Dad died."

Jimmy Eagle helped himself to an empty plate and began loading it with food. "How long you plan on visiting?"

Zane shrugged. "I'll probably leave in the morning."

"That's too bad. I would've enjoyed a nice, long visit." The old wrangler stuck out a hand. "I have to be up on the south range in an hour. Great seeing you, Zane."

"You, too, Jimmy."

Zane stepped into line behind Jesse and Wyatt and filled a plate, then followed them to their aunt's table.

Cora looked up with a smile. "Did I see you talking to Jimmy?"

Zane settled himself beside her at the picnic table. "He used to call me his little shadow. I dogged that man's footsteps when I was a kid. I can't remember him ever losing patience with me. Not once. No matter how many times I pestered him with questions. He didn't just give me the answers, he'd tell me the why of things." He shook his head, remembering. "Nobody else except Coot ever took that kind of time with me."

Cora gave a dreamy smile. "Oh, Coot had a soft spot for his grandsons, all right. He just couldn't do enough for the three of you. It almost broke his heart when two of his sons moved and took you boys away."

"Water under the bridge, Aunt Cora." Jesse shoved away from the table.

She looked up. "Where are you going, Jess?"

He paused to press a hand to her shoulder. "I just need some space. I'll see you when the crowd thins."

She watched him walk across the lawn, pausing every now and then to speak to one or two of the wranglers before continuing toward the house. She knew him so well. Knew that tight, closed look. He was angry and hurting. And there wasn't a thing she could do about it. It was something he'd just have to work through by himself.

She turned to Wyatt. "Tell me about your life since you left Montana."

"Would you like to hear about Tibet, or India, or would you prefer something more exotic, like the luxury yacht I helped crew in the South Pacific?"

His rogue smile, so like his father's, had her spirits lifting at once. "Why not tell me about all of them?"

"I hope you have a few days." He sat back. "Why don't I tell you about my last job, wrangling horses in Texas."

"Texas?" Cora looked startled. "Is that where you were when you heard about Coot?"

He nodded. "I guess you wouldn't have known that. I travel around so much I use a service for my messages. No matter where in the world I am, they can always find me."

"If only Coot had known you were back in the country." Cora looked down at her hands, clasped in her lap. "Why didn't you offer to work here, Wyatt?"

He thought about evading the question. After all, she'd been through enough, losing her only brother. But he owed her the truth. "I guess I didn't know if I'd be welcome, Aunt Cora."

"Oh, Wyatt." She laid a hand over his. "Why would you think such a thing?"

"My dad didn't exactly part company with Coot under the friendliest of terms."

"No, he didn't. But that had nothing to do with you, Wyatt."

He looked down at his aunt's hand covering his. Even though the fingers had grown a bit knobby, they were still the long, tapered fingers of an artist. He'd always been amazed that this sweet and seemingly spacey woman could take a blank canvas and turn it into a blaze of color, form, and energy. Within this quiet, unassuming woman lay a depth of passion that was shocking in its intensity.

"It had everything to do with me, Aunt Cora."

"Why do you say that?"

"Dad told me he left because he thought I was too much of a dreamer. He said he could see me becoming infected with the same poison that was killing his father."

"Poison?"

"Coot's obsession with the lost gold." He lowered his voice. "You have to admit, Aunt Cora, that it colored his entire life."

She nodded. "It did. And who knows? Maybe he'd have been better off without it. But this much I know." She closed her other hand on his. "If Coot had ever found his fortune, he'd have gladly given it all away to his three grandsons. You boys meant everything in the world to him."

Seeing the crowd beginning to thin, she got to her feet. "Would you mind coming with me now? I need to say good-bye to our guests."

With Zane on one side and Wyatt on the other, she made her way to the wide porch where she stood, flanked by her great-nephews, thanking the wranglers and townspeople who were taking their leave.

In the kitchen Jesse loosened his tie and poured himself a tumbler of Irish whiskey. Like his grandfather, he wasn't much of a drinker. But every New Year, and at the annual roundup barbecue, Coot would pour a round of whiskeys for himself and the crew, and offer a toast to the future.

"Life's all about the road ahead. What's past is past. Here's to what's around the bend, boys."

Jesse could hear his grandfather's voice as clearly as if he'd been standing right there. There had been a boyish curiosity about the old man that was so endearing. He'd truly believed he would live to find his ancestor's fortune. The anticipation, the thrill of it, had influenced his entire life. And it was contagious. Jesse had been caught up in it as well. It's what had kept him here, chasing Coot's rainbow, instead of going off in search of his own.

Not that he had any regrets. He couldn't imagine himself anywhere but here.

He crossed the mudroom and stepped out onto the back porch, hoping to get as far away from the crowd as possible.

Just as he lifted the drink to his lips, a voice stopped him.

"I thought I might find you out here."

He didn't have to see her to recognize that voice. Hadn't it whispered to him in dreams a hundred times or more?

His tone hardened as he studied Amy Parrish standing at the bottom of the steps. "What's the matter, Amy? Make a wrong turn? Lunch is being served in the front yard."

"I noticed." She waited until he walked closer. "I just wanted to tell you why I came back."

"To gloat, no doubt."

"Don't, Jess." She pressed her lips together, then gave a sigh of defeat. "I'm sorry about your grandfather. I know you loved him."

"Yeah." Her eyes were even greener than he remembered. With little gold flecks in them that you could see only in the sunlight. It hurt to look at them. At her. Almost as much as it hurt to think about Coot. "So, why did you come back?"

"To offer some support to my dad while he had some medical tests done."

His head came up sharply. "He's sick?"

She nodded. "The doctor in Billings sent him to a

specialist at the university. The test results should be back in a couple of days, and then I'll be going back to my job, teaching in Helena."

"I'm sorry about your dad. I hope the test results come back okay." He paused, staring at the glass in his hands because he didn't want to be caught staring at her. "So, I guess you just came here to say good-bye before you leave. Again."

"I just..." She shrugged and stared down at her hands, fighting nerves. "I just wanted to offer my condolences."

"Thanks. I appreciate it."

The breeze caught a strand of pale hair, softly laying it across her cheek. Without thinking he reached up and gently brushed it away from her face.

The heat that sizzled through his veins was like an electrical charge, causing him to jerk back. But not before he caught the look of surprise in her eyes. Surprise and something more. If he didn't know better, he'd swear he saw a quick flash of heat. But that was probably just his pride tricking him into believing in something that wasn't there, and hadn't been for years.

He lowered his hand and clenched it into a fist at his side.

She took a sideways step, as though to avoid being touched again. "I'd better get back to my dad."

"Yeah. Thanks again for coming."

She walked away quickly, without looking back.

That was how she'd left in the first place, he thought. Without a backward glance.

Now he could allow himself to study her. Hair the color of wheat, billowing on the breeze. That lean, willowy body; those long legs; the soft flare of her hips.

Just watching her, he felt all the old memories rushing over him, filling his mind, battering his soul. Memories he'd kept locked up for years in a small, secret corner of his mind. The way her hair smelled in the rain. The way her eyes sparkled whenever she smiled. The sound of her laughter, low in her throat. The way she felt in his arms when they kissed. When they made love...

He'd be damned if he'd put himself through that hell again.

He lifted the tumbler to his lips and drained it in one long swallow, feeling the heat snake through his veins.

"What's past is past," he muttered thickly. "Here's to what's around the bend."

Cora stood, flanked by Wyatt and Zane, until the ranch hands had returned to their chores and the last of the townspeople had driven away.

Dandy and his helpers began the task of cleaning up the remains of the luncheon.

"You need anything, Miss Cora, you let me know." Dandy looked up from his work as she walked past.

"Thank you for everything, Dandy." Cora led the way inside the ranch house.

Vernon McVicker was seated at the kitchen table, sipping coffee. He picked up a briefcase from the floor. "Where would you like to do this, Miss Cora?"

"Coot's office. I'll just go find Jess and the others. Why don't you boys go with Vernon?"

As she walked away Zane and Wyatt glanced at each other with matching looks of puzzlement.

The lawyer led the way down a long hallway to a large room at the rear of the house, which was obviously a masculine retreat. A massive wooden desk and leather chair stood in front of a stone fireplace. Floor-to-ceiling shelves filled with books and ledgers occupied two walls of the room. The windows looked out over a spectacular view of green rangeland, with the peaks of Treasure Chest Mountain in the distance.

While Zane and Wyatt settled into comfortable leather chairs, Vernon McVicker walked to the desk and opened his briefcase. Minutes later Cal Randall and Dandy Davis arrived, looking annoyed at being taken away from their chores. By the time Cora and Jesse entered, Vernon had a sheaf of papers carefully spread out before him.

He waited until all were seated before settling himself in Coot's chair and steepling his fingers on the desktop. "It was Coot's desire that his last will and testament be read in the presence of his sister, Cora, and his three grandsons, as well as his two trusted employees, provided they were all in attendance. Since all parties are present, I'll begin by reading the will, which, as you'll be able to tell from the language, was dictated by Coot himself. Afterward, I'll have a signed, dated copy for each of you, in case there are any questions."

He picked up a document and began reading. "To my ranch foreman, Calumet Randall, I leave the sum of three hundred thousand dollars, for his years of dedicated service to my ranch. Cal, if you choose to retire and use this money to build your own spread, I'll understand. But I'd be beholden to you if you could see fit to remain on as foreman for as long as the work pleases you. I want you to know that you'll always have a home with us at the Lost Nugget."

Cal, caught completely by surprise, swallowed loudly, then stared down at his hands.

"To my friend Thayer Davis..."

Every head in the room swiveled to stare at Dandy. At last, they knew his given name.

Jesse coughed.

Annoyed at the interruption, Vernon continued, "To my friend Thayer Davis, I leave the sum of two hundred thousand dollars for his years of fine cooking. I know you really wanted to be a wrangler, Dandy. If that's still your dream, maybe this money can make it happen. But you're one hell of a fine cook. If you're so inclined, I'd like you to stay on as ranch cook for as long as the work pleases you."

Dandy blinked hard. One fat wet tear rolled down his cheek before he quickly brushed it aside with the back of his hand.

"To my sister, Cora, I leave the house, which has been in our family for four generations, and all the furniture therein, along with the sum of three million dollars in order to maintain it. I know the money doesn't mean a thing to you, Cora, honey. But humor me. All I ask is that you continue to love and cherish this place. Oh yeah. And keep on painting all those godawful things you've been painting. I may not have told you, but I'm really proud of you, little sister."

Though she'd been apprised of the terms of her brother's will, Cora was forced to bite hard on her lip to keep it from quivering. It all seemed so final somehow, hearing Coot's words read aloud.

Vernon picked up a second document and continued reading. "To my grandsons, Jesse, Wyatt, and Zane. If you're hearing this, it means you all got together for my big send-off. That makes me happy, boys. It's all I ever wanted. Now here's the deal. Jesse, because you've always loved the ranch, it's yours. Except for the house, which belongs now to Cora, I want you to have the herd and outbuildings. As for the land, which totals over two hundred thousand acres, I leave that equally to the three of you, provided each of you agrees to live on the ranch and continue the search for the treasure that has consumed my entire life. You know what that treasure means to me. I want it to mean the same to each of you. Don't misunderstand. If any one of you wants to leave, for any reason, you'll be given the sum of half a million dollars, with no hard feelings. Well, maybe a few. There's a catch. If you go, you'll have no claim to any part of the ranch, or any part of the treasure, if and when it should be found."

Vernon McVicker set down the document and looked up. "Are there any questions?"

No one spoke a word. In fact, no one moved.

Jesse looked mad enough to spit nails. And why not? He'd spent a lifetime here, working the land alongside the wranglers and putting up with his grandfather's obsession. He had to feel a little like the good son finding out that the prodigals had returned to share in the bounty he'd helped create.

And what a bounty. No one could have imagined just how much wealth old Coot had amassed.

Vernon got to his feet and began moving among them with the intention of handing out documents. Except for Cora, they behaved like robots, reaching out silently to accept the paper he thrust into their hands.

He returned to the desk and snapped the lid shut on his briefcase. As he walked to the door, Cora pulled herself together and walked with him.

At the doorway he paused and turned. "Miss Cora has my number, if any of you would like to call with any questions." He glanced around at the stunned faces. "Good day."

There was no reply.

Cora touched his arm. "I'll see you out, Vernon."

"There's no need." He patted her hand. "I think it best if you stay here and tend the shell-shocked, Miss Cora."

She stood in the doorway and listened to the sound of his footsteps receding. Then she took a deep breath and turned to study the faces of the men who had been so deeply affected by her brother's last will.

Dandy was gripping the rolled document firmly in his hand as he approached. "I'm...needed in the kitchen. Could we maybe talk later?"

She nodded and watched him walk away. When she turned, Cal was beside her, looking grim.

"You knew about this?"

"Some. Not all."

"Do you want me to stay, Cora?"

"You know I do, Cal. But the choice has to be yours. You'll need a little time..."

He was shaking his head. "I don't need time, Cora. What Coot did was generous. More than generous. I'm... speechless. But right now I need to get up to the range." As he started past her he paused and leaned close to whisper, "I'm real glad you want me to stay."

Before she could respond he was gone.

She turned to the three men remaining.

Wyatt had walked to the window to stare at the spectacular scenery in the distance. He had his back to the others.

Zane was pacing like a caged tiger. Across the room. A quick turn. Then a dozen paces in the opposite direction. He looked so much like Coot at that moment, Cora had to swallow hard.

Jesse was standing beside his grandfather's desk, running his hand around and around the scarred wooden top.

It was his voice that finally broke the silence. "I always knew he was a crazy old coot."

The others looked at him.

His eyes were hot and fierce, his voice edged with steel. "He's spent a lifetime searching for a treasure that doesn't exist. And now he's sucking us into it, too. Luring us in with the dream of a fortune. But if you guys have any sense at all, you'll take the money and run." He turned to Wyatt. "Isn't that what you want? To use the money to go off to some exotic South Sea island?"

Wyatt shrugged, his eyes glinting with sudden humor. "I can't say it didn't cross my mind."

"And you, Zane." Jesse fisted a hand in the document. "This ought to give you enough clout in Hollywood to produce your own documentaries instead of working on someone else's."

"It might."

"So." Jesse tossed aside his grandfather's will and leaned a hip on the desk before crossing his arms over his chest. "Does that mean the two of you are leaving?"

Zane merely shrugged. Wyatt turned back to stare out the window.

With a hiss of impatience Jesse started for the door.

Before he was halfway across the room Zane's quiet voice stopped him. "I'm thinking I might stay."

Jesse turned with a frown. "Why?"

His cousin shrugged. "There's a lot of material for a fascinating documentary right here." A smile flitted across his face. "Maybe I'll call it *The Search for the Lost Nugget.*"

Wyatt threw back his head and laughed.

Jesse turned to him. "What's so funny?"

His cousin shrugged. "You could call it *The Search for Fool's Gold.* Hell, maybe I'll stay, too. I've always loved an adventure."

Jesse looked from one to the other. "This isn't a dude ranch. The work is long and tedious. It doesn't matter how much money Coot left you. If you stay, you'll be expected to pull your own weight."

Wyatt's smile faded a bit. "You're not the only one who knows how to work, Jesse. You might have spent a lifetime doing ranch chores, but I've crewed a yacht during some of the worst storms ever seen in the Pacific. I climbed Mount Everest when it was twenty below. I shepherded a couple hundred fugitives halfway across Darfur. I think I can hold my own here in Montana."

Jesse turned to Zane with a scowl. "How about you, Hollywood? How long do you think you'll last driving a truck and shoveling manure?"

Zane's tone was deadly soft, but the heat in his eyes betrayed his temper. "I guess you'll have to wait and see, cousin. According to the terms of Coot's will, we've just become equal partners. And apparently that doesn't sit very well with you, does it?"

"You got that right. But let's see how it sits with the two of you a month from now, when you've had a healthy dose of the real world."

Zane turned to Wyatt. "I'm willing to stick around for a couple of months, just to see if it's a good fit."

Wyatt nodded. "Count me in, cuz."

Jesse slammed out of the room, his footsteps echoing in the empty hall.

CHAPTER FOUR

Jesse climbed into one of the ranch trucks and tore across an open field, tires spewing sand and grass in his wake. He didn't know where he was headed, but it didn't matter, as long as it took him away from here. The last place he wanted to be was anywhere near Wyatt and Zane.

"Why, Coot?" He hissed the words between clenched teeth. "All these years we got along just fine after they left. You and me. We didn't need anybody else. Why did you have to drag them back into my life?"

At the top of a hill he brought the truck to a halt and stared at the sweeping vista spread out before him. Acres of rich green pastures, studded with thousands of cattle. He knew every pond and stream and grassy meadow. He'd spent his entire life nursing sick heifers, dragging himself through muddy fields in the aftermath of a violent rainstorm, or trudging through waist-high snowdrifts

caused by a sudden blizzard. Not because his grandfather had promised him a reward, but simply because he
loved doing it. And now everything was about to change
because crazy old Coot had made his grandsons an offer
they couldn't refuse.

They'd stay. Oh, yeah. They'd stay, with visions of a
fortune dancing in their heads. But they'd be nothing but
dead weight.

"I'm not saving their lazy asses, Coot. I didn't ask
them to be here, and I'm not going out of my way to make
it easy for them to stay."

He gunned the engine and the truck careened down the
hill, coming to an abrupt halt at the edge of the woods.

He slammed out the door and stopped dead in his
tracks at the sight of the horse and rider heading toward
him across a stream that snaked through the woods. The
roan mare picked her way carefully through the water,
managing to avoid the rocks and fallen trees that littered
the path. But it wasn't the horse that had him staring. It
was the rider.

Amy's hair streamed out behind her like ribbons of
gold. She rode a horse the same way he imagined she
taught her students. With that easy self-assurance that
came from having been born for this. There was a smile
of pure pleasure on her face. From her relaxed, contented
look, Jesse knew that she hadn't yet spotted him.

He decided to simply savor the moment. To study
her without having to school his features or hide his
pleasure.

It wasn't just because she was so easy to look at. There
were plenty of beautiful women in Gold Fever. But none
who stirred him the way she always had. From the first

time he'd seen her sitting in her father's truck, he'd been drawn to her.

Otis Parrish and Coot had been engaged in a shouting match. To spare his grandsons, Coot had waved the boys away. Wyatt and Zane had climbed onto their horses and hightailed it back to the house. But Jesse had brashly walked up to the truck where she'd been sitting, poked his head in the open window, and introduced himself.

Amy smiled and spoke her name, and he'd felt a flare of heat bursting inside him.

Unlike other girls, she hadn't blushed or stammered or flirted. And when her father had stormed back to his truck and climbed inside, gunning the engine, she'd turned to wave, leaving Jesse with his heart in his throat.

It seemed to be perpetually stuck there whenever he saw her.

He needed to remind himself that she'd been the one to leave without a word.

Even now, his heart was an open, gaping wound. He wasn't certain it would ever heal. But he'd be damned if he'd let her see him bleeding to death.

Spotting Jesse, Amy tensed and drew in the reins, slowing her mount to a walk.

"Didn't figure on seeing you out here." Jesse leaned against the hood of the truck and folded his arms over his chest.

"Just getting some air. We got a call, and Dad's test results are in. We're to meet his doctor late today. Then I'll head out tomorrow."

"You don't seem too worried about him."

She managed a faint smile. "I'm convinced he's too ornery to get bad news."

He couldn't help smiling. They had both tasted her father's temper. "I hope you're right. One last ride?"

She nodded. "Yeah. I've been missing Old Red." She leaned over to run a hand lovingly along the horse's neck. "And she misses me. She could hardly wait for the saddle."

He watched the movement of her hand and found himself sweating. There'd been a time when he'd felt those hands on him. Despite their time apart, he could still remember the way they felt. He could remember everything about her.

Resentment surged through him. The last thing he wanted was to remember anything about those times. About Amy. About the two of them.

"I saw Wyatt and Zane with your aunt at the funeral today." Amy slid from the saddle and stood watching as Old Red dipped her head to drink. "They haven't changed much. A little older, a lot taller, but I'd have known them anywhere."

"Yeah. Some things never change."

At his tone, she glanced over. "I'm sorry you have to go through this, Jess. I know how you felt about your grandfather. But he was their grandfather, too."

"Yeah?" He shoved away from the truck and jammed his hands in his pockets. "You'd have never known it by the way they treated him. Once they left, they never looked back."

"They were kids, Jess. They didn't have a choice."

"Last I saw, they were all grown up. And neither of

them bothered to visit the old man. Not once in all these years."

"They're here now. It's pretty obvious that once they heard about his death, they dropped everything to make it back for the funeral. Why don't you just concentrate on that, and make your peace with them before they leave?"

"I'd be happy to. If they decide to leave." He gave a grunt of impatience. "They're thinking about staying."

Her eyes widened. "Why?"

"Coot made them an offer that was too tempting to refuse. In his will he stated that they can leave with his blessing and a hefty sum of money, or they can stay, inherit a chunk of real estate, and continue his search for the lost fortune. They're both mulling over the option to remain here. I guess it's just too hard to pass up the chance to be a part of our famously crazy, dysfunctional family."

"Oh, Jess." Without thinking Amy put a hand on his. Squeezed. "I'm sorry you have to deal with so much on this sad day."

She looked up to see him staring at her in a way that had her throat going dry. She'd seen that look so many times, whenever he was about to kiss her. It always had the same effect on her, sending her heart into overdrive.

Annoyed by the feelings that rushed through her, she lowered her hand and took a step back before pulling herself into the saddle.

Before she could wheel her mount he caught the reins. Her head came up sharply.

"Thanks for your concern, Amy. I appreciate it."

When she said nothing, he added, "I hope your dad gets the good news he's hoping for. Safe journey."

He turned on his heel and climbed into his truck.

Amy watched as he gunned the engine and made a wide turn before heading back in the direction of his ranch.

She urged her horse into a run and wondered at the way her heartbeat kept time to the pounding of Old Red's hooves.

She'd thought, for just a moment there, that Jesse might haul her to the ground and kiss her. Or was it just wishful thinking?

She needed to get out of here. Out of the county and back to Helena where she wouldn't be close enough to Jesse McCord to be tempted to think about what might have been.

Jesse was doing plenty of thinking of his own. He'd driven out here to be alone, to deal with the pain of Coot's death. Amy's presence had brought another kind of pain—the pain of loss that had never been reconciled. And because they'd never dealt with what had happened between them, the wound had never healed.

She'd gone her way, without a word, and he'd been left to pick up the pieces of what passed for his heart. What kind of woman declared her love one night and was gone without a word the next morning?

There had been plenty of women since then, but none he'd allowed to get close. Once burned was enough. Only a fool would allow himself to get hurt like that again, and Jesse prided himself on being nobody's fool.

He wouldn't think about her. He'd had enough grief for one day.

He turned the truck into the barn and slammed the door hard enough to rattle the timbers as he headed toward the house.

"I made your favorite tonight, Miss Cora." Dandy set the platter of sliced meat loaf beside her plate before unloading the trolley containing mashed potatoes, gravy, green beans from the garden, and freshly baked biscuits.

The group seated around the table was subdued. Jesse made no attempt at conversation, keeping his attention fixed on his plate.

Across the table Wyatt and Zane directed their words to the ranch foreman.

"Thanks for the tour, Cal." Wyatt filled his plate before handing the platter to Zane, seated beside him.

"My pleasure. If you're going to be living and working here, I figured you'd want to familiarize yourself with the place."

"So many changes." Zane scooped potatoes from a bowl and made a crater in the middle before filling it with rich, dark gravy. "You've really gone high-tech on us."

"Some." Cal swallowed back a smile, remembering that it was Coot who'd taught his grandsons to do that so many years ago at this very table. His old friend had always enjoyed his potatoes smothered in Dandy's gravy. "Since you boys left the ranch, we've added computers and GPS, helicopters and all-terrain vehicles for the wildest stretches of land. But ranching is still hands-on, seat-of-the-pants dirty work best done by dedicated cowboys."

That had Jesse looking over at his cousins. "You two think you're up to it?"

Wyatt shrugged. "I guess we'll know soon enough." He grinned at Zane before turning to the weathered foreman. "You still planning on taking us up to the high country tomorrow?"

Jesse frowned at Cal. "You're sending them to Rafe?"

The old man nodded. "Zane and Wyatt said they'd like to jump in and lend a hand wherever they're needed. Rafe needs help with the herd."

"The last thing he needs is to babysit a couple of greenhorns."

Cora's jaw dropped. "Jesse..."

Before his aunt could say more, Wyatt held up a hand. "It's okay, Aunt Cora. Zane and I can fight our own battles." He looked over at Jesse and kept his smile in place, though his words were pure ice. "I get that you don't want us here. It must be a burr under your saddle to suddenly have to share what you've had all to yourself for so many years. But this was Coot's last wish. And I'm going to give it my best shot to make it my wish, too. For now, I intend to learn all I can about the operation of the Lost Nugget and see how I can fit in. *If* I can fit in," he added for emphasis. "Now if that sticks in your craw"—he gave a negligent shrug of his shoulders—"then you'll just have to swallow it or choke on it."

Jesse's scowl grew. He flicked a glance at Zane. "Does he speak for you, too, Hollywood?"

Zane set down his fork. "I don't need anybody to do my talking. I'm here by choice. I figure if I could survive three years of everything from the hottest stretches of desert to the frozen mountains tracking a herd of mustangs for our documentary, I can survive here. I'll stay or go on my own terms. And if you decide to try to push me out before I'm ready to leave, you'd better be prepared for a fight."

Jesse gave a bitter laugh. "A fight? You going to send for some movie extras to be your body doubles, Hollywood?"

Zane was on his feet, his hand fisted at Jesse's shirtfront. "Would you like to find out here and now?"

"I wouldn't want to mess up that pretty moviestar face." Jesse pushed away. "Excuse me, Aunt Cora. I think I'll head into town. I expect the company at the Fortune Saloon will be a whole lot more interesting than this."

As he slammed out of the house Cora took a calming sip of her iced tea before glancing at her nephews. "I know Jesse's hurting. But that's no excuse for his behavior."

"Don't worry about it, Aunt Cora." Zane reached across the table and caught her hand. "It's going to be a tough adjustment for all of us. I'm just sorry that it spoiled your supper."

She gave him a weak smile. "I really have no appetite tonight. But for Dandy's sake, I thought I'd try."

"I feel the same way." Zane nodded toward the doorway. "Why don't we give it up and take a walk outside before it gets too dark? Or would you rather just sit in the great room where we can talk?"

"The great room." Cora shoved away from the table. "It was always Coot's favorite room. We've been apart

too many years. I want to know all about the two of you."
She turned to Cal. "I hope you'll join us."

"Glad to." He nodded. "I'd like to do some catching
up of my own."

The four of them left the dining table and walked to
the great room, where a log blazed in the open four-sided
fireplace that dominated the center of the space. They
settled themselves comfortably in the overstuffed chairs
by the hearth. A few minutes later Dandy entered carrying a tray of frosty longnecks. After passing them around,
he made his way back to the kitchen, leaving the four to
their privacy.

Jesse drove like the very devil himself, leaving a trail
of dust in his truck's wake. By the time he reached town
the worst of his temper had evaporated. Still, he wasn't
ready to let go just yet. And so he nursed the simmering
anger, hoping to coax it back to flame.

He paused just inside the door of the saloon to allow
his eyes to adjust. A pall of smoke hung in the air. Added
to that was the smell of onions on the small grill behind
the bar, where burgers simmered in a lake of grease.
Violet Spence had her back to the door as she flipped the
sizzling meat patties before filling another drink order.

Through the smoky veil Jesse recognized the usual
patrons. Harding Jessup, owner of the hardware and plumbing supply store, was seated at the bar with Stan Novak, a
local building contractor. The two men were bent close,
deep in conversation, a set of blueprints between them,
which only confirmed to Jesse that the rumor he'd heard
about Harding's plans to add onto his store must be true.

Mayor Rowe Stafford was holding court in one corner with a cluster of the townsfolk who'd probably been there since returning from the funeral. By now they were well-oiled and hanging on his every word. Seeing Jesse, the mayor lowered his voice, and Jesse realized he was probably regaling the locals with one of his many tales of adventure with Coot. Though Rowe professed to be one of Coot's oldest friends, he was known to embellish his stories in order to make them just a bit more interesting than the original incident. And in most of the yarns that had been repeated to Jesse, it would seem that Rowe painted himself a hero and Coot nothing but an old fool.

At a table in the center of the room some of the wranglers from the Lost Nugget ranch were laughing and talking with several of the local women. When they spotted Jesse they beckoned him over, but he gave a quick shake of his head and sidled up to the bar.

"Hey, you sweet thang." Daffy Spence came up from behind and gave him a hard hug even before he'd parked himself on the bar stool.

Daffy and her twin sister, Vi, owned and operated the Fortune Saloon. Violet was as shy and sweet as her sister Daffodil was wild and crazy. The two women had bought the building when it was a grain and feed store in the 1970s. Once they'd turned it into a successful bar, they'd sold the grain and feed business to Orley Peterson, who relocated down the street.

The sisters took turns working the day and night shifts, except on the weekends when they worked together to handle the crowd. Both were stick-thin and wore their purple hair spiked, their eyes ringed with enough jet-black liner to give them the appearance of flirty raccoons. Their age was a source of constant speculation, though one thing was certain. Whatever their birth certificates said, they were still young and frisky enough to bed the occasional bartender or willing customer.

"You in need of a little sympathy, Jesse?"

"Just a beer, Daffy. And send a round to the guys over there." He indicated the table of wranglers.

"You bet." She rounded the bar and set a longneck in front of him before filling a tray for the others.

Violet hurried over to catch his hand. "I'm so sorry for your loss, honey." Her voice, whispery as a little girl's, trembled slightly.

"Thanks, Vi."

"Daffy and I were at the funeral, but we didn't stay for the luncheon. Had to hurry back and get ready for the afternoon rush."

"I understand." He glanced around. "Looks like business is good."

She nodded. "Most of 'em raised their first glass to Coot."

He lifted his bottle. "Then I'll do the same."

"We lost a good man."

Jesse saw her eyes tear up and prayed she wouldn't cry. He didn't think he could handle tears right now.

She sniffed. "Want a burger, honey? It's on the house."

"No thanks, Vi. But I appreciate the offer."

She patted his hand. "You want anything, Jesse honey, you let me know."

When she walked back to the grill he found himself

wondering if she and his grandfather had ever had a fling. Or would Coot have preferred her rowdy sister?

The direction of his thoughts had him scowling. He tipped up the bottle and took a long pull, hoping the taste of beer would wash away the bitter taste of loss.

"Hey, Doc. What'll you have?"

The sound of Daffy's voice had him glancing around. Dr. Frank Wheeler was just settling himself on the bar stool beside his.

"I'll have the same as Jesse." Dr. Wheeler's tufts of white hair and round, frameless glasses gave him an owlish look. He and Jesse exchanged a quick handshake. "Jesse. Sorry for your loss."

"Thanks, Doc."

When Daffy set down the longneck and walked away, Jesse shot him a sideways glance. "I saw Amy Parrish this afternoon. She said she and her father were seeing you today."

The doctor nodded gravely and took a long drink. "Just delivering the test results from the university hospital up in Billings."

"I guess Amy'll be halfway to Helena by noon tomorrow." He wondered why the words made his throat hurt.

Dr. Wheeler shook his head. "Doubt she'll be going anytime soon."

Jesse turned to study him. "Why's that?"

The older man shrugged. "Since Otis doesn't have any other family, he'll be depending on his daughter for support."

"Support?"

"Driving him to the clinic in town for his treatments.

Picking up his prescriptions. And pretty much holding his hand through this."

"How serious is it?"

Frank Wheeler stared down into his drink. "You know what the hardest thing about being a doctor is?" He looked up. Met Jesse's eyes. "Telling a man like Otis Parrish to get his affairs in order."

CHAPTER FIVE

Amy sat on the big porch swing, arms hugging her knees, staring into the darkness. Her father had gone into his room. A short time later she'd heard the creaking of his bed and knew that he'd retreated into sleep.

He hadn't said a word all the way home. Nor, for that matter, in the doctor's office. He'd listened in silence as Dr. Wheeler read the lab report and described the treatments suggested by the team of specialists in Billings. When Dr. Wheeler ended their meeting by telling him to get his affairs in order, she'd tried to take her father's hand. He'd shaken off her touch, but in that brief instant she'd recognized that it was as cold as the ring of ice that had begun to form around her heart.

How did others handle this kind of news about a parent? Did they cry? Get angry? Throw something? Some might urge a second or even a third opinion, or simply deny the truth. A few probably took a family trip around the world, hoping to store up memories for the harsh reality looming in their future. Did anyone else react like this? Or was she the only one in the universe to feel more like a statue than a human? She was numb. Her brain refused to function. She couldn't think. Couldn't even react. And so she sat, the swing motionless, staring without seeing the night shadows, the golden slice of moon, the glittering stars in the black velvet sky.

In her mind's eye she was four, teetering on a boulder to pull herself onto the back of her father's favorite stallion. While her parents watched in horror, she flicked the reins, sending the horse into a trot. She bumped up and down in the saddle, practically airborne, as the horse circled the corral. By the time her father managed to catch up with her and grab the reins, she was beaming with excitement.

"See, Daddy? I'm just like you."

He swore viciously, causing her smile to fade at his outburst. "Little fool. You could've been trampled."

"But I wasn't afraid, Daddy."

"You should've been. Fear's a good thing. It keeps us from jumping off cliffs."

"I didn't jump. I rode your horse. Just like you."

"Without my permission." He hauled her roughly from the saddle and swatted her backside before shoving her toward her mother, who was standing just outside the corral.

She wanted to cry, but even at that tender age she knew that it would add another layer to her father's anger. "You said I could ride when I was big enough." With hands on hips she faced him. "I'm big enough now."

"One more word and you won't be able to sit for a week. You hear me, girl?"

She looked up at her mother in confusion. "Daddy always says he wishes I was a boy. But then he gets mad when I try to be what he wants."

"Your father's going through a...difficult time." Her mother avoided Amy's eyes as she led the girl toward the house. "He fought with a neighbor, and I just gave him some bad news."

"Bad news?"

"You and I are going to stay with my sister for a while."

"Did Daddy cry?"

Her mother stopped, paused to kneel down, and managed a smile. "Your daddy doesn't know how to cry, honey. All he knows how to do is fight. Whether he's mad or sad or even when things are going fairly well, he just doesn't react like other men. But a good fight seems to clear the air."

"Did Daddy and I just have a fight?"

Her mother considered before she stood and hurried on toward the house, dragging Amy with her. "He'd have preferred a good knock-down, drag-out fight, but I suppose this was better than nothing."

At that, the little girl's spirits lifted. She hadn't completely failed. She'd managed to stay in the saddle. And she'd given her dad something he wanted.

That may have been the first fight Amy could recall. But it was far from the last.

She and her father had been butting heads almost from the day of her birth. She had long ago accepted the fact that she was fated to break every rule that Otis Parrish set, whether by accident or design. She'd lost count of the number and ferocity of their arguments.

But this time...this time, she thought with a sigh, all the fight seemed to have gone out of him, and she didn't know how to deal with it.

Her mother would have known just what to do. But ever since her mother's sudden death from a heart attack while Amy was away at college, nothing had been the same. She'd avoided coming home because it no longer felt like home. She and her father had grown more and more distant, and when, after graduation, she'd been offered a teaching job in Helena, she'd accepted with a sense of relief that it offered her the perfect excuse to stay away.

Now she was back, and she felt awkward and useless.

She looked up at the sound of an engine. Headlights momentarily blinded her. A truck door slammed and a tall figure bounded up the steps.

Amy sucked in a breath, then let it out in a whoosh when she recognized Jesse.

He was headed toward the front door but halted in midstride when he caught sight of her seated in the shadows. "You okay?"

Her heart was pounding again, but this time it wasn't because she'd been startled, but because of some other, deeper emotion. When she couldn't find her voice she merely nodded.

"Mind if I join you?" Without waiting for her reply, he settled himself on the swing beside her.

Their hips bumped and they both moved apart a fraction.

"You heard?" She studied his profile.

"I ran into Doc Wheeler at the Fortune Saloon."

"So much for doctor-patient confidentiality."

"The rules don't apply. This is Gold Fever."

"Yeah." She crossed her arms over her chest. "I should have known. Bad news and small towns."

"He wasn't spreading gossip. I asked and he told me." Jesse paused before adding, "How'd your dad take the news?"

"How should I know?"

He looked over. "Doc said you were there."

"Yeah. It was like watching a silent movie. All facial expressions and body language. But no dialogue."

"You two didn't talk? Not even on the long drive home?"

She shook her head.

"I'm sorry, Amy." She looked so defeated. He thought about taking her into his arms, but she'd probably slap him. "So, what're you going to do?"

"I don't know. I've been trying to sort things out. Dr. Wheeler said he didn't think Dad should be alone during the treatments. Since there's nobody else, I guess I'll take a leave of absence and ask the school district to get a substitute for me. After that, I'll just have to wait and see. If Dad responds to the treatments, I'll go back to Helena. If he doesn't..." Her words trailed off.

"Hey. He'll be fine."

"Don't." She covered her ears. "I'm not interested in empty platitudes."

"Then how about this?" He caught her hands. Held them fast when she tried to pull away. "Some people make it. Some don't. I'm betting your old man is ornery enough to survive anything."

That had her almost smiling, but the warmth of his touch

of her hands made her break contact. She didn't like the way her heart was pounding. To cover her feelings, she got to her feet and started pacing. "He is ornery, isn't he?"

"The toughest guy in the county." Jesse watched her stalk restlessly across the porch, then back. "If anybody can catch bullets in his teeth and spit them out, it's your father."

"Yeah." She released a long, slow breath. "I wish that were true. Oh, Jesse, when the doctor started talking about the series of treatments, I looked over at my dad and he looked so old and tired and beaten."

"Come on, now." Without thinking he stood and gathered her close. "This kind of diagnosis doesn't necessarily mean a death sentence. He's still breathing, isn't he?"

At his words she looked stricken. "What was I thinking? Here I am going on about my dad on the very day you've buried your grandfather. I'm sorry, Jess. At least Dad has a fighting chance." She touched a hand to his cheek. "You have to be reeling from the shock of Coot's death without any…"

The look in his eyes had her words trailing off. She recognized the smoldering heat. Had seen it often enough in the past to know exactly how unexpectedly it could build into an inferno.

Her heart nearly tumbled in her chest as his head lowered.

She braced herself, eager for his mouth to claim hers.

Instead, the moment seemed to freeze before he thought better of it and stepped back, clenching his hands at his sides.

"Guess I'd better be heading home. We've both put in a long day."

A breeze caught the end of her hair and he lifted a hand, tucking the errant strand behind her ear. His gaze held hers for just a moment longer before he turned away and bounded down the porch steps.

He opened the door of the truck and looked up. "If there's anything I can do..." He shrugged.

"Thanks."

She stood watching as the headlights receded. Within minutes the silence had returned, swallowing her in darkness.

Amy shivered. In that instant when his arms had encircled her, she'd had to fight a nearly overpowering urge to weep. She was so glad she'd managed to keep her composure. Especially since the expected kiss hadn't materialized. But she'd wanted, just for that moment, to allow him to be strong for both of them.

Fool, she thought with a rising sense of anger and frustration. He'd come here like a neighbor to offer her comfort, and she'd immediately begun to spin it into something more.

Whatever feelings had once been between them were dead and buried. Hadn't he made that abundantly clear years ago?

While she'd been feeling lost and alone in a brand-new town, struggling to get through crowded dorm rooms and confusing college classes, he'd been living the good life, dating every female within a hundred miles, according to the things she'd been told. And though she'd waited endlessly for him to contact her, he'd remained oddly silent, until, finally, she'd been forced to accept the message he'd been trying to send. Whatever feelings she'd had for him weren't returned.

The hardest lesson she'd ever had to learn was that Jesse not only didn't miss her, he didn't even think about her.

Out of sight; out of mind. At least on his part.

Just seeing him again had brought all the old emotions to the surface. It wasn't love, she cautioned. It was memory. Habit. Now that she was back in Gold Fever, she would have to remember to guard her fickle heart.

As she made her way inside she realized that now, after Jesse's visit, she felt even more desolate than ever.

Jesse let himself into the darkened ranch house and prayed he could make it to his room without running into anyone. He was in no mood to chat up his aunt or duel with his cousins.

He shed his boots in the mudroom and moved quickly through the kitchen. As he stepped into the great room he realized his mistake. In the glow of the fire two heads came up sharply.

Wyatt made a point of glancing at his watch. "Not even close to closing time yet. The Fortune Saloon run out of longnecks?"

"I decided to stop over at the Parrish ranch."

Now it was Zane's turn to glance meaningfully at his watch. "I guess this means you didn't get the warm reception you were hoping for." He chuckled at his little joke.

Jesse thought about ignoring Wyatt and Zane and heading off to bed without another word, but that would only give them a power over him they didn't deserve.

"Thought I'd pay a call on a neighbor who just got some bad news."

His cousins' smiles evaporated.

Wyatt spoke for both of them. "What was the bad news?"

"Otis Parrish got the results of his lab tests back late this afternoon, and he's facing some serious treatments if he hopes to live. Since Amy's his only kin, she's going to have to take a leave of absence from teaching to help him through the next few months."

"I'm sorry to hear that." Zane pointed to his beer. "Care to join us?"

It was on the tip of Jesse's tongue to refuse, but he found himself saying, "I guess I could use a cold one."

Zane left the room and returned a minute later with a frosty bottle.

Jesse took a long, slow pull before lowering it to his side. "Thanks. I was drier than I thought."

Wyatt glanced over from his position beside the fire. "How's Amy taking the news about her father?"

Jesse shrugged. "She's still in shock. Needs some time to sort through it."

Wyatt shook his head. "I don't blame her. When I heard about Coot, I felt like I'd been sucker-punched."

Zane nodded. "I know the feeling. I'd thought so many times about just packing up and driving out here, but the time never seemed right. Then, to get the news and know that I could never see him, never make it right between us..." He lowered his head.

Jesse wanted to remind his cousins that they'd had years to visit the old man if they'd really wanted to bridge the chasm left by old family feuds. Instead, he held his silence and took another long drink of beer.

Wyatt stared at the glowing coals of the fire. "It was the same when I heard about my parents going down in that plane. All of a sudden the most important people in my life were gone, and there was no way to bring them back. I spent years wandering the world, trying to make sense of it."

Jesse glanced over. "Did you? Make any sense out of it?"

"Some." Wyatt gave a dry laugh. "If I discovered anything, it's this: We have a certain amount of time, and we'd better use it wisely. When time runs out, there's no bargaining for more."

"That's profound." Zane yawned and drained his beer. "I wouldn't mind continuing this deep discussion another time, but right now, I need to get some sleep."

"You'd better both get some sleep." Jesse set aside his half-full bottle. "Rafe Spindler works his crew up in the hills like dogs."

"So I heard." Wyatt followed Zane toward the doorway before pausing and turning toward Jesse. "If you see Amy again, tell her that at least she's bought some time with her father. If there's anything they haven't resolved, now's the time."

"Yeah. I'll tell her." Jesse banked the fire before climbing the stairs to his room.

As he passed Coot's rooms, he resisted the urge to step inside as he often used to, just to talk over the day. He missed the old man with an ache that was so deep and physical, he held a hand to his midsection.

Upstairs he crossed the room and leaned a hip against the windowsill, staring at the canopy of stars in the midnight sky. He yanked his shirt over his head, intent upon tossing it aside. In that instant he became aware that it still bore the distinct fragrance of Amy.

On a moan he buried his face in the fabric, breathing her in, and felt a shudder pass through him.

He could lie to her, to his cousins, even to himself. But now, here, in the privacy of his room, in the dark of the night, in the depths of his own heart, there was no denying.

God, how he wanted her. Wanted her as much now as when he'd first held her in his arms all those years ago. In fact, since he was being completely honest with himself, he wanted her more. The need for her was a knife in his heart that nothing, not time, not distance, would ever heal.

On an overload of emotions he fell face-first across his bed, the shirt clutched tightly in his hand, praying for the release of sleep.

CHAPTER SIX

———◆◆◆———

Jesse tore open the driver's-side door of the truck and got slammed by a gust of wind and rain. He had to lean his weight against the barn doors to open them wide enough for the truck to pass through. He jumped back into the truck, drove it inside, parked it in a row of other vehicles, and then sprinted back into the rain to secure the barn door. By the time he made it to the house, his clothes were plastered to his skin. In the mudroom he levered off his muddy boots and hung his soaked hat and cowhide jacket on pegs by the door.

The weather this past week had been as surly as his mood.

Cora looked up from the table, where she sat sipping a steaming cup of tea. "I haven't seen you in a week."

"Been with Cal's crew mending fences." And putting as much distance as possible between himself and Amy.

"I missed you."

"Sorry." He felt a twinge of guilt. Her first days with her brother gone, and he'd left her all alone. Not that he'd have been any comfort to her, he thought with a trace of bitterness. He'd had his own demons to battle. Still, he wished he knew how to help his aunt get through her grief. God knew, he wasn't doing very well with his.

He spied the bulging travel case of paints and canvas standing in a corner. They always signaled another road trip for his aunt. "Where're you headed this time?"

"Treasure Chest."

At the mention of the distant mountain shaped like its name, Jesse arched a brow. "That's quite a hike, Aunt Cora."

"I'm not planning on climbing it. Just going to paint it. I think all those dark storm clouds will make an interesting background. Weather reports say they'll be around for at least three or four more days."

"Just what we need." He scowled. "More rain."

The old woman touched a hand to his sleeve. "You've been pushing yourself too hard, Jesse. With Wyatt and Zane up in the hills, why don't you take a few days off?"

"And do what?"

She smiled. He was so like Coot. Restless. Always on the move. "I don't know. Go for a walk or a ride. Maybe search for buried treasure."

"I'll leave that for the city slickers." He started toward the door. "Got to shower off all this range mud."

"Before you do that, would you mind helping me load my supplies?"

"You're leaving now? Before supper?"

"I asked Dandy to pack some food before giving him

the night off." She looked up suddenly. "Sorry. We didn't know whether or not to expect you."

"Doesn't matter about me." He shrugged. "I'll eat some of that glue Vi passes off as a burger at the saloon. When will you eat?"

"When I stop for the night." She laughed at her nephew's look of consternation. "After a lifetime with me, you have to know that I'm as crazy as my brother. Instead of gold, I keep chasing after art. I intend to be painting Treasure Chest by dawn's light."

Jesse picked up the box of supplies and paused to step into his boots before trailing her to her Jeep, buffeted by wind and rain. The back was loaded with a sleeping bag, a rifle, a cooler, a small cookstove, and enough supplies to see her through several weeks if necessary.

After loading the paint and supplies Jesse leaned in the open window. "You remembered your cell phone and charger?"

She nodded. "You sound like Coot. I'm fine, Jesse."

"Yes. You are. You're darned near perfect." He kissed her cheek. "Just remember to check in every day, or Cal and I will send the cavalry out after you."

"Yes, sir." She cupped his chin in one hand and gave him her sweetest smile. "While I'm gone, try to make peace with your cousins."

He stepped back, eyes steely. "Don't wish for miracles. Just stay safe."

"I'll be home in a week or two. Unless I run out of food or paint and canvas sooner." She put the Jeep in gear and pulled away, windshield wipers waging a furious war against the pounding rain.

Feeling as gloomy as the weather, Jesse trudged back to the house.

Up in his room he stood under the shower, letting the soothing warm water beat down on his head. After toweling dry he pulled on clean denims and rolled the sleeves of a well-worn shirt to his elbows.

In the mudroom he paused to slip into clean boots before heading for the barn. Minutes later he left a layer of mud in his wake as he drove the nearly hundred miles to Gold Fever.

Main Street was so littered with cars and trucks that Jesse had to drive to the very end of the line of businesses, alongside Harding Jessup's Plumbing Supply, to find a parking space. When he stepped inside the Fortune Saloon, he could see why. It seemed as though half the crew of the Lost Nugget was already there, eager to spend their paychecks.

"Hey, Jesse." Cal clapped him on the shoulder as he nudged his way toward the bar. "If I'd known you were coming into town, I'd've offered you a ride."

"No need, Cal." Jesse acknowledged the greetings from half a dozen men and women seated nearby before winking at Daffy behind the bar, who expertly flipped the cap off a longneck and handed it over the heads of several customers.

"You want a burger with that, honey?" Her rusty croak could be heard above the voice of Tim McGraw urging them to live like they were dying. The country-western singer was Daffy's latest crush, and her customers were subjected to marathon McGraw from morning to night.

"Yeah. Double onions."

"Double onions?" Burly Rafe Spindler looked up

from his seat at the bar. "I guess that means you don't figure on getting lucky tonight, McCord."

His words had everyone laughing, including Jesse, until he spotted Wyatt and Zane seated at the end of the bar. His smile faded as he ambled closer.

"Didn't expect to see you two in town."

Wyatt answered for both of them. "Couldn't pass up the chance to spend our first paycheck with the rest of the crew. We were told it was a rite of passage."

"It is. But I figured after a week up in the hills you two would be passed out in the bunkhouse. Or did you give up early so you could catch up on your beauty sleep before you went slumming?"

"I'll admit I'm a bit sore." Zane rolled his shoulders and grinned at the man beside him. "Jimmy here says I should be up to speed in a couple more weeks."

Jimmy Eagle nursed his soda. Even though he'd taken a lot of teasing over the years for choosing soft drinks over alcohol, he'd earned the respect of the wranglers for refusing to give in to their bullying. And while many of them had to drag out of bed for an early morning shift after a night in town, he was always clear-eyed and ready to face the day. "You keep working the way you did this week, son, and you'll have me thinking about retiring."

That had the wranglers from the Lost Nugget ranch laughing. They'd all heard Jimmy boast that he'd never slow down. His idea of heaven was to die in the saddle while bringing down one last herd from the high ground.

"It's going to take me a whole lot more months of wrangling to replace you, Jimmy."

"I'd say more like years." Stung by the easy camaraderie

between Zane and the weathered cowboy, Jesse tipped up his beer and took a long, steady pull.

"I don't know." Jimmy Eagle grinned at the two young men who had already begun to earn the grudging respect of the other wranglers. "You'd've been proud of your cousins, Jesse. Once they got the hang of it, the years melted away and they took to ranch chores like they'd never been gone."

Jesse gave a wry laugh. "You want me to believe our Hollywood pretty boy here was willing to get his hands dirty?"

Zane was halfway off the barstool when Wyatt's big hand pressed him down. His tone was low. "He's baiting you."

"Maybe I'm ready to take the bait."

Jimmy Eagle shot a quick glance at Jesse, who was rocking on his heels and staring daggers at his cousins. "Don't take it personally, son. He's been spoiling for a fight since Coot died."

"Oh, it's personal." Zane shoved aside his beer. "I'm more than willing to give him what he wants. He may have been able to beat me when he was twelve and I was nine, but that was too many years ago to count."

"You don't know..." Jimmy's head came up at a burst of raucous laughter from across the room.

Four strangers had been drinking steadily for the past couple of hours and their voices had grown progressively louder with every round of drinks.

"You know them?" Jesse nodded toward their table.

Jimmy gave a shake of his head. "Bikers, I'm thinking. I saw their motorcycles parked out back. Not from around here."

Vi turned away from the grill and held out a plate with a burger and a pile of her famous ranch fries, oozing grease. "Here you go, Jesse honey. Just the way you like it."

"Thanks, Vi." Jesse set aside his beer and lifted the burger to his mouth. Before he could take a bite one of the strangers, sporting a bushy beard and arms the size of tree limbs, strode across the room and snatched the burger out of Jesse's hands.

"What the hell?" Jesse looked more startled than angry. "What do you think you're doing?"

"We gave that old biddy our order half an hour ago. Since you just walked in the door, I figure this must be mine."

He started back to his table with Jesse's burger in his hand. Before he managed three steps Jesse spun him around and tore the food from his hand.

"Now you've gone and made me mad," the stranger said, then let loose with a string of oaths before throwing a punch.

Jesse ducked and managed to evade his fist. The burger slipped from his hand and landed on the floor.

Jesse looked down at the mess, then up into the cowboy's eyes. "Not nearly as mad as you've just made me. That was supposed to be my supper." His fist landed a direct hit between the stranger's eyes.

The biker, nearly a foot taller, barely blinked before jamming a fist into Jesse's midsection, leaving him grunting in pain. The man's buddies were on their feet now, cursing and egging him on.

One of them, with a beer belly hanging over the waist of faded denims, added to their laughter when he accused Jesse of fighting like a girl.

As they watched with the others, Zane turned to Wyatt. "Think we ought to lend a hand?"

Wyatt merely grinned. "Not our problem, cousin. Jesse was itching for a fight, remember? Now he's got one. I think he can handle this by himself."

The rest of the customers formed a circle around the pair. Some of them stood on their chairs, while others watched from barstools and tables. They gave the two men a wide berth, hoping for more action.

Jesse blew out a breath and straightened before landing a solid right cross to Bushy Beard's nose, sending blood gushing down the front of his shirt. The sight of all that blood had the crowd murmuring.

Before the stranger could recover, Jesse moved in with another blow to the man's jaw, snapping his head back.

For a moment the man looked dazed. He shook his head and staggered. That had his friends looking worried. Beer Belly was gesturing wildly to a beefy man in a ponytail and his remaining lanky friend. The three conferred, then moved in, circling Jesse.

Wyatt got to his feet so quickly he nearly kicked over his barstool.

Zane glanced up in surprise. "I thought you said this wasn't our fight."

"Those three just made it ours."

Beer Belly picked up his chair. Before he could lift it over his head, Wyatt tapped him on the shoulder.

He turned. "You want something, Surfer Boy?"

"Yeah. This."

The man found Wyatt's fist in his face. The chair clattered to the floor.

When Ponytail stepped up to help, fists raised, he found Zane directly beside him.

"Hey. Look at the pretty boy who came to join our party."

Zane landed a blow to his jaw that had him teetering backward.

The sight of the three McCords fighting the four strangers electrified the crowd. Even those who'd been trying to ignore the fight were now on their feet, watching avidly and calling words of encouragement.

"Behind you," Wyatt shouted.

Jesse ducked, and Bushy Beard's punch caught only air.

"Thanks." Jesse mouthed the word, then called to Zane, "Watch out."

Zane deflected the bottle that had come flying toward his head, then moved in to stop the lanky biker before he could toss a second one.

Without his friends to lend a hand, Bushy Beard realized he was in trouble. He'd picked the wrong cowboy to mess with. Desperate, he threw a punch that grazed Jesse's temple and was rewarded by a hard, stinging blow from Jesse's fist that sent him reeling.

Jesse turned to watch as Zane landed a solid punch to the lanky one's midsection. The man doubled up and hit the floor with a groan.

"Didn't know you had it in you, Hollywood." Jesse's grin faded when Zane pointed a finger. When Jesse turned, Bushy Beard had come back for more, landing a series of blows about Jesse's head that had his ears ringing.

When Beer Belly attempted to join in, taking aim with

a broken beer bottle, Wyatt caught the man's arm in a vicious grasp and began twisting until the bottle dropped to the floor, shattering into more pieces. Then Wyatt followed up with a fist to his jaw that rattled the man's teeth and caused his eyes to roll back in his head.

As he fell, Jesse threw a well-aimed punch at Bushy Beard that dropped him like a stone.

Both Wyatt and Jesse watched as Zane and Ponytail exchanged blows. Suddenly Zane took a fist to his eye and blinked furiously. He shook his head to clear it, then moved in with a series of blows. As the man brought his hands up to cover his face, Zane took advantage of the moment to take aim at his unprotected midsection. With a grunt of pain the man fell to his knees. Breathing hard, Zane waited, urging his opponent to get up so he could finish the job. Ponytail wobbled, then fell facedown on the floor.

After a few moments he lifted his hands in a sign of surrender. "I don't want to fight the three of you."

"You should have thought about that when you and your buddies decided to go four-on-one."

"We didn't mean anything by it. We had a few beers and just wanted to help a pal."

Jesse stared around at the mess. Broken chairs and bottles littered the floor, along with three unconscious cowboys.

"I expect you to pay the owners for the mess you made."

The man cowered before turning to Vi and Daffy. "Sorry for the mess, ladies." He reached into his pocket and withdrew a fat roll of bills. "I hope this will cover the cleanup."

Daffy accepted the money, then fixed him with a look of fury. "You owe my sister an apology."

"An...apology?"

"Your friend there called her an old biddy." In an aside she muttered, "Old biddy, indeed."

The man managed to choke out yet another apology. "Sorry, ma'am."

Anger gave Daffy's voice the rasp of a rusty gate. "Now take that"—she pointed to the three unconscious men—"trash out of our saloon. And see that you don't come back."

"Want to give him a hand?" Jesse turned to Zane and Wyatt, and the three of them began lifting, dragging, and nearly carrying the three cowboys toward the door. Once outside they dumped them unceremoniously in the mud and watched as Ponytail staggered off in search of their motorcycles. It took him nearly an hour to revive his friends enough to get them on their bikes.

When at last the rumble of their motorcycles faded into the darkness, the three cousins retraced their steps inside the saloon.

The crowd erupted into cheers before everybody returned to their beers.

Jesse wore a stupid grin on his face as he flexed his bruised, bloody knuckles. "That biker had the toughest hide I've ever encountered. I thought I'd broken my hand on his jaw."

"You think that's tough?" Wyatt leaned a hand on the wall until he could trust his legs. He gingerly touched his jaw and winced. "I'm lucky to have all my teeth."

Jesse turned to Zane, who had blood dripping from a cut over his eye.

"I think you're going to have a beautiful shiner by morning, Hollywood."

"Won't be the first time." Zane gave a short laugh.

"Yeah. I can see that."

Zane shared a grin with Wyatt. "Nothing like a good brawl to clear the air."

"Yeah."

Jesse looked from Wyatt to Zane, then surprised them both by dropping an arm over each of their shoulders. "Come on. Let's have a beer and some of Vi's awful burgers and fries."

"Better not let her hear you say that." Zane lowered his voice. "Poor thing's already had one insult tonight."

While the customers looked on with interest, the three cousins moved to a corner table, laughing like loons.

CHAPTER SEVEN

———◆◆◆———

Cora maneuvered her Jeep along the dirt road. The haunting strains of Debussy's "Clair de Lune" played by the London Philharmonic rose softly in the background. The soothing music seemed an odd contrast to the wild look of her. After a week of nonstop painting, her shirt and denims were spattered with paint stains. With Coot gone, she loved his cast-offs even more. They made her feel somehow closer to her brother.

She hadn't been to a beauty salon in years. These days she styled her own hair, which she'd allowed to go gray. In her younger days she'd gone through every color of the spectrum, from platinum blond to rich auburn to gothic black, hanging down her back almost to her waist. She'd been so proud of her crowning glory. Now, it all seemed too much trouble.

She knew how other people saw her. An oddball. A misfit. It never bothered her to be seen as a contradiction.

In her college years she'd traveled to France and Italy to pursue her love of art. Along the way she'd tasted the good life, had fallen in love a time or two, and had her share of heartbreak. And each time, through all the pain and heartache, she had found solace in her art.

She'd worked with some of the best and brightest in the art world, and had been offered apprenticeships that would have guaranteed her a grand life and a brilliant future. But she'd refused to accept the advice of the so-called experts. She needed to be here. Here on the land of her ancestors. It was a need so deep, so physical, she couldn't deny it. If some saw this land as raw and rough, Cora saw only the rugged beauty. And her great gift was the ability to convey that beauty on canvas.

When she'd first begun to paint the stark landscapes, she'd had no idea that so many would share her vision. After returning to Montana, she'd expected to live and die in obscurity. Then, when a local art dealer had seen her work and begged to be allowed to show it, she'd paid scant attention.

Her first show had given her such a thrill. It had been beyond her wildest dreams to see art patrons lavishing praise on her work and spending ridiculous amounts to own her paintings, while art critics around the world began raving about the rich, raw beauty of her work.

For Cora, it had never been about the money. Though that validated her success in art circles, it had always been about the need to express on canvas the rare beauty that she saw here, and then to share it with others.

She sighed. She'd needed this chance to reconnect with her work. To fill canvas after canvas with color and form and the vibrant life that was unique to her corner of the world. After the shock of Coot's death, and the arrival of her two nephews after so many years, she'd been feeling oddly disconnected.

"Oh, Coot." She veered off the dirt road onto the long dusty driveway that led to the ranch. "If only I understood men the way I understand art. I wish I knew what to do about our boys. I'm worried that the wounds are too deep, the chasm too wide, for them to ever be friends again."

As the ranch house came into view she slowed the vehicle to a crawl and let herself see it through the eyes of an artist. It was a handsome, sprawling building made of stone and aged wood that looked as though it had always been here. Rising to three stories, with tall windows to take in the breathtaking views of rolling meadows, evergreen forests, and soaring mountain ranges, it was an imposing sight. And yet, despite its size, it managed to be comfortable. Three generations had lived here together, and for a time, this house had been filled with love. Coot's three sons, their wives and children, had brought so much laughter to the old fortress. Then, one by one, his sons had left him.

Ben, the middle son, and his wife, Kelly, left first. They had craved a more adventurous lifestyle, and had taken their son, Wyatt, with them around the world, until the plane crash that had left a bitter son all alone, without the presence of his extended family. Judging from the places he'd been since then, Wyatt shared his parents' love of adventure. Cora wondered how long the spell of this place could hold him before he would have to once again cut himself loose from all that was familiar to explore the unknown.

Then Wade, Coot's youngest, had taken his wife,

Melissa, and son, Zane, to California, vowing to never again see snow or hear about the lost treasure. His untimely death left his son and young widow adrift. Melissa, who'd always hated the isolation of ranch life, had cut a wide swath through the smooth, slick Hollywood crowd before settling down with a famous director who had been, at the time, very married. Within a short time he'd moved on, leaving her for his young assistant. Through it all, poor Zane had been forced to deal with the loss of all that had once comforted him. Father, grandfather, ranch life. All denied him at a critical time in his life, while his mother ignored him to pursue her own pleasures.

Walker, Coot's firstborn, and his wife, Chris, had remained on the ranch with their son, Jesse. And although Walker never shared his father's passion for the treasure hunt, young Jesse's devotion to his grandfather more than made up for it. Walker's death, followed two years later by that of his wife, had brought Jesse and old Coot closer than ever. Theirs had been a bond forged out of desperate loneliness and need that nothing could ever break.

All the family ties had now been severed. Perhaps forever. And Cora could see no way to help heal the old wounds that had been festering for all these years. There was too much pain. Too much guilt. She found herself wondering if Coot had made a terrible mistake by tempting his grandsons with his vision of recovering the lost fortune. Look what it had already done to their family. The search for the elusive gold had completely consumed her brother, father, and grandfather. And now it looked as though it might destroy what little relationship was left between her remaining family members.

Was anything worth that price?

She circled the house and parked in the barn. Before she could exit the Jeep, Cal Randall approached, pulling a big wooden wagon that he'd made especially to transport her art supplies from her studio to her vehicle and back again.

"Cal." She gave him a bright smile. "With all you have to do, how could you see me coming?"

"I seem to have radar where you're concerned, Cora." He gave her a long, steady look. "You were gone so long I was beginning to worry."

She laid her hand on his arm. "You know I can take care of myself. I don't take foolish risks."

"I know." He closed a hand over hers. "But I worry all the same."

He began loading the freshly painted canvases, taking care to see that they were separated by tall wooden dowels.

The efficiency of his design never failed to please her. There was room for everything, from paints to finished canvases, with room to spare. Cal Randall had always been able to anticipate her needs and fill them before she could even express them. This wagon was no exception.

She lifted a sack of paint supplies from the passenger seat. "Lucky for me that you're here to unload all this. But if you're busy, I can handle it from here."

He caught her hand when she reached for the handle. "You go ahead, Cora. I'll see to this. Dandy's just getting ready to serve supper."

As he began hauling the wagon toward the house, she moved along beside him, matching her steps to his. Though she told herself she simply wanted to make conversation, it shamed her that she was reluctant to face her nephews. The tension between them made her feel so helpless.

Cal pulled the wagon into the mudroom and carefully hung his wide-brimmed hat on a peg by the back door before scraping the dirt from his boots. "You go ahead into supper and I'll set these in your studio."

"There's no need..."

"I don't mind. You may as well go ahead and get it over with." He gave her a gentle smile, and she realized that he'd been reading her mind.

She took her time washing at the big sink, using a brush to scrub the last of the paint from her cuticles. With a sigh she stepped into the kitchen.

Across the room Dandy was lifting a heavy roaster from the oven. The wonderful aroma of pot roast filled the air.

When he caught sight of her he beamed his pleasure. "Afternoon, Miss Cora. I was hoping you might get home in time for supper. I almost didn't make this, but Jesse's been asking for it for days."

"Then I'm glad, too, Dandy." She looked around. "Where's Jesse?"

He gave a nod of his head. "Great room, I'm thinking. He just got in from the north range about an hour ago."

"Wyatt and Zane?"

He shrugged. "They came down from the high country earlier today. Can't say if they're still here."

"Thanks, Dandy." She started toward the door, wondering if she and Jesse would be eating alone.

Even before she stepped into the great room, the sound of voices raised in a heated debate had her stomach clenching. Not alone, she thought. She'd stepped, once more, right into the thick of battle.

Zane and Wyatt were standing by the bank of windows, facing Jesse, who stood with his back to her.

Jesse's words had her stopping in her tracks. "...hate to admit it, but there's nothing as satisfying as a good down-and-dirty saloon brawl."

She studied Zane's black eye and her nerves started jumping. As if hateful words weren't enough, her nephews had now resorted to physical violence.

Oh, Coot. Where will this all end?

"Hey, Aunt Cora." Wyatt was the first to notice her.

As he hurried over, she saw the bruises on his cheek, the slight limp in his gait.

Her smile fled. "Who did this?" She touched a hand to his face when he bent to brush a kiss over her cheek.

"Never did hear his name." He pointed to a chilled longneck resting on a tray on the sofa table. "Care to join us in a beer while we rehash last week's donnybrook?"

"Fighting." She accepted the cold beer from his hand and took a long swallow before turning to Jesse. "Your cousins may not be aware of it, but you certainly know how I feel about that."

"Couldn't be helped, Aunt Cora." Jesse's face bore a bruise from cheek to jaw. "A guy's got to defend himself."

Zane nodded in agreement. "Especially since his attacker was the size of a mountain."

"His attacker?" She looked from Zane to Jesse to Wyatt.

"Some obnoxious biker who decided he'd help himself to my supper." Jesse drained his beer. "I figured I'd put him in his place and get back to my own business, but then his drunken buddies decided to join in. If it hadn't been for Wyatt and Zane, they might have wiped the floor with what was left of me."

Cora let out a quick breath. Not cousin against cousin, as she'd feared. "You three fought with strangers at the saloon?"

"Like I said, it couldn't be helped. We didn't start it, Aunt Cora."

Zane laughed. "But we definitely finished it."

For emphasis he raised his hand, and both Wyatt and Jesse slapped his palm in a high five.

Feeling a little dazed, Cora dropped into the nearest chair and studied the three young men, who were chuckling over their shared barroom brawl. She could still see three little boys who would come in from the fields covered in mud and laughing like loons over some silly adventure they'd shared. She blinked and saw them as they were now, three handsome, headstrong young men who had been on the verge of war.

And a battle with strangers had turned the tide.

They might not yet be the best of friends they once were, but a night's shared adventure had them stepping back from that impenetrable wall of anger. For now, she thought with a smile, she'd settle for a truce.

She stood and set aside the nearly full bottle.

"Where're you going, Aunt Cora?"

"I thought I'd shower. Will I see any of you at supper?"

"I'll be there." Jesse shot her a wink.

"Me, too." Zane tipped up his beer.

"I wouldn't miss it." Wyatt was grinning.

"I'll be right down." As she started up the stairs, her heart felt lighter than it had for many a day.

Oh, Coot. Maybe there's hope for us after all. At least they're all on the same team for now.

It may be true that she didn't understand men. But this much she knew. Their shared bruises had given them something in common. They were actually speaking to one another without bitterness. And wasn't that a wonderful thing to see?

"You throw a mean left hook." Over supper, Cal glanced at Zane. "Last week you didn't look like that was your first bar fight."

"It wasn't." Zane buttered another soft-as-air roll. He'd have paid a fortune for this meal at one of California's trendiest restaurants.

"Hard to believe you spent your time in seedy bars in Hollywood." Jesse grinned over the rim of his cup. "I figured you for fancy dinner parties and those pansy drinks with exotic names."

Zane was feeling too mellow to take offense. "I've had my share of those, too."

"Then where'd you learn to fight like that?" Cal was enjoying the new sense of camaraderie, and he could see that Cora was enjoying herself, too. The old cowboy wanted to keep the cousins talking, hoping they might find more common ground.

"From Jesse and Wyatt." Zane polished off the roll. "A good thing, too. My first day at middle school in Beverly Hills I came home with a black eye and was grounded for a month."

"Why'd you fight?" Wyatt's mouth watered when

Dandy stepped into the room and began passing around a plate of homemade chocolate chip cookies.

"It started with the usual bullying. Some kid made fun of my boots and jeans and got his friends to call me Cowboy, which soon turned into the whole class calling me Cow Patty."

"Ouch." Jesse winced. "Sorry I had to add to it by calling you Hollywood."

Zane shrugged. "Hey. I've been called worse. It wasn't worth fighting over. But if stupid name-calling wasn't bad enough, the same kid accused my mother of sleeping with his father."

That had everyone going quiet.

"I hope you gave as good as you got." Jesse was scowling.

"Oh yeah. I bloodied his nose and shredded the sleeve of his designer shirt."

"Good. Little liar had it coming." This from Wyatt.

Zane stared down at his plate. "Yeah. It was pretty satisfying. That is until I found out later he wasn't lying."

They all gaped at him.

"Not that she ever admitted it. But soon enough it was common knowledge. The next thing I knew, there was a very messy, very public divorce, and my tormentor was my stepbrother." He moved his food around without tasting it. "I learned to be damned good with my fists."

"Well." Feeling the weight of the sudden silence around the table, Cal cleared his throat and turned to Cora. "How was the weather up at Treasure Chest?"

"Cold and rainy." She shot Cal a grateful look. "But I got some great paintings."

"Good." He patted her hand before shoving back his

chair. "Sorry to run, but I promised to head on up to the north ridge before dark."

Zane scraped back his chair and stood. "Mind if I ride along?"

Cal studied the young man whose eyes bore a haunted look. "Not at all. I'd be grateful for the company."

Zane rounded the table and softly touched his lips to his aunt's cheek before following the old cowboy from the room.

Behind them, those still seated around the table had gone suddenly somber.

When the door closed behind Cal and Zane, Jesse let out a long, slow breath. "Guess I'll have to alter my view of life in sunny California. I figured my little cousin spent all his time lying around pools and ogling chicks in bikinis. Who knew he had to fight his way through middle school?"

He turned to Wyatt. "I hope you fared a little better."

Wyatt merely shrugged before scraping back his chair. "Maybe I'll tell you about it some time. For now, I promised to lend a hand out in the barn."

As he started away Jesse pushed back from the table. "Why don't I join you?"

They called out their good-byes to their aunt before heading for the back door.

Cora watched them leave, sipping her tea in silence. She carried her steaming cup to the great room, where she stood by the bank of windows watching a glorious sunset. But her mind wasn't on the beauty of the scene. Zane's words played through her mind.

How painful had it been for Zane to suddenly find himself alone and facing the taunts of strangers? He couldn't have been more than twelve.

Suddenly she felt an unmistakable presence next to her and a smile spread across her face.

"You know, Coot, it occurs to me that our boys are a lot more like you than I realized. You used to say there was nothing like a good fight to clear the air. I believe I see your hand in all this."

CHAPTER EIGHT

W ould you like to sit in the chair, Dad, or would you rather go in to your bed?" Amy helped her father from the truck and up the steps of the house.

Once inside he motioned toward the bedroom, and Amy hurried ahead to turn down the covers.

It worried her to see him moving so slowly, as though he'd aged ten years since leaving the local clinic after his first treatment. Dr. Wheeler had warned her that a side effect of the treatments was lethargy, but she hadn't been prepared to see her father asleep beside her during the entire ride home.

"I'll start some soup. It'll be ready by the time you wake from your nap."

"Thanks, Amy girl." He eased himself down on the edge of the mattress, kicked off his shoes, and fell back heavily against the pillows.

She watched helplessly for a minute before turning away.

In the kitchen she dragged out one of her mother's heavy stockpots and began assembling the ingredients for chicken soup. A short time later, while the soup simmered, she looked around for something to occupy her time.

She paused in the neglected family room and smiled as she studied the framed photographs on the mantel. There was her mother, Sarah Miller Parrish, as a young bride, standing proudly beside her tall, solemn husband. Amy studied another photo of a beaming Sarah holding her infant daughter. The joy of proud, new motherhood was evident in those laughing green eyes. Mother and daughter shared so much more than the color of their eyes. There was the shared dimple in their left cheek. A yen for pasta. A deep and abiding love of this ranch.

Amy picked up the family photo taken at her graduation. How could they have known it would be the last one of the three of them together? Scant weeks later her mother had taken the call from her beloved sister, Morgan, in Helena, begging her to come and tend to her during her illness. There was no way Sarah would have refused. Morgan had been Sarah's refuge during her stormy marriage, and was the only family she had. Amy and Sarah had packed hastily in the night and started the long drive to Helena, never dreaming that they would be gone the entire summer.

By the time her aunt Morgan had gone to her eternal rest and Sarah returned to Gold Fever, Amy started college in Helena alone.

Alone.

It was, she thought, the one word that best described her life. Even with Colin, a friend and fellow teacher who occasionally took her to dinner or to staff parties, she never really felt like part of a couple the way she had with Jesse.

Not that she minded. She was very good at being alone. And now, of course, she had her pupils. She missed the start of a new school year. This had always been her favorite time, setting up her classroom, greeting her students and their parents, seeing to it that newcomers were made to feel welcome. She had a real talent for teaching. She was one of those rare people who loved the challenge of making the lessons come alive. She thrived on the endless chatter. She took particular pride in seeing a student suddenly begin to shine because of her praise.

Amy picked up a load of laundry and headed for the small, enclosed room between the kitchen and the garage. It had once been an open walkway until, at her mother's urging, her father had added walls and a roof. Her mother had been delighted to move the washer and dryer from the damp basement to this sunny location.

Now the room had become a catchall for discarded newspapers and magazines, old clothing, and mismatched boots, all of which were piled on shelves and spilled over onto the floor, covering every available inch of space.

"Oh, Mom," she sighed. "You were always so neat. Too bad Dad lacks that gene."

With the first load of laundry in the washer, she picked up an empty box and began filling it with junk. While she worked she thought about Jesse. She'd thought of little else since his visit that night.

Was it just because she was back staying in her

childhood home that she was unable to shake the image of Jesse McCord? His presence had unleashed a tide of buried feelings. His arms around her, making her feel safe and protected. His strength that made her want to let go of all her worries and trust him to be strong for both of them. His tenderness that brought her to the verge of tears.

That potent male energy simmering just below the surface had always been her downfall. Even in her teens, when her father had made it abundantly clear that the McCords were to be avoided at all costs, she'd been drawn to Jesse and he to her. Though she'd been forced to sneak around behind her father's back, making her feel like a cheat, she hadn't been able to resist any chance to be with him.

His visit the night of her dad's diagnosis was no exception. She'd wanted him to kiss her. To crush her in his arms and kiss away all the tears and fears. Instead, he'd chosen to walk away, leaving her confused and frustrated.

The old Jesse would have taken what he wanted. And she'd have gladly given. She paused in her work. Maybe, she thought, they had both done some growing up while they'd been apart.

She tossed another pile of newspapers into the box and was reaching for more when a handwritten slip of yellowed paper caught her eye.

She read the words: ... *trail to the treasure points to* ... The rest of the page had been torn away. At the bottom were more words, but these were blured, as though the paper had been water-soaked: ... *going to try that next chance I* ...

She turned the paper over and saw the doodles.

Squiggly lines that could have been a child's drawing of a mountain peak or a crude graph of sorts.

"Coot." Like everyone in Gold Fever and the surrounding area, Amy had seen examples of old Coot's journal. Pages had been turning up for years, ever since the old man had begun keeping a record of the places he'd searched for the lost treasure. Like an absentminded professor, Coot would make notes to himself on scraps of paper, along with his own personal directions, before putting them in his pocket to copy when he returned home. Except that the slips of paper often fell from his pocket along the trail and were lost or retrieved by strangers. Some people, recognizing them as Coot's property, would make it a point to return them to their rightful owner. Many more simply tossed them away or, like her father, added them to the junk pile.

Had it been an accident on her father's part? Or had it been deliberate?

The thought had her pausing in her work. In her mind she went back to the day when she'd watched her father face off against Coot McCord, fists raised, voice a roar of fury.

"If you or your sons set foot on my land again, I'll blow your heads off. You hear me, McCord?"

"Wade told me what you saw, Otis, but it wasn't the way it looked."

"I know what I saw. His telling you different doesn't make it so."

"Your wife fell off her horse. Wade happened to be nearby and helped her, is all."

"And kissed her in the bargain."

"So you say. According to Wade, she was crying after

the fall. He used his handkerchief to dry her tears. He swears he would never touch another man's wife."

"I'm not a fool, McCord. Your youngest son has a reputation for chasing the ladies. All ladies. But what's mine is mine." A vein throbbed at his temple and his face had grown red with rage. "So be warned. You so much as set foot on my land, you'll pay. Now get out of my sight. And if your boy ever comes near my wife, I won't be responsible for what happens."

"You're a damned fool, Parrish." Coot's fury was more than a match for Otis's.

Amy had sat frozen in the truck, listening to every hateful word. Then, without warning, Jesse had been there, peering at her through the open truck window, introducing himself. In that instant she'd been utterly charmed by that rogue smile, that boyish bravado, and more than a little relieved to have a distraction from the ugly scene playing itself out before them.

When her father had slammed back into the truck and taken off, laying down a trail of dust as he drove away, she'd seen Jesse in the side-view mirror lift his hand to wave. She'd turned and waved in return.

The child she'd been hadn't understood the significance of what she'd witnessed. But as she grew older she realized just how long and deep that festering anger lay.

She'd heard the rumors that her mother once had been wildly in love with Wade McCord, Coot's youngest son, and he with her. But like so many young lovers, they had drifted apart, and each had married someone else.

Apparently, Otis wasn't willing to let a long-dead romance die in peace. To save face, he later attempted to sue over infringement of water rights, which the judge had

disallowed as a frivolous lawsuit. But it had been a cover
for her father's jealousy. That long-ago incident had been
the actual trigger. And it went a long way in explaining
why he'd refused to allow Coot to buy him out, as Coot had
purchased the land of many others in the area whose poor
ranches had stood in the way of the old man's search for the
lost treasure. What was worse, that had been the cause of
the chasm that had grown between her father and mother,
continuing long after it should have been dead and buried.

Dead and buried.

Like her mother. Like Coot and his sons. Like the feelings she and Jesse had once shared.

Amy glanced at the slip of paper in her hand. She had
no doubt that her father would have tossed this in the
trash rather than pass it along to Coot's family. She read
the blurred words again before tucking the page in her
pocket. This belonged to the McCords. It was only right
that she return it to them.

As she continued cleaning, her heart felt suddenly
lighter. It wasn't, she told herself firmly, because she now
had an excuse to see Jesse again. It was simply because
she felt better knowing she was doing the right thing.

She would head out after her dad was awake and comfortable. Old Red needed the exercise. The ride would be
good for both of them.

Jesse wrestled the fence post into the hole he'd dug,
then took a pair of pliers from his hip pocket and began
tightening the wire that he'd cut from the rotted, discarded original post.

Hearing the sound of hoofbeats, he paused to glance
up, squinting against the glare of sunlight.

"Hi, Jesse." Amy hoped her voice didn't reveal her nerves. All the way over to the Lost Nugget ranch she'd rehearsed a casual conversation. Now, seeing him, shirt damp, muscles rippling, she felt tongue-tied and jittery.

"Amy." He reached up and removed his wide-brimmed hat, slapping it against his thigh as he wiped sweat from his brow.

"Looks like hard work." She slid from the saddle, keeping hold of Red's reins.

"Somebody's got to do it."

"I thought you had a machine for this."

"We do. If there's a line of fencing down. But for one broken fence post, it's just easier to do by hand."

He moved closer to run his open palm down Red's muzzle. The mare whickered, causing him to smile. "She remembers me."

"Of course she does. You always brought her a carrot."

"With good reason. It kept her from whinnying and alerting your dad that I was around."

They both grinned at the memory.

"Speaking of Dad..." Amy reached into her pocket. "When I was cleaning house, I found this."

Jesse read the slip of paper, then turned it over and studied the doodles.

"Coot's." His voice was little more than a whisper.

She nodded. "I recognized it as his and figured you'd want it."

He stared at the torn yellowed paper, studying each word with a look of naked pain that had her heart breaking for him.

"I'm sorry, Jesse." She laid a hand over his. "Maybe I shouldn't have brought it."

"No. You were right to come. I appreciate it." He tore his gaze from the paper and looked at her. "I'm just a little...bruised, and still missing him. How's your father?"

She was touched that he could think of her troubles at a time like this. Touched and grateful. She had a desperate need to talk to someone. "He had his first treatment today, and it really knocked him down."

"Is he in the hospital?"

"No. The doctor said it was safe to drive him home. He slept for nearly two hours. When I brought him a bowl of soup, he barely managed a few sips before he threw it up."

"Is that a normal reaction to these treatments?"

She shrugged. "A nurse at the clinic gave me a list of things to expect. Weakness, lethargy, extreme fatigue, and nausea are just some of them. But it scares me to see him down like this. He's always been so tough."

Jesse saw the fear in her eyes. Without thinking, he reached a hand to her cheek. "Your dad's a scrapper, Amy. Tough as nails. But right now he's dealing with a new opponent, and he's going to need some time to figure out his best strategy for fighting the battle."

"What if he never figures it out? What if he just gives up?"

"Hey." He drew her into the circle of his arms, sensing that she was struggling to hold back the tears. "You're scared. He's scared. But you've got each other."

"I feel so alone. He doesn't talk to me. He won't confide in me, Jess." Her voice vibrated against his throat, sending a thrill all the way to his toes.

He caught her chin, forcing her to meet his look. "You just have to give it time, Amy."

"What if time is running out?"

He ran a thumb over her trembling lips. "Then you'll have to be strong enough for both of you. But I'm betting, once these treatments take over, he'll come out of this stronger than ever."

She drew in a long, unsteady breath. "Oh, I hope you're right." She gave a toss of her head. "I miss our fights."

That had Jesse grinning. "Now that's something not every daughter could say."

She managed a shaky smile. "I guess it does sound silly. But at least when we were fighting I could say what was on my mind. Now I find myself monitoring every word so I don't add to his misery."

"Maybe you should try a little tenderness."

She flushed. "I don't know how. Besides, we've spent a lifetime arguing. If I start to go all mushy on him now, he'll figure he's been given a death sentence."

Jesse chuckled, and Amy realized how much she'd missed the sound of it. He had a warm, rich laugh that wrapped itself around her heart and squeezed until she felt her throat go dry.

"Know what you need?" He caught her hand and started toward the house in the distance.

She felt the jolt of electricity that shot along her spine when he kept her hand in his. "What?"

"A cup of Aunt Cora's tea."

Amy dug in her heels. "I don't want to interrupt her if she's working."

"You couldn't if you tried. When she's painting, she's in another zone." He tugged her along, and she picked up her pace to match his long strides, the roan mare following close behind. "But most afternoons she takes a break from her studio. We'll just see if she's around."

At the back door he took the reins from Amy's hand and tied Old Red at the hitching post before leading the way inside.

Like everyone who'd ever visited the Lost Nugget, she knew the routine, scraping her boots in the mudroom and pausing to wash at the big sink before stepping into the kitchen.

Dandy looked up from the stove. Spotting Amy, his face was wreathed in smiles as he wiped his hands on a towel before hurrying over to catch her hands in his.

"How good to see you, Amy. It's been too many years."

"Yes, it has, Dandy. It's good to see you, too. I saw you at the funeral, but I know you were too busy to notice me." She breathed deeply. "Something smells wonderful."

"Beef stew. If you'll stay for supper, you can see if it tastes as good as it smells."

"I wish I could." She took a step back. "Dad will be expecting me to get home in time to make his supper."

"I heard about his illness. Tell him I send my best."

"Thanks, Dandy." Amy felt herself relaxing in this courtly man's presence. He'd been part of the McCord ranch since she was a kid. Despite her father's nasty temper and harsh treatment of the McCord family, they'd never held it against her. She had always been warmly treated by everyone here.

Jesse spied the China teapot on the counter. "Aunt Cora's tea?"

Dandy nodded. "I was just about to add a sugar bowl and creamer to the tray before taking it in to her."

"I'll take it. I invited Amy to join us."

"Then you two go ahead, and I'll bring the rest. Your aunt's in the great room."

Amy held the door while Jesse carried the tray with the tea service. Cora stood by the bank of windows, staring out at the mountain peaks in the distance.

"Aunt Cora, look who's come to visit."

At Jesse's words Cora turned and hurried across the room to embrace the young woman. "Oh, Amy. How good to see you."

Amy poured herself into the hug, knowing this woman's words came from the heart. "It's good to see you, too, Miss Cora."

The older woman held her a little away. "How is your father?"

"I'm not sure. He had his first treatment today, and he slept all the way home. Then he napped for another two hours or more."

Cora led her across the room, where they settled side by side on a comfortable sofa. "From all I've read, that's to be expected."

"He looks..." Amy lifted her palms, then folded them nervously in her lap. "He looks defeated."

"I'm sure that's how he's feeling right now. In a battle for his life, and it seems the illness is winning. But as his strength returns, I think you'll see a significant improvement in his attitude."

"Oh, I hope you're right."

Cora watched as Dandy entered carrying a second tray, on which rested additional cups and saucers, as well as a plate of cookies still warm from the oven. When he'd filled three cups with tea, he passed them around and placed the plate of cookies on a coffee table.

"If you need anything else, just let me know," he called as he took his leave.

"Thank you, Dandy." Cora sipped and sighed with pure pleasure. "Nobody makes a more perfect cup of tea than Dandy."

"Not to mention his cookies." Jesse reached for one, ate it in three bites, then took a second one and forced himself to eat it more slowly, savoring every bite. "Mmm. Chocolate chip. The chocolate is still hot and melting." He held out the plate to Amy. "Come on. You know you could never resist Dandy's cookies."

She took one and ate it slowly. By the time she'd finished, she was smiling. "I'd forgotten how good these really are."

Jesse pulled the yellowed slip of paper from his pocket. "Amy found this and thought we'd want it."

He handed it to Cora, who studied it in silence. When she'd turned it over, she smoothed out the wrinkles and continued holding it in her hand, as though unwilling to let go of something that had once been held by her brother. It took several moments before she was able to compose herself.

"I wish we had a bit more. It's so vague, it could be just about any mountain peak in the area."

Jesse nodded.

Amy set aside her tea. "I found it among a pile of old newspapers. Before I toss any of them away, I'll go through each one carefully to see if there's more."

"That would be grand." Cora continued to hold it as

she gently led the conversation back to Amy's father. "How often will you need to drive Otis to the hospital?"

"Twice a week until the doctors can determine how much he's capable of tolerating. They'll add as many treatments as possible until they feel they have this under control."

Cora studied the young woman. "That's a lot of responsibility to handle alone."

Amy managed a weak smile. "I'll be fine."

"Yes, you will." Cora placed a hand over Amy's. "I hope you'll remember that we're not just neighbors, we're friends. Please let us know what we can do to help."

Amy was shaking her head. "I wouldn't..."

Cora interrupted. "I know. The feud. That's all in the past."

"Not in my father's mind."

Cora held up a hand. "You know, I've always felt a bit sorry for your father."

"Sorry for Dad?"

The older woman nodded. "Think about it. For three generations your land belonged to your mother's family. With no sons, your grandfather was considering selling it to Coot rather than let it fall into the hands of strangers. But then your mother came home with her new husband, and Otis agreed to farm his wife's property. Even now, there are old-timers in Gold Fever who refer to your ranch as the Miller place."

Amy went very still, absorbing her words. "I knew all this, of course, but I never considered the fact that my father may have felt like nothing more than a caretaker of Mom's land. Thank you, Miss Cora. I guess I never gave it enough thought."

"Then think about this, too. At times like these, old feuds need to be put aside. Any one of us would be more than happy to drive Otis to town when you're not able, or to sit with him if you need a break."

Amy met her look and read the concern in her eyes. "Thank you, Miss Cora. I appreciate that." Not that her father would ever permit it. But it helped to know that these good people could look beyond the past to the future.

She stood. "Now I'd better get home and start supper."

Cora got to her feet and gave her a hard hug. "Don't be a stranger, Amy. You're always welcome here."

"Thanks. You'll never know how much I've needed this."

Amy quickly turned away, hiding the tears that sprang to her eyes.

Jesse followed her from the room.

As they stepped into the kitchen, Dandy pointed to a linen-wrapped package on the counter. "I hope that'll fit in your saddlebag."

At Amy's arched brow he said, "Beef stew. And some of my cookies."

"Oh, Dandy." Amy crossed the room to give him a big hug.

Before she could reach for the parcel, Jesse picked it up and led the way to the back door. Once outside he tucked it into her saddlebag and untied the reins.

"I'm glad you came, Amy."

"I knew you'd want Coot's note."

"It means a lot to me. And even more to Aunt Cora."

She nodded. "I could see that." She paused, considering

her words before asking, "Are you thinking about continuing the search for the treasure?"

He shrugged. "Some days I think I want to, and other days I figure I'll leave that to the city boys."

She heard the disdain in his tone. "Still not friends?"

"Things are better, but there's a lot of baggage between us."

She met his eyes. "You could be talking about us, instead of Zane and Wyatt."

"I guess I could be."

He stepped closer, keeping his eyes steady on hers.

Her heart started racing.

A breeze caught her hair and he lifted a hand to smooth it back. "But, except for the ending, our baggage was all good." Instead of pulling away he kept his hand there. His thumb stroked her temple and he could feel the way her pulse leaped. "Maybe some time we could talk about..."

"Hey, Amy. Long time."

At Zane's voice both their heads came up sharply and they stepped apart with matching looks of guilt.

Zane and Wyatt came striding from the barn, crossing the distance between them to give Amy a quick hug.

"Zane." She embraced him before turning to Wyatt. "How good to see you both."

"You look fantastic." Zane gave her a long look that had Jesse doing a slow burn.

"How's your father?" Wyatt asked.

"Not good today. He had his first treatment at the town clinic. Ask me again in a week, and maybe I'll have better news."

"Good. You'll let us know?"

She nodded and pulled herself into the saddle.

To Jesse she said, "Thank Dandy again for the food. Even if Dad can't enjoy it, I know I will."

With a wave she urged Old Red into a leisurely trot.

Feeling frustrated, Jesse stood watching until horse and rider disappeared over a ridge.

When he turned, he found Zane and Wyatt grinning like conspirators.

"I think," Zane said with a laugh, "our timing was just about perfect."

"Yeah." Wyatt slapped Zane on the back. "One minute more and the poor fool would have been right back where he started years ago."

"It's a good thing you've got us here to save you, cuz." Zane dropped an arm around Jesse's neck.

Before Jesse could shove him away, Wyatt chimed in. "Oh, no. Don't thank us. We're only too happy to save you from temptation."

The two slipped their arms around his shoulders, dragging him toward the house and laughing.

CHAPTER NINE

J esse?" As she moved about her bedroom, Amy hoped her tone sounded sufficiently businesslike over the cell phone. It had been three days since she'd been to his family ranch. Three days of replaying in her mind every word he'd spoken, every look they'd shared. Three days of regretting the arrival of Zane and Wyatt at the very moment when she'd been certain that Jesse intended to explain about their abrupt parting. And maybe kiss her in the bargain.

She'd swallowed bitter disappointment on the ride home and reminded herself over and over that she was behaving like one of her students with a first crush.

"Hey, Amy."

She caught the note of surprise laced with pleasure in his voice. "Hey, yourself. I've been going through my dad's stuff, and I've found a few more bits of paper that you might be interested in seeing."

"That's great. I can't stop over right now." Amy could hear a truck's horn sounding and the whoosh of passing traffic in the background. "I'm on my way to town."

"If you're going to be there awhile, I could meet you somewhere. I'm just about to drive Dad to the clinic."

"Do you have to stay with him during his treatment?"

"No. I'll have about two hours to be on my own."

"Great. Why don't we meet at the saloon at noon? We'll see if the daily special is edible."

That had Amy laughing. "All right. I'll see you there."

She dropped her cell phone into her purse and went off in search of her makeup. Not that she was going to fuss just because she was seeing Jesse, she reminded herself. But it wouldn't hurt to take a few extra minutes before she headed to town.

When she walked out to the truck, her father was already in the driver's seat and waiting impatiently, engine idling.

"What kept you, girl?"

She shrugged. "I just had to get a few things." She swallowed back her surprise at seeing her father at the wheel.

Before she could fasten her seat belt he put the truck in gear, the wheels spitting gravel as he headed along the winding driveway.

He glanced over. "I'll need you to pick up some supplies at Orley Peterson's. I wish I could handle it myself, but..."

"I've got the list."

He handed over a blank check. "No more credit. Fill in the amount and get a receipt."

She studied the familiar signature before tucking it into her pocket. "Why don't you want to buy on credit? Isn't that the way we've always done it?"

"I don't want to leave you with any debt."

Her heart did a quick plunge, all the way to her toes. "Dad, I don't think..."

"No need to think. I've done enough of that for both of us. Tonight, if I can keep my head out of the toilet long enough, we'll go over the books so you have a handle on how things stand with the ranch."

"I have a pretty good..."

"You don't have a clue. But it's time I laid it all out so you won't have to deal with any surprises."

Amy bit back any further protest. This was the first time her father had opened up even a tiny crack in that wall he'd built. If it got him talking about his illness, his fears, it would give her a chance to do the same.

"Okay." She turned to stare out the side window. "Tonight's fine with me."

They drove the rest of the way into town in silence.

Amy hauled a four-wheel, flatbed cart along the aisles of Orley Peterson's Grain & Feed, wrestling sacks from shelves. Because their ranch was too small to qualify for free shipping, Otis Parrish had opted to haul his supplies himself rather than pay the additional fee. Though her muscles protested, she reminded herself that it was an excellent workout. If Violet and Daffy had anything decent on today's menu, she could eat her fill without a thought of the calories.

"Morning, Amy." Orley Peterson stood behind the counter, checking a packing slip while a trucker waited for approval. "Be with you in a minute."

Orley was as round as he was tall, his plaid shirt stretched tautly over his bulging middle. His bald head glistened with sweat, and his double chin jiggled with each movement as he checked the figures, scrawled his signature on the paper, and handed it to the trucker before turning to Amy. "How's your dad?"

"Fine. I left him at the clinic for another treatment."

Orley walked around the counter and began scanning each sack with a handheld device. "How's he tolerating the treatments so far?"

Amy shrugged. "They leave him weak and sick. Just when he starts to feel a little better, it's time for another one."

"Yeah." He circled back behind the counter and rang up the sale. "My wife's sister had the same reaction."

"How's she doing?" The minute the words were out of her mouth, Amy regretted them, but it was too late to take them back.

Orley didn't quite meet her eyes. "That'll be three hundred and seventy-five."

He seemed surprised when she took the check from her pocket and filled in the amount, but he accepted it without a word before handing her a receipt.

As she started to pull the cart he stopped her. "Where's your truck?"

"Out front."

"You got anything else to do in town?"

She nodded.

"Then you go ahead, and I'll load this stuff in your truck later."

She smiled. "Thanks, Orley. I appreciate it."

"No problem. And Amy?" he called to her retreating back.

She turned.

"My wife's sister is in remission. They're not calling it a cure, but she's got her hair back, and her strength. For now, that's more than enough."

She wanted to hug him. Instead she just flashed him a smile. "That's good to hear. Thanks again, Orley."

The Fortune Saloon was doing a standing-room-only business. Their nearest competition was a tiny diner at the other end of town. Despite the good food, the surly owner of the Grizzly Inn, Ben Rider, drove away as many customers as he attracted. Most folks would rather eat the greasy burgers offered by Vi and Daffy, just for the chance to enjoy their bawdy humor. These two sisters, with their outrageous style and brash demeanor, were the darlings of the town of Gold Fever.

Jesse, seated at a corner table, spotted Amy the minute she stepped through the doorway. She paused to look around before spying him and giving him a bright smile.

He resented the fact that his heart rate shot up at that exact moment. He set down his coffee and sat back, enjoying the look of her, hair wind-tossed, cheeks pink as she started weaving her way among the tables.

She paused to speak with Mayor Rowe Stafford, and the two exchanged a laugh before she moved on to talk to Stan Novak, who was having lunch with Ledge Cowling. The way the two men had been huddled over a sheaf of papers, Jesse figured Stan was angling for another loan. It was common knowledge in town that the construction business was down.

At the next table Amy was flagged over by Delia Cowling, who was lunching with Harding Jessup.

"You alone? If so, you can join us." Delia indicated the empty chair at their table.

"Thanks, but I'm joining someone."

Amy tried to move on, but Delia already had a firm hold on Amy's sleeve. "I hear your daddy's not doing so well."

"He's fine. Just a little weak. Thanks for asking." Amy resisted the urge to tug her arm free and waited until the older woman lowered her hand before making her escape.

Amy passed only two tables before stopping yet again, to speak to Rafe Spindler and Cal Randall, on a break from their ranch chores. The two were close enough for Jesse to hear Amy's response to their questions about her father's health.

"...doing fine. He's at the clinic right now having another treatment."

"You be sure and give him our best," Cal said as she thanked him and moved on.

Jesse got to his feet when she reached his table and held her chair. She sank down gratefully.

"Thanks." She gave a long, slow sigh.

"I never gave a thought to the number of times you must be called on to answer the same questions about your father."

She smiled. "I don't mind. Really. It's nice to know so many people care. But sometimes I feel like I'm climbing a mountain."

"Yeah." He started to reach for her hand, then stopped as Daffy approached.

"Hey, Amy." The older woman wrapped her arms around Amy and gave her a warm hug, which Amy returned. "How you doing, girlfriend?"

"Fine now. I always love your hugs."

"That's what I'm here for. Your mama was the first friend Vi and I made when we came to Gold Fever. And she remained our best friend until she was gone. So now you're stuck with us whether you like it or not."

"I love both of you." Amy waved to Vi, who was standing over the grill behind the bar.

"The feeling's mutual." Daffy pulled a pencil from her purple hair. "Something to drink, honey?"

"Iced tea, please, Daffy."

"You got it. Know what you want for lunch yet?"

Jesse shook his head. "What's the special today?"

"Vi and I are calling it the Fortune Five. Turkey, ham, pastrami, corned beef, and cheese in an onion roll, drizzled with our special dressing. The deluxe comes with fries or slaw."

Jesse winked at Amy, who nodded.

"We'll give that a try, Daffy. And slaw on the side."

Daffy glanced at Amy. "You letting him order for you, honey?"

"He knows what I like." The minute the words were out of her mouth she felt her cheeks grow hot. Especially since Delia Cowling, who was staring at their table, was close enough to overhear every word. Whatever they said, Amy knew, would be repeated all over town by tonight.

"I just bet he does." Daffy slapped Jesse's shoulder. "This good-looking cowboy sure does know how to please the ladies." Still cackling at her little joke, she hurried away to call their order to her sister, Vi.

A short time later Jesse and Amy were devouring their lunch like two starving ranch hands.

Midway through, Jesse glanced over. "You forget to eat breakfast again?"

Amy flushed. "Yeah. Too many ranch chores to see to."

"You ought to have help."

"I can manage."

"I know. But between running the ranch and driving your father into town for these treatments, you have to be running on empty."

She shrugged. "I'm okay with it."

"I could loan you somebody from our ranch."

"I said I'm fine." She instantly hated the edge she'd let creep into her voice.

He sat back and sipped his coffee, knowing better than to push. "You bring those papers that you found?"

"Yeah." She reached into her pocket and handed over the discolored slips of paper. "They were stuck between a bunch of newspapers and magazines. If I hadn't been looking, I'd have never spotted them." She watched the way Jesse studied each word, each line and squiggle. Wouldn't she do the same, if someone found an old note of her mother's? "Do they make any sense?"

"No."

"I thought this was interesting." Amy leaned close and pointed to a torn scrap of paper with the words *possible cavern beneath rock ledge.*

Jesse breathed in her scent and struggled to concentrate. It wasn't easy, when she was this close. He remembered that she used to dab some kind of light floral perfume between her breasts. The mere thought of it had him sweating.

"Yeah. Fascinating. But not much help. There are so many rock ledges in these hills, it would be impossible to know which one he meant."

Their heads came up sharply when Delia Cowling swooped down on their table. "Those look like some of crazy old Coot's notes. Where'd you find them?"

Before Amy could respond Jesse shot the old woman a grin. "Now how'd you see them from where you were sitting, Delia?"

"I recognized that yellow paper. Folks have been finding Coot's notes for years now. In fact, I've found a few of my own."

"You don't say?" Jesse arched a brow. "I don't recall Coot ever telling me you'd turned in some of his notes."

"Well I have. Now and then."

"Now and then? Where'd you find them?"

She took a step back. "Here and there. They used to fall out of his pockets and blow all over Montana."

"Well, if you find any more, I'd appreciate it if you'd return them to me. For sentimental value, you understand."

"Sentimental? I hear Coot promised your cousins a share in his estate if they'd stay and join in the treasure hunt."

"Who told you that?"

"I can't recall. Is it true?"

"They're still here, aren't they?"

The old woman shot him a knowing look and quick-stepped back to her table.

"Now you've done it," Amy whispered. "You know she'll tell the entire town that you and your cousins are still interested in finding Coot's treasure."

He grinned at her. "You mean she isn't going to buy my claim of being sentimental?" He gave a casual shrug of his shoulders. "It doesn't matter what gossip she spreads. Half the town already knows. And the other half will hear all about it by tomorrow."

They shared a laugh before returning their attention to the strips of paper and the faded words.

"Does the drawing on the other side help?"

Jesse turned the paper over, studying the crude lines before giving Amy a quick grin. "No help to me. But then, most of Coot's notes never made any sense, except to him. He had his own secret code."

"Maybe Miss Cora can decode them."

"Worth a try." He shoved the papers into his pocket and picked up his cup, staring into the coffee as though searching for answers to all life's questions in its depths. "Coot was so sure he'd find the treasure."

"And now he has you and your cousins in on the hunt."

He gave a grunt that could have been a laugh or a sneer. "Aren't we a fine bunch to go treasure hunting? A surfer, a Hollywood pretty boy, and a hotheaded cowboy."

Hotheaded and hot-blooded, she thought. "But what if you find it?"

He looked over and saw the spark of excitement in her eyes. "Hey. Don't tell me you're getting caught up in this?"

To his amazement, instead of denying it, she fell silent.

He shook his head. "I'll be damned. Coot just got himself another convert."

"I'm not saying I believe. Well..." She chuckled. "I'm not saying I don't believe either. But think about it, Jess. All that gold, just lying somewhere out there for more than a hundred years. Doesn't it seem reasonable that the ancestors of the man who found it originally ought to be the ones to find it again?"

"Reasonable." He gave a rough laugh. "Now what makes you think anything in this life will have a reasonable ending?"

"Some things do."

"Name me one."

She saw the heat in his eyes and felt her cheeks color. He wasn't thinking about the lost treasure now. They both knew it. They had a history together. Because of Jesse, she'd defied her father's rules, had lost her heart to the enemy, and had eagerly joined him in planning a future together. But their story had ended badly, because he hadn't cared enough to contact her even once through the years she'd been away at college. He'd cut her off without a word. No explanation. No sugarcoated apology. Just stony silence, making it abundantly clear that he'd had a change of heart.

So much for all those sweet dreams she'd spun around him.

"Can't think of one, can you?" Jesse's tone hardened. "While you're looking for a happy ending, all I'm seeing is twists and turns along the way."

Hearing him, Daffy paused beside their table to refill Jesse's coffee and drop the bill for their lunch beside his plate. "Honey, my philosophy is this: Life is supposed to take all these twists and turns so that we're forced to slow down and enjoy the passing scenery instead of just racing along a boring, straight, narrow stretch of highway to get where we're going. Some folks may want to cruise a fancy new highway. Me? I'll take twists and turns along a rutted country road any old time."

Jesse surprised her by getting to his feet and planting a kiss on her cheek.

She touched a hand to the spot. "Now what's that for?"

"For being your absolutely brilliant self. I love your philosophy, Daffy."

Looking slightly dazed, she walked away.

Jesse dropped some money on the table before catching Amy's hand. As he led her from the saloon, he continued holding her hand, while every customer turned to stare and then to whisper.

Talk about twists and turns. She was having a hard time keeping up with his mercurial moods.

Amy hoped his unexpected gesture hadn't left her looking as dazed as Daffy.

CHAPTER TEN

———◆———

W here're you parked?" Jesse continued to hold Amy's hand as they walked away from the Fortune Saloon.

Was he just doing it to taunt Delia Cowling and the other gossips in town? Amy wondered. Or had he, in his haste to escape the saloon, just forgotten what he was doing? Though she was puzzled, there was no denying that she liked it. And that annoyed her, since she considered it a silly weakness on her part. Did she need a man holding her hand to make her feel special?

"End of the street." Amy pointed.

If half the town had been in the saloon for lunch, the other half seemed to be milling about the sidewalk on their side of the street. Jesse was forced to let go of her hand and trail behind her when they met up with a cluster of people just entering the courthouse after their lunch break.

"Hey, Jesse. Amy." Judge Wilbur Manning, toting his

ever-present attaché case, paused. "I heard about your father, Amy. How's he doing?"

"He's just started his treatments. But so far, he seems to be doing fine."

"You give him my best, you hear?"

"I will. Thanks." Amy nodded.

The judge turned to Jesse. "How're your cousins adjusting to life in Gold Fever again?"

"So far, they seem to be enjoying the chance to play cowboy."

"This is the place to do it." The judge chuckled before starting up the steps of the courthouse.

As Jesse walked beside Amy he muttered, "So much for trying to keep any secrets in this town. Especially from the judge, who knows everybody's business."

"These people care about us."

He grinned. "And they feel that it entitles them to know every little detail of our lives."

When they came to Amy's truck, she nodded toward the sacks loaded in the back. "Thanks to Orley, I only have to wrestle these one more time."

"I could follow you home and unload them in the barn for you. It'll only take me a few minutes."

"I can handle them, Jess." She paused. "Besides, there's no reason to add to my dad's guilt about not being able to do things himself."

Jesse could see her point. A man like Otis Parrish was used to handling his own chores. As hard as it would be seeing his daughter struggling to do his work, it would be twice as painful to see a McCord lending a hand. Her old man could hold a grudge better than anybody else Jesse could think of.

"What time do you have to get back to the clinic?" Jesse leaned a hip against the door of her truck, reluctant to end their time together.

Amy glanced at her watch. "The treatment is over by now, but Dad always needs a few minutes to rest before tackling the ride home."

He reached a hand to an errant strand of her hair, tucking it behind her ear.

At the familiar gesture, heat spiraled all the way to her toes, annoying her yet again. Jesse McCord had always had an easy way with the ladies. She had to keep reminding herself that the gesture meant no more to him than breathing.

Jesse's tone softened. "I wish there was a way to make this easier for you. I wish I could..."

"Hey, Jesse." Rafe Spindler's voice had them looking up.

The husky cowboy was standing on the sidewalk, squinting against the noon sunlight.

"Cal wanted me to tell you that I need to beef up my crew on the north range. I thought maybe, seeing that you're"—his voice was heavy with sarcasm—"all one big happy family now, you'd like to join Zane and Wyatt for a couple of days." His look turned sly. "That'll give me a couple of nights to win back the stallion you won from me in last night's poker game. He was the best saddle horse I've ever..."

Jesse gave a quick shake of his head. "Can't do it. I've got too much to do in the next couple of days. Call Jimmy Eagle and see if he can spare some hands from the south pasture."

Rafe glanced from Amy to Jesse with a knowing

smirk. "Yeah, I can see you're going to be real busy in the coming days. And nights."

"You've made your point, Rafe. Now beat it."

"Yeah. Wouldn't want to crowd you."

As he sauntered away, Jesse clenched his hands into fists in silent fury. Rafe was another one who knew everybody's business and enjoyed letting them know it.

Huffing out a breath, he turned back to Amy. "Is this some kind of conspiracy?"

She merely shrugged at the absurdity of it. The interruptions were endless, but so was Jesse's flirting.

"I swear this is some evil plot to keep us apart. A few days ago, back at the ranch, it was Zane and Wyatt. Today, it's all these well-meaning citizens who keep interrupting. All I wanted to do was"—he leaned close—"say a proper good-bye."

"Oh, Amy. Glad you're still here." Orley Peterson came rushing out of the store, holding a parcel in his outstretched hand. "Be sure to give this to your father."

Amy couldn't help laughing at the look on Jesse's face as he jerked back. "Thanks, Orley. What is it?"

"An antibiotic he ordered for his heifers." He grinned at Jesse. "Hey, Jesse. Good to see you."

"You, too, Orley."

Jesse watched the older man waddle away.

When he turned back, Amy had already opened the truck door and slid into the driver's seat before dropping the parcel beside her.

She turned the key in the ignition.

Before she could put the truck in gear Jesse stuck his head in the open window. His voice was a low growl of frustration. "Would it be okay if I stop by later tonight to see you?"

"I guess so." She nodded. "I'd like that."

He felt a sense of relief. "Good. So would I." He'd had no intention of taking no for an answer. If she'd refused, he'd have found an excuse to see her anyway.

He stepped back as she checked for traffic, made a quick U-turn, and headed along the street toward the clinic.

Jesse jammed his hands in his pockets, watching her truck move along Main Street. It was a good thing she'd agreed to see him tonight, or his head might have exploded.

He was happy to let his cousins cool their heels on the north range, babysitting a herd of cattle. As for him, he had a challenge of a different sort in mind.

He needed to sort out just what was going on inside his head. Not to mention his heart.

He'd thought he could live without her. He'd learned all kinds of tricks to keep himself from dwelling on what he'd lost. He managed for years to throw himself into the tough, demanding ranch chores, working killer hours alongside the wranglers so that he could sleep. But even in sleep his mind refused to give him peace. She was there in his dreams, taunting him, teasing him.

Now she was back and he found himself wanting to see her again. In fact, if he was to be perfectly honest, it was more than just a want. These feelings for her were a need. He needed to see her, even though he knew there was a chance that she'd be gone in a short time, back to the life she'd made for herself in Helena. A life that didn't include him.

It was a risk he was willing to take.

That probably made him the biggest fool in the world.

Amy stepped out onto the porch, her head still spinning from the rows of figures she and her father had gone over in his ledgers. Though he may not have wanted to talk about his illness, it was plain that he'd given it a lot of thought. Aware of his mortality, he'd taken great pains to arm his daughter and only heir with as much information as possible. To that end they'd discussed the exact acreage owned, the number of buildings and the repairs that would be needed in the coming year, and the amount of county, state, and federal taxes owed, as well as expected income from the sale of cattle.

Amy now had a handle on their income, expenses, and maintenance fees. And though money would be tight, she was comforted by the knowledge that she wasn't in any danger of losing all that her father had worked so hard to manage through the years.

Besides discussing their finances, he'd said something that had caught her by surprise.

"You realize this ranch was never mine, girl."

She'd looked up at him. "What's that supposed to mean?"

"When I married your mother, she made it clear that she intended to see her family's ranch passed along to the next generation. Whether you return to teaching or stay on the land, it's still yours to do with as you please."

"Don't be silly, Dad. You worked it alongside Mom for more than thirty years. That makes it yours."

"I had no illusions about it ever being mine. Long

after I'm gone, the land will remain your legacy. I know it would please your mother if I kept it as a working ranch. But the future of this place will be squarely in your hands."

In her hands.

There seemed to be way too much in her hands these days.

Amy lifted her head to study the full moon rising above the peaks of Treasure Chest in the distance.

It was one of those perfect autumn evenings. Though the day had been warm, there was a chill in the air as the last of daylight faded, bringing a hint of what was to come.

Amy draped her mother's faded old afghan around her shoulders. It gave her such comfort to have something of her mother's.

She loved autumn here in Montana, just as her mother always had. Loved the burnished gold of the aspens. Loved watching the mist rise up off the lakes as late-morning sun began to heat the chilly waters. She felt energized by the thought of a solitary morning of fishing when the cooler water brought walleye and trout up from the depths to practically leap onto her hook.

Though she missed her students, she had to admit that she was beginning to appreciate the chance to leave the daily routine behind and return to her roots. Especially since it meant a return to...

She looked up at the sudden flash of headlights in the distance. Jesse. The mere thought of him had her heart doing cartwheels. Damn him for having this effect on her after all this time.

Long before she heard the crunch of tires, she'd

discarded the afghan and was down the steps, waiting at the end of the driveway as he stepped from his truck.

"How's your dad?"

"He only got sick twice on the ride home this time. He was able to keep down some broth when we got here and then slept for an hour. So that's all good."

While leading Jesse up the steps to the porch swing, she paused. "Isn't it strange how quickly things can change in our lives? I can't imagine another time when I would consider any of this as good news. Not long ago it would have been impossible to imagine my father spending one day tired, nauseous, or weak. He was so strong. So confident. Now he seems to grow a bit more frail every day. For supper he managed a couple of bites of a grilled cheese sandwich, and he had just enough energy to stay awake for a while before calling it a day."

"He's asleep?" Jesse sat beside her, giving the swing a nudge with his foot.

She nodded, struggling to ignore the press of his shoulder and hip to hers. "Those treatments really knock the wind out of his sails. But the nurse at the clinic assured him this was only temporary, and that he'd bounce back."

"Hold on to that thought." He squeezed her hand and absorbed the quick rush of heat he always felt when touching her. Instead of letting go, he continued holding it lightly in his as the swing rocked gently back and forth.

"I will. I'll take all the assurances I can get." She looked up at the canopy of stars. "It's funny how a life-and-death situation puts everything in perspective."

"Yeah. I guess the little things just fall by the wayside."

"Most of them." She sighed. "Before Dad went to bed, he went over the ranch accounts with me."

"Is that good or bad?"

She gave a shrug of her shoulders. "He's been so silent, so distant, I was convinced that he was in complete denial about the seriousness of his illness. Now I realize he's been doing some heavy-duty thinking."

"That sounds good to me."

"It is. But the poor guy had to figure out how to talk to me, how to bring me up to speed on his finances, how to plan ahead on keeping the ranch going without his help. And all without Mom here to act as mediator." She looked over. "It was always Mom who kept the two of us from ripping each other into shreds."

Jesse sandwiched her hand between both of his. "The main thing is, he did talk to you. And I take it he did it without fighting."

"He did." She studied their joined hands, enjoying the connection. She'd missed this. Missed him more than she'd ever allowed herself to admit. "And now that he's opened that door, I intend to keep it open, even if I have to pester him with questions on a daily basis. I'm not going to let him shut me out again."

"I know just how you feel." Jesse's words, though spoken softly, held a thread of steel.

She looked up to see his eyes, hot and fierce, fixed on hers, and felt the jolt to her heart.

"Whatever happened between us is in the past, Amy. We can't undo it. But I don't want to be shut out again."

"Jess…"

He touched a finger to her lips to still her words. "Hear me out."

The press of his finger against her mouth had her heart stammering. She couldn't have managed a word if she'd wanted to.

"I'm sorry that it was bad news that brought you back. I wouldn't wish that on anyone. But I'm not sorry you're here now. The minute I saw you at Coot's funeral, I had the sense that you and I had been given a second chance."

She gave a wry laugh. "Is that why you were so warm and inviting that day?"

"I deserve that." He swore under his breath. "I was trying to deny what I was feeling, what I am feeling. I'm hoping you feel the same way."

He waited, staring into her eyes with a look that implored even while it challenged.

She hadn't expected such honesty. But now that he'd been forthcoming, how could she be less so?

"I didn't know what to expect, Jess. I guess I still don't know exactly how I feel about being back here. I've made a life for myself in Helena. I love my work. Have some good friends..."

"Any in particular?"

She shrugged. "A couple."

"Any marriage proposals?"

She shook her head. "Not so far." She thought about Colin, the history teacher. They'd been spending a good deal of time together, and she knew it was getting serious, at least on Colin's part. As for her, she'd been holding back, and she didn't even realize it until now. Was Jesse the reason?

"But you don't hate me?" His words sent her thoughts scattering.

"I came close." She sighed. "But I couldn't hate you, Jesse."

"Then why did you...?" He paused, considering his words carefully. He wanted desperately to know why she'd left him without a word. But he worried that if he brought up the past, he would end up right where he'd been stuck these past years. Hurt, angry, and distant. He was sick and tired of such feelings.

Instead, he drew her close. Against her temple he murmured, "For now, I'll be satisfied that you don't hate me."

With no warning he lowered his head and touched his lips to hers. He hadn't planned this, but now that he'd started, there was no way he could stop.

Dear God. She tasted even better than he'd remembered all these years. Wild and sweet and as cool, as fresh as a mountain stream. This reality was far better than any of the memories he'd stored up. And there'd been enough of them to rob him of too many nights of sleep to count.

Amy responded with the same shocking hunger, wrapping her arms around his waist and throwing herself fully into the kiss.

She'd always loved kissing Jesse. Those firm, practiced lips. That hot, clever tongue that could tease and tempt until she forgot everything else. And those hands. Those rough cowboy's hands that could stroke and soothe and coax until she was mad with need. Hands strong enough to break her, but when they went all soft and easy, as they were now, moving over her slowly, carefully, as though afraid she might break, they had her flesh and bones melting like hot wax. These same hands had always been there to hold her and keep her from falling.

He kissed her long and slow and deep, until they both were fighting for air. The heat between them felt as though they'd been thrust into a furnace.

The need for her was so sharp and deep, he found himself sucking in a breath on the pain. "God, Amy. I've never stopped wanting you."

"I..." She broke free, filling her lungs, struggling to calm her ragged breathing. "I need a minute."

"Time is the last thing we need. We've wasted far too much already." He drew her close and touched his lips over hers. "I just need you."

"Wait." She pulled a little away, her head spinning, hating the way her body strained toward his. It shamed her that with a single kiss all the old feelings were back, and stronger than ever. "I don't even know how long I'll be here. It could be months or just a few weeks. And then I'll be leaving again."

Not if he had anything to say about it.

Aloud he merely said, "Let's not think about the future or dwell on the past. Let's just think about today. Tonight. Now."

When she opened her mouth to argue he stopped her. "Life doesn't pass out guarantees. But for whatever time you're here, Amy, let's make the most of it."

He cradled her face between his big hands, kissing her eyelids, the tip of her nose, the corner of her mouth, drawing out each butterfly kiss until her heartbeat pounded in her temples, drowning out any negative thoughts she might be harboring. "I've missed you so much, it's like one big ache in my heart."

She knew a thing or two about aching hearts. She sighed and wondered that hers didn't burst clear through her chest. "Damn you, Jesse. You always could win me over with tenderness."

He grinned. "I was counting on it."

"You're one cocky cowboy. Think you're smart, don't you?" She stared into those laughing eyes and felt her heart do a slow dip.

Why did Jesse McCord have to be her weakness?

He caught her hand, drawing her up from the porch swing. "We could go out to the barn. For old time's sake."

His words were like a dash of water.

Her smile faded, and a sad, haunted look crept into her eyes.

"I don't make love for old time's sake, Jess. Not even with you. I think you should go."

He knew he'd crossed the line and cursed himself for his foolishness. "Let me stay awhile."

Before she could refuse he whispered, "Please, Amy."

She stared into his eyes. "No pressure?"

He shook his head. "No pressure." He sat back down and was relieved when she reluctantly sat beside him.

He nudged the swing into a gentle motion and stared up at the moon.

"Oh, Jess." Her sigh seemed to rise up from somewhere deep inside. "I'm so worried about my dad. I wish I had more family to share this with. There are times when I feel so alone."

"You're not alone, Amy." He wrapped a big arm around her shoulders and tucked her up against him.

They fit together like two pieces in a puzzle. Perfectly.

Against her ear he whispered, "I want you to know that you can count on me."

"Thank you." She closed her eyes, breathing him in, loving the feel of him beside her.

They sat that way for long, silent minutes, while the swing moved back and forth, and the stars winked above them.

Though he wanted her more than he'd ever wanted anyone or anything in his life, he knew that he would have to bank his needs in order to tend hers. And what she needed right now was tenderness, trust, and a feeling of safety. If those things were all he could give her for now, he would have to be satisfied with that.

As the minutes ticked by, he glanced at her head resting lightly on his shoulder, eyes closed, breath warm against his neck. She was so exhausted by her father's illness and the never-ending ranch chores, she'd fallen asleep.

Jesse realized that, though he should have been feeling really frustrated, he was, instead, feeling almost content.

Just holding her, watching her sleep, he thought with a smile, was bringing him more happiness, more peace, than he'd known in years.

Maybe, when her life became more settled, they could resolve whatever had gone so wrong between them and move on. Or maybe it would all end as it had before.

He just hoped he didn't go slowly mad while he waited.

CHAPTER ELEVEN

Jesse awoke with a start and realized that both he and Amy had fallen asleep on the swing. He glanced down at her head, still resting against his shoulder.

She looked so peaceful here. The worry about her father, the million and one ranch chores, all were forgotten as she lost herself in sleep.

Careful not to wake her, he reached for the afghan lying at their feet. Drawing it over them, he tucked it around her shoulders.

She sighed and snuggled closer. His pulse did a quick dance. He was fully aroused. The thought of waking her with a slow, easy kiss had the blood pounding in his temples. He had no doubt he could wake the slumbering passion within her while she was still in the throes of sleep.

Though he was sorely tempted, he drew back, watching her. It wouldn't be fair to take advantage of her in this state. She was exhausted by the burdens she was being forced to carry these days. Besides, though he wanted her desperately, he wanted the decision to be hers alone. If they made love... *when they made love*, he mentally corrected, he wanted her fully engaged, as eager and hungry as he would be.

This time, he thought with a little frown, there would be no second thoughts. No regrets.

No regrets.

Hadn't he lived with regret every day since Amy had left Gold Fever without a word?

They would get past that, he vowed, or he'd die trying. He wanted her to want what he wanted.

What he wanted. He sighed and lifted his head to study the path of a shooting star. He knew from his childhood here on the ranch that it wasn't possible to get everything he wanted in this life. As a boy he'd lost his cousins, who were also his best friends. He'd lost both his parents. And now Coot. Still, he realized that he'd been lucky to have a chance to grow up as he did, surrounded by so many caring people.

Right now, he would give up everything he had for the chance to get back the years he and Amy had lost.

"Jesse." Amy jerked awake and lifted her head from his shoulder, staring around in confusion.

In that brief instant she'd seen the way he'd been looking at her with a strange, almost haunted look. It was unsettling to realize that he'd been studying her without her knowledge. "How long have I been asleep?"

He glanced at the moon. "Most of the night, I'd say."

Despite the warmth of the afghan tucked firmly around

her, she felt a trickle of ice along her spine at the thought of having spent the night in his arms. "Sorry."

"I'm not."

She looked over, expecting him to say more. Instead he continued watching her with that wary look.

"You work so hard all day, Jess. The last thing you need is to spend the night on my porch swing."

"There's no place I'd rather be."

He smiled then, and her heart actually fluttered.

"I should get inside."

"In a minute." He closed a hand over hers. "I want to be with you, Amy. But I need to know what you want."

She looked away, unable to meet that steady gaze. "I'm not sure what I want, Jess."

"Then you take your time until you're sure."

"You don't understand. My first concern has to be my father."

"I know that. I'm not pushing for your answer right now. I'm not going anywhere. When you're ready, I'll be waiting." He looked up, watching the first faint light of dawn beginning to streak the sky. "Want to catch a few more winks before you start your day?"

She chuckled, but seeing his warm invitation, she moved closer and laid her head on his shoulder. Knowing there was no pressure on her to make a decision had her sighing with relief. "This is nice."

He nuzzled her hair. "Yeah."

"Your arm ought to be numb by now if it was around me all night."

"My arm's just fine. Never better."

She closed her eyes, loving the feel of his calm, steady

heartbeat. "Good. Maybe, since you offered, I'll just take a few more minutes before I think about those chores."

"I'll call you later, Amy, just to see how your father's doing." Jesse dropped his cell phone into his shirt pocket.

Beneath a spectacular sunrise, they stood beside his truck.

She touched a hand to the dark stubble at his cheeks and chin, which only added to his appeal. "I have to get inside. Dad will be awake soon."

"You realize that sooner or later you'll have to tell him that you're seeing me."

She lifted her chin. "Am I? Seeing you?"

He caught her chin between his thumb and finger and met her questioning look. "Damn right you are."

She grinned. "I guess that answers my question. But I'm not ready to tell Dad yet. He has enough to deal with. I can't add to his problems right now."

"I understand." He bent his head to give her a quick kiss. Then, thinking better of it, he gathered her into his arms and lingered over her lips until they were both struggling for breath. "That's so you'll think about me from time to time."

She managed a shaky laugh over the tightness in her throat. "You kiss me like that too often and I won't be able to think of anything else."

"Promise?" He hauled her up against his chest.

"Oh, yeah."

"Good. That's my plan."

She lifted her face for another kiss and wasn't disappointed.

When at last he climbed into his truck and closed the door, she stepped back and waved as he backed the truck away and turned it in the opposite direction before heading down the long gravel drive.

She waited until he was out of sight before walking to the house. As she climbed the steps she thought about the night they'd spent together. Together and yet not together. Strange. But she felt at peace knowing that he'd been content to just hold her.

She didn't like the fact that all the old feelings were back and, if possible, even stronger. How would she deal with them? It was too soon to act on those feelings. She just wasn't sure that anything could ever come of them. There were too many barriers between them. Not just her father's resentment against anyone in the McCord family, but also because of their past. Neither of them had spoken about their long separation, or the reason for it.

They were tiptoeing around things. Neither of them had wanted anything to spoil the mood, and so they'd deliberately avoided bringing it up. Still, it was there between them. And sooner or later they would have to deal with it if they hoped to move forward.

Forward?

What was there for them as they moved forward? Great sex in the barn? Wasn't that what Jesse had suggested last night?

She paused on the front porch, staring at the fiery ball of sun rising above the mountain peaks in the distance. Sex with Jesse would be great. Better than great. Fantastic. Earth-shattering. And the truth was, she wanted it. Wanted him.

But for now, while she dealt with her father's serious

health issues, there wasn't room in her life for any thoughts about the future. She'd have to think about it later. Much later, when her life was more settled.

She hurried inside and started the coffee before heading back to the barn for morning chores.

Jesse swore as he drove his truck into the barn and caught sight of Rafe Spindler talking to a cluster of cowboys. He'd expected them to be gone by now.

Their heads came up sharply and they turned to watch as he stepped out of his truck. He recognized Cal Randall, Jimmy Eagle, Zane, and Wyatt among them and cursed his lousy timing.

"Catching an all-nighter?" Rafe sauntered over, his big, beefy face wearing a mean grin.

Ignoring the question, Jesse turned to the others. "I figured you'd be up on the north ridge by now."

"I bet you did." Rafe wasn't about to let this go. "Now I see why you couldn't lend a hand with my crew."

Enjoying the flare of anger in Jesse's eyes, he decided to push a little harder.

His eyes glittered. "I could've made myself a fortune taking bets on how long it would take you to score with Amy Parrish. I could tell by the look on both of your faces at the old man's funeral that it was just a matter of time."

Jesse's hand was at his throat before he had time to blink. With a fistful of Rafe's shirt he dragged him close, his eyes hot and fierce. "That old man was my grandfather, and he had a name. You want to talk about him, you call him by name, you hear?"

Rafe tried to pull away, but Jesse's hand tightened.

"I asked if you heard me."

Rafe swallowed hard. "I hear."

Jesse twisted the fistful of shirt, drawing Rafe's face even closer. "As for Amy Parrish, I don't see that she's any of your business. Not now. Not ever. You got that clear?"

Rafe gave a barely perceptible nod of his head, all that he could manage in that tight, choking grip.

Jesse lowered his hand and spun away.

"Let's get moving." Rafe's shouted order had the cowboys scrambling to climb into a line of trucks that were idling in the barn.

As Jesse started to walk away, Zane and Wyatt followed him to the door of the barn.

When Wyatt dropped a hand on his shoulder, Jesse spun around, fire in his eyes, until he realized that it wasn't Rafe.

"What?" His voice was a snarl.

Wyatt lowered his hand and his voice. "There's a rumor going around town that Amy found some more of Coot's notes."

"I guess it's like Amy said. There are no secrets in this place."

Zane glanced at Wyatt before turning to Jesse. "Is it true?"

"Yeah." Jesse dug his hands in the pockets of his jeans and pulled out the crumpled slips of paper. "They were mixed in with some old newspapers, just like the others."

"Do they make any sense?"

He shook his head. "No more than any of the dozens of others that have been found over the years. A few words, a couple of doodles, but no clear pathway to anything. But even though they don't make any sense, both Amy and I are feeling pretty good about this latest discovery. In fact, we're thinking of joining forces to continue Coot's search."

The two cousins shared a long, speculative look.

It was Wyatt who finally spoke. "We've been talking about it. We both decided that we'd like to study the papers. If you and Aunt Cora have no objections."

Jesse surprised himself and them by giving a negligent shrug of his shoulders. "I'm sure Aunt Cora will welcome your input."

"And you?" Zane shot him a challenging look.

Jesse met his look. "I won't object. Hell, Coot invited you in. Who am I to say otherwise?"

As he started to turn, Wyatt lifted a hand to Jesse's hair, smoothing out the clumps of bed-head.

"Next time you sleep over, you might want to at least give your head a shake before you drive home." He shot Jesse a wide grin. "So long, cuz. When we get back in a day or two, we'll take a look at Coot's old journal and notes and see if we can make any sense of them. Maybe, if we all put our heads together, we can come up with a plan."

"Fine." Jesse watched as his cousins sauntered away and joined Cal Randall and Jimmy Eagle in one of the ranch trucks.

He should have been glad that they were heading up to the north ridge, where they'd be out of his hair for a couple of days. But he couldn't help wishing he'd arrived home a little sooner, or a lot later. With little to occupy the cowboys except cattle and weather, they enjoyed every little bit of gossip they could uncover. Word of Amy's papers was proof of that. It was already spreading like wildfire. Jesse had no doubt that Rafe Spindler would spin out this latest tidbit as far as he could, enjoying every little minute of his self-importance while he told and retold his story of Jesse's nightly romp with the daughter of his grandfather's sworn enemy.

Because he wasn't about to take any more chances, he tossed his head like a shaggy dog and ran his hands through his hair before heading to the house. No sense broadcasting his night to Aunt Cora and Dandy, too.

It occurred to him that he wasn't nearly as angry about being caught sneaking home at dawn as he ought to be. And, wonder of wonders, he wasn't even upset about the fact that his cousins had decided to intensify the search for Coot's fortune.

Maybe all this warm, fuzzy mellowness had to do with the fact that he'd spent the night with Amy in his arms.

Just sleeping beside her made him feel better than he'd felt in years.

He couldn't wait to do it again.

CHAPTER TWELVE

———◆———

This is nice." Cora looked around the dinner table at her three nephews. Cal had gone into town with some of the crew. "I believe this is the first time we've all been together in a week or more."

Earlier in the day Zane and Wyatt had returned, bewhiskered, weary, and caked with mud after their stint with the wranglers from the north ridge. Jesse had ridden in at nearly the same time after lending a hand with a crew mending fences on the south ridge.

Now, freshly shaved, showered, and dressed in clean clothes, they were enjoying a meal of Dandy's best stuffed pork chops and garlic mashed potatoes.

Cora set aside her napkin. "How about taking dessert in the great room?"

"Good idea, Aunt Cora." Jesse pushed away from the table.

Dandy, busy spooning chocolate sauce over devil's

food cake topped with ice cream, looked up. "You folks go ahead and I'll bring it, along with a pot of coffee."

Jesse held the door for his aunt, who was trailed by Zane and Wyatt.

They settled on two facing sofas in front of a roaring fire. The three men stretched out their long legs, enjoying the warmth and peace after the frantic pace of these last few chore-filled days.

After Dandy delivered a tray of desserts and coffee, they sat for long minutes in companionable silence enjoying the rich confection, washing it down with strong, hot coffee.

Wyatt glanced at the others. "This might be a good time to start sorting through Coot's journal."

If Cora was surprised at his remarks, she was even more surprised when Jesse agreed. He left the room and returned minutes later carrying an old shoe box, then dumped the contents on the coffee table between them. Besides the yellowed slips of paper, there was a small, pocket-sized notebook bulging with handwritten notes.

At Wyatt's raised eyebrow, Jesse grinned. "This was Coot's idea of a file cabinet."

"Yeah. I'd say that suits old Coot."

At Zane's words, the others burst into laughter.

They looked up when Dandy knocked before opening the door. "You have a visitor. Amy Parrish is here."

"Oh, Amy." Cora was on her feet and hurrying across the room as Amy entered.

"Is this a good time?" Amy returned the warm hug from the older woman.

"There's never a bad time for a visit, my dear. Come." Cora caught her hand and led her toward the sofas.

Jesse stood back, staring at her while his cousins offered their greetings.

"Good to see you again, Amy." Zane kissed her cheek.

"Hi, Amy." Wyatt kissed her other cheek.

"Hi to both of you." She looked across at Jesse and held out her hand. "I just found another slip of paper that looks like the others. I thought since Dad is asleep for the night, I'd bring it over."

"And just in time." Instead of taking the paper, Jesse caught her hand in his.

Amy wondered if the others could see her heart in her eyes, or the sparks that seemed to flare at their simple touch.

Jesse winked. "We were about to start sorting through Coot's journal. Want to join us?"

She began to back away, shaking her head. "This should be a private, family thing. I'll just go."

Jesse wasn't about to let go of her hand just yet. "Didn't you tell me just the other day that you were starting to believe in Coot's treasure hunt?"

She flushed. "I did. But..."

"Stay. Please." Cora laid a hand on Amy's shoulder and guided her to sit beside her on the sofa.

Without further protest Amy sat and was soon as caught up in the puzzling array of papers as the others.

"What a mess." Jesse sat back, studying the mountain of paper, then glanced over at Wyatt. "What are you doing?"

Wyatt was already turning each slip of paper faceup across the length and width of the coffee table. "I thought we'd treat this like a picture puzzle."

"What a fine idea." Getting into the spirit, Cora joined him in setting out each slip of paper, laying the pieces end to end until they filled the entire coffee table.

While they worked, Zane stood a little away, his trusty camera recording every word and movement.

Since moving in, half a dozen shipments of equipment had arrived for him. Video cameras, movie cameras, filters, lights. His suite was beginning to look like a Hollywood soundstage, complete with editing equipment and a soundboard.

Jesse looked annoyed. "I can't think while that camera is stuck in front of my face."

"Then stop thinking and just smile. You wouldn't want to be edited out of my documentary, would you?"

Jesse gave the camera an exaggerated grin before returning his attention to the puzzle.

Amy was studying a torn piece of paper, when suddenly she reached across the table and held up a second one. "Look. These torn edges match exactly. They have to be from the same note."

Everyone stared as she held the two pages close and read, "Finished with...buttes." She looked up. "He may have meant the Gold Rush buttes. They're the closest buttes to your ranch."

Jesse nodded. "You're right. And it sounds as though he meant to say there was no further need to search there. At least that's what 'finished with' means to me."

"I agree. Let me try something." Wyatt left the room. Minutes later he returned carrying a much-folded, oversized map of the ranch and the surrounding area.

At their questioning looks he explained, "While I was traveling the world, I wanted to remind myself of the place where I'd been born. So I've carried this with me."

He wasn't aware of the looks that were exchanged by the others as he smoothed out the map on the floor, then marked off the Gold Rush buttes. "If we agree that this area has already been searched and yielded nothing, we'll mark it off so we can concentrate on other areas."

Zane peered over his camera. "I could make a clear plastic overlay on my computer and print it out. That way we could see at a glance where Coot finished searching and what areas he missed. It would certainly simplify our hunt."

After a moment of charged silence, there was a renewed sense of excitement as they began searching through the papers for more matching edges.

Jesse looked over at Wyatt. "What made you think of a puzzle?"

His cousin shrugged. "In my travels around the world I've always been fascinated by primitive stick drawings. No matter what the culture, the people found a way to communicate. And those left behind to sort through those drawings have usually had to rely on piecing them together to form the big picture." He shrugged. "It just seemed to make sense to set out all of Coot's papers and then sort through them." While he spoke, his gaze searched the jumble of papers on the coffee table.

"Like these." Jesse held up two pages smeared with dirt and badly wrinkled in an identical fashion. "This one goes with this. I'm sure of it." He studied them. "The only words here are *north cliffs*."

Cora's eyes sparkled. "Oh, my. I wonder if Coot

meant that he wanted to search those cliffs? Or if he'd already searched them and found nothing?"

Jesse laid a hand over hers. "We won't know unless we find another piece to this page telling us what he meant. But at least we can see a pattern beginning to form."

"Yes. Oh." Cora touched a hand to her heart. "If only Coot were here to show us the way."

Zane, taking a close-up shot of the map and papers, aimed his camera at her. "He is here, Aunt Cora. He's here in every word and drawing. In every torn scrap of paper. Once we figure out his shorthand, he'll show us all the places he's already searched, so we won't have to duplicate his trail. And maybe, just maybe, when we put them all together, he'll show us the way to the treasure."

"I don't believe I've ever seen your aunt so excited over anything other than her art." Amy stepped out into the darkness and walked beside Jesse to her father's truck.

"Yeah. I'm feeling a little excited myself. Of course"—he shot her a sideways glance—"that could be because of the pretty woman next to me." He caught her hand. "I wish you could stay."

"Now that could prove interesting. Let's see. How would I greet your family when I walked downstairs in the morning? Hi, Miss Cora. Zane. Wyatt. My...um... truck wouldn't start, and I thought rather than tinker with the engine, I'd just sleep with Jesse. Oh, good morning, Dandy. What's for breakfast?"

Jesse burst into laughter. "Yeah. They might not buy your story. But you know what? They wouldn't say a word. You'd be as welcome in the morning as you were tonight."

Though she had joined him in laughter, she sobered. "They did make me feel welcome. I'm so grateful for that. Through all the troubles between my dad and your family, they've always been kind and considerate where I was concerned. I only wish my dad could make an effort to do the same for you."

Jesse dropped a hand on her shoulder. "Don't push, Amy. Give him time. Right now he's dealing with some major issues."

She nodded, relieved that Jesse was willing to be patient. "As for the treasure hunt, I never really gave it much thought before. But now that I've seen your grandfather's papers, and watched the enthusiasm grow between you and your cousins, I have to admit that I find it really exciting. No wonder Coot spent a lifetime searching. The thought of finding lost treasure is so tantalizing."

"Almost as tantalizing as your lips." He brushed his mouth over hers and they both absorbed the flare of heat.

Was it just the excitement of this night, with all the talk of lost treasure and the thought of taking up Coot's search? Or was there something else going on here?

He'd thought that once he'd made the decision to slow things and allow Amy time to chart her own course of action, some of this wildfire raging inside him would cool. But if anything, it was burning hotter than ever. Maybe he'd just try to nudge her along.

Against her mouth he muttered, "I'd give up a treasure for you, Amy."

"Oh, sure." Despite her thrill at his admission, she drew away a little, determined to keep things light. "You say that now. If you and your family ever find that treasure, I'll remind you of those words, cowboy."

"I've never meant anything more." He gathered her close and lingered over her lips until they were both sighing.

Reluctantly Amy pulled away, keeping a hand at his chest. "I'd better get home. Will I see you soon?"

"You bet." He kissed her one more time for good measure before holding open the door of her truck. "Wild horses couldn't keep me away from your door."

Though she was thrilled at his remark, she was determined to remain composed.

"Night, Jesse." She blew him a kiss and started away.

Jesse watched until her taillights were just a blur before turning back to the house.

Inside he made his way to his room. He pried off his boots and kicked them aside before unbuttoning his plaid shirt and tossing it over the arm of a chair. Barefoot and shirtless, he walked to the bank of windows that looked out over the foothills of Treasure Chest Mountain. He loved the look of it, silhouetted against the night sky, its peaks gilded by the light of a half-moon. These mountains and hills and this glorious land hid a million secrets. And somewhere, they hid a fortune in gold that had once, for a few precious hours, belonged to his ancestors.

Though he'd never shared old Coot's hunger for the lost treasure, he could understand the desire to retrieve what was rightfully his. After all, that treasure had cost the lives of Coot's father and grandfather. To be perfectly honest, Jesse thought, it had cost all of them a great price. Coot's sons, weary of their father's obsession, had abandoned him. Coot had been denied watching two of his grandsons grow to manhood, and Jesse had been denied his cousins and closest friends at a critical time in all their young lives. And all because of a lost treasure that could possibly remain lost for another century.

Though they were a long way from regaining what they'd once had, this late-night session had been a pleasant interlude. An uneasy truce in their family feud. Maybe, he thought, old Coot hadn't been as foolish as he'd first appeared when the will was read. At the time, they'd all recognized his clumsy attempt to entice them to stay. But maybe there was more to it. Maybe the sly old man had hoped that the search for the treasure would be a catalyst for them to learn how to be a family once more.

Yawning, Jesse lowered the shades and turned off the light before kicking off his jeans and stretching out on the bed.

He found himself wishing that Amy could be here in his arms.

He should have followed her home.

Could've. Should've. Would've.

The thought had him alternately smiling and frowning as he drifted into sleep.

CHAPTER THIRTEEN

The town of Gold Fever was buzzing with the gossip that the McCord boys had decided to follow in their grandfather's footsteps and chase the elusive dream.

"Are they so foolish they've forgotten the curse?" Delia Cowling was holding court in the Fortune Saloon while many of the lunch crowd gathered around.

Delia's brother, Ledge, nodded. "Took the lives of three generations of McCords. I guess that's not enough for them. They'd like to gamble away what's left of 'em. But what the hell. It's their lives to risk."

Rafe Spindler and Cal Randall, in town to pick up supplies, couldn't help but overhear as they shook the dust from their hats and ambled toward their table.

Rafe hung back, letting Cal walk ahead while he remained beside Delia's table. "From what I've seen, it looks like Amy Parrish has agreed to join forces with them."

Rafe's words had everyone muttering as they gathered around him.

"You sure of that?" Delia's eyes were as big as saucers.

Rafe ignored Cal's scowl of disapproval. Cal Randall was a stickler for keeping ranch gossip away from the town. The old man knew the rumors about Amy and Jesse were all over the Lost Nugget. Why shouldn't they be repeated in town? Too bad if Cal didn't like it. Rafe might work for the McCord family, and Cal might be his boss on the ranch, but here in town, Rafe reasoned, he was his own boss. And this town was his lifeblood. Besides, it wasn't often he found himself the center of attention. He puffed himself up, enjoying his moment of fame.

He raised his voice a fraction, so everybody could hear. "From what I've heard, Amy found some of Coot's old notes and drawings in her family's trash."

Delia snorted. "Trash, is it? I'm not surprised. Her pa made no bones about the fact that he hated the whole pack of McCords. What better way to show his true feelings than to hide Coot's precious notes? Why would he hand over any papers to them? Especially if the papers would prove helpful in their foolish search."

Rafe nodded. "Exactly. Amy found them and turned them over to the McCords. But then, I'm not surprised." His tone lowered for dramatic emphasis.

Everyone bent close to hear.

"She and Jesse have been getting really cozy, if you know what I mean. I saw him coming back from her place at dawn."

His words brought the desired reaction. Delia hissed out a breath. Ledge rolled his eyes and his lips thinned into what was the closest he ever came to a smile. A couple of the others exchanged knowing looks.

"And Amy's truck has been at the McCord ranch a couple of nights, too."

Delia crossed her arms over her chest. "If Otis Parrish knew about this, he'd pack his daughter off to Helena without another word."

"Seems to me he did that once." Harding Jessup grinned. "But she's not a teenager now, Delia. She's all grown up and in charge of her own life. Plus, she's become a mighty fine teacher, I hear."

Delia clucked her tongue. "She's still living under Otis's roof. He has every right to expect her to respect his feelings. This is a fine way for a daughter to behave while her father is dying."

"Now, Delia." Orley Peterson patted her hand to silence her. "You don't know that Otis is dying."

"He's in treatment, isn't he? Has anybody asked Doc Wheeler what his chances are?"

"Not my business." Mayor Rowe Stafford turned toward another table, having heard enough to pass along to any and all who would listen. And he had no doubt there were plenty willing to listen when it came to news concerning the McCord boys. "I don't think you ought to make it yours either. Besides, Doc wouldn't tell you even if he knew."

Delia watched him and Orley leave, then gathered the others closer to whisper a few choice words before breaking up the crowd and leading the way toward her table.

Daffy approached, pencil in hand, and fixed Delia with a hawk's stare. Her rusty voice lowered a notch.

"You folks going to eat, or are you already filled up on gossip?"

Delia looked as though she'd sucked a lemon. "I suppose you're going to claim you're above a little gossip?"

"Not at all. I hear enough of it every day to make my ears bleed. But most of it's like that old greasy stuff we scrape off the grill. When it's fresh and clean, it cooks a heap of chicken and fries, and we love sharing. When it gets old, the only thing it's good for is the critters out back. The stuff you're talking about is old as the hills, and too rancid for my taste. I doubt even the critters would care for it."

"If you're through spouting your folksy words of wisdom"—Delia cut her off with a wave of her hand— "I'll have the special."

"Make that two," her friend said.

"Two specials," Daffy shouted to her sister, Vi, manning the grill. "With a side of our best fries, cooked in... fresh oil."

She walked away, humming to herself, while many in the room struggled not to laugh out loud.

Still, with the seeds of gossip sown, it was only a matter of time before speculation, jealousy, and outright lies would begin to blossom.

"You doing okay, Dad?" Amy helped her father from the truck and up the steps of their house.

"Fine. Just help me to my room, girl." Every word was an effort, and he was sweating profusely despite the cold wind that swirled around them.

Once he was settled into bed, Amy headed toward the

barn to finish her chores. A glance at the distant field had her puzzled. The hill that should have been dotted with cows was oddly empty.

She started across the field at a run, spotting a section of fence that was down. There was no sign of the cows.

Frantic, she raced back to the barn and saddled Old Red.

Horse and rider followed a creek that ran between the Parrish property line and that of the McCord ranch. Several miles distant Amy came upon her cows, some standing leisurely in the stream and drinking, others grazing on a nearby hillside, mingling with the McCord herd.

Cal Randall spotted Amy and drove his truck across the field.

In a courtly gesture he whipped his wide-brimmed hat from his head. "Afternoon, Amy. Something I can do for you?"

"I'm sorry, Cal. I just found a section of my fence down and"—she waved a hand—"my herd wandered down here while I was in town seeing to my dad. I'll get them home as fast as I can."

"I'll get some of the wranglers to give you a hand."

She slid from the saddle. "There's no need..."

He stopped her with a hand on her arm. "No sense herding them home until that fence is mended, or you'll just have to do it all over again tomorrow. First let me see that fence. When it's properly repaired, I'll have my men bring your herd back. In the meantime, why don't you just head home and tend to your pa."

When she realized that she couldn't win the argument, she let out a long, deep sigh. "Thanks, Cal. I owe you."

He gave her a smile. "Not at all. That's what neighbors are for."

As soon as Cal pulled up to the Parrish fence line, Jesse, Zane, and Wyatt clambered down from the truck and began assembling their tools.

Zane pulled his ever-present video camera from his pocket and began filming each word and movement.

Jesse looked over at him. "Okay. I get that you're going to document every damned thing we do, but can you lend a hand first?"

Zane gave one of the famous McCord grins. "I figure you two are doing such a great job, I'll just sit this one out."

"Like hell." Jesse tossed a pair of leather gloves, hitting Zane in the face. "Put these on and get to work."

"Yes, sir." Laughing, Zane joined them.

Cal tucked his cell phone into his shirt pocket before exiting. "I told Rafe to start rounding up the Parrish herd. This isn't much of a break. We ought to have this done in an hour or two, and by then he can have those cows back. We'll have this wrapped up before dark."

It occurred to Cal that these three cousins worked well together. Despite the years apart, despite the teasing banter, they still shared a similar work ethic. The minute he'd phoned Jesse about Amy's problem, Zane and Wyatt had volunteered to help. Now the three dropped to the ground, examining the length of fencing that was lying in the dirt.

"Look at this." Jesse's voice was sharp as he turned to the ranch foreman. "Cal. Take a look. What do you think?"

The old man knelt beside him and ran a hand along the surface of the metal links. "These don't look broken to me."

Behind them, Zane grabbed up his camera and began recording everything.

Jesse's eyes narrowed. "Yeah. These don't look like they were pulled apart by a surge of cattle, or eroded by weather. The links aren't jagged or worn. They're too smooth, the pattern at either end of the break too similar."

"Cut?" Zane spoke the word they were all thinking.

"Looks like." Cal continued running his hand over the edges, as though hoping to prove his theory wrong.

"But why?" Wyatt looked around. "Who would benefit from this?"

"Nobody that I can see." Cal sat back on his heels. "This kind of thing is usually done when somebody wants to free a herd worth stealing. Lure them far enough away from the ranch so nobody can hear the trucks pulling up in the night. The Parrish herd is too small to be worth stealing. Besides, the only place the cows could wander is onto McCord land. And anybody hoping to rustle cattle has to know that we have cowboys keeping watch day and night."

Zane looked from the old cowboy to his cousin. "So, the Parrish herd would actually be safer on our land than they would be here?"

"Exactly."

Jesse turned to Cal. "Why don't you drive up to the house and tell Amy what we found. While we get this fence mended, she'd better phone Sheriff Wycliff and make a report. Even though it isn't exactly a crime, it looks a lot like harassment. Either this is the result of an old grudge, or it's some kind of cruel prank. Poor Amy. As though she doesn't have enough on her mind right now."

Cal hesitated. "Don't you think you should be the one to tell her?"

Jesse gave a weak smile. "Her father might be awake. He's apt to toss me off the property without even bothering to ask why I'm here. I don't think he's ever had a beef with you, has he?"

Cal shrugged. "We're civil whenever we meet."

"That's good enough for me."

When Jesse said nothing more, the old cowboy gave up the argument and climbed into the truck.

Even before the dust had settled, Jesse, Zane, and Wyatt were hard at work mending the fence.

Whenever Zane and Wyatt glanced over at Jesse, his eyes were narrowed, his look grim. It was obvious that he had a lot on his mind. And none of it pleasant.

A raw, bitter wind, dubbed an Alberta clipper by the locals, blew in from the north, reminding the ranchers of the winter they would soon be facing. What few leaves had clung tenaciously to the aspens were now torn loose to fly through the air like golden snowflakes.

Amy pulled on a parka and headed toward the barn to begin the morning chores. After gathering a basket of eggs in the henhouse, she mucked out stalls and forked dung and straw into a wagon before tackling the milking.

Outside, the wind rattled the big door and whistled against the windows of the hayloft.

The barn creaked and groaned, complaining like an

old woman. The sound sent shivers along Amy's spine. She could actually feel the old structure bending and swaying.

She picked up the heavy buckets of milk and started toward the door. Just as she opened it, a gust of wind blew her nearly backward. She heard a crash as loud as a freight train and turned in time to see a massive timber beginning to fall.

As if in slow motion she saw the main rafter separate from the roof and swing downward.

Dropping the buckets, she stumbled backward through the open doorway just as the timber came crashing to the ground. It smashed the walls of an empty stall, barely missing the row of cows at a trough as it landed with such force it sent a shudder through the old barn that rattled the walls and windows.

For long moments Amy was too stunned to react. She sat numbly in the dirt, staring at the destruction, seeing it all through a haze of disbelief. Then, realizing the enormity of what had just occurred, she got to her feet, and, despite the nerves that sent a trembling through every part of her body, she ran as fast as she could to the house. By the time she reached the back door, the breath was burning in her lungs, and tears of anger and confusion filled her eyes.

"I'm really sorry to bother you with my problems." Amy met Jesse, Wyatt, Zane, and Cal at the door to the barn. "But I didn't know who else to call."

"You did the right thing." Knowing they had an audience, Jesse contented himself with a hand to her shoulder.

He pulled open the door. As they crowded inside, they surveyed the damage in silence.

Zane plucked the video camera from his pocket and began recording.

Wyatt walked closer to the smashed trough. "It's lucky that this happened when you were almost out the door. Any closer, and you could have been crushed."

Amy nodded. "That timber has been here since my grandfather built this barn. Who would have believed that a gust of wind could topple it?"

Cal and Jesse knelt to examine the ancient wooden beam, and both looked up at the same instant.

In a low voice that only Jesse could hear, Cal muttered, "I'm no carpenter, but I know one thing. This was no accident. Anybody with half a brain can see that this was sawed nearly all the way through. Feel how clean this break is."

While Jesse ran his palm over and over the wooden beam, his mind was working overtime.

He got to his feet. "Amy, I know you have to take your father into town for his treatment. We'll stay here and check on any structural damage."

"You think the barn might collapse?"

He gave a quick shake of his head. "I hope not. But we'll need to check it out. I'll call you later with a report."

She glanced at her watch and turned away reluctantly. "I'm sorry to leave you with all this."

"That's what we're here for," Cal assured her.

When she was gone, Jesse's forced smile fled as he plucked his cell phone from his pocket and called the sheriff.

CHAPTER FOURTEEN

———◆◆◆———

Hours later, after Sheriff Wycliff had gone over every inch of the scene, he walked outside, trailed by Jesse and his cousins.

He paused beside his truck. "This doesn't look like an accident. And now, coupled with the damaged fencing, I'm inclined to agree that somebody is out to do Otis Parrish harm. I'll go through my records to see if I can find anyone who has had a problem with him." He shifted his gaze to Jesse. "You realize, of course, that the McCord family will be at the top of that list."

Jesse nodded. "As far as I'm concerned, that feud between Otis and Coot died with Coot."

"Maybe. Maybe not. I can appreciate that you don't want Otis upset right now, while he's going through these treatments. But we all know he's a hothead. He's probably made plenty of enemies over the years. After I go through my files, I'm going to need to speak with him, even if it upsets him. He and his daughter have to be made aware of any danger."

Jesse shrugged. "You do what you think is right, Ernie."

When the sheriff's truck disappeared in a cloud of dust, Cal walked from the barn, wiping his hands on his pants. "It doesn't look like there's any structural damage, but I asked Stan Novak to bring his construction crew over for a better look. They'll be here within the hour. I'll have them go over this place with a fine-tooth comb."

"Thanks, Cal." Jesse looked back at the barn. "Who would want to hurt Amy or her father?"

Wyatt turned up the collar of his parka against the wind. "You heard Ernie. Otis Parrish is a hard man to like. I'm betting he knows a dozen people who wouldn't mind seeing his ranch fail, and Otis along with it. It's just a shame that Amy has to be painted with the same brush as her father."

"We're making headway." Wyatt added another flag to the clear overlay on his map, while Jesse filed the notes they'd already matched into a manila folder.

Zane recorded the action with his newest addition, a tiny handheld video camera small enough to carry in a shirt pocket. It was the size and thickness of a credit card. He'd tested the quality of the pictures and sound and was pleased with the professional results. It was, he decided, well worth the outrageous sum he'd paid.

Amy and Cora sorted through the rest of the slips of paper that littered the tabletop.

They had agreed to work together to whittle down the number of places Coot may have hunted for the treasure, in order to chart a path for future searches.

It was Jesse's suggestion that they meet one or two evenings a week, schedules permitting, to keep Amy's mind off her father's illness. They gathered in the great room around a roaring fire and struggled to identify as many of Coot's notes as they could.

The pile had already dwindled, though there were still a dozen or more slips of paper that made no sense whatever. They decided to place all those slips in an envelope for future reference, while they concentrated their energy on the facts at hand.

"You can see where Coot was headed." Wyatt ran a finger along the map, showing a definite trail from the Beartooth Mountain Range, across the Gold Fever River that crisscrossed their land, snaking ever closer to the foothills of Treasure Chest. "If we're correct, Coot had already scoured this part of McCord land, and was narrowing his search to this."

"That's a mighty big 'if,'" Jesse said with a chuckle. "Even when he was alive, nobody could fathom old Coot's mind. How're we supposed to believe that we can figure him out now?"

"It does seem logical," Cora mused aloud. "I agree with Wyatt that there appears to be a direct line from there to here."

"I'll trust your artist's eye, Aunt Cora. But that still leaves a couple thousand acres of McCord land to search." Jesse looked up. "A pretty daunting task for the five of us."

"At least we're five times as many as Coot. There was only him searching." Cora's eyes grew dreamy, as they always did when she spoke of her brother. "And he never doubted that the fortune would be found one day."

"One day could be in the twenty-third century." Jesse winked at Amy. "When some multinational mega-conglomerate comes in here and decides to blast through all these mountains and rivers. Of course, they might find nothing but gold dust."

That had everyone laughing, lifting their moods considerably.

Amy got to her feet. "Time to head home and check on my dad."

Jesse stood. "I'll follow you."

"There's no need." She touched a hand to his arm. "You and your cousins put in a full day."

She bent to brush a kiss over Cora's cheek before heading to the door, with Jesse trailing behind.

Outside, she paused beside her truck. "It's nice to see you and Zane and Wyatt working together on this."

"Yeah." He gathered her close and softly kissed her lips. "But this is a hell of a lot nicer. This is what really charges my engine."

She laughed before climbing behind the wheel of her father's truck. "Will I see you tomorrow?"

He shrugged. "Hard to say. With weather coming in, we need to get the rest of the herds down from the hills." He reached inside the open window and caressed her cheek. "If I had my way, I'd leave the ranch chores to the others and just spend all my time with you."

"That might be hard to do right now." She sighed. "Dr. Wheeler called and said he thinks it's time for Dad to increase the treatments."

"How often will you need to go to town?"

"We're adding a day next week, to see how Dad tolerates that. If he does well enough, they may add yet another. That would mean driving to town four times a week instead of only two."

"That's bound to raise hell with your ranch chores."

She sighed. "I'll just have to manage."

Jesse stepped back. "Let me know what happens."

"I will. Night, Jesse." She put the truck in gear and headed into the darkness.

Jesse watched until she rounded a curve in the long driveway before heading inside and up to bed. He'd put in fourteen hard hours today, and his body was screaming for rest. He was asleep as soon as his head hit the pillow.

It took five rings of Jesse's cell phone to break through his sleep-shrouded mind. Eyes closed, he fumbled for it on the night table. In the dark he snapped it open, without bothering to see who was calling. "Yeah?"

"Jesse?"

Amy's voice sounded breathless. He sat up and switched on the light, studying the clock. Not even midnight. No wonder he was so addled. He'd been asleep less than an hour. "What's wrong?"

"My tire blew."

"Where are you?"

"A couple of miles from home. Just over Gold Strike Pass. I hated waking you. I know I could leave the truck here and walk home, but..."

He was already across the room, retrieving his clothes. "It's too cold to walk that many miles, especially in the middle of the night. Stay in your truck. I'll be there to pick you up in no time."

"Thanks, Jesse."

He rang off and fumbled into his clothes and boots. Minutes later, shrugging into a sheepskin jacket, he raced to the barn and climbed into his truck.

Amy stepped out of the truck to survey the tire. A blast of frigid air had her hunching into her parka. Though the calendar said October, this was a sample of what was to come. Folks had a saying around here: Winter came to visit early in Montana, and it always overstayed its welcome.

With her hands jammed into her pockets, she fingered her cell phone and thought about calling Jesse back. She'd hated waking him, knowing the hours he was putting in on ranch chores lately. Maybe she would tell him to go back to sleep. If she jogged at a steady pace, she'd be nearly home by the time he got here anyway. What was the point of both of them losing sleep?

She smiled in the darkness, thinking about the sound of his voice, husky with sleep. She could picture him in her mind, dressing too quickly and fumbling around for his keys.

When the clouds of sleep had cleared, he'd sounded genuinely concerned about her. It was comforting to know that she had someone to rely on. Someone she could call on, even at this hour, and trust that he would keep his word.

There was no way she would have called her father for help. The last thing she wanted was to add to his worries.

She decided not to call Jesse back. By now he was probably dashing to the barn to retrieve one of the ranch trucks. Besides, just thinking about him had her wanting him. Maybe, as long as he was awake anyway, they could make the most of the night. Why keep fighting what they both wanted?

She was chuckling when she heard the sound of an engine racing at high speed.

It was way too soon for Jesse to be here, even if he could fly.

"What...?" She turned.

There were no headlights piercing the gloom, but even as she watched, a truck came roaring at her in the darkness.

She leaped out of the way, falling over rocks that lined the road and tumbling down a slight embankment. Behind her, up on the road, she could hear the sound of metal scraping metal, and the distinct sound of shattering glass. From the impact, it would appear that a vehicle had smashed directly into hers.

For a moment all the breath was knocked out of her and she lay still, wondering what had just happened.

She got to her knees, breathing deeply, struggling to clear her mind.

Was this a random drunk who'd made a wrong turn and ended up on this desolate stretch of road? Was the driver hurt? Dead?

"Oh, my God. Hang on."

She made it to her feet and was just about to scramble back up the embankment when she heard the sound of a vehicle door opening. A tiny slice of light split the darkness before the door was slammed shut. In that instant she caught sight of a man's silhouette on the road above her. A man holding a rifle.

Her heart nearly stopped.

Most folks around here carried a rifle in their vehicles, and had several more in their houses and barns. It was as natural as having a tractor, or a spare can of gas close at hand.

But why was this guy carrying a gun while checking out a crash he had caused? Did he see her as a threat?

She remained very still, hearing the crunch of footsteps on gravel. A beam of light flashed and she could see someone peering through the windows of her shattered truck.

He hadn't yet spotted her. Maybe over the sound of his truck's engine, he hadn't heard her calling out. And just maybe, that was a good thing.

Her heart was racing like a runaway train. The fall had left her feeling dazed, but she was suddenly alert. And terrified.

If he was drunk...if he saw her as a threat...he might be tempted to shoot first and ask questions when it was too late.

She couldn't take a chance on showing herself. Not in the presence of this unknown.

Turning away, she set out across the barren hills toward home.

She'd gone no more than a few hundred yards when she heard the slam of a car door and an engine roar to life. From the sound of it, the vehicle was picking up speed, and still there were no headlights to tell her exactly where it was. She knew only that it was closing in on her.

She began running in a zigzag pattern, but the truck continued to draw near.

Was this some drunk's cruel game? Or was this threat somehow connected to the things that had been happening at her ranch?

How could the driver pick her out in the darkness? Yet, she could tell, by the way the sound was growing closer, that he was deliberately trailing her, and he would soon overtake her.

She ran until her breath was burning a path of fire down her throat, but like a laser, the vehicle continued to close in on her.

Not a game. A deadly reality. This was no accident. He was chasing her in the hope of running her down. And by the way he was weaving and gaining, he was very determined, and very familiar with the area.

Amy veered to her left and raced down a dry gully, with the vehicle roaring in the darkness behind. When she knew that it was too close to outrun, she waited until the last second, then twisted to her right, ducking behind a huge boulder.

She heard the screech of brakes and felt a wave of earth and stones rolling over her as the driver stood on the brakes to keep from crashing into the boulder. Before the vehicle had even come to a stop she was racing across a flat stretch of land and up an incline, desperate to escape this madness.

She was halfway to the top when a truck came roaring over the hill, heading directly toward her, its headlights blinding her.

She let out a cry and flung an arm over her eyes. Now she would be caught in the cross fire of two crazed drivers.

As she turned to flee, she heard the truck's door slam and Jesse's voice calling, "Amy. Wait."

Hurried footsteps had her heart hammering as a hand clutched her arm, spinning her around.

"Oh, God. Jesse. Thank heaven it's you." She couldn't say more over the terror that had her by the throat.

"What's this about?" He could feel the erratic tattoo of her heart. Could feel the tremors that rocked her, while she struggled to calm her ragged breathing.

"He tried to run me over."

"Who?"

"I don't know. I need a minute." She sucked in deep draughts of air, fighting for calm.

They both looked up at the roar of an engine as the other vehicle took off in the darkness.

When the sound of the engine faded away, Jesse led her to his truck and helped her inside.

By the interior light he could see how pale she was, and the absolute terror in her eyes.

Though Jesse's first instinct had been to follow the vehicle and try to overtake it, he had to think about Amy and what she needed. And so he gathered her into his arms and held her until the tremors faded. And though he wanted to swear and pound his fists in frustration, he merely listened in silence as she told him what had just happened.

His eyes narrowed with fury when she looked up at him.

"At first I thought it was just some drunk who'd made a wrong turn and was lost. When I saw his rifle I was afraid that, in a drunken haze, he might try to shift the blame onto me for the accident because he plowed into my disabled truck. But then he began chasing me across the hills..." She struggled for calm. "I don't care how drunk he is, he can't possibly think this is all my fault."

Jesse clenched his jaw. "There are some pretty mean

drunks in this world. I've been forced to fight my share of them."

Amy drew in a ragged breath. "You don't understand. It was scary enough when he crashed into Dad's truck. But when he started after me..." She gave a shudder. "This was deliberate, Jesse."

Jesse lifted her face, pressing soft kisses to her mouth, her cheeks, her tear-filled eyes. "The main thing is, you kept your wits about you and got away."

"I hate to think what would have happened if you hadn't gotten here in time."

"Shh." He kissed her mouth and could taste her fear. "Don't think about that now. You're safe. He's gone."

He enfolded her in his arms, staggered by the depth of emotion that swamped him.

He'd thought, when he'd found her truck damaged and had seen those deep gouges in the dirt, that she'd been injured in an accident and the other party was taking her for help. But then he'd heard that far-off engine and a sea of endless blackness, and he'd feared that someone had taken her against her will.

If he hadn't made it here in time...

He shoved aside the thought and concentrated on the only thing that mattered. Amy was safe.

By now the drunk was no doubt halfway across the wilderness, and would probably wake in the morning so hung over he wouldn't even be able to remember what had happened or how he'd damaged his vehicle.

If, in fact, this had been the actions of a drunk. Amy thought it was a deliberate act. He had no reason to doubt her.

Jesse gathered Amy close, needing to feel her safe

beside him. Safe. Maybe, if he'd been here sooner, she could have been spared all this. He'd lost her once before, and he couldn't bear the thought of losing her again. They'd been given a second chance at something rare and precious.

As he drove toward her ranch, he whispered a prayer of thanksgiving that he'd been in time to save her from a stranger's wrath.

CHAPTER FIFTEEN

———◆◆◆———

"Whoa." Zane looked up from his morning coffee as Jesse stepped into the kitchen. "You look like hell."

"And a cheery good morning to you, too." Jesse straddled a chair and scowled into the steaming cup Dandy placed before him.

Cal Randall, having learned years earlier to gauge the moods of the various family members, kept his thoughts to himself. Across the big kitchen table Cora wisely watched and listened without comment.

Zane dug into his pancakes. "I thought I heard a truck leave last night after Amy was gone. Did you go into Gold Fever to party?"

"This was no party." Jesse shot a look at his aunt. "Amy had a blowout on the way home last night. She called for help, but before I could reach her somebody plowed into her truck, then chased her clear across hell's half acre."

His statement had everyone's attention. Around the table, they all sat up straighter, staring at him with worried eyes.

Cora touched a hand to her nephew's arm. "How is Amy?"

"Scared, but otherwise fine."

"She has a right to be scared." Wyatt's eyes narrowed. "If some idiot chased me in the dark, I'd be pretty freaked. I can't believe you left her alone with only a sick father for company."

"She ordered me to leave. So I spent the night in my truck at the end of her driveway. With all that's been going on at the Parrish ranch, I'd say this can't be considered the random work of some drunk. Although we can't rule it out until we see what the sheriff thinks." Jesse sipped his coffee, hoping to chase away the cobwebs of sleep that lingered.

Zane pushed aside his coffee. "We need to figure out who has a grudge against Otis Parrish."

Jesse frowned. "As Ernie Wycliff said, our family would be at the top of that list."

Zane and Wyatt exchanged a look before Zane said, "I'm betting the list is a long one. Over the years, Amy's father hasn't exactly endeared himself to a lot of people in Gold Fever."

Jesse nodded. "Look, I know Otis Parrish is a tough old bird. But nobody with half a brain would blame Amy for the sins of her father."

Wyatt thanked Dandy for the plate of bacon and eggs before glancing at Jesse. "At least nobody you know of."

Jesse drained his cup and got to his feet.

"Where are you going?" Cora called to his retreating back.

"To town. My first stop will be to see if Vi and Daffy saw any drunken cowboy stumble out of their place last night with murder in his eyes."

As he started toward the door Zane shoved aside his half-eaten breakfast. "I'm coming with you."

Jesse turned. "Why?"

Zane shrugged. "Sometimes a second pair of eyes and ears can come in handy."

Wyatt smashed his bacon and eggs between two pieces of toast, making a messy, oozing sandwich he could carry with him, before shoving away from the table. "Make that three pairs of eyes and ears."

As they left, Cora exchanged a look with Cal and Dandy. "Poor Amy. No wonder Jesse is so furious. But I'm worried about that anger of his. If he doesn't control it, he could find himself in trouble."

Cal gave her a gentle smile. "He has a right to be angry. And worried. Whatever's going on, the threat to Amy and her father is real."

Cora nodded.

Cal added, "But I wouldn't worry about Jesse, if I were you. He'll be just fine. And look at the bright side of this incident. Just weeks ago he was ready to take on both his cousins and wipe the floor with their hides. Now he and Zane and Wyatt are chasing a common enemy. I'd say those three working together make a pretty formidable team."

Cora sat back, her breakfast forgotten as Cal's words sank in.

She nodded. "They were awfully quick to come to Amy's defense, weren't they?"

"Just like their grandfather," Dandy added. "The McCord hasn't been born who could resist a challenge."

By the time Cora returned to her studio, she'd put aside her fears and was humming a little tune, buoyed by the fact that her nephews seemed to be growing closer with each passing day.

"I know it isn't much, Coot." She paused, her hand holding the artist's brush in midair. "But every day that our boys work together brings them closer to the way things used to be." She sighed. "Oh, how I hope they can find their way back to that happy, joyous place of their childhood."

"Well now." Daffy, wearing a T-shirt that read HELP WANTED: ONLY SEXY COWBOYS NEED APPLY, and a pair of jeans two sizes too small for her skinny hips, looked up when Jesse, Zane, and Wyatt stepped into the Fortune Saloon. "You boys get tired of Dandy's fancy food up at your ranch?"

While Zane and Wyatt chuckled, Jesse got right to the point.

"Somebody tried to run Amy over last night, after hitting her parked truck on the side of the road."

Hearing him, Violet left the grill, wiping her hands on a big apron as she approached. "Oh, honey, that's just awful. Was Amy hurt?"

"Just scared. The driver roared away when he spotted my truck heading toward him."

Vi sucked in a breath. "Thank goodness you were there to scare him off."

Daffy frowned with concern. "And you're wondering

if we had any cowboys here last night that could've been drunk enough, or mean enough, to do this?"

"Yeah."

She gave a quick shake of her head. "No strangers. We had the usual. Ledge Cowling was in, along with Harding Jessup and Orley Peterson. The doc was here, and Mayor Stafford. A couple of others. But nobody got drunk or disorderly. Nobody sulking or brooding. Though your names did come up a time or two."

At Jesse's arched brow she added, "Just the usual speculation on whether or not the three of you really intend to take up where Coot left off." She gave them each a probing look.

Wyatt chuckled and lifted his hands in a sign of surrender. "Guilty."

Vi gave a little gasp of surprise. "It's true, then?"

Daffy turned to Zane. "You, too, Hollywood?"

He shook his head at the nickname that Jesse had flung in anger. It would take time and hard work before this town would forget his years in California. "Guilty as charged."

"It runs in the family." Daffy gave a shake of her head, sending purple spikes fluttering. "You're all crazy as loons."

She turned to Jesse. "I may as well tell you that there were bets being made on you and Amy, too."

"Bets?"

"On whether the two of you will hook up or crash and burn like last time. Odds are in favor of crashing and burning, by the way."

At the look on Jesse's face, Wyatt slapped him on the back. "Now this is the town of Gold Fever that I remember as a kid. No secrets here. Everybody not only knows your business, but knows it better than you do."

Jesse unclenched his jaw long enough to say, "Thanks for that wealth of information, Daffy. If you think of or hear about anybody who has a grudge against Amy or her father, I'd like you to call me."

"You know I will, honey." Daffy touched Jesse's cheek. "For all our teasing, you know that Vi and I love that girl like our own. Ever since her mama passed, we've worried and fretted over how she'd survive her daddy's temper. Oh," she added with a grin. "We love you, too. Almost as much as we love Amy."

He closed a hand over hers. "Thanks, Daffy." He kissed her sister's cheek. "Vi."

As the three cousins strolled out of the saloon, Violet and Daffy stood watching, wearing matching looks of appreciation at their tight, sculpted backsides in those faded denims.

Jesse climbed into the truck and waited while Zane and Wyatt crowded into the passenger side.

"What now?" Wyatt asked.

Jesse shrugged and put the truck in gear. "I'll stop at the sheriff's office. See if he has anything to go on. When I drove Amy home last night I asked her to phone Sheriff Wycliff first thing this morning and file a report. Maybe he can think of something that I've overlooked."

An hour later, after an uneventful meeting with the sheriff, they realized they had no more information than when they'd left the ranch.

Wyatt broke through the somber mood that had settled over them. "At least you've notified the law. As Sheriff Wycliff said, by now the predator driver of that truck is awake and aware that he messed with the wrong woman. If he has any sense, he'll be long gone by this time tomorrow. And if he was just an angry drunk, it'll be an even longer time before he gets behind the wheel of a truck after he's been drinking."

"I'm still not sure that Amy was the real target."

At Zane's remark, Jesse looked over. "Otis?"

"It has to be." Zane nodded. "He's probably insulted more people in Gold Fever than any other citizen. I'm betting there's a laundry list of people who wouldn't mind seeing him and his ranch fail."

Wyatt nodded. "I'm with Zane on this. If someone's holding a grudge against Otis, there's no better way to hurt him than by hurting the person he most loves."

His words, spoken casually enough, had Jesse reeling as a new thought struck.

Wyatt studied Jesse's ashen features. "You look like you've just been struck by lightning. What're you thinking?"

"It's something you just said. What better way to hurt someone than to threaten the person they love? What if the object of all these threats isn't Otis, or Amy, but somebody else who cares about her—like me?"

"Okay." Wyatt gave this some thought. "So, who in town would want to hurt you?"

Jesse shrugged. "The only people I can think of that I've had any real trouble with are those bikers."

Wyatt shook his head. "Strangers."

"Strangers to us. But they could have learned my name from anyone in town."

"Do you think they're angry enough to want to get to you through Amy?"

"I don't know yet. But I intend to find out everything I can about them. Who they are, where they live and work, and what they were doing in town the night of the fight."

Jesse plucked his cell phone from his pocket and dialed the sheriff's office. After filling the lawman in on his thoughts, he listened before saying, "Thanks, Ernie."

He turned to his cousins. "The sheriff will see what he can find out about those bikers." He braked, turned the wheel sharply, and headed the truck in the direction they'd just traveled. "We need to go back to the saloon and see if Daffy or Vi can remember anything about them." He hissed out an impatient breath. "I wish now I'd filed a complaint against them the night of the fight. At least Ernie would have their names, addresses, maybe even where they work."

Wyatt was shaking his head. "I don't know, Jess. This just doesn't look like the sort of thing a couple of angry strangers would do. Why would they go to all the trouble of finding out about Amy and then set up these accidents? If they wanted to even the score, they could just follow you from the Fortune Saloon some night and leave you dead along the highway."

Zane shrugged. "Maybe they're afraid of facing him in another fight."

"As I recall," Wyatt said with a grin, "they'd have wiped the floor with him if you and I hadn't stepped in to help."

"I was doing fine."

At Jesse's offended tone, Wyatt and Zane grinned.

"Okay, Superman." Zane slapped Jesse on the back. "Next time we'll just stand back and let you rid the world of all the evil villains."

That had Jesse joining in the laughter. "Okay. I'll admit I was glad to have you guys lending a hand."

"You mean a fist," Zane said, still laughing.

"Not to mention a jaw." Wyatt touched a hand to his jaw and pretended to wince.

That only made them laugh all the harder.

It was, Jesse realized, good to be able to laugh, considering all that was going on in his life.

And for that he had Coot to thank. Though he wasn't quite ready to believe that his cousins could ever become his best friends again, there was no denying that it was nice to have someone to share his concern over all the strange things happening.

Jesse adjusted his sunglasses. "Since we're going to be quizzing Daffy and Vi about what they know about those bikers, we may as well have lunch there."

Zane nodded in agreement. "Especially since I passed up Dandy's breakfast. Wyatt was smart enough to bring part of his along for the ride, but right now my stomach's so empty, it wouldn't matter if Vi was serving raw steer, I'd order a plate of it."

"Now this is much better'n raw steer." Zane took a big bite of his burger.

"You mean it isn't raw?" Jesse studied the red meat oozing blood.

Zane took another bite. "I like it rare."

"Rare is one thing. That looks like Vi never even bothered to kill it before serving it."

Zane ignored him and polished off his lunch in a couple of satisfying bites.

When the three were finished, Vi and Daffy approached the table.

"You wanted to talk to us about those nasty bikers?" Daffy glanced around to make certain that no one at the nearby tables was in need of a coffee refill.

"Just to see if there's anything you can recall. Something they might have said that would give a hint as to where they work or where they were headed that night."

Daffy gave a shake of her head. "Honey, the only thing I know for certain about them is that if they ever show their faces in our place again, I'm calling Sheriff Wycliff right away."

Jesse patted her hand. "That's what I'd recommend, Daffy. And after you phone him, phone me. I'd relish a chance to ask them a few questions."

When he got to his feet Vi said, "Folks in town have already heard what happened to Amy."

Her sister nodded. "I heard Delia Cowling telling some folks that now that Amy has aligned herself with the McCords to hunt old Coot's lost fortune, she'll have to expect to deal with the curse. Most folks around here figure she brought this on herself."

"Brought this…" Jesse stared around at the familiar faces. "Where is Delia? I'll give that old gossip a piece of my mind."

"Now, honey." Violet laid a hand over his. "If you confront her, you'll just add to her self-importance."

He was beyond hearing. When he spotted the self-proclaimed town historian sitting with Rowe Stafford, Harding Jessup, and Orley Peterson, he stormed over to their table. The four looked up.

"Well." Delia sipped her tea before saying, "We were just talking about you."

"I'll bet you were." His tone was low with anger. "Let's get something clear. I don't believe in the curse. What happened to Amy Parrish is neither supernatural nor accidental."

"You don't say?" Delia set down her cup with a clatter.

"You heard me. This was no accident. It was a deliberate attempt to hurt her. And I mean to find out who's behind it and why."

The mayor pushed aside the last of his lunch. "If I were you, I'd be very careful about saying such things without proof."

"Oh, I'll have proof."

"Don't you think that ought to be Ernie Wycliff's job?"

"I do. And I've already told the sheriff how I feel. But I intend to do what I can to lend a hand."

"As mayor, I must advise you to step aside and let the law handle this, Jesse."

"As a...friend of Amy's, I'm afraid I can't do that, Rowe."

Delia hadn't missed that slight hesitation. Her blackbird eyes looked sharper than ever, while her tone was sugar-sweet. "My, my. Does Otis Parrish know about your...friendship with his daughter?"

"I'm sure he'll hear about it before I'm halfway home." Jesse turned and headed toward the door, where Wyatt and Zane stood waiting and watching.

He could feel every pair of eyes in the room following his movements. His jaw was clenched so hard his teeth ached.

Before he was halfway to the truck, the saloon was buzzing about the latest proof that quick-tempered cowboy Jesse McCord was building up a head of steam and headed toward a satisfying no-holds-barred fight with someone, anyone, in order to clear the air.

CHAPTER SIXTEEN

Jesse?" Sheriff Wycliff's voice was punctuated with static over the cell phone. "The state police sent an investigative team to the Parrish ranch to check out that beam. While they were at it I asked them to check that section of fencing that was down. They won't have any conclusive evidence for a couple of weeks, but one of the inspectors told me privately that it certainly looked deliberate rather than accidental."

"Thanks, Ernie. I appreciate the call. I know you'll relay their findings as soon as you can."

"You bet. In the meantime, I sure wish I could spare someone to keep an eye on Amy and her father, since I don't have anything at all in my files on those bikers. But with only Harrison helping me days, and his daughter, Charity, manning the phone at night, there's just nobody left."

"I understand. My crew and I will keep a close eye on things."

"I know you will. You call if you see anything out of place."

When the sheriff hung up, Jesse stood a moment, staring at the foothills of Treasure Chest in the distance. Then he made his way to his truck.

"Jesse." Amy stepped out onto the porch, carefully closing the door behind her. "We just got home from the clinic." She glanced over her shoulder. "Dad's asleep. He's having an awful reaction to the latest treatment."

"I'm sorry." He motioned toward the path leading to the barn. "Let's walk and talk."

As she moved along beside him, Amy kept her gaze averted. "Sheriff Wycliff talked to us about the accidents. Dad said he doesn't know anybody who would want to hurt us or scare us."

"I talked to Ernie, too." Jesse stuck his hands in his back pockets to keep from reaching out to her. The need to hold her, to protect her, was almost overpowering. "He feels that the threats are real, and that you have to take steps to stay safe."

"I promised him that I'd be careful, and call him the minute I see anything out of the ordinary."

"I don't think that's enough."

At Jesse's words, she stopped. "What do you suggest?"

"That you and your father come and stay at our place." Seeing her mouth open to protest, he added quickly, "I know. It would be awkward for your father, but I think if you persuade him that it's what you want, he'll go along."

She gave a vehement shake of her head. "You know

how stubborn he is. My wanting something wouldn't change his mind. Besides, knowing his pride, I'd never put my father in a position of having to accept help from your family."

"To hell with your father's pride." Without thinking he caught her arm and felt the current of electricity that shot between them. He fought to keep the anger from his tone. "Listen to me, Amy. This wasn't meant to just hurt or scare. You could have been killed by that beam. Then there's that nighttime incident. We both believe it was deliberate. It could have been deadly."

She shook off his hand, though it cost her. "I won't deny that I'm afraid. And I don't want to fight with you, Jess. I know you care about us. But this just isn't going to happen. I'm not asking my father to leave his home. He's fighting for his life. And we're finally starting to bridge a chasm that's been between us for years. Now you're asking me to push him into accepting help from your family. It's all too much. I can't do it."

His eyes narrowed. "Can't? Or won't?"

She saw the hard, tight line of his mouth and wished with all her heart that she could find a way to reconcile the differences between them.

"I won't ask it of him, Jesse." Seeing his quick flash of temper she struggled to soften the blow. "But I do thank you for your offer."

He looked as though she'd just slapped him. The sorrow in his eyes had her fighting to keep her voice from breaking. "Now I'd better see to my chores before my dad wakes up."

Jesse watched her shove open the barn door. He wanted, more than anything, to drag her into his arms and tell her everything would be all right. But how could he say the words to her when he didn't really believe them?

Someone wanted to hurt her. He was certain of it. And though he wanted to toss her over his shoulder and drag her kicking and screaming to a place of safety, he was helpless to do more than watch her walk away.

Damn her father's stubborn pride. And damn the daughter who was just as tough. They were two of a kind.

He strode back to his truck, more determined than ever to find out what this was all about.

The woman he loved was in trouble, and he was feeling helpless to do anything to help her.

The woman he loved.

He stopped dead in his tracks and absorbed the shock to his system.

Yes, by God. It was time to stop denying the truth. The woman he loved. Hadn't he loved her for years while grieving the loss of her?

Well, she was back now. And in harm's way.

He didn't need the state police or Sheriff Wycliff to hold things together.

He'd do it himself.

He drove away in a cloud of dust, mulling a plan of action.

Amy poured herself a mug of spiced tea and carried it to the front porch. With the afghan around her, she sat and sipped and tried to let the cares of the day slip away. It wasn't easy. She and her father, though not close, had declared a sort of truce. He still refused to discuss his illness, but he had become resigned to allowing his daughter to see his weakness. He permitted her to help him to bed, to feed him when he was too weak to feed himself, to lay out his clothes. Beyond that, their only common bond was the ranch. And the memory of the woman they'd both loved.

"Oh, Mom." She closed her eyes.

Though her father had danced around these frightening, annoying incidents, declaring them more a puzzle than a danger, he was willing to discuss any problems she had with the operation of the ranch. So they discussed milk production, and the cost of feed from Orley Peterson, which offset what they had harvested. They talked about replacing the weatherstripping on the doors and windows, and how much they would pay Stan Novak each month for the repair of the damage from the fallen beam. It would take them six months to completely pay off that debt. •

More than that, her father had spoken about her mother. She'd waited so long to hear him express any feelings of love for the woman who held such a special place in her heart. He hadn't said much.

"I miss Sarah." He'd said it with a sigh, and then, realizing what he'd admitted, he'd added, "You know, girl, I never really appreciated her until she was gone."

Hearing it, Amy had fought back tears.

Why had it taken him so long to say those words?

She was relieved that her father had finally fallen asleep. He'd had a really tough afternoon after his latest treatment.

She drained her cup and tipped her head back with a sigh. A sliver of moon gleamed in the night sky. A canopy of stars looked close enough to touch. She wished she could just drift among them, high above this world of worry and work.

A silly, foolish wish.

She hurried inside and deposited her cup in the sink, then pulled on a warm parka before hurrying out to check the barn before turning in for the night.

Ordinarily she wouldn't bother. The cows and horses weren't going anywhere. Nor the barn cats. But she'd promised Jesse that she would take extra precautions.

Jesse.

She hated that she'd sent him away hurt and angry. But what he was asking of her was impossible. She'd meant what she'd said to him. She had no intention of asking her father to put aside his pride and take help from the McCords. This illness was enough of a blow to his dignity.

Still, it rankled that she and Jesse had parted in anger.

It wasn't the first time. But right now, when they'd been working so hard at repairing the rift, it was even harder to bear.

She absorbed a quick blow to her heart at all the turmoil whirling inside her mind as she slid open the barn door and stepped inside. In a purely reflexive manner she glanced toward the high, steepled roof, where a new beam had been installed by Stan Novak's crew. Just then, out of the corner of her eye, she saw movement in one of the empty stalls. Her head swiveled in time to see the tall figure of a man getting to his feet.

"No!" She let out a yelp and reached for a pitchfork. Before she could wield it like a weapon Jesse closed the distance between them and caught her wrist.

"Jesse." His name came out in a whoosh of air. "Oh, God, Jesse."

"Sorry." Seeing her distress, he tossed aside the pitchfork and gathered her close, running his hands over her hair in an effort to soothe. "I didn't mean to frighten you."

"Frighten me?" She pushed free of his arms to look into his eyes. "You scared me half to death. My poor heart nearly stopped. What are you doing here?"

He was wearing that cocky grin that always did such strange things to her heart. A grin, and not much more. He'd shucked his shirt and boots, and was barefoot and naked to the waist. His faded denims rode low on his hips. A lifetime of ranch chores had left him more toned than any physical fitness expert. Just looking at him made her mouth water.

"Since you wouldn't move over to my ranch, I thought I'd just settle in here and keep an eye on things."

"Settle in...?" She huffed out a breath. "You were planning on sleeping in the barn?"

"It wouldn't be the first time." His smile grew. "I seem to remember you sleeping here with me a time or two."

Her heart gave another quick jolt. If the sight of all that muscled flesh wasn't enough, the reminder of what they'd shared had her breath backing up in her throat.

"You're..." She was at a loss for words. "You're crazy. You can't just give up your bed and move into the barn permanently."

"I never said it would be forever. Just until we find out who's trying to get our attention, and why."

"That could take weeks. Months. In the meantime, do you expect to just commute back and forth between your ranch and mine?"

He kept his eyes steady on hers. "If that's what it takes to keep you safe."

"Oh, Jesse." She felt a lump growing in her throat, and she knew if she wasn't careful she might find herself weeping at any moment. "You can't do this."

"Who's going to stop me?"

She took a step back and stiffened her spine. "I am. I'm ordering you to leave."

"Just like that?"

"Just like that."

There was a moment of silence, and Amy watched a flicker of emotion cross his face. In the gleam of moonlight, she caught the half-smile that curved his lips. She recognized that look. Not just humor, but determination. He was digging in his heels. How could she have forgotten that Jesse liked nothing better than a challenge? And she'd just tossed down the gauntlet.

"All right, Amy." He crossed his arms over his chest. "Make me leave."

She gaped at him.

"Throw me off your property."

"You know I can't physically remove you."

"Then I guess you'd better come up with a better way to persuade me. Maybe you'd like to kiss me until I'm too weak to remember why I'm here."

Oh, it was so tempting. "Are you laughing at me?"

He relaxed his features until there was no hint of a smile. "What if I am?"

"I'm not fooled by that pose, McCord." Her voice rose fractionally. "You think you're so smart."

He held out his hands, palms up. "I'm just trying to be agreeable."

"Like hell." She slapped his hand and assumed her best teacher voice. "You're playing a cat-and-mouse game. And I refuse to be the mouse."

"Okay. I'll be the mouse. You can be the cat." He leaned a hip against the wooden rail of the stall. "Go ahead, Ms. Parrish. Make your first move. Pounce."

When she stood perfectly still, his hand suddenly snaked out, snagging her wrist.

"Time's up. Now it's my turn. And believe me, I know how to pounce." With a growl in his throat he dragged her close.

"Jesse, don't you dare..."

His mouth covered hers, swallowing her protest.

Splinters of fire and ice collided along her spine, leaving her trembling. She'd never forgotten the feel of that hard, sculpted body pressed to hers. It was the most exquisite torture.

His lips moved over hers, seducing, sending her pulse racing. When his mouth left hers to explore her neck, her throat, she closed her eyes and gave herself up to the pure pleasure of the moment.

"Why are you wearing all these clothes?" He slid the parka from her shoulders before drawing her close and raining kisses across her cheek to her ear, where he plunged his tongue inside, driving her half mad with need.

"Jesse."

It was all she could manage before he gathered her firmly into his arms and kissed her long and slow and deep, while his hands, those clever, work-worn hands, began a lazy exploration of her body. When his thumbs found her nipples, they stroked until, her breathing ragged, she pushed away, dragging air into her starving lungs.

"Oh. That's right." His lips curved. "I'm supposed to leave. That is, if that's what you really want."

"You devil." She couldn't think. What she wanted and what she knew she ought to do were in direct conflict. She needed to send him away. It was the sensible thing. But now that he'd touched her, and kissed her, and had her fully aroused, there was nothing else she wanted but him. Just him. The thought of giving in to her desire had her mind clouding, her heart beating overtime.

"You were saying?" His grin was back, causing her poor heart to stutter.

"What I want…" Need won out over sense. She'd never had a lick of sense where Jesse McCord was concerned. "Is the same thing you want, and you know it."

Feeling bold, she lifted a hand to the buttons of her old denim work shirt.

Jesse's eyes followed every movement.

She slipped the shirt from her shoulders, revealing a nude, lace-edged bra that barely covered her breasts. "So, if you've had a change of heart, McCord, speak now, or suffer the consequences. But I warn you, if you try to leave here, I'll have to kill you."

This was one of the things he'd always loved about her. The way she lifted her chin, defying any challenge. There had always been a fearlessness in Amy Parrish that spoke to a brashness in his own soul.

He managed a husky laugh, though it nearly choked him. The sight of all the cool, pale flesh had the blood draining from his head and rushing to another part of his anatomy.

"I'd be a fool to risk death. Do with me what you will, Ms. Parrish."

With a laugh she wrapped her arms around his waist and ran hot, wet kisses down his chest to the flat planes of his stomach.

She felt his muscles quiver before he clamped his hands at her hips, lifting her off her feet.

With their eyes level, he covered her lips with his and whispered inside her mouth, "Woman, you know exactly how to drive me mad."

Very slowly he lowered her to her feet, allowing her body to brush his before fisting a hand in her hair. His mouth was almost bruising as he nearly devoured her with a kiss so intense she could do nothing more than hold on as he took her on a wild roller-coaster ride.

Oh, this was what she'd wanted. This was what she'd craved with a gnawing hunger and raw desire. A touch, a kiss that melted away all the years and the fears until they were nothing more than a blur of vague memories.

He kissed her until they were both gasping for air.

As she started to pull back he kissed her again. Inside her mouth he growled, "Before we're through, I'll make you forget everyone and everything except me. And this. Just this."

"How could I ever forget? I had the best teach..." Her words were cut off with a kiss that spun on and on until, driven by half-crazed need, he turned and drove her back against the rough door of the barn, his body straining in desperation against hers.

He lifted his head and fixed her with a look so hot, so fierce, she couldn't look away.

"No more teasing, Amy. No more jokes. Tell me you want this as much as I do."

She didn't hesitate this time. "I want this, Jess. I want you..."

His mouth closed over hers, stealing her words, her breath. Stealing her very heart.

CHAPTER SEVENTEEN

J esse." It was the only word Amy could manage as his mouth continued taking her higher with each kiss.

His body was pressed to hers, pinning her firmly against the door.

"Shh." He nibbled her lower lip while his hands, those clever, work-roughened hands, moved over her.

Despite the frigid air in the barn, her flesh was so hot she wondered that she didn't set off sparks and start a major fire.

This was what she'd wanted. What she'd hungered for. His hands on her. His mouth on hers. This knife-edge of excitement that had her breath burning her lungs, her pulse throbbing in her temples.

Jesse unhooked her bra and watched the lace drift to the floor. His lips curved into a wicked grin. "You've moved up in the world. What happened to those plain white cotton underthings?"

"In case you haven't noticed, I've grown up."

"Oh, yeah. I've noticed. It's not something I could ignore." His hands dipped to the snap at her waist, and her faded jeans joined the rest of her clothes.

His smile grew. "Why, Miss Parrish, is that a thong?"

"A gift to myself when I started teaching school."

He roared with laughter as he stripped it aside. "I'll never be able to look at you dressed like a schoolmarm again without seeing this in my mind."

His laughter faded as he lowered his head and covered her mouth with his, while his hands moved over her, slowly driving her mad.

She needed to get her hands on him. Her fingers played with the hair on his chest and she thrilled at the ripple of muscle beneath her touch as her hands moved lower, across his stomach. When she reached for the metal button at his waist, he helped her, until his clothes joined hers at their feet.

At last they were free, with no more barriers. Free to feel, to taste, to savor. And they did. With murmured words and soft sighs they lost themselves in the pure pleasure of the moment.

As his mouth moved over hers, he sensed that this kiss was different from all the others. Always before she'd held back, as though unwilling to admit to the depth of her feelings. Now she poured herself into it. Heart. Mind. Soul.

That freed him to do the same. To show her, with each touch, each press of his mouth to hers, just how much she meant to him.

His hands at her shoulders were almost bruising as he gathered her close, desperate to feel her, flesh to flesh, all the while savoring her lips. He couldn't get enough of the wild, sweet taste of her. The press of her body to his had the blood roaring in his temples. The need to take her hard and fast nearly staggered him. In order to slow down he changed the angle of the kiss and felt the quick jolt of nerves race through his system.

"Do you know how long I've dreamed of this?" He drew back, his eyes steady on hers.

She saw the hint of danger in those eyes and felt a sudden flare of heat deep inside. She'd always loved this dark, dangerous side of Jesse. "How long?"

"Every day since you left." He ran hot, wet kisses down her throat, sending delicious sensations skittering along her spine. "And when I saw you again, the dreams were back, stronger than ever."

She drew his head up, needing to feel his mouth on hers. "Kiss me, Jesse."

He did as she asked, with a hunger that had their hearts thundering.

"I need you to touch me, Jesse. Take me." She hated that her voice was trembling, but there was no way to hide the need.

"Oh, I intend to. But I won't be rushed. I've waited too long. Wanted this too much."

He dipped his head and closed his lips around one erect nipple, nibbling and suckling until she felt her legs buckle.

"Jess." She clung to his waist and would have fallen if she weren't pinned between his body and the rough wood of the barn.

"Afraid?"

"No." She tried to laugh, but it sounded more like a sob.

"You ought to be." His eyes held hers. "You can't even begin to imagine all the things I've dreamed of doing with you. To you."

Her chin came up in the defiant way he'd always loved. "Show me."

His strong, clever hands began moving over her, driving her and himself slowly mad.

She wrapped her arms around his waist. He could hear her labored breathing, the pounding of her heart like a runaway herd of cattle.

With teeth and tongue and fingertips he moved over her at will, kissing her face, her throat, teasing her nipples until she moaned and writhed, desperate for release from the madness that had overtaken her.

She let her head fall back, giving him easier access.

Except for their sighs, and the sound of their labored breathing, the night had grown still. The air around them seemed charged with the same electricity that flowed between them.

He pressed soft, feathery kisses down her neck, pausing at the sensitive hollow between her neck and shoulder. When she shivered and sighed, moving catlike in his arms, he moved lower, to circle her breast with his tongue.

Her purr of pleasure had his pulse rate climbing.

Just as she began to relax in his arms he found her hot and wet. Without warning he took her up and over the first peak. At her stunned expression, he gave her no time to catch her breath as he took her higher, then higher still.

She was wonderful to watch. He saw her eyes widen in surprise, then seem to glaze over as the waves of sensation rolled over her, carrying her along in their tide.

"Jesse." Her eyes snapped open and she clutched at him as he brought her to the edge yet again.

Her arousal deepened his own, and he knew that he couldn't hold out much longer.

Heat rose up between them, pearling their flesh, clogging their throats.

His hands cupped her hips, dragging her firmly against him. He lifted her and she wrapped her legs around him as he drove himself into her. That unleashed a firestorm of passion that took them over completely. Their breathing shallow, their heartbeats thundering, their bodies slick, they began to move, to climb, as though scaling a high, sheer cliff.

The world beyond this barn no longer mattered. A night owl called to its mate. A horse nickered in a nearby stall. They were beyond hearing. The perfume of fresh-cut hay, the earthy scents of cattle and dung drifted on the air, but they took no notice.

There was only this man, this woman, and this incredible need that had them climbing toward a distant star. With shuddering breaths and urgent whispers they moved to a rhythm as old as time.

"Amy. Look at me. I need to see you."

At the sound of her name she struggled to focus on his face. All she could see were his eyes, hot and fierce, fixed on her. All she could hear was his heartbeat, thundering wildly, matching hers.

"Jesse. Dear God, Jesse."

With unbelievable strength they moved together, climbing ever higher until, in one last burst of strength, they reached the pinnacle.

Soaring through space, they shattered into millions of glittering pieces as they drifted back to earth.

"You okay?" Jesse pressed his forehead to hers, waiting for his world to settle.

"Fine." It was all she could manage over a throat clogged with tears. To hold them at bay, she lifted a hand to his cheek.

Jesse had always been able to take her to places nobody else could even imagine. She'd wondered if, after their years apart, it would be the same. Now she had her answer.

He felt so good here in her arms. She thought she could stay this way all night, just so, flesh to flesh, heartbeat to heartbeat.

Pure heaven.

He moved his head a fraction so he could see her face. "Sorry. I didn't mean to go so fast."

"Fast?" She managed a throaty laugh. "If you'd made me wait any longer, I'd have died."

"I feel like I already did." He brushed his mouth over hers. "I've died and gone to heaven. And I don't ever want to go back to earth."

She wrapped her arms around his neck and kissed him long and slow and deep.

When at last she lifted her head she muttered, "Jesse?"

"Hmm?"

"Would you mind moving a little? This barn wood is awfully rough on my bare backside."

"Oh." He chuckled. "Sorry about that." Still holding

her in his arms he turned and carried her to the stall, lowering her to his bedroll in a mound of hay.

"Umm." When he'd settled himself beside her she sighed. "Much better."

"Let me make it up to you." He drew her close in his embrace and began rubbing her back.

"Oh, that's so nice."

"I'm sure I can do better." With his hands still massaging her back, he began running nibbling kisses across her face. Against her temple he whispered, "Baby, you still rock my world."

"I'm glad." She found herself smiling dreamily. She turned to him, wrapping her arms around him. She buried her face against his chest and breathed him in. There was something so wonderfully, potently male about him. Everything about him was achingly familiar.

"Why?" His fingers combed through her hair.

"Why what?" She was still floating, still drifting among the stars, barely able to focus.

"Why are you glad?"

"Oh." Her smile grew. "Because you rock my world, too."

"I do?"

"Um-hmm."

When he lowered his mouth to her throat, she sucked in a quick breath. "That tickles."

"Good. Part of my plan to see if I can get you to let me have my way with you again."

"Oh, right. This soon?" She looked up. Though he was grinning, she could see the glint of fire in those eyes. "Who do you think you are? Superman?"

He threw back his head and laughed. "Since I've been accused of that twice lately, I think it only fair that I try to prove I can live up to that name."

"Careful. I might believe you're serious."

"Believe it. I'm about to show you all the amazing, superhuman things I can do, as long as you're not in any hurry to send me home."

"You still want to stay?"

"I do." He had that look in his eye. Not as hungry as before, but more wolfish. Hunger laced with knowledge. "I feel I ought to redeem myself."

"Redeem?" Her fingers played with the hair on his chest, and he felt his stomach muscles tighten at her mere touch.

"I was...eager. Too hungry. Starved, in fact. I moved too fast. Now that we got that out of the way, I'd like to show you that I can take my time."

"Really?" She couldn't help laughing at his serious tone. "You need to prove that you have staying power?"

"Something like that. Especially since I plan on being here all night." He rubbed his mouth over hers before bringing his lips to the sensitive column of her throat, and was rewarded with her sudden intake of breath. "I thought I'd show you..."

He began nibbling his way down her body, between her breasts, down her stomach, and felt the way her heart took a sudden quick bounce before beginning to race as his lips moved lower still. "...All the things I've been wanting to do with you since you returned to Gold Fever."

"Jess..." The protest died on her lips as he followed his words with bold action.

"Oh, Jess." That was all she could manage before being taken on a slow, glorious ride to paradise.

At the sound of a rooster crowing up in the hayloft, Amy stirred. The first thing she saw when she opened her eyes was Jesse, leaning on one elbow, staring down at her.

"Morning." She yawned, stretched, then went very still as he bent to press a kiss to her lips.

"That's just about the nicest sound in the world."

"What is?"

"Your voice. All warm and sleepy." He brushed a strand of hair off her forehead. "And seeing you like this is just about the prettiest sight in the world."

"Careful. You keep up those compliments and I won't be able to get my head through the doorway."

"Then I'll just break down some timbers to make way for my favorite girl."

That had her shaking her head. "Who are you, lavishing praise like this, and what have you done with that brash cowboy I once knew?"

"Jesse McCord is a changed man. In the space of one night some gorgeous female kissed away all his rough edges and turned him into a sweet-talking gentleman."

"Think it will last?"

"I'm betting on it."

"We'll just have to see." She sat up and spied her clothes lying in a heap near the barn door.

He snagged her wrist before she could stand. "Where're you going?"

"Time to get up and dressed and ready for the morning."

He allowed his gaze to move slowly over her. "I like you better like this."

"I just bet you do, cowboy. That's why I'd better get dressed before you get any ideas."

"Give me five more minutes."

Amy laughed. "That's what you said last night. A number of times, in fact. But you know what happened each time I gave you five more minutes."

"Yeah. And it's about to happen again." He drew her into his arms and kissed her until she could feel her bones begin to soften, and her resolve begin to slip.

"Jesse."

"You know you want to."

"Mind reader." With a sigh she wrapped her arms around his neck and gave herself up to the pleasure he was offering.

Amy and Jesse lay in a tangle of arms and legs, pleasantly sated.

"You warm enough?" Jesse lay with one arm behind his head, the other around Amy, who was snuggled against his chest.

"Any warmer and I'd set this hay on fire."

They both laughed before Amy sat up. "Jesse, I need to say something."

At the seriousness of her tone he sat up beside her and took her hand in his, linking their fingers. "Okay."

She stared down at their joined hands. "I can understand that my sudden departure right after graduation was a shock to you."

"That's an understatement..."

She touched a finger to his lips. "It was a shock to me,

too. My aunt was my mother's only family, and I couldn't let Mom drive up to Helena alone."

"Of course you couldn't. But..."

Again she stopped him. "I never thought we'd be gone the entire summer, but Aunt Morgan's illness lingered, and then..." Amy shrugged. "She was gone, and it was time for college to begin, and I found myself swamped with new classes and new friends, and grieving the loss of my aunt and the loss of you..."

It was Jesse's turn to still her words. "You wouldn't have had to lose me if you hadn't shut me out, Amy. I tried to find out where you were..."

"You couldn't have tried too hard. I told you everything in my letter."

He shook his head. "There was no letter."

She looked bewildered. "It may have happened in the middle of the night, but I'm sure I didn't dream it. I wrote you."

"And I'm telling you I never got a letter from you."

"Look, I get that there's been a lot of time between then and now. Time can blur a lot of images." She paused, thinking of all the hours she'd spent waiting by the phone, by the mailbox, waiting, hoping, dreaming. Crying her heart out.

Her tone hardened. "If you insist that you never got my letter, all I can do is insist that I wrote you. Are you implying that I'm lying?"

"I'm not calling you a liar, Amy. I'm just telling you that I never got a letter."

Though it didn't make any sense, she took one look at the exhaustion in his eyes and let out a huge sigh of exasperation, fully aware that this was going nowhere fast. "Can we talk about this another time? I really have to get dressed. Dad will be awake soon, and he'll need some breakfast."

His lips curved into a dangerous smile and the hungry glint returned to his eyes. "What about what I need? I love it when you get all heated with temper."

At his teasing tone, her smile returned. "You're a very greedy man."

"Can you blame me? For years I've been on a starvation diet. Now I have this glorious, wonderful feast, and I can't seem to stop myself."

"Speaking of feasts..." Coming to a sudden decision, she pushed herself free of his arms and crossed the barn before picking up her clothes. "You're coming in to breakfast."

Jesse got to his feet, unmindful of his nakedness. "Are you serious?"

She turned and sucked in a breath at the beauty of his body. He was all muscle and sinew from years of tough ranch chores. And that fabulous body was all hers, she thought with a sudden shock of recognition. To enjoy as she had all night.

She stepped into her jeans and buttoned her denim work shirt. "I guess, if you're going to spend your nights in our barn..."

"With you."

She looked over. "If you're going to spend your nights in our barn with me," she added for emphasis, "I won't sneak around behind my father's back. We're not a couple of kids now, Jesse. I intend to be honest and up front with my dad."

"He might decide to throw me out."

"He might. Are you up for it?"

He tugged on his jeans and boots and plaid shirt before crossing to her. Tipping up her chin he brushed his lips over hers. Then he gave her one of those heart-stopping smiles. "I'd walk through fire for you, Amy. And I'm guessing it won't get much hotter than what I'm about to face in your house. If you're ready, so am I."

Together they walked hand in hand out of the barn and up the path to the house.

CHAPTER EIGHTEEN

———◆———

Jesse paused in the doorway while Amy moved around the kitchen, snapping on lights, cranking up the heat.

At the sound of her father's voice calling to her, she turned. "Make yourself comfortable while I help my dad through his morning routine."

Alone in the kitchen, Jesse began opening cupboards until he located Amy's stash of pots and pans. Then he rummaged through the refrigerator and hauled out eggs, cheese, bread, and assorted vegetables. Rolling up his sleeves, he set to work, humming to himself.

By the time Otis Parrish and his daughter walked into the kitchen, the table had been set and Jesse was busy turning sausage links in a heavy skillet.

"What the hell...?" Otis stopped dead in his tracks.

"Morning, Mr. Parrish." Jesse gave him a quick smile before turning his attention to the omelet he had cooking in another pan.

"You made breakfast?" Amy peered over his shoulder. "Oh, that smells fabulous."

"It'll taste even better." He winked. "If you get that toast, everything's ready."

He crossed to the table and began dividing the omelet into three portions. When he noted that Otis was still standing in the doorway he added, "Better enjoy this while it's still hot."

Giving Amy's father no chance to argue, he returned to the stove and began scooping sausages onto a platter.

"And you made coffee." Amy breathed in the wonderful fragrance before filling three cups and placing one beside each plate.

When Otis dropped weakly onto his chair, she added lamely, "Dad, I hope you don't mind, but I've invited Jesse to join us for breakfast. Of course, I invited him before I realized he'd be the one doing the cooking."

The two shared a grin, while Otis merely glared.

As Amy picked up her fork her father slammed a hand down on the table. "Stop this foolishness and tell me what this is about. You said a McCord was here. You didn't tell me he'd be in my house, making himself at home."

"I tried to tell you, Dad. Jesse's worried about the accidents..."

Jesse held up a hand to stop her. "Mr. Parrish, I talked things over with Sheriff Wycliff, and he agrees with me that these weren't accidents. Someone is deliberately targeting you and your daughter."

"What business is that of yours?"

"You're my neighbor. That ought to be enough of a reason. But there's another. I care about your daughter. What happens to her is my business."

"Are you suggesting that I can't take care of my own?"

"I never said that. But right now, your first priority has to be taking care of your health."

He saw Otis wince, and he wished there had been an easier way to say it. But there it was, laid bare. Now Otis would have to deal with it.

"So, while you're busy regaining your health, I've decided to do what the sheriff and his deputy can't, for lack of time and manpower."

"By sitting in my kitchen and eating my food?"

The older man's temper had Jesse grinning. "Not exactly what I had in mind. But since I'm here, why don't you taste my special omelet and see if you still object."

Otis glowered. "I don't need some smart-mouthed McCord telling me what to do."

"Suit yourself."

"Dad, the least you can do is eat something." Amy tasted the egg mixture and gave a sigh of pure pleasure. "Oh, this is delicious. Where'd you learn to cook like this, Jess?"

"I guess all those years of Dandy's good cooking just rubbed off. Once in a while I look over his shoulder, just to get an idea of how to stay alive if I'm up at one of the bunkhouses during a storm. I haven't mastered his corn bread yet, but I can get by with the essentials, like eggs and meat and potatoes."

Out of the corner of his eye he saw Otis take a taste of his omelet. Though the older man never said a word, he soon cleaned his plate. Then he sat back, sipping strong, excellent coffee, his eyes narrowed on Jesse.

The color had returned to the older man's skin. Skin

that just minutes earlier had been the color of chalk. The food had given him renewed energy.

"How long have you been here, McCord?"

"Since last night."

Otis set his cup down with a clatter. "You spent the night under my roof?"

"I slept in the barn, Mr. Parrish."

Just as Otis began to relax, Amy added, "That's where I found him when I went out to check on the herd."

His gaze shifted to his daughter. "Last night."

Her chin came up in that infuriating way she'd had since she was no more than a toddler. She'd spent a lifetime challenging him and his authority.

"That's right."

"And when did you come back to the house, girl?"

"This morning." She met his eyes, refusing to look away.

He hissed out a breath. "You know how I feel about the McCords."

She nodded. "You've always known how I feel about Jesse."

He shot a quick glance at Jesse's face, then returned his attention to his daughter. "You know I could order you to leave my house, girl."

"I know." She held her breath.

"And maybe I would, if I didn't need you right now."

Need. Not love. His choice of words was an arrow through her heart.

He took no notice of her pain. Now that he'd given in to his anger, he couldn't seem to stop himself.

"I never thought I'd see the day that my daughter would give up the warmth and comfort of her own bed to sleep in the barn like an animal. With a *McCord*." He spat the word like a curse.

"It's my choice."

Amy watched as her father shoved away from the table. With an effort he got to his feet, leaning heavily on the back of his chair. He fixed Jesse with a look of pure hatred.

"You may be a good enough cook. But you'll never be good enough for my daughter. And if you know what's good for you, you'll never set foot in my house again."

He turned and walked slowly, painfully from the room.

At the table, neither of them spoke until they heard the slam of the bedroom door.

Jesse reached across the table and caught Amy's hand. It was cold as ice.

"I'm sorry, baby."

She shook her head. "Don't be. This isn't just about you. You heard what he said. He needs me. That's all. Just need. Well, that's not good enough for me. When he's strong enough to get along without me, I'll be gone again. And this time for good."

"Amy..."

She pulled her hand free. "Don't, Jess." She managed a weak smile. "You were right. That was an excellent breakfast. You cooked, so I'll clean up."

He walked to her chair and pressed his hands on her shoulders, holding her when she tried to stand.

"Sit and enjoy your coffee. I'll have this mess cleaned up in no time."

She was too drained to argue.

True to his word, in short order he had the kitchen gleaming.

When he'd hung the kitchen towel on a hook by the door, he crossed to her and kissed her forehead. "Time to head home and see to my chores. I'll see you tonight."

"You heard my dad."

"He said not to set foot in his house. He didn't say anything about the barn."

She merely nodded.

When she heard the sound of his truck, she stood and walked to the back door.

What had she done? At a time when her father was most vulnerable, she'd hit him with the hardest news of all. She'd let him know that she had chosen to give her love to the grandson of his enemy.

Her love.

She put a hand to her middle and leaned heavily on the door. She did love him, desperately, though she hadn't planned to. Instead of feeling good about the knowledge, she was feeling more miserable than ever.

No matter the outcome, she could see no happy ending to this situation.

Jesse drove like a man on a mission, sending up a cloud of dust as he sped along the dirt road leading to his ranch.

Otis Parrish was a hardheaded fool. Couldn't he see what his careless words were doing to his daughter? That he was fighting a deadly illness didn't give him the right to unload his temper on Amy. She'd already given up a career she loved to come home and take care of a thankless old man who seemed to enjoy picking a fight with her. How much more should she be asked to endure?

As he tore up the driveway and headed toward the

barn, he was forced to stand on the brakes when a vehicle came lumbering up from behind the barn.

"You idiot!" Jesse slammed out of the truck, itching for a fight.

Rafe leaned a head out the stake truck's window. "You ought to know by now that ranch implements have the right-of-way around here. Where's your brain this morning?"

Zane and Wyatt ambled out of the barn, trailed by Cal and Jimmy Eagle. All of them looked up as Rafe jumped out of the truck.

"Why should I bother to ask? You probably left your brain in the same place you've been parking your body. Over at the Parrish ranch."

That had everyone laughing, until Jesse grabbed Rafe by the front of his shirt and hauled him up until their faces were mere inches apart.

"What I do and where I sleep are none of your business."

Rafe slapped his hand away. "I don't see why I should be any different. Everybody in Gold Fever knows about you and Amy shacking up."

After building up a head of steam over Otis's treatment of Amy, Jesse's blood was hot to fight. And Rafe and his smart mouth made him the perfect target.

Jesse charged him, driving him back against the barn door. While the others watched in silence, Rafe brought up his knee, catching Jesse in the groin.

"Let that be a lesson, Jess. You fight me, you're going to regret it."

"Uh-oh." Wyatt turned to Zane. "I'm betting that got Jesse's attention. I wouldn't want to be Rafe now."

Zane shrugged. "I don't know about that. Rafe's got fifty pounds on Jesse. Ten says Jesse's going down for the count."

Wyatt dug into his pocket and held up a bill. "You're on."

Jesse threw a quick, hard punch to Rafe's chin, snapping his head back.

In retaliation Rafe brought a fist into Jesse's gut, doubling him over. When Jesse straightened, he shook his head to clear it before pummeling the stocky man with a series of blows that had both men struggling for breath.

While they fought, several other wranglers stepped out of the barn and crowded around, making bets on the outcome.

Jimmy Eagle shook his head, refusing to get caught up in the gamble.

Rafe landed another solid blow before Jesse lunged forward, taking him to the ground. The two men rolled over once, then twice, each getting in their licks.

Jesse was the first to regain his footing. He stood, wheezing in shallow breaths as he fought to clear his head. Seeing Rafe sitting in the dirt, blood oozing from a cut over his eye, he reached out a hand to help him up.

Rafe stared at his outstretched hand for several long seconds before slapping it aside and easing slowly to his feet.

His anger spent, Jesse wiped an arm over the blood oozing from a cut over his eye, smearing it down the side of his face. "You pack a mean punch, Rafe."

The wrangler shot him a look of pure venom. "Some of us didn't grow up on a big, fancy ranch, having people around to watch our backs. I learned to make sure my first punch did the job, in case there wasn't a second one."

Cal stepped between them. "Fun's over, boys. Time to get to work."

As Jesse turned toward the house, Wyatt slapped him on the back. "As far as fights go, it was okay, though I'd have landed a few more blows before calling it quits."

Laughing, Zane added, "Me, too. Still, this was a great way to start the day."

When they stepped into the mudroom, the three took pains to wipe their boots and wash their hands.

As they turned away from the sink Wyatt gave a quick shake of his head. "Uh-uh. I think you'd better get rid of the blood before you set foot into the kitchen, just in case Aunt Cora happens to be there."

Jesse followed his cousin's advice and winced when he touched the cut over his eye.

Zane grinned. "I think it's your turn to have a lovely shiner."

"Won't be the first time." Jesse punched his shoulder good-naturedly.

The three were grinning as they walked into the kitchen. Seeing it empty, they relaxed and helped themselves to the last of the hot coffee.

Wyatt leaned a hip against the counter. "So, does Otis Parrish know you were there?"

Jesse frowned. "Otis knows and is beyond furious."

Just then Cora stepped into the kitchen and stopped at the sight of her nephew's dirt-stained clothes and his face bearing bloody cuts. "Jesse. Are you saying Otis Parrish did this to you?"

"No, Aunt Cora." Jesse set down his coffee mug and poured a mug for his aunt. "I think I'd better explain."

He led the way to the big table and sat, waiting until

they were settled around it before filling them in on all that had happened.

Nobody spoke until Jesse had finished.

It was Cora who said, "How long do you think you can continue working the ranch here, and then spending your nights in the Parrish barn?"

Jesse shrugged. He'd been asking himself the same question.

"We could spell him."

At Wyatt's words, they turned to stare at him.

Wyatt glanced at Zane. "We could take on more of your chores during the day. Or, we could take turns sleeping in the barn. And we can certainly ask the crew here to keep an eye on the Parrish ranch whenever they're nearby."

Jesse shook his head. "I don't like the idea of asking everyone to do double duty."

Cora laid a hand over his. "That's what family does in time of trouble." She glanced around the table. "If Coot were here, I know he'd be proud of the way you three are coming together to solve this problem." She pushed away from the table. "I'll be in my studio if you need me. But I want Amy and Otis to know that they're welcome here."

Jesse brushed a kiss over her cheek. "Thanks, Aunt Cora. I doubt that Otis will accept your offer. But it will mean a lot to Amy."

When their aunt was gone, the three remained at the table, discussing their options.

Now that his anger was spent, the depth of Jesse's worry was obvious to both Zane and Wyatt.

When he finally made his way to his room to shower

and dress for the day, Wyatt and Zane bent their heads close.

"Jesse's a hardheaded cowboy. He really thinks he can handle all this alone, but he can't. Nobody can." Zane drained his cup and set it in the sink.

"You're right." Wyatt followed Zane from the house to the barn to begin their daily chores.

As they worked they made a pact. They would do all they could to lend a hand in whatever way possible until this crisis was resolved. Even if it meant that all of them had to go without sleep.

CHAPTER NINETEEN

Y ou don't like my pot roast?" Dandy stared at Jesse's plate, still heaped with beef and garden vegetables and potatoes swimming in rich brown gravy. "It's always been one of your favorites."

"I'm just not hungry."

Dandy narrowed his eyes. "You sick? Or in love?"

Cora looked across the table at her nephew. "Aren't you feeling well, Jesse?"

"I'm fine, Aunt Cora."

Wyatt and Zane shared a private smile.

Cora pushed away from the table. "Dandy, we'll have our dessert in the great room when Amy joins us."

She left the room, trailed by her three nephews.

By the time Amy arrived they had already laid out the dozens of slips of yellowed paper and were busy trying to match them up.

"Sorry I'm late." Amy hurried across the room and paused to kiss Cora's cheek before greeting the others.

Jesse took her hand, linking his fingers with hers, relieved that he'd managed to talk her into continuing their treasure-hunt meetings. It was the perfect way to get her mind off her troubles.

"We've found a few more matches. Nothing earth-shattering, but we're definitely seeing a pattern. See this?" He held up the slips they'd already paired.

Amy's smile widened. "I'm so glad. I know, with enough time, we'll be able to figure out exactly where Coot was heading in his search."

Cora studied their joined hands and felt a lightness around her heart. She'd known, of course, that Jesse still carried a torch for Amy. What she hadn't been certain of, until now, was that it was reciprocal. The light in Amy's eyes was all the proof she needed to know that these two shared the same strong feelings.

Love.

It was what she wanted for each of her nephews. A love strong enough to see them through life's good times and bad.

She'd had her share of lovely romances. A suave, sophisticated museum director in Italy. A wild and reckless sculptor in Paris. The very thought had her smiling. But though she'd fancied herself in love any number of times, and had her heart broken more than once through the years, Cora had never experienced the sort of deep, soul-stirring love that her brother, Coot, had enjoyed with his beloved Annie, and it was one of her biggest regrets. That kind of love was rare indeed.

Amy glanced at Wyatt. "Have you done any more with that clear overlay?"

"Yeah." He moved it over the map and they studied it in silence.

"I don't think there's any doubt now." Amy traced a finger over the path he'd drawn from the slips of paper they'd matched. "Coot was definitely closing in on Treasure Chest Mountain."

"I have to agree with you, dear." Cora had to blink away the mist that suddenly sprang to her eyes. "I believe Coot is still showing us the way."

They paused in their work when Dandy entered with a tray of fudge brownies topped with vanilla ice cream and warm caramel sauce, along with a pot of coffee. After passing around the plates of dessert and cups of coffee, he left them alone.

"Oh." Amy took a first taste of brownie and sighed with pleasure. "Finding Coot's treasure would be a wonderful bonus. But for now, I'll settle for just this."

Jesse, sitting on the hearth with the warmth of the fire to his back, smiled in agreement. It wasn't the sweet confection he was admiring, but the woman facing him.

He was more than happy to give up another night's sleep to stay in her father's barn, as long as she was there to spend the night in his arms.

Jesse arrived home to find Wyatt and Zane waiting for him in the ranch kitchen. They had been talking quietly, heads bent in earnest conversation. They both looked up when he entered the room.

Wyatt studied Jesse's red-rimmed eyes and fresh growth of stubble. "You look like hell. Do you ever sleep?"

"Not if I can help it. What about you? Do you ever work? I saw the crew heading out when I drove in."

"You'll owe me an apology for that after you hear what I've dug up."

Jesse poured himself a mug of coffee and dropped down onto a kitchen chair. "Okay. What've you dug up?"

"On my world wanderings, I've met some…interesting characters. One of them, Archie, is a private detective and bounty hunter."

"A bounty hunter." Jesse came close to snickering, but seeing the intense look in his cousin's eye, he held himself back. "And what did this bounty hunter tell you?"

"He did a little sniffing around and got a lead on our bikers."

Jesse set down his mug with a clatter. "How'd he do what the law couldn't?"

"I didn't ask. All I know is that he found them."

"Where the hell are they?"

"Just listen." Wyatt held up a hand to silence him. "They claim someone contacted them online and invited them to Gold Fever to earn some serious money. When they got to town, Buck, the beefy guy who's the leader, received a call on his cell from someone who used an electronic device that modifies the voice. Buck couldn't tell if he was talking to a man or a woman, or even a human. He said it sounded like an android from some cheap sci-fi flick. He was asked if he and his buddies would be willing to kill someone for a great deal of money. They claim they flat-out refused. Then they were offered a sum of money to break a few of some cowboy's bones."

"Mine?" Jesse's eyes went wide.

Wyatt nodded. "They figured it was easy money. But Buck claimed that when Zane and I joined the fray, all bets were off. By the time we were through with them, our bikers decided to leave town without payment, and stated they would never be back."

"You believe them?" Jesse's coffee was forgotten.

Wyatt shrugged. "What reason would they have to lie?"

"Can your pal Archie find out who contacted them? And why?"

Wyatt gave a shake of his head. "He said it's like looking for the proverbial needle in a haystack. Using an Internet connection, it could be anybody, anywhere. So the better question is, who do you think it is? Who would want you dead?"

Jesse mulled that before saying softly, "I don't know. I'm sure I've made some enemies in my life, but I can't think of anybody who hates me enough to want me dead. And if it's me they're after, why are they using Amy?"

Wyatt glanced at Zane. "We think it's because she's your weakness. Now that their plan A failed, they've decided that they don't just want you dead, they want you to suffer."

"There's something else," Zane added. "Amy and her dad are completely isolated over at their place. Nobody around for miles."

"So whoever wants to get me finds a way to lure me to Amy's, then he knows exactly where to find me."

Wyatt's tone was low. "That's the way we figure it."

Zane nodded in agreement. "If our theory is correct, you're falling right into their trap. You've got to persuade Amy and her father to move over here until we find this madman."

Jesse gave a short laugh. "I'd have a better chance of seeing hell freeze over. Otis may be feeling weak, but not where we're concerned. If anything, his hatred is stronger than ever. And Amy won't leave him alone while he's fighting a serious illness." He stood, hoping a shave and a shower would help clear the thoughts that were spinning through his brain. "Since I can't afford to leave Amy alone at the mercy of whoever is doing this, it looks like I'll just have to be more careful while I'm at the Parrish ranch. At least until I figure out who wants me dead."

As he strode away, Wyatt and Zane watched with matching looks of concern.

Wyatt turned to Zane. "You ready to give up some sleep, cuz?"

"Won't be the first time." Zane picked up the camera that was never far from his reach. "I'll take first watch tonight. I've been meaning to try my new night lens. I hear the Parrish ranch has some great views of Treasure Chest Mountain."

"Keep your cell phone charged, and have my number and Sheriff Wycliff's on speed dial. You see anything suspicious, you call first and ask questions later."

The two conspirators parted to begin their morning chores.

The night had turned frigid. The truck's headlights illuminated a whirl of snowflakes dancing across the road, whipped into a frenzy by a bitter wind.

In Jesse's truck Amy cranked up the heater and huddled inside her parka. "I watched your aunt Cora's face tonight while we were working on Coot's trail. I'm so glad we're doing this, Jess. It's giving her such pleasure to be involved in her brother's treasure hunt."

He nodded thoughtfully. "I've noticed. I guess I was so caught up in the pain of my own loss, I forgot just how much Coot's death affected her. He was her big brother. The guy she always turned to. She has to miss him every day."

"I never heard how he died. I only know what the townspeople had to say. And most of them figure it was the curse."

"The curse." He huffed out a breath. "He was doing his usual thing, climbing around the foothills of Treasure Chest, when he fell. Probably the result of a rock slide, since there were a lot of loose rocks around him when we got to him."

"How did you know he was in trouble?"

"He phoned Cal on his cell. Didn't want to worry Cora. Said where he was, and that he'd taken a bad fall. Cal phoned Marilee Trainor for a medical backup, then we all headed out to the site of the fall. We were too late."

She heard the catch in his voice and laid a hand over his on the wheel.

They drove the rest of the way in silence. When they drove into her yard, Jesse stopped at the front porch.

She glanced over. "Why are you stopping here? You always park your truck behind the barn."

"The night's too cold for you to sleep in the barn tonight. You go ahead inside."

She drew close. "I'd rather sleep with you. We can generate enough heat to keep from freezing."

He chuckled against her temple. "Yeah. We're good at

that. But you need to sleep in a warm house tonight. In your own bed."

He stepped out of the truck and walked around to open her door. When they paused at the front door he drew her close for a quick, hard kiss, while the bitter wind blew swirls of snow in their faces.

Amy shivered. "You're right. It's too cold. Why don't you stay inside with me?"

He grinned. "It's bad enough that a McCord is sleeping in your father's barn every night. I won't add insult to injury by invading his home." He lingered over her mouth, wishing he could just ignore this damnable code of honor and take her up on her invitation. "Good night, Amy. Sleep well."

"Night, Jesse. Will you come up to the house for breakfast before you leave in the morning?"

He shook his head. "You said your father has another treatment tomorrow. No point in adding to his discomfort. Now," he said, turning her around, "be sure you lock your door."

He waited until he heard her throw the lock. Then he climbed back into the truck and drove it to the barn.

With the wind whistling around the roof and rustling the hay in the loft, it promised to be a long, cold night. Not that it mattered. As long as he could be here, close to Amy, keeping her safe from harm, he'd endure whatever discomfort the universe sent his way.

Chapter Twenty

———◆———

Amy checked on her father, relieved to find him snoring softly. Today's treatment had left him weak and nauseous as always, but by suppertime he'd begun to feel some of his strength returning. The doctor suggested that he may have turned a corner and was now beginning to rebound. The news had given both father and daughter a great deal of hope.

She tiptoed from his bedroom and made her way to her own room. Before she could begin to undress she heard a soft tap on the back door.

Jesse. She gave a delighted laugh. He'd had a change of mind. Hadn't she told him it was too cold to sleep in the barn?

She raced to unlock the door and threw it open. "Jess..."

Rafe Spindler took a step inside, his stocky body filling the open doorway.

Startled, she simply stared at him. "Rafe. What are you...?"

His hand snaked out, catching her roughly by the shoulder. "You're coming with me."

"With you?" She was more indignant than afraid. "Does Jesse know you're here?"

"Not yet. But he will."

He tossed an envelope to the floor.

For a moment she merely watched as it skidded across the kitchen tile. Then she looked up, her tone pure ice. "Leave my house this minute, Rafe."

"Shut up." He jammed a hand in his pocket.

"Now you listen..." Her words died in her throat as she caught sight of the glint of something as he withdrew his hand from his pocket.

He was holding a small, silver handgun, aimed directly at her heart.

He saw the way she looked around wildly, searching for something, anything, with which to defend herself.

"You got two choices. Come with me now, without a fight, or"—he waved the gun in the direction of the hallway—"I blow your old man's brains out while he's sleeping."

"My father...No. Wait. Do whatever you want, but leave him out of this."

"I figured you'd see it my way."

With a moan of despair she allowed her hands to be tied with a leather cord before being dragged to Rafe's idling truck. Once inside he tied the end of the cord to his own wrist, assuring that she couldn't leap to freedom.

Agitated, staring around with the eyes of a wild man,

he stomped on the pedal hard enough to send snow-covered gravel flying.

Zane left his truck parked in the hills and started hiking toward the Parrish ranch. While he picked his way in the moonlight, he turned his camera on the moon-washed countryside, already dusted with snow.

Breathtaking.

He loved the look of it, at times stark and forbidding. At other times, with the canopy of stars hovering over the tips of Treasure Chest, it looked like a Hollywood set. Too perfect to be real.

At moments like this he had to remind himself that he was really here, back in the place his heart had never left.

California had all that golden, liquid sunshine. But Montana had everything he'd ever wanted. Space. Grandeur. And right this minute, with snow falling in his hair and coating his lashes, a winter wonderland that was like no other place on earth.

The cell phone in his pocket vibrated, and he paused to see who was calling him.

He flipped it open. "Hey, Wyatt. What's up?"

"You at the Parrish ranch?"

"Almost. Why?"

"Keep a close watch. I just heard something I didn't like."

"What's that?"

"I thought I'd join in the poker game out in the bunkhouse. Figured I might hear a little gossip."

"And?"

"The buzz is that Rafe Spindler has been smarting for

some time now over the loss of his favorite stallion to Jesse in a card game."

"Everybody knows that. You think he'd hold a grudge against Jesse over a horse?"

"Maybe. Maybe not. But there's more. There are rumors that Rafe has been gambling somewhere other than on the ranch. Some of the guys in the bunkhouse tell me he's been spending a lot of his nights away. Rarely gets in before morning. Maybe he goes to town, though I couldn't find anybody who's seen him there. I phoned Daffy. She and Vi claim he hasn't spent an evening in their place for a week or more. I even checked the Grizzly Inn, and Ben Rider hasn't seen Rafe in over a month. There's talk of some high-stakes gambling at a ranch somewhere far enough from town so nobody sees where the trucks are parked."

"You think he's been gambling to try to win enough money to buy back his stallion?"

"I don't know. It could be. Or maybe he has a gambling problem. Hell, maybe he's just looking for a little excitement. A lot of wranglers get the itch. Whatever the reason, I thought I'd pass along the fact that he's mad as hell over the loss of that stallion."

"I can see, if he's still simmering over his stallion, why he'd enjoy a good fight with Jesse. But that doesn't explain why he'd be threatening Amy and her father. I can't see a man going to this much trouble over a horse." Zane swore as he lost his footing on a rock. "I'm almost at the ranch."

He lifted his camera and stared through the night lens. At first he wasn't sure what he was seeing. Then, as it became clearer, he swore again. "There's a cloud of snow, as though a vehicle is hightailing it out of there. No tail-lights that I can see. Call Jesse and see if it's his truck."

As he tucked away his phone and started running toward the ranch, Zane prayed that the churned-up snow he'd just seen through his camera lens was caused by Jesse's truck, and not that of a stranger bent on doing harm.

"Jesse."

Zane pulled up short when he saw Jesse looming up out of the darkness, running out of the barn.

Jesse's breath was coming hard and fast, as though he'd fought his way through a nightmare. He was still pulling on his jacket. "Wyatt said you saw someone?"

"Someone in a big hurry."

The two cousins raced toward the back door of Amy's house. Seeing it standing open, they ran inside.

Jesse headed for Amy's room. Finding it empty he raced down the hallway to her father's room.

Shoving open the door he shouted, "Amy? You in here?"

Her father sat up, sleep-fogged and disheveled. When he caught sight of Jesse he heaved himself out of bed. "Have you gone crazy? What in the hell are you doing here in the middle of the night, McCord?"

"Looking for Amy."

"She isn't with you?"

Jesse tore from the room, shouting over his shoulder, "I left her here half an hour ago."

"Jesse." Zane handed his cousin the envelope he'd found lying in the middle of the floor.

As he took it from Zane's hand, Jesse's heart nearly stopped.

In Rafe's childlike scrawl were written the words *she's dead.*

He tore open the envelope and read the crude note inside.

> *Come alone. Cliffs of Treasure Chest.*
> *You bring help, she's dead.*

Crushing the note in his fist before tossing it aside, Jesse spun away and raced toward his truck in the barn, leaving Zane and Otis Parrish to stare after him with matching looks of stunned surprise.

Jesse drove like a madman. What was this about? Why would Rafe Spindler do a thing like this? Had something inside the cowboy snapped?

It didn't seem like a random or spontaneous act, but rather something he'd given a lot of thought to. Still, it was so out of character for Rafe. He had a mean temper when he was pushed, but he'd never been dangerous.

Until now.

Amy. Dear God, Amy.

The thought of her, alone and frightened, had his jaw clenching. If Rafe hurt her in any way, he'd kill him. Or by God, he'd die trying.

Though he wasn't a man who prayed often, he found himself storming heaven with but one thought: *Keep her safe. Please, keep her safe.*

By the time Zane had raced back to his truck parked in the hills and returned to the Parrish ranch, Otis Parrish was dressed and pacing the front porch.

As the older man climbed into Zane's truck, it occurred to Zane that Otis was fighting valiantly to hold himself together. The interior truck light illuminated his sickly pallor. The poor guy was being forced to fight two battles at once. A deadly illness, and the threat of real physical harm to his daughter. No wonder he was as pale as a ghost.

To offer him some hope, Zane said softly, "Wyatt has already phoned Sheriff Wycliff, who's contacting the state police to ask for their help."

The older man smoothed out the wrinkles from the note Jesse had tossed aside. "He told Jesse to come alone or he'll..." He couldn't bring himself to say the word.

"Wycliff knows that. I told Wyatt what the note said, and Wyatt relayed the information to the sheriff."

"If that madman harms my daughter..." Otis's voice was choked with a combination of fear and rage. "Amy told me that your family offered us shelter. I couldn't bring myself to accept help from them, but I should have agreed to let Amy go to your ranch until this was resolved. This is all my fault."

"I'd say the fault is Rafe's. And believe me, Mr. Parrish, if anyone can stop Rafe and save Amy, it's Jesse."

Otis stared out into the darkness. "I wish I had your faith. I wish..." His words trailed off as he fought the fear that clutched at his heart and squeezed until he could scarcely take a breath.

"Tell me what this is about, Rafe." Amy clung to the door of the truck as it bumped up a steep incline and lurched, with stomach-churning speed, headlong down the other side.

She was shivering so hard her teeth were chattering. Rafe had given her no time to grab a parka. Her thin shirt and denims offered little warmth against the frigid night air that whistled past the truck's windows.

Rafe was taking no chances on being stopped. He avoided the roads and instead kept to the wild countryside, his headlights extinguished. He navigated by the light of the moon, and at times barely avoided crashing into darkened boulders.

She had a flashback to that night when she'd fled for her life across this very stretch of landscape. "It was you!"

"You don't know what the hell you're talking about." He kept his gaze firmly fixed on the path in front of them.

"I know you tried to run me over. Why?"

He shot her a quick glance before returning his attention to his driving. "Believe me, if I wanted to run you over, you'd already be dead."

"Then why were you chasing me?"

"How do you know I wasn't just having some fun?"

"Fun?" She turned to face him. "There's more going on here. I don't believe you."

He made a choking sound that could have been a laugh or a sneer. "You think I care what you believe? I was told to scare you good."

Her head came up sharply. "Told? Who told you?"

"Shut up."

"No. I have a right..."

His hand shot out, slapping her so hard her head snapped to one side and stars danced before her eyes.

"Now maybe you'll keep your mouth shut. I got nothing more to say."

As they continued their way across the rough terrain, Amy blinked back tears as she thought about her father and Jesse, her two fierce protectors, and the helplessness they would feel when they learned that she'd been taken while they slept.

At least, she thought with a sob lodged in her throat, they were safe.

Swallowing back her fear, she stared around at the darkened landscape. This was no time for tears. She couldn't let fear paralyze her. She needed to think. To plan. To concentrate on any means possible of escaping this nightmare.

She vowed to do whatever it took to stay alive. She was smart and she was strong. There had to be a way out.

She saw the bulge of the handgun in Rafe's pocket and shivered. She couldn't afford to think about what was awaiting her. All that mattered was that, for now, she was alive. When the time came to face whatever this madman was planning, she needed to be ready to fight for her life.

CHAPTER TWENTY-ONE

J ess." Wyatt's voice on the cell phone sounded as though he'd been running a marathon. He'd already filled Jesse in on what little they knew about Rafe's gambling problems. Now he had more unpleasant news. "Cal just told me that Rafe's stallion is gone. Jimmy Eagle thinks Rafe could have stashed the horse and some essentials in one of those canyons. He might be planning on dumping the ranch truck and taking off across the hills on horseback."

Jesse's mind started racing. "Rafe grew up in these hills. He could elude the police and hide out in the wilderness for years."

"Yeah, that's what we're thinking." Wyatt paused. "We've alerted the sheriff and the state police. They're hoping to get into position without Rafe spotting them."

"You tell them to back off. Keep their distance. I can't afford to have that nutcase going off half-cocked and hurting Amy."

"They know that. But if they can get a couple of sharpshooters in a position to pick him off, the odds get a little better."

"I'll take all the advantages I can get." Jesse saw the foothills looming in the darkness and charged ahead toward the distant cliffs. "Just so they know what's at stake here."

What's at stake.

Amy. Just the thought of Rafe hurting her had the blood in Jesse's veins turning to ice. He would do whatever was necessary, pay whatever price was required of him, to see her safe.

He was going into this blindly. All these miles, and he hadn't come up with a single plan. He had a rifle in the truck. Anyone who lived on a ranch of this size had one or more. But what good was a rifle if Rafe was holding a weapon to Amy's head?

Why? There were pieces to this puzzle that just didn't fit.

What had caused Rafe to snap? What would he possibly gain by hurting them?

Jesse needed to know what was going on in Rafe's mind. Maybe, just maybe, when they stood face-to-face, he would understand. For now, he had no clue.

He knew one thing. He couldn't afford to let himself think about all the things that could go wrong. He would concentrate instead on how to get Amy free. Unless that happened, his own life wasn't worth a damn.

Amy stood shivering in the night, ankle-deep in snow at the high elevation, her wrists bound tightly to a tree limb above her head. Rafe stood a little away, intently watching the road far below through night-vision binoculars.

He'd chosen an isolated spot near the cliffs, where he could see for miles. The ranch's four-wheel-drive vehicle had brought them halfway up the hill. At that point they'd abandoned the truck and walked the rest of the distance.

So what, she mulled, did he plan to do with her? Rape? Hold her for ransom? With either choice, she would be a witness to his crime. A liability. She would be a loose end he couldn't afford to have around.

That thought had her scalp prickling.

There would be no bargaining for her freedom. Rafe had already decided her fate. But why? What was the point of all this? He wouldn't go to these lengths just to frighten her.

Jesse.

She remembered the envelope Rafe had tossed on the floor. This wasn't about her. He'd used her as the bait to get Jesse alone.

She saw twin pinpricks of light pierce the darkness. As she watched, the lights drew nearer, and her heart plummeted.

She heard a door slam and Jesse's voice shouting out her name. It bounced around the cliff walls and echoed down the canyon.

"Answer him." Rafe crossed to her and pressed the pistol to her temple. "You heard me, answer him."

"What are you going to do if I refuse? Shoot me?" She clamped her mouth shut, taking comfort in even this small act of defiance.

"Suit yourself." He turned and cupped his hands to his mouth. "She's up here."

Amy waited, straining in the silence, praying that Jesse would keep his distance. Her heart was pounding in her temples.

Suddenly she made out a shadowy figure. In the swirling snow, Jesse was walking toward certain death. She had to warn him.

At the top of her lungs she shouted, "It's a trap, Jesse. Don't come any closer. Tell the sheriff…"

Rafe's hand closed over her mouth and nose, cutting off her breath. Unable to fight him, she kicked and bit, but he continued holding her tightly until spots danced in front of her eyes. There was a strange buzzing in her ears, and she could feel herself beginning to fade. The need for air caused her to go limp in his arms.

Just when she thought she would surely suffocate, he released her and lifted the gun to her temple as Jesse stepped into the clearing.

Amy stood, sucking in deep draughts of air, watching helplessly as Jesse advanced toward his fate.

"Okay, Rafe." Jesse took in the scene and fought an overwhelming urge to run to Amy and gather her close. The sight of her, arms tied to a tree limb over her head, the cold barrel of a gun pressed to her temple, tore at his heart. "I'm here."

"Take off your parka and turn your pockets inside out."

Jesse did as he was told.

"Now turn around. I need to see if you thought you'd be cute and hide a weapon in your waistband."

Jesse turned, then turned back. "Satisfied?"

When Rafe gave a barely perceptible nod of his head, Jesse added, "You can release Amy now."

Rafe's lips curled in a sneer. "You'd like that, wouldn't you?"

"Whatever this is about, it doesn't involve Amy."

"That's right. It doesn't. But you've made it pretty clear to everyone that she matters to you. That's why I knew you'd come. I'd be a fool to release her just yet."

"And you're no fool, are you?"

"That's right."

"Tell me what you want, Rafe."

"Not me." He peered into the darkness until he spotted what he was looking for. "Him."

Jesse turned in time to see a beam of light moving from behind a mound of snow-covered rocks. As the light drew closer he could make out a tall figure holding a high-powered lantern and leading a horse.

The horse's saddlebags bulged. Behind the saddle was a bedroll.

"You got him." Rafe crossed to the man and took the reins.

"Just like I said I would." The man removed his wide-brimmed hat, slapping it against his leg to remove the dusting of snow.

Jesse stared at the thatch of gray hair combed straight back, and the long, lean face with its sad hound-dog expression.

His grandfather's lawyer had always looked deceptively bored. Disinterested. Now his eyes glittered with a look that was frightening to see.

Madness? Vindictiveness? Pure hatred?

"Vernon?"

Vernon McVicker ignored Jesse as he watched Rafe lovingly examine his stallion.

Rafe looked over at the lawyer. "I delivered him just like I promised. Has my debt been erased?"

"Is that what this is about, Rafe? I heard you were gambling." Jesse looked from Rafe to the lawyer. "How much did Vernon stick you for?"

"None of your business."

"I don't see why it should matter whether or not I know, since you're obviously planning on riding off into the wilderness."

"That's right." Rafe stood a little taller. "My brother taught me to play poker when I was no more'n eight or nine. I've had men tell me I'm one of the best players they've ever met."

"Is that what the high rollers said?"

"You bet. Tell him, Mr. McVicker. I won nearly every hand. The first two weeks, I couldn't lose."

Jesse's hands fisted at his sides. "So you started betting more than you could afford. And that's when the cards turned against you, and you found yourself losing every hand."

Rafe's eyes narrowed. "Who told you?"

Jesse shook his head. "It's the oldest con in the world, Rafe. He set you up from the beginning. Letting you win, so he could sucker you into upping the ante and losing more than you could afford." He paused to let his words sink in, then lowered his voice like a conspirator. "So it was Vernon who planned these incidents at the Parrish ranch? And Vernon who told you to terrorize Amy out on the range? Did Vernon offer to erase your debt if you did just one more little thing for him?"

"Shut up, Jesse."

"Did he also tell you that you could just ride away

from this with clean hands? Didn't it ever occur to you what this is really about?" Jesse turned to Vernon. "Tell him, counselor. Tell him why you set him up."

Vernon calmly faced Rafe. "Everybody knew how much you hated losing that stallion. It wasn't much, but I figured it was enough of a motive to satisfy the sheriff."

"And while the law is chasing Rafe, what do you get out of all this?"

"What I've wanted from the beginning." Vernon gave a chilling smile. "A chance to search for Coot's gold without interference from any other... interested parties."

"What about my aunt and cousins? Do you think killing me will end their interest in the search?"

"I figure once you're... eliminated, they'll lose their appetite for the hunt. Lord knows, Coot never did. I listened to him for years, charting the trails he'd taken, the dead ends he'd dealt with, keeping a detailed map for my own sake. I waited as long as I could, hoping he'd get too old to continue searching, or die. When that didn't happen, I just had to help him along."

"What're you saying?" Jesse's eyes narrowed in stunned surprise at the lawyer.

"I've been trailing Coot for years, until I got sick and tired of waiting for the old man to step aside. When I saw him climbing one of Treasure Chest's cliffs, I figured a little rock slide would be a convenient way to eliminate him."

Jesse's voice was filled with shock and rage. "You followed Coot and... killed him?"

"The mountain killed him. I just greased his trail with a few well-placed rocks. As for following him, I've been doing it for years, hoping he'd lead me to the gold."

"You bastard! My grandfather trusted you. Trusted you with all his business."

"So will your aunt and cousins. I figure dealing with another death in the family will curb any appetite they may have for the family treasure."

"And you'll just happen to have some legal papers drawn up for them to sign when they withdraw from the search, pretending to be from Coot, making the treasure fair game for anybody who happens upon it?"

The lawyer threw back his head and laughed. "You're smarter than I gave you credit for, Jesse."

"And Amy? Why did you involve her in this?"

"Just call it killing two birds with one stone. The Parrish ranch is a bit too close to these foothills for my taste. Since Coot's trail was edging closer and closer, I figured I'd eliminate any more witnesses while I continue my search."

Jesse looked over at Rafe. "Do you still believe he's going to let you ride out of here? Think about this, Rafe. By now the entire ranch knows what's happening. By tomorrow the whole town will know. Whether or not you're the one to pull the trigger, you've become an accessory to a murder. Montana isn't big enough to hide a killer."

"All I did was erase a gambling debt. The rest of this isn't my business. What Mr. McVicker does after I'm gone has nothing to do with me." Nervous, Rafe put a foot in the stirrup. "I know this country better'n anybody. Once I lose myself up in these hills, nobody will ever find me." He pulled himself up into the saddle and touched a hand to the brim of his hat.

Vernon lifted his hand. "I'm afraid Jesse's right again.

You've been set up, Rafe. You see, I need you here so that when the law finds Jesse and Amy, they'll also find you. Dead, of course. And the case will be closed as easily as Coot's death."

Instead of a salute, he took careful aim with his pistol and fired.

Rafe's eyes went wide with surprise. His body stiffened before he tumbled to the ground and lay perfectly still, while his lifeblood drained into the snow around him.

Stunned and reeling, Amy gave an involuntary cry of horror. Her shoulders shook as she sobbed silently at the sight of such cold, calculated murder.

Vernon crossed to Rafe's body to check for a pulse.

Using that instant of distraction, Jesse was on him before he could blink, driving him back against a tree.

Stunned, Vernon shook his head, then pistol-whipped Jesse with such force that blood spurted from his temple.

The two men fell to the ground and rolled around in the snow.

Jesse's fist connected with Vernon's nose, sending a river of blood flowing down his parka.

The lawyer brought a knee into Jesse's groin, doubling him over. Through a haze of pain, Jesse saw Vernon getting to his feet. Jesse kicked out a foot, sending him sprawling.

When the gun slipped from Vernon's hand and dropped into the snow, Jesse gave a vicious kick, sending it flying.

As it skidded across the clearing, both men made a mad dash and fell on it.

Vernon's hand closed over the icy metal and he fired.

The sound of the explosion echoed and reechoed through the hills.

Jesse's body jerked, and his hand reached automatically to his chest.

Vernon staggered to his feet, still holding the gun, as blood spilled from beneath Jesse's parka. "Last chance to say good-bye to your girlfriend, Jesse."

He took careful aim at Jesse's heart.

"No!" Amy's cry had Vernon turning slightly, sending his second shot wide of its mark as she used the tree limb to pull herself up and kick out with both feet.

The thrust caught the lawyer by surprise and sent him sprawling.

Amy looked over at Jesse, lying as still as death. "Oh, Jesse. Please don't die. Get up. Please, Jesse, get up."

Jesse could feel himself fading. He knew he had to finish this before he passed out. He had to get to Vernon and take possession of the gun for Amy's sake. But though he moaned and struggled to move, his body refused to respond.

Amy watched helplessly. There was so much blood mingled with the snow.

As Amy mentally willed Jesse to move, she saw Vernon get slowly to his feet, wearing a look of smug victory. In his hand was the glint of the pistol as he aimed it at her. "I didn't realize you were such a fighter. Too bad it was a wasted effort. Time to finish this. Starting with you."

Amy watched, mesmerized, as his finger curled around the trigger. Inside her brain she heard the click. Though her first impulse was to squeeze her eyes tightly shut, she forced herself to face down her killer.

"You'll have to look me in the eye..."

An explosion of sound echoed through the cliffs and canyons.

Amy waited for the pain she knew would follow. Feeling no pain, she numbly waited for death to claim her.

Instead, as she watched in disbelief, Vernon's eyes went wide with the shock of recognition. His gun slipped from his hands as he seemed to fall forward in slow motion. With a cry she watched as the lawyer's body sank into the snow beside Jesse, an ever-widening pool of blood spilling from the bullet wound in his back.

When she looked up, the area was swarming with uniformed deputies and state police officers, all of them moving carefully around the crime scene, looking like actors in a dark movie.

Sheriff Wycliff led the charge, shouting out orders.

At this moment, none of them mattered. All that mattered to Amy was the fact that Jesse lay crumpled in the snow, as still as death, blood flowing from an ugly, gaping wound and staining the ground around him.

CHAPTER TWENTY-TWO

————◆————

"Cut her down." Sheriff Wycliff's voice had one of the uniformed officers following orders.

Amy let out a cry as the blood began flowing once more through her numb limbs.

She couldn't feel her feet as she raced to Jesse's side and dropped down in the snow. "Is he...?" She couldn't speak the word. All she could do was stare in horrified fascination as several officers knelt beside Jesse's body, checking for vital signs.

His limp body was lifted onto a portable gurney and the straps secured.

Finally one of them spoke. "He's not dead, ma'am, but I'm betting he feels more dead than alive right now. That gunshot has to be causing him some big-time pain."

"Alive?" Amy's heart began beating again as she grabbed hold of his hand, needing desperately to feel the connection. "Jesse, can you hear me? Oh, Jesse, you're alive. Stay with me, Jess. Please, stay with me."

"I'm...here." His lids flickered but remained closed. "McVicker?"

"He's dead. Killed by a police sharpshooter."

"You—" Jesse's teeth were chattering so hard he could barely get the words out. "You okay?"

His eyes opened, and he stared up pleadingly at Amy.

"I'm fine, Jess. Save your strength now."

One of the uniforms helped her into a heavy parka. But when she saw Jesse's gurney being moved, she raced to keep up.

As they bumped along the rutted path, he clenched his jaw at the pain that jolted through him. So much pain. As though he'd descended into hell and his entire body was on fire.

Amy continued holding his hand as she kept pace with the officers carrying the gurney. "There's a plane waiting to take you to town as soon as we get you down the mountain."

Pain had him drifting in and out of consciousness. The sight of his suffering nearly broke Amy's heart.

As they neared the plane, Amy recognized Marilee Trainor and felt a wave of relief.

Marilee was an emergency medical worker who partnered with the local and state law enforcement agencies, flying ranchers in need of medical services to the town's clinic. More serious accidents were taken by medevac to the hospital in Helena.

"Amy. You look like you've been through a war." Marilee caught her in a bear hug.

"That's what I feel like." For a moment Amy leaned

against her, soothed by this young woman's quiet competence.

Marilee turned to her patient. "Hey, Jesse. Got yourself shot, I hear."

"Mmmm." It was all he could manage.

"He's freezing." Amy caught his hand, which was cold as ice, despite the mound of blankets that enveloped him.

"Shock. This will help." Marilee withdrew a syringe from her black bag and shoved aside the blankets, injecting it into his vein.

By the time he was secured in the rear of the small plane, with Amy and Sheriff Wycliff on either side of him, Marilee had the engines revving and they were soon airborne.

In no time they arrived at the rodeo grounds on the far side of town, where an ambulance was waiting to transport them to the clinic.

Inside, Dr. Wheeler and his staff whisked Jesse away to an examining room to assess the damage.

"How about you, Amy?" One of the nurses studied the blood that stained Amy's clothes.

"I wasn't shot. This is Jesse's blood. Please see to him. He's in so much pain."

"Then take this." The nurse removed Amy's police-issue parka and draped her in a heated blanket before walking away.

Amy turned to face the chaos that had already reached fever pitch and saw Jesse's aunt Cora hurrying toward her. She wasn't surprised that Jesse's family was here waiting when the ambulance arrived.

"Oh, my dear." Cora wrapped Amy in a warm embrace and began to weep softly.

Instead of being soothed, Amy found, to her dismay, that she was the one doing the soothing. This sweet old woman had already been through so much with the recent loss of her brother. How she must have suffered over the threat to her beloved nephew.

Framing the old woman's face in her hands, Amy whispered, "Jesse's going to be fine, Aunt Cora."

"I know he's young and strong. But a bullet..."

"You can't think about that. You just have to trust that he's in the best possible hands." Amy wiped Cora's tears with her thumbs and looked toward Cal, who, sensing her discomfort, turned Cora into his arms, where she continued to weep silently against his shoulder.

Wyatt enveloped Amy in a bear hug. "The police are hailing you as a hero."

"Hero?" She gave a long, deep sigh. "All I did was survive. That doesn't make me a hero, Wyatt."

Zane stepped close to wrap her in his arms. "All I know is you and Jesse made it back from hell. That makes you both heroes in my book."

"Oh, Zane. Wyatt." She stepped back and took in a long, deep breath. "I was so scared. And the truth is, I'm still afraid."

"Hey." Zane patted her hand. "Vernon's gone. Rafe, too. There's nothing to be afraid of now."

She shook her head, then lowered her voice so that Cora wouldn't overhear. "It's Jesse. I'm afraid for him. There was so much blood. So much." She dragged in a ragged breath. "He has to be all right. He just has to."

Hearing the thread of panic in her tone, Wyatt and Zane led her away from the others.

"Jesse's going to be just fine, Amy." Wyatt tipped

up her face. "He's always been the toughest McCord of all. Now you just have to believe in him a little longer."

She nodded and swallowed the lump in her throat that felt like a boulder.

"Amy..." At the sound of her father's choked voice she turned.

He was standing alone, apart from the others, staring at her with a look that tugged at her heart.

"Dad." She stepped toward him. "I didn't know you were here."

"Zane brought me. He took me to the McCord ranch first, where we could stay in contact with the state police. As soon as we heard about the shooting, we drove to the clinic. We wanted to go out to Treasure Chest, but they told us you would be brought here. For a minute I thought..." He swallowed and tried again. "I was so afraid you might have been the one shot."

"You must be relieved to know it was Jesse."

"That's not what I meant." He frowned. "But I deserve that. I haven't been fair to him, or to you. I just want you to know..." His voice nearly broke. "I want you to know how much I love you, Amy."

"Oh, Dad." Touched by his admission, she stepped into his arms and he held her to him, his face pressed to her hair, his shoulders shaking slightly as he gave in to the emotion that rolled over him in waves. "I love you, too, Dad. I've always loved you."

It occurred to Amy that she and her father hadn't been this close in years. Even his serious illness hadn't been able to bring them together the way this crisis had.

When he could trust his voice Otis said, "I'm proud of you, girl. So damned proud."

"Thank you." She stayed in his arms for long minutes, reveling in this newly discovered bond.

At last she pushed slightly away, dreading the fact that her next words just might sever their bond. "I need to tell you something, Dad, even though it will hurt you. When I thought I'd lost Jesse, I realized just how much he means to me. What I'm feeling for him is real. I know you'll never approve, but I have to be honest, not only with you, but with myself. I love him, Dad. I'm not going to give him up, even to please you."

"I understand, girl. And I'm grateful for your honesty." He looked away, mulling over what he was about to say. "Maybe it's time I was more honest, too."

Though she wondered at his words, there was no chance to question his meaning. The door opened and Dr. Wheeler strode into their midst.

Everyone flocked around him.

"How is Jesse?" Cora's tone was pleading.

"Jesse's fine. The bullet didn't hit any vital organs. It was fired at such close range, it passed directly through the flesh of his arm. That's why there was so much loss of blood. An entry wound and an exit wound. But he's strong and healthy. He'll be up and moving in no time. In fact, we'll probably send him home tomorrow, if he promises to remain quiet and take the drugs we prescribe."

His gaze skimmed the crowd before he spotted Amy standing with her father. "Amy, Jesse isn't going to give us any peace until he sees you."

While the others hugged and exchanged high fives,

Amy made her way through the crowd and stepped into the examining room.

After the level of noise in the outer room, the quiet seemed a little unnerving.

Amy moved silently toward the examining table.

Jesse lay as still as death. At the sight of him her heart contracted.

As though in church her voice became a whisper. "Jesse?"

His eyes opened. "Oh, Amy. You look so good right now."

He lifted a hand and winced at the sudden, shocking pain.

She caught his hand, holding on for dear life. "How bad is it?"

His words were slow and thick. "Just a twinge now and then. Doc Wheeler has me all shot up with something."

"Then I guess getting shot up is good."

He grinned. "I never thought about that. But yeah, it's nice to have the pain gone. Doc said it'll be back tomorrow with a vengeance. But each day it'll get a little easier. He'll be sending me home tomorrow." He closed his eyes a moment before adding, "You know how good that sounds? Home. For a little while, I doubted I'd ever see home again."

"Shh." She placed a finger on his lips. "Don't talk about it."

When she started to lift her hand away he caught it and pressed it to his lips. His eyes opened and he gave her one of those heart-stopping grins. "My brave, fierce Amy. You were amazing."

She shook her head. "I didn't do a thing. I was so scared, I couldn't even think."

"Baby, you saved my life."

"And you saved mine."

"We're quite the pair." He was still grinning when she suddenly flung herself across his chest and began to weep.

"Hey, now. What's this about? It's all over, Amy."

"Oh, Jesse. I thought you were going to die."

Now that the floodgate had been opened, she couldn't seem to stop the flow. "I didn't even mind so much about my life. But when I thought he'd killed you, something inside me just snapped."

While her tears dampened the front of his hospital gown, Jesse wrapped his good arm around her and held on, content to just lie here holding her close, feeling her heartbeat inside his own chest.

Outside, the din faded as the crowd dispersed and the clinic staff returned to their routine. In Jesse's room, Amy crawled up beside Jesse, needing to feel him warm and safe and alive beside her. The two figures remained locked in each other's arms.

When the door to the examining room opened, Amy looked up, expecting to see Dr. Wheeler. After Jesse had finally fallen asleep, she had pulled a chair alongside his bed, where she could sit and hold his hand without disturbing his rest. She'd had this desperate need to remain connected with him, afraid to let go for even a moment.

As her father advanced toward the bed, Jesse's eyes snapped open.

"Sorry to wake you." Otis cleared his throat. "Doc says you're going to be fine."

Jesse nodded.

Amy looked over. "You should go home, Dad, and get some sleep. You'll need to be back here later today for another treatment."

"I know. Zane's waiting out there to drive me home whenever I'm ready. And he said for you not to worry about bringing me into town for my treatment. He'll pick me up."

Amy felt a wave of relief, mingled with surprise. When had her father begun to accept help from a McCord?

"Then why...?"

He stopped her with a lift of his palm. "I need to talk to Jesse. Alone."

Amy was already shaking her head. "He's been through too much..."

Jesse squeezed her hand. "It's okay. I'll bet you could use some coffee."

"I don't want..."

She saw the quick shake of his head and gave a sigh. "I guess I could use some caffeine."

Otis watched until she stepped out of the room before turning to Jesse with a long, deep sigh. "All her life, Amy has always been scrupulously honest, even when she was telling me things she knew I didn't want to hear. It was her most infuriating quality. But I've always secretly admired her for it. Now I owe her the same honesty." He walked closer. "I'm the one who sabotaged your romance years ago."

Jesse shrugged, though it cost him. "You had a right

to want to protect your daughter from someone you considered an enemy."

"That's what I told myself. But no matter how I try to justify what I did, it was still wrong."

"As I recall, it was Amy who left me right after graduation without a word, sir. Not you."

"Amy never left you, Jesse."

Jesse blinked.

"As you know, my wife's youngest sister, who lived in Helena, called to say she'd been diagnosed with a... terminal illness. Much like mine." He clenched and unclenched his fists, the only sign of his agitation. "So Amy agreed to go to Helena with her mother. They left in such a hurry, there was no time for her to let you know, so she left a letter for you in the mailbox."

Jesse frowned. "A letter? That's what she was trying to tell me in the barn. I never got a..."

"I took it out of the mailbox. It was a long, passionate letter, which I read. And then destroyed. When you came to my ranch looking for Amy, I shamelessly lied and told you she'd gone for good, that she wanted to sever all ties with you before starting a new life at college. And when she complained about having never heard from you, I told her that you'd been seen all over town with other girls." He heaved another sigh. "I told a string of lies, and they had the desired effect. You ended up hating Amy for leaving without a word, and Amy was hurt and angry with you for never answering her letter, and never making an effort to contact her, all the while seeing other girls."

Jesse was silent for so long, Otis hung his head. "I realize there's no way for you and Amy to get those years back. I'm truly sorry. And I know there's no way to make amends. I'm just relieved to learn that my daughter still loves you, as she said, whether I like it or not."

"She told you that?"

Otis nodded. "She did."

"It had to be hard for you to tell me all this."

Otis shrugged. "I thought it would be, but the funny thing is, I feel better now. I know it's too much to ask you to forgive me, but I'm still glad I finally did the right thing. I'm only sorry it took me so long."

"So am I." Jesse extended his hand. "I accept your apology, Otis. And I hope that someday you can accept my friendship and that of my family."

Otis stared for long moments at Jesse's hand before shaking it. "After what happened tonight, I'd be a fool to hang on to all those old hostilities. You and your family treated me like a neighbor, and not as the enemy. If you're willing, I'd like...I'd like to be your friend."

Jesse studied the older man's bowed head. "If you're willing, Otis, I'd like to be something more."

As Otis shot him a questioning look, Jesse added, "It would please me to be your son-in-law. In case you haven't noticed, I've never stopped loving your daughter. And I intend to ask her to marry me, if that meets with your approval."

The door fell inward with such force, Amy nearly stumbled. "Did he give his approval?"

The two men looked over at her and she felt her cheeks redden. "Okay, I admit it. I was listening at the door." She advanced on her father, hands on her hips. "You read my letter to Jesse and then burned it? And let me believe all these years that he didn't care about me?"

"Now, girl..."

"Don't you 'now, girl' me. I want you to know how many tears I shed, how much pain your lies..."

Taking pity on the old man, Jesse moaned. "Amy. Help me."

At once both Amy and her father gathered around the bed.

"Where does it hurt?" Amy demanded.

"Here." Jesse touched a hand to his chest.

She moved his hand away. "Maybe you've opened up your stitches."

"It isn't that."

"Maybe you need another shot for pain."

"Not that either." He caught her hand and placed it over his heart. "This is where I hurt."

"Your heart?" She looked terrified.

"Yeah. I think there's only one cure."

"What?"

"You have to agree to marry me."

She stepped back. "Jesse, this isn't funny."

"I agree. It's deadly serious. Now, you need to stop fighting with your father long enough to give me an answer. I've already accepted his apology, and he's given his approval. All we need now to make it final is your answer."

She glanced at her father, who was smiling. "You... actually approve?"

He nodded.

She turned to Jesse, who winked.

"Oh, Jesse." She leaned down to brush a kiss over his mouth. "I never could resist that charm."

"I was counting on it." As she started to straighten, he cupped a hand around her head and drew her back for another kiss. "Wait. You didn't answer me. Will you marry me, Amy?"

"Yes. Oh, yes. Yes, a million times yes."

"I think that was a yes." He winked at her father. "It will mean that you won't be able to return to Helena to teach."

She gave him a wide smile. "Then it looks like I'll have to find some students around here. Or maybe we could have a few of our own to teach."

Jesse couldn't think of anything he'd like better. "You know we were destined to be together, don't you?"

"There were times when I wasn't at all certain of it. But now, I know for a fact that this is our destiny."

Then they were laughing together, and kissing, and whispering words that only they could hear.

As Otis walked from the room he saw Wyatt and Zane standing in the open doorway, watching the scene and straining to hear every word.

Wyatt slapped Otis on the back, while Zane pumped his hand.

"Welcome to the family," they called in unison.

"Let's get you home," Zane said.

Wyatt held the door. "Looks like we've got a wedding to prepare for, neighbor."

EPILOGUE

———◆———

Otis Parrish turned at the sound of Amy's bedroom door opening. His eyes widened. "Are you wearing that to the wedding?"

She glanced down at her faded jeans and denim shirt. "You think, just because you're wearing that fancy suit, these aren't good enough?"

He caught sight of the long plastic bag hanging over her door and felt a wave of relief. "Okay, I get it. You're going to dress at the McCord ranch."

"I don't want to arrive all wrinkled. I'll dress in Jesse's suite just before the ceremony." She tossed him the keys. "Now that you've finished your treatments, you can drive." She took up the heavy bag. "And I'll just sit back and try to remember to breathe."

He paused and touched a hand to her cheek. "Things will probably get too crazy later, so I'd like to say this now. I'm proud of you, girl. For the way you took care of me through this...thing." Though the doctor had told him he was in remission, he still couldn't talk about his illness. "And for the way you handled Rafe Spindler and that cowardly lawyer's attack."

She closed a hand over his. "Thanks, Dad. And I'm proud of you for admitting the truth to Jesse."

"Took me long enough."

"Better late than never. You won't mind that I'll be living on the McCord ranch?"

He shrugged. "Whither thou goest, and all that. Besides, I've already been enjoying the benefits of being on the good side of that family. They really know how to treat their friends. Orley Peterson delivered our grain free of charge."

Amy arched a brow. "Did he say why?"

"He said since he was delivering to the McCord ranch, our place wasn't out of his way. I guess he sees us as part of their family now, and he doesn't want to offend his biggest clients."

"Don't let it go to your head."

"I'll do my best to remain humble."

As Amy opened the passenger door, her father put a hand on her arm. "I keep thinking how much your mother would have loved this day. You do her proud, Amy girl."

Her eyes brimmed. "Thanks, Dad."

Her heart felt lighter than air as they headed toward the Lost Nugget.

Wyatt, Zane, and Jesse stood in the middle of the great room, staring around as the florist delivered a dozen different vases and urns filled with roses, lilies, and trailing ivy.

"The place looks and smells like a damned greenhouse."

At Wyatt's remark, the three of them shared a laugh.

Dandy was shouting orders to the cowboys he'd coaxed to be his assistants as they set up steam tables for the buffet to be served in the dining room.

A hairdresser had his assistants running up and down the stairs as he sent them out to his van at least half a dozen different times to fetch gels, lotions, sprays.

A seamstress from town was making last-minute repairs on dresses and searching frantically for an iron and ironing board.

Wyatt watched it all with a look of astonishment. "Is there some kind of crazy rule that says all women have to go overboard for weddings?"

"Looks that way." Zane slapped Jesse on the back. "Just think, cuz. The whole town, in fact, half the state of Montana, is thriving this weekend, getting rich quick, and all because of you."

Jesse merely grinned. "I'm happy to make them all rich, as long as they make my bride happy." He lowered his voice. "I've got to see Amy. Just for a minute. Then I'll meet you outside. You know where."

Wyatt exchanged a look with Zane. "We'll be there."

Cora heard a chorus of laughter in the hallway and peered out her bedroom door. Daffy and Vi were just walking toward her, with the seamstress following behind.

"Well?" Daffy paused to pose, her hand on her hip. "What do you think of the gowns Amy picked out for us?"

"They're lovely." Cora looked from Daffy, in bright crimson, with a scooped neck and slit in the ankle-length skirt that displayed a great deal of leg, to Vi, in palest pink, with a scalloped neckline and flirty, ruffled hem. "And they suit each of you perfectly."

"Our Amy is one sly girl. When she asked us both to be her maids of honor, we nearly fainted."

"I'm so glad she asked you. You've been good friends of hers through good times and bad. And when her mother died, you two made a difference in her life."

"It's easy to be a friend to someone like Amy. I surely do love that girl." Nerves caused Violet's voice to be even softer and breathier than usual. "I just hope I don't faint halfway through the ceremony."

"Maybe you ought to," Daffy said in her rusty voice. "With those gorgeous cowboys Wyatt and Zane standing with us, I just might pretend to faint myself, just so I can be scooped up in those strong, muscled arms."

While they shared a throaty laugh, Daffy glanced at her watch. "We'd better hurry. The bride's waiting for us to help her into her gown." She paused. "Miss Cora, Amy will want you to see her as soon as she's dressed."

"Just call me when she's ready." Cora watched them dance away and returned to her room to finish slipping into her shoes.

A short time later she heard the knock on her door.

"Miss Cora?" Amy stepped into the room, wearing a strapless wedding gown of white silk that fell in a fluid line to her ankles. Her hair was worn long and loose. At her ears were the diamond earrings that Jesse had insisted on buying her for an engagement gift.

"Oh, my." Cora put a hand to her throat. "Amy, honey, you're just about the most beautiful bride I've ever seen."

"Thank you." Amy held out a white satin box. "This is for you."

"For me? Why?"

"Since my mother isn't here to share this day with me, I'd like you to be my honorary mother."

"Oh, Amy." Cora's eyes swam with sudden tears. "You and Jesse will always be like my own children." She opened the box and stared at the double strand of perfect pearls with a small, jeweled clasp.

She turned to hide her tears. "Will you fasten this for me?"

Amy drew the pearls around her throat and closed the clasp.

Cora studied her reflection in the mirror. It was the perfect accessory for the pale pearl silk gown she'd chosen. "I love them. You know I'll cherish them always, just as I'll always cherish you as my own."

"Thank you. I guess I should call you Aunt Cora now." Amy softly kissed the old woman's cheek, while Daffy and Vi looked on.

At a knock on the door Daffy hurried over to find Jesse just about to enter.

She stepped up to block his way. "You can't see the bride before the ceremony."

"Daffy, do you want to live to see another day?" Jesse's eyes looked as hot and fierce as if he were facing another gunman.

Violet giggled like a schoolgirl. "I think, sister, you'd better let the man in."

Daffy turned. "Amy?"

Amy nodded.

Daffy stepped aside and Jesse started in, then halted in midstride when he caught sight of the vision in white.

Seeing the look that passed between Amy and Jesse, Cora walked to the door and motioned for the other two to follow. When she pulled the door closed, neither Jesse nor Amy noticed. They had eyes for only each other.

Amy walked to him and lifted a hand to his cheek. "What's wrong?"

"Nothing. Not a single thing is wrong now." He let out a long, deep sigh. "It's all so right." He caught her hand between both of his and lifted it to his lips. "Do you know how much I love you?"

"Not as much as I love you."

"How did we get so lucky?"

"The fates were kind."

"Remind me to thank them later. For now…" He leaned close and brushed a soft, butterfly kiss on her lips.

There was a knock on the door and Violet called, "Amy, honey, we need time to finish in there."

Amy laid a hand on Jesse's cheek. "You need to get downstairs."

"I'll be there waiting." He started to walk away, then turned back. "I almost forgot. Carry this with your bouquet."

She looked at the keychain he handed her. "A rainbow?"

"It was Coot's. I always carry it for good luck. I figure today, getting you as my wife, I've already had more than my share."

Amy felt a mist of tears and tucked the rainbow into her pretty nosegay of white roses and trailing ivy. "For luck. Maybe it will bring us closer to the treasure."

He paused. "You realize that the search will earn you a lot of nasty jokes in town. Folks will say we're both crazy."

"I know that. Isn't that what they always said about Coot? But I intend to continue helping you search for the treasure. Folks can say anything they want, as long as I know you love me."

"I always have. I always will." He tucked a strand of hair behind her ear. "I'll leave you alone with the women for now. I'll see you in front of the preacher. I can't wait to start our life together."

Together. It was, Jesse thought as he started down the stairs and past the smiling guests, just about the happiest word in the world. And no threat, no mythical curse, could have any power over the two of them, as long as they were together.

Outside, the snow fell like a thick, white curtain. In the distance, hovering just above the peaks of Treasure Chest, hung a shimmering rainbow.

Jesse paused to look at it, then, grinning, started toward the small plot of land that his grandfather had considered sacred ground.

"Hey, cuz." Wyatt's long hair flowed over the collar of the leather duster he wore over his tuxedo, giving him the look of a cowboy straight out of the Old West.

As Jesse stepped into the small, fenced gravesite of their grandfather, Zane held up a bottle of fine Irish whiskey. "I figure you might want some of this for courage."

Jesse shook his head. He'd pulled on a sheepskin parka against the snowfall. "It doesn't take any courage to marry the girl of your dreams. Frankly, I can't wait."

"What I can't wait for"—Zane, wearing a denim jacket over his tux, grinned—"is for the formal part of the ceremony to be over so we can enjoy all that great food Dandy's been cooking for days. Have you smelled that kitchen?"

The three men were laughing as Cal Randall walked up, a small wooden box tucked under his arm. He opened it and began passing around cigars, cupping his hands around a flame while each of them puffed, until the air was redolent with the rich fragrance of tobacco.

While Zane brought out one of his video cameras and began filming, Wyatt filled four tumblers with whiskey and handed them around.

"Zane and I thought this was the right time to tell you that our grace period is up. We've decided to stick around for good and continue the search for the treasure."

Jesse looked from Zane to Wyatt. "You're both crazy. You know that?"

They chuckled, low and deep in their throats.

"It's a family trait," Wyatt said with a laugh.

"Yeah." Jesse offered a handshake to each of them. "Thanks. I know I behaved like a real jerk when you first came here."

"Now that you mention it..." Wyatt and Zane shared a laugh.

Jesse joined them. "I couldn't have said this a short time ago, but I'm really glad you're staying. I feel as though I got my best friends back."

They stood, cigars in hand, and lifted their glasses while Cal said, "Your grandfather would be a happy man today. And not just because it's your wedding day, Jesse." He cleared his throat and stared around at the three cousins. "Coot spent a lifetime searching for his family's treasure. But he made no secret of the fact that he considered his family the greatest treasure of all. When your daddies left and took part of his family away, they took part of his heart, too. I think now, finally seeing his family reunited, and willing to take up his search, he'd be the happiest man around."

Jesse's voice became solemn. "Here's to Coot."

"To Coot." The others lifted their glasses before drinking.

Jesse fought the lump in his throat as he intoned Coot's favorite words. "Life's all about the road ahead. What's past is past. Here's to what's around the bend, boys."

For long moments the only sound was the sighing of the wind as snow fell around them.

"Here's to you and Amy, Jesse." Wyatt lifted his glass. "You've been through tough times together. Here's hoping the road will be a little smoother around the next bend."

They drained their glasses and headed toward the ranch house.

Cal remained at the grave, watching the three cousins, tall, rugged, handsome, hearing their voices, their laughter, carried on the breeze.

He lifted his glass. "You did it, you old son of a bitch. You did the impossible. You brought them together by the sheer force of your will. Now you'd better see to it that they succeed in finding that treasure."

He downed his drink in one long swallow. "Here's to what's around the bend, my friend."

Then, shaking the snow from his wide-brimmed hat, he pulled it low on his head and made his way to the house to celebrate this memorable day with this remarkable family.

MONTANA
DESTINY

To my beautiful daughter, Mary Margaret

And to her beautiful daughters, Caitlin, Ally, Taylor, Isabella, and Maggie

And, of course, to Tom, my fearless protector

And a special thank you to Gary Fitzsimmons for his generosity in sharing his valuable expertise in the field of emergency responders.

PROLOGUE

Gold Fever, Montana—1992

Hang on, Clint." Twelve-year-old Wyatt McCord hung
on the wooden fence at the town's rodeo grounds, shouting
encouragement to the cowboy fighting to stay in the saddle
of the meanest bucking bronco on the rodeo circuit.

Beside him, his cousins, Jesse and Zane, watched wide-
eyed as the rider was tossed high in the air before landing
facedown in the dirt. While two cowboys in clown cos-
tumes distracted the crazed animal, a handler hustled the
cowboy through a gate to safety.

"Wow!" Eleven-year-old Zane looked properly impressed.
"Did you see how close he came to being trampled?"

"He didn't stick long enough to qualify." Wyatt couldn't
hide his scorn.

"You think you could?" Jesse, at fourteen the oldest of
the three, shot his cousin a knowing look.

"Maybe not now. But I bet a couple of years from now,
I'll do better'n old Clint."

Jesse spit in the dirt, the way he'd seen his grandfather's wranglers do along the trail. "I'll take that bet. A couple of years from now." He shared a grin with Zane. "And I'm betting we'll be picking you up out of the dirt and hauling you home in pieces."

"Not me. Haven't you heard? I'm Superman." Wyatt watched as the next cowboy climbed atop the rail, preparing to drop into the saddle when the gate opened. "I figure if I'm going to carry on Coot's name, I'd better be good at everything I try. Especially in this town."

"Why bother?" Jesse looked around at the sea of faces in town for the annual rodeo, completely unaware of the cluster of preteen girls who watched from a distance, sighing over him and his cousins. "They all figure our grandpa's crazy anyway. Why should we bother trying to impress them?"

"It's not about them." Wyatt turned away from the railing as yet another cowboy bit the dust.

His two cousins followed.

The three cousins looked more like brothers, with the same dark, curly hair and the McCord laughing blue eyes. They and their families shared the sprawling ranch house that was home to three generations of McCords. Homeschooled, they were best friends. Their bond, forged since birth, was wide and deep.

"It's about proving to Grandpa that we don't feel the same way as the folks here in town do. They might call him a crazy old coot, but we know better. Our ancestor's treasure really is out there somewhere. And we've got to be stronger, and smarter, so that when the day comes that we can join Coot in his search, we'll be ready."

Zane stopped and studied the booth selling corn dogs

and chili fries. "I'd be a whole lot stronger and smarter with a couple of those."

Laughing, the three pooled their money and invested in as many dogs and fries as they could afford.

They sat cross-legged in the shade and polished off their lunch, believing, with all the innocence of youth, that the only life they'd ever known could not possibly end, even though the fabric of their family had already begun to unravel. All three of them had heard voices, often late at night, raised in protest. Grumblings about too much togetherness. Complaints about the restrictions of ranch life. Coot's once-loyal sons were being asked to choose between a father's lifelong search for lost treasure and the needs of wives who yearned for a future far from the Montana wilderness.

Unknown to these three carefree boys, this would be the last rodeo they would share for many years to come.

CHAPTER ONE

***

Present Day

W yatt." Amy McCord turned to watch as her husband's cousin paused at one of the food booths set up at the rodeo grounds. "You've already had two corn dogs. Don't tell me you're buying another one."

"All right. I won't tell you." Despite his faded denims and scuffed boots, with his hair blowing in the wind, Wyatt McCord looked more like an eternal surfer than a cowboy. "But I can't get enough of these." He took a big bite, closed his eyes on a sigh, and polished off the corn dog in three bites.

Wiping his hands down his jeans he caught up with his cousins, Jesse and Zane, and Jesse's bride, Amy.

Their grandfather's funeral had brought the cousins together after years of separation. Now the three had begun to resolve years of old differences and were quickly becoming the same inseparable friends they'd been in their childhood.

Wyatt glanced around. "Where did all these people come from? It looks like half of Montana is here."

Jesse grinned. "Gold Fever might be a small town, but when it's rodeo time, every cowboy worth his spurs makes it here. In the past couple of years it's become one of the best in the West."

The four paused at the main corral, where a cowboy was roping a calf. While they hung on the rail and marveled at his skill, Zane whipped out his ever-present video camera to film the action. During his years in California he'd worked with famed director Steven Michaelson filming an award-winning documentary on wild mustangs. Now he'd become obsessed with making a documentary of life in Montana, featuring their ongoing search for a treasure stolen from their ancestors over a hundred years ago.

The search had consumed their grandfather's entire adult life, causing the people who knew him to give him the nickname Crazy Old Coot. He'd embraced the name, and in his will, he'd managed to entice his three grandsons to take up his search, no matter where it might lead them.

Jesse looked over at a holding pen, where riders were drawing numbers for the bull-riding contest. "There's one you ought to try, cuz." He laughed at Wyatt's arched brow. "It doesn't take just skill, but a really hard head to survive."

"Not to mention balls of steel," Zane remarked while keeping his focus on the action in the ring.

Wyatt merely grinned. "Piece of cake."

Jesse couldn't resist. He reached into his pocket and withdrew a roll of bills. "Twenty says you can't stick in the saddle for more than ten seconds."

"Make it a hundred and I'll take that bet."

Jesse threw back his head and roared. "Cuz, you couldn't stay on a bull's back for a thousand."

"Is it a bet?" Wyatt sent him a steely look.

"Damned straight. My hundred calls your bluff."

Wyatt turned to Zane. "You're my witness. And you might want to film this. I doubt I'll offer to do a repeat."

Without waiting for a reply he sauntered away and approached the cluster of cowboys eyeing the bulls.

Half an hour later, wearing a number on his back and having parted with the fifty-dollar entry fee, he stood with the others and waited his turn to ride a bull.

While he watched the action in the ring he noticed the ambulance parked just outside the ring. In case any fool wasn't already aware of the danger, that brought home the point. But it wasn't the emergency vehicle that caught his attention; it was the woman standing beside it. There was no way he could mistake those long, long legs encased in lean denims, or that mass of fiery hair spilling over her shoulders and framing the prettiest face he'd ever seen. Marilee Trainor had been the first woman to catch Wyatt's eye the moment he got back in town scant months ago. He'd seen her dozens of times since, but she'd always managed to slip away before he'd had time to engage her in conversation.

Not this time, he thought with a wicked grin.

"McCord." A voice behind him had him turning.

"You're up. You drew number nine."

A chorus of nervous laughter greeted that announcement, followed by a round of relieved voices.

"Rather you than me, cowboy."

"Man, I'm sure glad I ducked that bullet."

"I hope your life insurance is paid up."

Wyatt studied the bull snorting and kicking its hind legs against the confining pen, sending a shudder through the entire ring of spectators. If he didn't know better, Wyatt would have sworn he'd seen fire coming out of the bull's eyes.

"What's his name?" He climbed the wood slats and prepared to drop into the saddle atop the enraged animal's back.

"Devil. And believe me, sonny, he lives up to it." The grizzled old cowboy handed Wyatt the lead rope and watched while he twisted it around and around his hand before dropping into the saddle.

In the same instant the gate was opened, and bull and rider stormed into the center ring to a chorus of shouts and cries and whistles from the crowd.

Devil jerked, twisted, kicked, and even crashed headlong into the boards in an attempt to dislodge its hated rider. For his part, Wyatt had no control over his body as it left the saddle, suspended in midair, before snapping forward and back like a rag doll, all the while remaining connected by the tenuous rope coiled around his hand.

Though it lasted only eight seconds, it was the longest ride of his life.

When the bullhorn signaled that he'd met the qualifying time, he struggled to gather his wits, waiting until Devil was right alongside the gate before he freed his hand, cutting himself loose. He flew through the air and over the corral fence, landing in the dirt at Marilee Trainor's feet.

"My God! Don't move." She was beside him in the blink of an eye, kneeling in the dirt, probing for broken bones.

Wyatt lay perfectly still, enjoying the feel of those clever, practiced hands moving over him. When she moved from his legs to his torso and arms, he opened his eyes to narrow slits and watched her from beneath lowered lids.

She was the perfect combination of beauty and brains. He could see the wheels turning as she did a thorough exam. Even her brow, furrowed in concentration, couldn't mar that flawless complexion. Her eyes, the color of the palest milk chocolate, were narrowed in thought. Strands of red hair dipped over one cheek, giving her a sultry look.

Satisfied that nothing was broken, she sat back on her heels, feeling a moment of giddy relief. That was when she realized that he was staring.

She waved a hand before his eyes. "How many fingers can you see?"

"Four fingers and a thumb. Or should I say four beautiful, long, slender fingers and one perfect thumb, connected to one perfect arm of one perfectly gorgeous female? And, I'm happy to add, there's no ring on the third finger of that hand."

She caught the smug little grin on his lips. Her tone hardened. "I get it. A showboat. I should have known. I don't have time to waste on some silver-tongued actor."

"Why, thank you. I had no idea you'd examined my tongue. Mind if I examine yours?"

She started to stand but his hand shot out, catching her by the wrist. "Sorry. That was really cheesy, but I couldn't resist teasing you."

His tone altered, deepened, just enough to have her glancing over to see if he was still teasing.

He met her look. "Are you always this serious?"

Despite his apology, she wasn't about to let him off the

hook, or change her mind about him. "In case you haven't noticed, rodeos are a serious business. Careless cowboys tend to break bones, or even their skulls, as hard as that may be to believe."

She stared down at the hand holding her wrist. Despite his smile, she could feel the strength in his grip. If he wanted to, he could no doubt break her bones with a single snap. But she wasn't concerned with his strength, only with the heat his touch was generating. She felt the tingle of warmth all the way up her arm. It alarmed her more than she cared to admit.

"My job is to minimize damage to anyone who is actually hurt."

"I'm grateful." He sat up so his laughing blue eyes were even with hers. If possible, his were even bluer than the perfect Montana sky above them. "What do you think? Any damage from that fall?"

Her instinct was to move back, but his fingers were still around her wrist, holding her close. "I'm beginning to wonder if you were actually tossed from that bull or deliberately fell."

"I'd have to be a little bit crazy to deliberately jump from the back of a raging bull just to get your attention, wouldn't I?"

"Yeah." She felt the pull of that magnetic smile that had so many of the local females lusting after Wyatt McCord. Now she knew why he'd gained such a reputation in such a short time. "I'm beginning to think maybe you are. In fact, more than a little. A whole lot crazy."

"I figured it was the best possible way to get you to actually talk to me. You couldn't ignore me as long as there was even the slightest chance that I might be hurt."

There was enough romance in her nature to feel flattered that he'd go to so much trouble just to arrange to meet her. At least, she thought, it was original. And just dangerous enough to appeal to a certain wild-and-free spirit that dominated her own life.

Then her practical side kicked in, and she felt an irrational sense of annoyance that he'd wasted so much of her time and energy on his weird idea of a joke.

"Oh, brother." She scrambled to her feet and dusted off her backside.

"Want me to do that for you?"

She paused and shot him a look guaranteed to freeze most men.

He merely kept that charming smile in place. "Mind if we start over?" He held out his hand. "Wyatt McCord."

"I know who you are."

"Okay. I'll handle both introductions. Nice to meet you, Marilee Trainor. Now that we have that out of the way, when do you get off work?"

"Not until the last bull rider has finished."

"Want to grab a bite to eat? When the last rider is done, of course."

"Sorry. I'll be heading home."

"Why, thanks for the invitation. I'd be happy to join you. We could take along some pizza from one of the vendors."

She looked him up and down. "I go home alone."

"Sorry to hear it." There was that grin again, doing strange things to her heart. "You're missing out on a really fun evening."

"You have a high opinion of yourself, McCord."

He chuckled. Without warning he touched a finger to

her lips. "Trust me. I'd do my best to turn that pretty little frown into an even prettier smile."

Marilee couldn't believe the feelings that collided along her spine. Splinters of fire and ice had her fighting to keep from shivering despite the broiling sun.

Because she didn't trust her voice, she merely turned on her heel and walked away from him.

It was harder to do than she'd expected. And though she kept her spine rigid and her head high, she swore she could feel the heat of that gaze burning right through her flesh.

It sent one more furnace blast rushing through her system. A system already overheated by her encounter with the bold, brash, irritatingly charming Wyatt McCord.

"A hundred bucks, cuz. And judging by that spectacular toss over the rail, I'd say you earned it."

Wyatt tucked the money into his pocket. "It was pretty spectacular, wasn't it? And it worked. It got the attention of our pretty little medic."

Jesse, Amy, and Zane stopped dead in their tracks.

Amy laughed. "You did all that to get Lee's attention?"

"Nothing else I've tried has worked. I was desperate."

Jesse shook his head in disbelief. "Did you ever think about just buying her a beer at the Fortune Saloon? I'd think that would be a whole lot simpler than risking broken bones leaping off a bull."

"But not nearly as memorable. The next time she sees me at the saloon, she'll know my name."

Zane threw back his head and roared. "So will every shrink from here to Helena. You have to be certifiably nuts to do all that just for the sake of a pretty face."

"Hey." Wyatt slapped his cousin on the back. "Whatever works."

Zane pulled out a roll of bills. "Ten says she's already written you off as someone to avoid at all costs."

Wyatt's smile brightened. "Chump change. If you want to bet me, make it a hundred."

"You got it." Zane pulled a hundred from the roll and handed it to Jesse. "Now match it, cuz. I was going to bet that you can't persuade Marilee Trainor to even speak to you again. But just to make things interesting, I'm betting that you can't get her to have dinner with you tonight."

"Dinner? Tonight? Now you're pushing the limits, cuz. She's already refused me."

"Put up or shut up."

Wyatt arched a brow. "You want me to kiss and tell?"

"I don't say anything about kissing. I don't care what you do, after you get her to have dinner with you. That's the bet. So if you're ready to admit defeat, just give me the hundred now."

"Uh-oh." Wyatt stopped dead in his tracks. "Is that a dare?"

Amy stood between them, shaking her head. "You sound like two little kids."

Wyatt shot her a wicked grin. "Didn't you know that all men are just boys at heart?"

He reached into his pocket and handed Zane a bill before he strolled away.

Over his shoulder he called, "I'll catch you back at the ranch. You can pay me then."

He left his cousins laughing and shaking their heads.

CHAPTER TWO

———— ❖ ————

Marilee stepped from the shower and turbaned her hair in a towel before slathering her fair skin with lotion. After toweling her hair she stepped into a pair of boy-style boxer shorts and tied a cotton shirt at her midriff.

Leaving her damp hair streaming down her back in a riot of tangles, she padded barefoot to the tiny kitchen of her apartment and set a kettle on for tea. After rummaging through the refrigerator, she decided her supper would have to be a peanut butter and jelly sandwich. She was too tired to bother with a grilled cheese. That would require taking out a pan, turning on the burner, and watching to see that she didn't burn it. Too much wasted energy.

While she waited for the water to boil, she sank down onto a barstool at the tiny kitchen counter. It had been a good day. Except for a run to Dr. Wheeler's clinic with an out-of-towner who needed stitches, there'd been no serious injuries. No broken bones. No head injuries. During rodeo time, this was considered a very good day indeed.

Rodeo. The very word had her smiling. She loved the sights and sounds and smells of the fairgrounds. Reveled in the people and animals and pageantry. Like the men and women who followed the circuit, she appreciated the athletic ability required to win an event. The professionals were superb athletes. But she also enjoyed the pure freedom expressed by the ordinary cowboys who showed up year after year just to compete with fellow wranglers. Not for fame, or money, or trophies, but for the pure love of the sport.

She loved mingling with the men and women who spent their lives doing the backbreaking work required to keep a ranch going. These were the people to whom rodeo meant the most. The same men and women who competed in hog-tying, calf-roping, and bull-riding for sport did the same thing all year on their ranches, not for sport but out of necessity. They honed their skills in the real world, far away from the glamour of these few days in the limelight.

In many ways this lifestyle was far removed from the life she'd lived growing up. Maybe that was why Gold Fever satisfied her so. After a lifetime of enduring the strict military code that had colored her childhood, she felt as though she'd somehow stepped into an alternate universe, where the only rules were those she set for herself.

She loved being in charge. Loved choosing the path less traveled by most of her friends. As a girl forced to pull up stakes at a moment's notice, she'd dreamed of putting down roots and staying long enough to really know the people around her. Though many of the ranchers in these parts rarely made the long drive to town, they always remembered her name and offered their hands in friendship. These were good, hardworking people, and she felt fortunate to live among them and call them friends.

When the kettle whistled, she sighed and heaved herself to her feet. Before she could reach it, there was a knock on the door.

While she tried to decide which one to deal with, there was a second knock. Curiosity won out, and she chose to ignore the kettle and see who was at her door at this late hour.

After peering through the tiny hole, she opened the door. "What are you . . . ? How did you find out where I live?"

"This is Gold Fever, remember? Everybody knows everything about everybody. I could have asked a dozen people, and they'd all know that Marilee Trainor lives in the apartment above the emergency medical garage on Nugget Street in downtown Gold Fever." Wyatt brushed past her and placed a cardboard box on the kitchen counter.

She barely remembered to close the door before following him. "Just a minute. I don't recall inviting you in."

"You didn't. I invited myself."

She stared at the box. "Is that pizza?"

"It is. But if you'd like me to leave . . ." He picked up the box and made a move to go.

"Wait." Without thinking, she put a hand on his arm. And became instantly aware of the ripple of muscle beneath the shirt sleeve.

He paused. "Hungry?"

Relieved to let go of him, she put a hand to her middle. "Starving. But I was too tired to do much about it."

He reached over and lifted the whistling teakettle off

the burner. "That's piercing. How can you stand it?" He turned to her. "Now, what were you saying? Did I hear you say 'Come on in, Wyatt'? 'I'm so thankful that you came along just in time to save me from starvation'?"

Though she wanted to laugh at his silly sense of humor, she managed to stop herself just in time. "I told you I wanted to be alone."

"And you will be. I'm leaving. Right after you guess what's on the pizza."

"I don't play games."

"Your loss. Try to guess anyway."

"Why don't I just peek?"

As she reached for the lid he put a hand over hers. "First, tell me what you like."

There it was again. That sizzle of electricity from the mere touch of him. "All right. I'll play along. But just to get you moving toward the door. The only things I like on my pizza are sausage, mushrooms, green pepper, and onion."

"Your wish . . ." He lifted the lid and she stared in surprise.

"Who told you?" Before he could say a word, she held up a hand. "Never mind. As you said, this is Gold Fever. Ask half the town what I like on my pizza, and they could probably tell you."

"Or, I could be a really gifted mind reader."

She couldn't hold back the laughter. "You could be. But I'll stick with door number one. What's in the bag?"

"Wine." He lifted it from the slim bag and pulled a corkscrew from his pocket.

At her arched brow, he grinned. "Just in case you didn't have one."

"My my. What a handyman. You do think of every-thing, don't you?"

"I try. Glasses?"

"You're assuming that I'm inviting you to stay."

"I'm assuming that you're as hungry as I am, and that the smell of this pizza is driving you crazy."

"You're right." She pointed to the cupboard above the stove. "The glasses are there."

He filled two stem glasses and handed one to her before leading her to the little sofa across the room.

"Here. Put your feet up. You've put in a long day."

"I have. And I will." She propped her feet on a little footstool and lifted the glass to her lips.

In his best Anthony Hopkins imitation, Wyatt purred, "A nice little glass of Chianti to go with the fava beans and the body I'm about to cut up for you."

She was still laughing as he rummaged in her cupboards and found two plates. Minutes later he settled himself beside her, and they ate and drank in companionable silence.

"Oh." Marilee sat back with a sigh. "I can't even tell you what that tasted like. I think I inhaled it."

"I know what you mean." Wyatt filled their plates a second time and topped off their glasses. "Now we can actually take our time and enjoy."

She did. And then followed up with a third slice of pizza before sitting back with a sigh of satisfaction while sipping her wine.

She glanced over. "I should be mad. I told you I wanted to be alone."

"Okay. I can take a hint." He started to get up. "I'll leave you now."

"Too late." She put a hand on his arm. "I've already accepted your hospitality. Now I invite you to accept mine."

He turned to her with a smile. "I was hoping you'd say that."

She studied him, from the wild mane of dark hair to the scuffed boots propped up beside her bare feet on the hassock. "Are you always so pushy, McCord?"

"What you call pushy, others might call confident."

"A rose by any other name . . ."

"Is what you remind me of."

She blinked at his sudden change of direction.

Before she could say a word he merely smiled. "One of those pale English roses, all cool and pink, with drops of dew still on the petals." He leaned close and breathed her in. "You smell like crushed roses."

"Body lotion." Her heart was hammering, and that knowledge had color rising to her cheeks. Damn him.

"I smelled you as soon as I walked in. You had my head swimming."

There was that smile again. She'd have called it cocky, except that it was beginning to grow on her. Or else she was a lot more tired than she realized. No energy left to fight. Yeah. That was the reason.

"I'll give you this, McCord. You certainly know how to think on your feet. I'm betting you've managed to use that line to get all kinds of girls to do your bidding."

"It's a curse, but I've learned to endure it." He topped off her glass and then his own. "Would you like me to start some coffee?"

"Not this late. The caffeine will have me tossing and turning all night long."

"Okay." He crossed one ankle over the other and leaned

his head back against the back of the sofa. "I like your place. It looks like you."

"All prim and tidy?"

"I was going to say fascinating." He pointed to the exotic piece of silk displayed in a simple black-lacquered frame hanging on the opposite wall, and the ornate shelves displaying a collection of Oriental masks and woven baskets. "Looks like you've done some traveling."

She nodded. "An Army brat. I never stayed in one school long enough to learn my classmates' names. My father said I was getting a better education than all those kids who lived in one town all their lives."

"That's one way of looking at it. How'd you end up in Gold Fever?"

She shrugged, uncomfortable talking about herself. "My mother and I came here after . . . my dad died, because her only living relative was here."

He'd noticed her slight hesitation. Did he detect an issue between Marilee and her father? Or was he reading more into this than was here? "A relative? Somebody I know?"

"Reese Trainor."

"I didn't know her well, but I remember that she ran a boardinghouse here in town."

"That's right. She was a third cousin. After she died, my mother moved on to Florida. She wanted me to join her, but I'm glad I chose not to."

"Why?" He was watching her eyes while she spoke. He loved the way they sparkled in the lamplight.

"Mom's passed away now, too. I would have been alone again. After a lifetime of traveling, it's nice to finally sink some roots." She looked over and saw him watching her. "I guess that sounds crazy."

He shook his head. "Not at all. I've been gone a long time, but I never stopped missing this place. The minute I returned, I knew I was home to stay."

"Oh, yeah. On your family's crazy treasure hunt." At his arched brow she added, "Big news in Gold Fever."

"Why do you call it crazy?"

"Isn't that what they said about old Coot?"

He laughed. "Runs in the family. I take it you're not a believer."

"Not at all."

"Even though you were dispatched to Treasure Chest Mountain after Vernon McVicker killed Rafe Spindler and tried to kill Jesse and Amy, as well? You still don't believe there's really a lost fortune?"

She shivered, recalling the grisly scene when one of the wranglers from the Lost Nugget Ranch was shot and killed by Coot McCord's trusted lawyer, who was in turn brought down by a team of sharpshooters from the state police. It was an ugly, twisted scheme designed to derail the McCord family from continuing their search for the lost treasure.

"Maybe your grandfather's lawyer believed in the treasure. Or maybe he just went off the deep end. Frankly, I don't care one way or the other how the rest of you spend your lives. But I think the whole lost-treasure lore is nothing more than a really good yarn."

"I'll accept an apology when you're forced to eat those words." He looked up. "Speaking of eating, we're not finished yet. There's dessert in that bag."

"Dessert?" Her head came up sharply. "What did you bring?"

"Tiramisu. Guaranteed to be the gooiest, yummiest confection you'll ever sink your teeth into."

"Bring it on."

As he got to his feet she carried her wine to the bar and set it aside before putting the kettle on the stove. Minutes later, with two huge slices of dessert, they perched on barstools and devoured every crumb before washing it down with steaming cups of tea.

He held up his cup. "Decaf?"

"Naturally. I'd like to get a little sleep tonight."

"I know something that will relax you even more than a cup of tea."

At his offhand remark she glanced over.

His lips quirked. "I give really great back rubs."

"I think I'll stick with tea."

"Your loss." He filled the sink with hot, soapy water and proceeded to wash their dishes.

Marilee picked up a linen towel and stood beside him, drying.

"Are you always this handy in a stranger's kitchen?"

He looked over at her. "I don't consider you a stranger. But in my travels, I've learned that I'm a more welcome guest if I clean up after myself."

"Where have your travels taken you?"

He shrugged. "I've been to a lot of places. Both here in the country and around the world."

"Was your father in the Army, too?"

He rinsed a plate and handed it to her. "Both of my parents suffered from wanderlust. They just had to see every exotic place they'd ever read about. I was still a kid when they pulled up stakes and left the Lost Nugget. I turned into the typical rebellious teen. I let them know, in every possible way, just how furious I was that they'd uprooted me and taken away my greatest pleasures in life.

My cousins, who were my best friends. My grandfather, who was my hero. And this countryside, that was as familiar to me as these rooms are to you."

"How did you rebel?"

He gave a laugh. "Think about every rotten thing a teen can do, and I did them all. Dropped out of school. Experimented with wine, women, and song. Explored cults, religions you've never heard of, and even lost myself in a few mountains and jungles."

"I'm sure that got their attention."

He shared her laughter. "Yeah. They got the message that I was mad as hell. Thankfully, I finally woke up to the fact that it was my life I was about to ruin, and not theirs. I finished college, tried my hand at a few respectable jobs, and made my parents proud before they died."

"I'm sorry, Wyatt. How did they die?"

His hands stilled. "Plane crash. They were off on another world adventure, this time to South America. When I got the word, I had just signed on as a counselor for troubled teens. I tendered my resignation and made a trek to Tibet to meditate for a month with some monks. Then I returned to civilization and decided to spend the rest of my life doing exactly as I pleased."

"And what is it that pleases you?"

"I thought I'd spend my time wandering the world. Funny how life hands us all these little surprises." He rinsed the last of the forks before draining the water from the sink and drying his hands. "When I got the message that Coot had died, I knew I had to come back. And the minute I got here, I knew I was home for good."

"Just like that?"

He smiled. "Just like that."

"It wouldn't have anything to do with the chance to find Coot's lost treasure?"

"The treasure you don't believe in." He shot her a dangerous smile. "I'm sure that has something to do with it. Coot made it possible for me to stay, and to feel useful. But I'm not sure now if I could have ever left. The pull of this place has always been strong. The minute I returned, I knew I was in over my head."

"Yeah. Me, too, but probably for a very different reason. You're here because it's home. I'm here because I always wanted one. And since my parents wouldn't make one for me, I decided to make one for myself."

He turned to study her. "Lots of Army brats feel at home all over the world."

"I'm sure I could have, too, if my parents had ever tried to make a home for us. My father . . ." She shrugged. "He was into issuing orders and having them followed to the letter. My mother and I were his troops, and when he didn't like what he saw, we paid for it."

"Your mother allowed that?"

"My mother bought into it. I doubt she ever made a simple decision in her life without my father's approval."

"And how did their daughter fit into all this?"

She smiled. "You know that rebel you talked about, who broke the rules and his parents' hearts?" When Wyatt nodded she added, "I fought my whole life for the right to make my own decisions and live with the consequences. It was a long, hard battle, with me acting like an out-of-control car and my father the brick wall I kept hitting. Until the day that wall crumbled, all I could do was keep revving my engine and dreaming of one day having my own power."

"And now you have it. Was it worth the fight?"

"I'll tell you when I quit fighting." Marilee hung the damp towel on a hook by the stove. When she turned, she stifled a yawn.

At once Wyatt turned away. "Time to head back to the ranch."

She followed him to the door. "Thanks for feeding me."

"Anytime." He stared at her mouth.

Seeing the direction of his gaze, she absorbed a jolt that brought a rush of color to her cheeks.

She leaned in slightly, anticipating his kiss. "Night, rebel."

"Good night, Marilee."

"My friends call me Lee."

"Yeah. That's what Amy calls you. Lee." He tried it, then shook his head. "Sorry. I think I'd like to be more than your friend. But for now . . ." He touched his hand to her cheek, then turned and stepped through the doorway. "Good night, . . . Marilee."

The way he said her name, soft, almost a whisper, reminded her of a prayer.

She closed the door and latched it, all the while listening to the sound of his footsteps as he descended the outer stairs.

Her face felt flushed from his touch. To cool it, she pressed her forehead to the door and listened to the roar of the engine as he gunned his Harley. Lights flashed across her windows for a brief moment as he turned his motorcycle toward the distant ranch.

She'd been pleasantly surprised by Wyatt McCord. Oh, she'd seen him often in town, hair streaming behind him on his bike, or at the Fortune Saloon, surrounded by his family or a crew of wranglers from the ranch. She'd written him off as too handsome, too privileged, and probably completely self-absorbed.

Instead, he'd been funny and charming and interesting to talk to. And he was a good listener. She'd opened up to him the way she rarely opened up to anyone.

She smiled. It hadn't hurt that he'd brought her favorite pizza.

As she switched off the lights and made her way to her bedroom, Marilee decided that she was going to have to change her opinion of him. The brash, bold, annoying rebel was a man of many surprises. And the fact that he hadn't tried to turn his visit into an all-nighter was another point in his favor.

He hadn't even tried to kiss her.

As she made ready to sleep she had to brush aside the feeling of frustration over that. The truth was, a part of her had wanted him to. Another part was afraid he might.

Had she somehow conveyed her feelings to him? Maybe, she thought, he really was a mind reader.

She was too weary to puzzle over it.

After the day she'd put in, she was asleep as soon as her head touched the pillow.

CHAPTER THREE

The morning sky outside the kitchen window of the Lost Nugget Ranch was a clear, cloudless blue when Wyatt swaggered into the big ranch kitchen whistling a little tune.

That had the others looking up with interest.

"Sounds like you had a good night." Zane turned to his cousin as he helped himself to a glass of freshly squeezed orange juice from the counter before taking his seat across the table. "Does this mean you won the bet?"

Their great-aunt Cora, Coot's seventy-year-old sister, was seated across the table from rugged, white-haired Cal Randall, longtime foreman of the Lost Nugget. Cal was devoted to the ranch and to the woman seated across from him.

Though Cora was a world-renowned artist whose wild-life paintings sold for outrageous sums of money, she continued to live a simple life in her childhood home, where she was more comfortable wearing her brother's cast-offs than her own clothes. In the town of Gold Fever she was known as an odd eccentric, as out-of-step as her crazy brother had been.

Cora's head came up, and she studied her nephews with interest. "What bet?"

Jesse heard the note of disapproval in her tone. Their aunt, who willingly shared her home with her nephews, detested gambling. "Wyatt bet me a hundred dollars that he'd be having dinner last night with Marilee Trainor."

Wyatt gave a smug smile. "I'll take that hundred now, if you don't mind."

"Not so fast." Zane glanced around at the others. "What proof do we have that you actually won? For all we know, you could have stopped off at the Fortune Saloon for one of Daffy's greasy burgers before driving back to the ranch."

"I could have. But then I wouldn't be able to describe Marilee's apartment in detail."

Amy took that moment to enter the room, looking pretty in fresh denims and a gauzy shirt. She paused to brush a kiss over Jesse's cheek before taking the seat beside him. "I've been in Lee's apartment dozens of times. Go ahead, Wyatt. Describe it."

"Small, efficient kitchen with two barstools." He arched a brow. "Where we shared tiramisu and decaf tea. Cozy sofa along one wall, with a little fancy embroidered footstool. A lot of interesting artifacts collected on her life of travels as an Army brat. Exotic silk framed in black on one wall, and lots of masks and baskets on her shelves."

Amy nodded before saying to the others, "He nailed it."

"Yeah. But what proof do we have that he actually ate there?" Jesse shot his cousin a triumphant look.

"I suppose I could demand an autopsy, to prove what the poor victim ate at her last meal." That had everyone around the table grinning at his outrageous sense of humor. "But since that seems a bit radical, you'll have to take my word for it. We shared a pizza with her favorite toppings—sausage, mushrooms, onions, and green pepper—as well as a bottle of Chianti and, to top it off, tiramisu."

"Be still my heart." Amy mockingly touched a hand to her heart. "What single woman wouldn't welcome a man bearing such gifts?"

Wyatt shot her a killer grin. "My thoughts exactly."

"Oh, you're good, cuz." Jesse slapped him on the back while Zane handed over his money.

"Of course, as pretty as she is, Marilee has a flaw."

They all waited as Wyatt sipped his coffee.

"Okay, cuz. Out with it." Zane leaned forward.

"She thinks Coot deserved his nickname. She doesn't believe there ever was a fortune, and that anybody who's willing to join in the search for it is just as crazy."

Jesse laughed. "Is that all? Hell, half the town of Gold Fever figures we're all loony. I wouldn't be surprised if they're taking bets to see which one of us crashes and burns first."

"So," Zane asked casually, "does this mean you've lost interest in pretty little Marilee Trainor?"

"Not at all." Wyatt glanced around the table. "I figure I'll just have to pour on a little more charm until she's willing to see the light."

"I think I ought to warn you." Amy nibbled a light-as-air biscuit. "Lee is well-liked by everyone in Gold Fever, and she returns the sentiment. She genuinely likes people, and they're drawn to her. But she's really careful about letting anyone get too close. She guards her friendships, and she's single by choice."

"So, you're saying I'll have an uphill climb."

Amy smiled. "More like an impossible climb."

"Thanks for the warning. I love a challenge."

Jesse turned to Zane. "This should prove interesting. Maybe we ought to take a couple more bets."

Throughout all of this, Cora sat back sipping her coffee and enjoying the easy banter between her grandnephews. When Zane and Wyatt had returned to the Lost Nugget Ranch for her brother's funeral, she'd feared their relationships had been too badly damaged to ever be repaired. Now the old friendship they'd once enjoyed had blossomed anew, and they had once again become the easy, fun-loving family she'd hoped they could be.

Cal Randall winked at Cora across the table. "Who do they remind you of, Cora?"

"Coot." She glanced around, meeting their smiles. "You're all so much like your grandfather. I find myself thinking several times a day how much he would have enjoyed all this."

"He is enjoying it, Aunt Cora." Jesse circled the table to brush a kiss over her cheek. "He's the one who set the terms and conditions in his will, and he knew exactly what he was doing. Thrown together again, we had to learn to swim or sink. Nobody but Coot would have been so sly. You don't think he'd leave all this behind without sticking around to watch, do you?"

Cora blinked away the tears that sprang to her eyes before touching a hand to her nephew's cheek. "You're right, of course, Jess. I feel him here so often."

"Me, too." He straightened and caught his bride's hand. "Come on. I promised you a grand tour of the property."

"Tour?" Cora looked puzzled. "I would think, growing up right next door to our ranch, you'd know this land as intimately as you do your father's place."

"We're scouting locations to build our own ranch." Amy blew a kiss to Cora and allowed herself to be led from the room.

Zane looked around the table. "Why would anyone want to leave this to build their own?"

Wyatt shrugged. "You think we're in the way? Maybe the newlyweds aren't getting enough privacy."

Zane winked at his aunt. "Or maybe they're thinking about adding to the nest."

They all saw the sudden light that came into Cora's eyes.

Cal got to his feet. "I'm heading up to the north range. Either of you interested in riding along?"

"I'm up for it." Zane was on his feet, touching a hand to the ever-present movie camera in his shirt pocket.

"I think I'll go, too." Wyatt polished off the last of his omelet and turned to the cook. "Great breakfast, Dandy."

"Wait'll you try my dinner. Slow-cooked roast beef tonight, with garden vegetables."

"I'll be here." Wyatt called.

Zane's voice drifted from the mudroom where he was busy taking a wide-brimmed hat from a hook by the door. "Count me in."

When they were gone Dandy topped off Cora's cup. "Nice to see the house alive with all those young stallions, Miss Cora."

She nodded. "I was just thinking the same thing." She picked up her cup and started toward the door. As always, she was wearing her brother's old overalls and a paint-stained shirt. "I'll be in my studio, Dandy."

The cook was already busy cleaning off the table, the countertops, the floor. He wouldn't stop, she knew, until the kitchen sparkled. It was his trademark, and everyone at the Lost Nugget Ranch had learned to respect his rules. No dirty boots leaving marks on his floor. No dirty hands at the table. No hats allowed past the hooks on the mud-room wall.

They were all willing to do whatever it took to keep the obsessively neat Dandy happy so that he was free to make the best food in the state of Montana.

As she headed toward her studio, Cora's heart felt light. Could it be that Jesse and Amy were thinking about starting a family? Though she couldn't imagine this house without Jesse here under the same roof, it was enticing to think about another generation growing up on this land she and her brother loved with such passion.

Once inside her barnlike studio she set to work, her mind focused on capturing the intricate light she'd seen just before the sun dipped beneath the peaks of Treasure Chest Mountain. Though her paintings fetched obscene amounts of money in the international art world, Cora never thought about that. Her only concern was capturing the beauty of her beloved countryside on canvas. It was her pride, her passion, her life.

As always, she was soon lost in her latest work of art.

Marilee showered and dressed, all the while sipping coffee and listening to the drone of news on the local

TV station. After clipping her cell phone to her belt, she headed downstairs to spend a pleasant hour cleaning her rescue vehicle. Although it was owned by the county, she took pride in always having it ready for any emergency. That meant a full tank of gas, along with a fresh supply of linens, blankets, cots, and first-aid supplies.

Parked alongside it was her ancient truck, which she drove when she was on her own time.

When the rescue vehicle was clean, she drove to the clinic, also owned by the city of Gold Fever, and staffed by Dr. Frank Wheeler and Elly Carson, his trusted nurse-practitioner.

Marilee stepped inside the clinic and breathed in the familiar scent of disinfectant.

Elly looked up from the phone and waved without missing a beat of her conversation.

"Are the spots on Timmy's stomach flat or raised, Paula?" She paused. "Uh-huh. Oozy?" She winced. "Okay. Chicken pox. You'll have to keep him quarantined." She laughed. "I know, Paula. And I'm sure he was contagious for the past forty-eight hours, which means half the class will be down with it in the next week or so. Can't be helped. You'll have to miss work until Dr. Wheeler says you can send him back to school. He'll want to see him first. Call when the rash is gone."

She hung up, grinning. "Poor Paula Henning. She said she'll go stir-crazy if she can't leave her ranch. I can hardly wait to talk to Kristy O'Conner and tell her that one of her students has come down with chicken pox."

"Now I remember why I didn't go into teaching." Marilee opened a cabinet and began filling a plastic tub with supplies. "Any emergencies?"

Elly gave a shake of her head. "A quiet night for a change. I bet, after all those hours at the rodeo, you were glad for the break."

"Yeah." Marilee decided not to mention her visitor. Though Elly was a good friend, she wasn't ready to share this with her yet. Everybody in Gold Fever loved knowing everybody else's business, almost as much as they loved sharing it with the world. At least for now, she would keep Wyatt McCord to herself. Besides, she reminded herself, it wasn't as though anything was going to come of it.

When the phone rang, Elly picked it up and gave her usual cheerful response. "Morning. Gold Fever Clinic." In the blink of an eye her tone changed to that of a professional. "Is she bleeding? No, Frances. Don't try to move her. Stay with her. Marilee is here now. She'll be right over. Is the front door unlocked? Five minutes. Stay put."

She replaced the receiver. "Delia Cowling didn't answer her door when her neighbor Fran Tucker got there for coffee. Apparently Delia took a fall in her basement. She's lucid and isn't bleeding. That's all I know."

Marilee turned away, hugging the plastic tub of supplies to her chest. "I'm on it."

Elly put a hand on her arm. "A word of warning, Lee. I don't know if you've had much contact with Delia, but you certainly know her reputation. She's practically made a career out of being nasty. With that vile temper of hers, you'll need to handle her with kid gloves."

"Thanks. I'll keep that in mind." Marilee headed for the door. "I'll report in as soon as I've determined the extent of her injuries."

Minutes later she was pulling up outside the home of the woman who proudly called herself the town's historian. Delia Cowling knew everything that had gone on in Gold Fever for the past sixty years. And was more than happy to share her knowledge with anyone willing to listen. That was why most who knew her well referred to her not as the town historian, but as the town gossip, who had managed to offend nearly everyone in Gold Fever with her wicked tongue at one time or another.

Thankfully, Marilee thought as she climbed the steps of the neat white frame house and let herself in the front door, she'd never personally been on the receiving end of Delia's famous temper.

The smell of coffee wafted from the kitchen.

Though she hadn't been in Delia's house before, Marilee quickly located the open door leading to the basement stairs.

"Delia?" She descended the stairs. "Frances?"

"We're down here."

The lights were on, and Delia lay on the cold, damp cement floor, surrounded by the littered contents of an upended box.

An afghan had been tossed over her.

"She was shivering when I found her." Fran Tucker knelt beside her neighbor, looking absolutely terrified. "I ran upstairs to call the clinic and grabbed this. I hope it's okay."

Marilee nodded as she removed the afghan and began a quick examination of the woman on the floor.

"Any pain, Delia?"

"Of course. How do you think you'd feel if you fell? I hurt all over." Her voice trembled.

Marilee probed gently. "Where is the worst pain?"

"My ankle. I slipped and tried to catch myself, but I went down so fast there wasn't time. And then I heard a knocking on my door, and I was terrified that whoever was there would just give up and leave me down here." Her voice rose. "I could have died down here and nobody would have even known."

"Hush now, Delia." Her neighbor stood, wringing her hands. "You're not going to die."

"But I could have."

Hearing the bubble of hysteria in her tone, Marilee was quick to soothe. "Thank heavens for good neighbors."

Delia nodded. "I was so grateful to see Fran coming down those stairs."

Her neighbor shrugged. "I felt like an intruder letting myself in like that, without an invitation. I know how Delia guards her privacy." Her tone became more accusing. "It wouldn't be the first time that she ignored my knock and refused to come to the door."

"Sometimes I just don't feel like company." Delia's tone was sharp.

"More often than not." Frances brought her hands to her hips, ready to do battle.

Marilee decided to intervene before these two went at each other's throats. "What made you come inside, Fran?"

"I thought I heard Delia calling for help. Once I stepped inside, I was able to follow the sound of her voice."

"Apparently you had some angels on your side, Delia."

"Angels? More like demons, sending me flying like this."

Marilee was accustomed to patients babbling. It was a good sign that the adrenaline was kicking in. But in Delia's case, the quick temper was a sign she wasn't badly hurt.

Marilee did a quick check of the older woman's vitals. Though her blood pressure was a bit high, that was to be expected under the circumstances. Fortunately, except for some swelling in her ankle, she seemed in very good condition.

"Nothing's broken. I'm going to get you up slowly. Don't do a thing. Just let me do the lifting, all right?"

"If you say so." Delia's tone was petulant as she was helped to a sitting position.

Marilee noted her pallor and gave her time to clear her head before taking the next step. "Frances and I are going to get you up those stairs."

"I can do it myself. I've been climbing those stairs for more than sixty years."

"Not today. I insist you let us help." Marilee's tone was firm.

With Marilee on one side and her sturdy neighbor on the other, they got the older woman up the stairs and to her bedroom.

Once there Marilee got Delia comfortably into bed before retrieving supplies from her vehicle and wrapping the ankle.

"Dr. Wheeler will want to take a look at this."

Frances caught Delia's hand. "I'll take you over there later today. Do you want me to stay with you, or would you rather rest?"

Delia looked away, clearly annoyed at being helpless and at the mercy of others. "If you don't mind, I think I'll sleep a bit. We'll have coffee another time."

Frances nodded. "I'll turn off the coffeemaker and we'll start a fresh pot later."

"There's no need . . ."

Delia's voice trailed off when she realized her neighbor had ignored her protest.

She turned to Marilee. "I can't believe this happened. I've always been so careful when I go downstairs. That old cement floor is cracked and dangerous. But Frances had been bragging about her excellent spiced-apple cake that had taken a blue ribbon at the fair, and I went in search of my mother's old recipe, hoping I'd find it in my keepsake box of her things."

"Were you thinking of competing with Frances in this year's competition?"

Delia blushed, her only admission of guilt. "The next thing I knew I was slipping. I remember grabbing onto the edge of the shelf to stop my fall, but I caught a cardboard box by mistake and then I was down. No fool like an old fool."

Marilee placed a hand over Delia's. "Don't beat yourself up over it. These things happen. That's why they're called accidents. At least nothing's broken."

"Oh, my." Delia touched a hand to her throat and gave a gasp. "My mother's locket. It must have broken free when I fell." She clutched Marilee's wrist. "Would you mind going downstairs to find it? It's a small gold heart on a chain. It means the world to me."

"I'll look for it. You rest now." Marilee pulled the bed linens over her patient and made her way down the stairs.

"What a mess," she muttered as she looked around.

It was obvious that Delia had tried to break her fall by grabbing hold of the stash of old boxes that littered the shelves. The one she'd managed to snag had broken open, spilling yellowed letters and documents all over the floor.

It wasn't going to be an easy matter to find one small locket and chain in all this mess.

"Just part of the job," Marilee sighed as she dropped to her knees and began trying to make order out of the chaos.

She set the empty box in the middle of the mess and began picking up the papers, placing them one by one in a neat pile inside. She was nearly done when she came to a torn scrap of yellowed paper. Underneath it lay Delia's locket and chain. Tucking the jewelry into her pocket, Marilee was about to add this paper to the pile when her eye caught the word in a large scrawl.

Gold.

She paused to read more and made out the words:

Can't believe my good fortune. I found gold nuggets the size of a man's fist.

Marilee's heart started pounding. Everyone in Gold Fever talked about the diary kept by Nathanial McCord, the McCord ancestor who had originally found the treasure in 1862 at Grasshopper Creek. Though much of his journal had been found, there were thought to be many more pages missing.

She studied the paper, which was worn, wrinkled, and water-stained. Could this be part of that journal? If so, what was it doing in Delia Cowling's basement, in this old box of papers?

She picked up another paper. Though it didn't appear to be nearly as old as the first, it contained crude drawings of hills, with X's marked over certain ones, and notations about possible places to hide a fortune.

Electrified, Marilee sat back on her heels.

Though this was none of her business, she felt a need to ask Delia about what she'd found.

Keeping these two pages, she placed the box and its contents back on the shelf before making her way up the stairs.

In the bedroom, Delia was sound asleep.

Marilee stood for several seconds before coming to

a decision. She set the old woman's locket and broken chain on the night table and then made her way outside to phone a report to the clinic.

As for the papers in Delia's possession, no matter what reason she might give for having them, Marilee believed the McCord family had a right to know about their existence.

Though she had steadfastly refused to believe that old Coot McCord's hunt for his ancestor's lost treasure would ever lead to anything, she couldn't deny the quick little flutter around her heart. Maybe it was the thought that she could add to the lore of the lost treasure.

Or maybe, she thought with a sigh, it was simply because she'd come up with the perfect excuse to see Wyatt McCord again.

CHAPTER FOUR

———◆———

Marilee parked the rescue vehicle in the garage before climbing into her old, battered truck. Digging out her cell phone, she dialed the medical clinic.

At the familiar voice she said, "Elly? I'm headed out to the Lost Nugget Ranch."

At Elly's note of concern, she was quick to reply. "Oh, no. Don't worry. Nobody's sick or hurt at the ranch. I just have something that needs to be delivered."

She knew she was being deliberately evasive, but there was no way she could explain. "I hope you and Doc don't have to make a run while I'm gone. But if you do, I wanted you to be prepared. You know where I keep the spare keys."

She could hear the smile in Elly's voice on the cell phone. "You give Miss Cora my best, you hear?"

"I sure will. I'll check back with you on my way home." Marilee tucked away her cell phone and turned up the radio, singing along with Taylor Swift at the top of her lungs. With the windows open and her hair blowing on the breeze, she felt a bubble of happiness that wasn't entirely caused by the gentle weather or the brilliant sunshine. Part of it was, she knew, the fact that she was about to see Wyatt. And part of it was simply that she was enjoying the aura of mystery and anticipation surrounding the papers she'd found in Delia's basement.

"Hey, Cal." Wyatt's voice from the bed of the truck had Cal and Zane, seated in the cab, glancing out the back window. "Could you be a little more careful going over this rise?"

He had both arms around the bawling heifer that they'd found tangled in barbed wire. After a quick examination of the injuries, Cal had decided to bring the heifer in to the main barn, where they could keep an eye on her while her injured leg mended.

Zane aimed his camera out the open window, capturing the image of his cousin, shirtfront stained with the heifer's blood, trying his best to calm the frightened animal while the truck rocked from side to side, taking the dips and curves at breakneck speed.

"Hold on. We're almost there." Cal sped through an open gate and took the last hundred yards like Mario Andretti.

Zane leaped out to open the barn door. The truck came to a halt inside, and within minutes a couple of the wranglers had the heifer in a stall, where Cal and a grizzled cowboy knelt, applying an antibiotic to the cuts.

Wyatt and Zane watched until the animal was treated before they headed out into the sunlight.

Marilee's old truck wheezed to a stop and she stepped out.

One look at Wyatt's shirt, covered in blood, had her racing toward him. "You idiot. What did you do this time? Try to ride one of the bulls out on the range?"

He was too startled by the sight of her, all tidy and springtime-fresh, to do more than gape. Then, as he realized what she was talking about, he stared down at his bloody clothing before shooting her that killer smile. "All in a day's work, ma'am."

"Get that shirt off and let me look at the cuts."

"Can't wait to get me naked, is that it?"

She was already reaching for the buttons of his shirt, while Zane stood to one side, watching and grinning.

"See what happens, cuz?" Wyatt went very still while she fumbled with the damp fabric. Though he was cracking jokes, he couldn't completely ignore the little thrill that raced up his spine when she freed first one button, then the next. "I feed a woman, and right away she wants to undress me. It's been the story of my life."

Marilee parted his shirt, then seemed startled by the absence of blood on his chest.

"What . . . ?" She stared again at the bloody shirt, then looked up to find him grinning from ear to ear.

"A poor helpless heifer got caught in some barbed wire. We brought her back for observation. But I didn't want to spoil your chance to do your Florence Nightingale routine."

Though she drew back and huffed out a breath, she couldn't help laughing at herself. "Okay. You got me." She looked over at Zane, who joined in the laughter. "Hi. I'm Marilee Trainor."

"Nice to meet you, Marilee. Zane McCord. You already know my cousin, the jokester. He makes quite an impression, doesn't he?"

"Oh, yeah." She tried not to stare at the ripple of muscle she'd bared during that comedy routine.

"What brings you all this way?" Wyatt tucked his hands in his back pockets to keep from touching her and rocked on the heels of his boots. "Thinking of feeding me?"

"I suppose I do owe you dinner. But I'll leave that for another night." She pointed to her truck. "I brought something I think will interest you and your family."

"Why don't you bring it inside?" He started toward the back porch. "I'll just wash up and dig out a clean shirt."

She watched him saunter away and had to admit that his backside looked as good in those faded denims as his bare chest had just seconds ago.

When she realized that Zane was watching her, she turned away to fetch the papers from her truck. Minutes later she and Zane walked into the kitchen.

Zane handled the introductions. Afterward, Dandy welcomed her with a choice of iced tea or lemonade.

She stared at the plate of fruit. "Did you actually squeeze fresh lemons?"

He looked offended. "Is there any other way?"

She shared a laugh with Zane. "I see you haven't heard of instant lemonade."

Dandy sniffed. "That's for amateurs." He handed her a frosty glass with a slice of fresh lemon decorating the sugar-dipped rim.

By the time Wyatt had returned from his room, tucking a clean shirt into his waistband, she was sitting at the kitchen table, sipping lemonade and talking with Zane and Dandy.

"I passed Aunt Cora in her studio and told her you'd come by for a visit." Wyatt snagged a glass of lemonade from the counter and pulled up a chair beside Marilee's. "She's cleaning up before coming to say hi."

Cora bustled into the kitchen, still wiping her hands on a rag that reeked of paint thinner. "Marilee. How grand to see you." She tucked the rag in the back pocket of her bib overalls as she rounded the table and engulfed the young woman in a bear hug. "It's been too long."

"Yes, ma'am. It has." Marilee kissed the older woman's cheek. "How're you doing, Miss Cora?"

"Fine. It's been quite a comfort to have these boys back home." Cora glanced around the table, her smile radiant as she took in Wyatt and Zane.

"Elly wanted me to say hi. She sends you her best."

Cora accepted a glass of lemonade from Dandy before settling herself at the table beside Zane. "How's Elly's husband, Mac?"

"According to Elly, Mac's as ornery as ever."

The two women shared an easy laugh just as Jesse and Amy came strolling into the kitchen.

When Amy spotted Marilee she danced across the floor to hug her.

After returning the hug Marilee held her a little away and gave her old friend a long look. "Marriage agrees with you."

"Thanks." Amy shot a quick glance at her husband. "Jess and I have been scouting locations for our spread."

"You're leaving the Lost Nugget?"

"Oh, no." Amy was quick to correct her. "Jesse could never leave here. But we thought we'd start looking for a site to build our own house. Not right away, but maybe in a year or two."

Out of the corner of his eye, Wyatt saw his aunt give

a long sigh. To her credit, her smile remained in place. A year or more would definitely give her time to get used to the idea of Jesse moving. He'd lived his entire life in this house, and he was more like a son to her than a great-nephew.

Jesse held Amy's chair and handed her a glass of lemonade before sitting down beside her. "I didn't see your rescue vehicle, so I guess this is a social call." He glanced beyond her to Wyatt and arched a brow. "What brings you out to the Lost Nugget, Lee?"

The look hadn't been lost on Marilee. It was obvious that Jesse, not to mention the rest of his family, was aware of Wyatt's nighttime visit to her apartment.

So much for keeping secrets.

She felt her palms sweating. It was difficult for her to comprehend so many people living in such close quarters. All of them here, under this roof, and knowing one another's business.

Knowing her business.

It occurred to her that as an only child she wasn't at all prepared for this big, open, inquisitive family. What's more, having moved so often, she'd rarely had a chance to develop the sort of close friendships that allowed her to share her most intimate thoughts and feelings with other people. In fact, she had become very good at keeping people from getting too close.

She felt, as she had so often in the past, like an outsider. Not really connected to anyone, and especially these people who seemed so comfortable with one another.

With an effort she pulled herself back from her troubling thoughts. "I had an emergency call this morning. Delia Cowling took a fall in her basement."

Cora lowered her drink. "I hope she's all right."

"She's fine. A sprained ankle, but nothing broken except her mother's locket. After making her comfortable I went back downstairs to hunt for the locket and chain. She'd overturned a box of old papers, and while cleaning them up I found some things I thought just might be of interest to all of you."

Because Wyatt was beside her, she handed the papers to him and watched as he read the first, then the second.

He shot her an incredulous look before handing them over to his aunt. As soon as she looked at the first page she let out a cry, and the others left their places at the table to crowd around her and read over her shoulder.

"This"—Cora lifted the stained, wrinkled paper—"has to be part of Nathanial's diary." She turned to her nephew. "Jesse, would you mind fetching that box from Coot's room? You know the one I mean."

He raced from the room and returned minutes later bearing a leather-bound box. Lifting the lid, he removed the crumbling notebook.

Cora studied it almost reverently as she explained to Marilee. "This is what remains of Nathanial McCord's diary. Some of it was found in the rotted cabin he shared that winter in 1862 when he and his father, Jasper, came to Montana to seek their fortune."

Wyatt picked up the thread. "Over the years a lot of the pages were lost, blown about the countryside by storms. But from what we've read, fourteen-year-old Nathanial was close to starvation and half-frozen when he stumbled onto a fortune in gold nuggets at Grasshopper Creek."

Marilee gasped. "I guess that would go a long way to ease his hunger and cold."

"You bet." Wyatt grinned. "The only trouble is, it was stolen that night at a room above the saloon, and Jasper was murdered."

Cora nodded. "At the time, everybody believed the crime was committed by Grizzly Markham, a fearsome miner who'd been drinking with Jasper and listening to him boast of his newly discovered fortune. Jasper had foolishly allowed everyone in the saloon that night to see the nuggets. When young Nathanial woke in the morning to find the fortune gone and his father's throat slashed, he set off to avenge his father's murder and retrieve the gold."

Marilee was clearly caught up in the tale. "I guess he wasn't successful, or you wouldn't still be searching."

Cora's voice lowered to a hush. "Markham was found weeks later, dead in the same manner as Jasper, and the gold missing. Some said Nathanial had his revenge. Others pointed out that he was only a boy, not capable of such a thing. Whatever the truth, Nathanial spent the rest of his life searching for the gold, which he believed to be stashed somewhere nearby, and which we still consider our legacy." She held the newly discovered page next to the open notebook and waited for the others to see what was so obvious.

Jesse swore under his breath. "Look at the scrawled handwriting. And the size and texture of the paper. It's a perfect match."

The others crowded around.

"And this." Cora held up the second paper. "It's undeniably Coot's. Everyone in this town is familiar with his doodles and drawings and markings."

Jesse's eyes narrowed on Marilee. "How did Delia Cowling explain what these were doing in her basement?"

"She was asleep. I . . ." Marilee spread her hands. "I knew I had no right to bring these out here, but I just thought you had the right to know about them."

Seeing her embarrassment, Wyatt laid a hand over hers. "You did the right thing. And now it's up to us to find out how these came to be in Delia's possession."

Around the table, the others nodded.

Marilee met his stare. "I'll need to go with you when you talk to her. I owe her an explanation for daring to take something of hers without permission. This was totally unprofessional. A medic is expected to treat the patients and their possessions with respect." She turned to the others. "And even though I felt this would be a matter of importance to all of you, I still had no right to reveal her secret without her knowledge and explicit permission."

Cora spoke for all of them. "Marilee, you have the respect of everyone in this community. I can't imagine that Delia would find fault with what you did."

Wyatt shrugged. "How can you be so sure of that, Aunt Cora? If Marilee made the connection to our family with only a glance at these papers, why wouldn't Delia have done the right thing years ago and returned them to their rightful owners? Unless," he added, "she had every intention of keeping them a secret."

"For what reason?"

At Jesse's question, Wyatt's tone lowered. "That what I intend to find out. We all thought, after that incident with Vernon McVicker, that he'd been acting alone. What if there were others who coveted the gold?"

Jesse nodded. "I agree. But I'm finding it pretty hard to believe that Delia Cowling would have been involved in some sort of conspiracy."

Zane set aside his lemonade. "We need to find out the truth."

Jesse glanced around. "I say we confront Delia now."

His two cousins nodded.

Cora lifted the lemonade to her lips and drank. "I believe I'll wait here while you confront Delia."

When Jesse frowned, she set down her glass and met his look, as though daring him to argue with her decision. "Delia and I haven't spoken in years. I intend to go back to my studio and finish my work before the light fades." When she saw that her nephew was about to protest, she said firmly, "You can let me know what you find out when you return."

"Yes, ma'am." He caught Amy's hand. "I'll drive."

Zane picked up his video camera and followed.

Behind them, Wyatt called, "I'll ride along with Marilee."

When they were settled in her truck he stretched out his long legs and watched her drive as she followed behind Jesse's ranch truck.

"Last I heard, you didn't believe in old Coot's lost fortune." Wyatt shot her one of those mellow smiles when she turned to look at him. "Am I mistaken, or have you had a change of heart?"

Marilee couldn't help laughing. "I would have been the last one in this town to believe in the McCord pipe dream. But that old paper really got to me. Just reading the word *gold* had me sweating." She shook her head. "I still can't believe I'd violate my own code of ethics like that and bring you something of Delia's without her permission."

"Except that this doesn't belong to Delia Cowling. It's ours. Plain and simple. And she'd better have a really good explanation for having those papers locked away in her basement for all these years, or she'll be answering to Ernie Wycliff."

At the mention of the police chief, Marilee's hands tightened on the wheel of her truck.

She'd opened a real can of worms. And now, ready or not, she would just have to deal with it.

CHAPTER FIVE

———✦———

Jesse, always the hothead, was out of his truck and sprinting up the walkway to Delia's house before the others had even exited their vehicles. By the time they joined him, he was frowning.

"Delia isn't answering the door."

Marilee checked her watch. "She's probably at the clinic. I told her to have Dr. Wheeler check her ankle. Her neighbor Frances Tucker offered to drive her."

They trailed back to their trucks and headed over to the clinic across town.

Elly was just tidying up one of the examination rooms when they strode inside.

She looked up. "Which one of you needs to see the doctor?"

Marilee stepped around the others. "Nobody here needs to see Dr. Wheeler. We're looking for Delia Cowling."

"Oh." Elly stepped to the sink and washed her hands with disinfectant soap. "She's gone. Nothing to worry about. Doc said it was just a bad sprain. But she'll have to stay off her foot for a while. Frances agreed to drive her to Shelbyville to stay with her cousin." Elly chuckled. "Her poor cousin. Delia was already feeling grumpy when she arrived. By the time she left, she was indulging in a huge pity-party. I hope her cousin has some Valium."

Marilee arched a brow. "Did Dr. Wheeler prescribe it for Delia?"

Elly shook her head. "Not for Delia. For her cousin. By the time Delia leaves, she's going to need it. That woman's mean mouth would give the angels a headache."

Though Marilee enjoyed Elly's joke, the others weren't laughing.

Jesse gave a hiss of impatience. "Did Delia say when she was coming home?"

"Not exactly. I guess she'll lean on her cousin until she can easily put her full weight on that ankle." The nurse glanced from Jesse to Zane to Wyatt, who wore matching looks of disgust. "Something wrong?"

"Nothing." Marilee was quick to smile. "We had something to ask her, but it can wait until she gets back in town."

"All right then." Elly began switching off lights as she trailed them to the front door. "It's been a full day. Doc was heading home, and I'm on my way to meet Harding Jessup over at the hardware store. He swears his newest faucet is guaranteed not to leak. I'm going to hold him to it. This will be the third replacement in a year."

When she left, the three cousins paused outside the clinic, feeling a letdown after the adrenaline rush they'd experienced earlier.

Jesse looked around. "I guess there's nothing to do but wait until Delia gets back."

Zane nodded.

Jesse turned to Marilee. "Thanks again. I really appreciate what you did."

"I wish it could have been more."

He shrugged. "It's not your fault that Delia decided to leave town." He caught his wife's hand. "I'm starving. Want to eat in town or head back to the ranch?"

Amy looked up at him. "I'd rather go back. I think Aunt Cora will want to hear how our meeting went."

"You're right." He looked over at Zane. "Coming with us?"

"Sure thing." Disappointed that the adventure hadn't turned out as he'd hoped, Zane tucked his video camera in his pocket.

As they started toward the truck, Wyatt held back and touched a hand to Marilee's shoulder. "I can ride back with them, and save you a trip. Or if you'd like, I'll spring for supper at the Fortune Saloon."

She grinned. "I believe I owe you a meal. If you stay, I'll buy."

"We'll flip for it later." He held the door for her, then circled around and climbed into the passenger side. "But remember, if I stay, you'll have that long drive back to the ranch, and then home alone."

She laughed. "I'm a big girl. I think I can handle it."

He shrugged. "Your call."

As the others settled into the ranch truck, he motioned for Zane to lower the window.

Cupping his hand to his mouth he shouted, "I'll catch you back at the ranch later."

Marilee couldn't miss the wide smiles on his cousins' faces. They thought Wyatt McCord was going to get lucky.

Maybe he was. And then again, maybe he wasn't. She had no idea how the night would end. She was allowing Wyatt McCord to get too close, too quickly. She'd been there a time or two before and had been burned every time. Now that she felt stronger and wiser, she had no intention of simply falling into a relationship. But there were times, like right now, that she could feel herself sliding along, unsure of where she might land. And that bothered her much more than she cared to admit, because she was a person who needed to be in charge of every aspect of her life.

Still, he was such fun to be with. And what was the harm in having a little fun? She hadn't felt this comfortable with a man in a very long time.

Comfortable? Who was she kidding? Whenever she was with Wyatt, she was forced to deal with all kinds of strange, new emotions, not one of which was comfort.

The sudden tingle along her spine meant she was beginning to realize that she may have stepped into something over her head.

She intended to take this slow and easy. Tonight was nothing more than a meal and a few laughs. After that, she would just have to take charge and see that she didn't allow the night and her charming companion to take this to a level she wasn't prepared to deal with.

"Why, just look at you, big as life." Daffodil Spence, who owned the Fortune Saloon with her sister, Violet, opened her arms as Wyatt sauntered through the doorway.

As expected, he returned the embrace and kissed her cheek. "Hey, Daffy. How's business?"

"It just got better with you here, honey." She turned to include Marilee. "Well, don't you two make a pretty picture." Her smoky, rusty-nails voice lowered. "You two want to be seen? Or would you rather sit in the shadows?"

Wyatt leaned close, as though delivering a state secret. "Find us a dark corner, Daffy."

"You got it, honey." She winked at him and led the way through the smoke-filled room.

Though Wyatt and Marilee had hoped to be invisible, there was no escape from the curious stares of the townspeople. They were forced to pause at each table to speak a few words. There was the mayor, Rowe Stafford, who was, as always, surrounded by a cluster of old cronies hanging on his every word. At the next table was Stan Novak, a local building contractor who had let it be known around town that he was furious with the McCord family for not releasing any of their vast holdings for development. Their next stop was to speak with Orley Peterson, owner of the grain and feed store, who'd been talking to Judge Wilbur Manning about suing a local rancher who refused to pay for a year's worth of supplies. Sheriff Ernest Wycliff was sitting with his deputy, Harrison Atkins, and Harrison's daughter, Charity, who handled the emergency phone at the jail during the night shift.

Daffy led them past the busy pool tables, where several cowboys from the Lost Nugget Ranch were engaged in matches with cowboys from nearby ranches. They smiled and waved at Wyatt, and he returned their greetings.

Daffy skirted the small, empty dance floor and moved on to a far corner of the cavernous room. "This dark enough for you, honey?"

"Perfect." Wyatt waited for Marilee to slide into the booth before settling himself beside her.

"You want to start with a couple of chilled longnecks?" Daffy dropped two menus in front of them.

Wyatt glanced at Marilee, who nodded.

When Daffy returned, she set the beers down and slid into the opposite side of the booth, kicking off her spike-heeled shoes and wiggling her toes.

"Been on my feet for eight hours now. Thought I'd just sit here while you two decide what to order."

"What're the specials?" Marilee asked.

"Vi started a pot of chili at noon. Right about now it's hot enough to start a fire in your gut that won't burn out until next Friday." She threw her head back and laughed at her own joke. "She's also got barbecued ribs, chicken, and her pound-and-a-half burger with onions, mushrooms, peppers, and cheese." Without missing a beat she added, "I recommend the ribs. They're so tender they're falling off the bone."

"I'll have that." Wyatt turned to Marilee. "How about you?"

"Absolutely. With a side of Vi's famous onion rings."

"You've got good taste, honey." Daffy winked. "In food and in men."

As Daffy walked away, Marilee chuckled. "You realize," she said as she lifted the frosty bottle to her lips and drank, "that Daffy was practically drooling when she looked at you."

"She drools over every cowboy that walks through the door. Now if you'd drool"—he touched a finger to her jaw—"my ego would definitely be stroked."

"I doubt your ego needs stroking. I'm thinking you have a very high opinion of yourself, rebel."

He gave an easy laugh. "Does this mean you're not going to buy into my shy-guy routine?"

"Not likely."

They sipped their beers and watched the ebb and flow of customers, some drinking, some eating, some playing pool or darts. When Daffy delivered their meals, they both dived in.

"Um." Marilee closed her eyes on the first bite of soft-as-butter ribs. "Daffy wasn't kidding. These are the best."

Wyatt nodded. "I'll never let Dandy know, but these are every bit as good as his." He reached for an onion ring. "Of course, it could be because I haven't eaten a thing since breakfast."

"Did you say breakfast?" She sighed and touched a hand to her middle. "I even forgot about that."

"No wonder you're starving. I can see that I'm going to have to feed you more often."

"Somebody ought to." She laughed. "Food's not high on my list of priorities."

"What is?" He sat back, sipping his beer and watching her eyes. He loved the light that sparkled in them.

"My independence. I fought long and hard for it."

"So you've said."

"And my job. I'm really happy when I'm doing whatever I can for the people of this town."

"Why a medic?"

"I was always patching up something or somebody. I remember a friend when I was about seven. He fell off the monkey bars at school. I knew instinctively that he shouldn't try to stand. I sent one of our classmates to find a teacher. I went with him to the nurse's office, and I held his hand until the ambulance arrived to take him to the hospital to cast his broken leg."

"That's pretty young to be so smart."

"I guess it was. I was always stumbling across wounded animals in the woods or backyards. My mom got sick at the sight of blood. She'd get weak and have to go sit down and rub her hands together until the sickness passed. I was determined to be just the opposite. I seem to have this sixth sense about injuries. I don't panic. I don't sweat. I just . . ." She looked over at him. "I just do what's needed."

"Why not go back to school and become a doctor?"

She shrugged. "I've thought about it. I don't know why, but I'm not sure I want to go that far with it. I really enjoy my life the way it is. I like the freedom this job gives me. It allows me to see a lot of the countryside. And it pays me enough to afford the plane I keep out at the airport."

"The plane is yours?" He sat up. "I figured it belonged to the town or the county."

She shook her head. "It's all mine. It doesn't have a lot of bells and whistles, but it gives me a lot of pleasure." She glanced over. "Would you like to go up in it some time?"

"I'd like that." He gave a snort of laughter. "I might have to white-knuckle it, but I'd still like it."

"That's natural enough, considering how your parents died."

He nodded. "Until their accident, I was able to fly any-where without a thought. Since their crash, I have a few issues with flying."

She laid a hand over his. "I'd say you have good reason to have some issues."

He absorbed the warmth of her touch. "I've flown since then. Plenty of times, as a matter of fact. But every time, on takeoff, I feel the butterflies. Then, once I'm airborne, I get past it. How about you? Any fear of flying?"

"None. As long as I'm at the controls, I don't have any second thoughts."

"A woman who likes to be in control." He closed a hand over hers. "I like that."

Marilee absorbed the quick little flutter of awareness. Wyatt McCord did have a way about him. And probably knew exactly what he had and how to use it.

To fill the silence she said, "I don't get as much flying time as I'd like. But whenever I get a chance to make money while flying, I leap at the offer."

"Who pays you?"

She shrugged. "The town. The county. Sometimes the state or even the federal government. But mostly it's businessmen who need me to pick up something in a distant town and deliver it the same day. With gas so expensive, I never refuse the offer to fly at someone else's expense." She looked over. "Want to join me the next time I'm flying on business?"

"Yeah. I'll be your copilot."

"You're on."

They both looked over at the roar of laughter coming from two cowboys engaged in a game of darts. When the last dart was tossed, one of the players reached into his pocket and withdrew a handful of bills, which he slapped into the palm of the other player before storming away.

"Wow." Marilee chuckled. "Now there's a happy loser."

"And an even happier winner." Wyatt nodded toward

the second player, who walked away whistling while he stuffed his winnings in his pocket.

"Do you play?" Marilee drained her beer.

"A little. You?"

She nodded. "I've played a time or two."

"To sweeten the pot, let's play for the bill. Loser pays. You willing?"

She thought about it for less than an instant before saying, "Okay. You're on."

Wyatt slid from the booth and caught her hand.

Minutes later they stood at the line, each one prepared to toss a single dart. The one with the higher score would become the first player of the match.

"Ladies first." Wyatt stepped back and watched as Marilee tossed her dart, landing in the inner circle for a triple.

He arched a brow. "I'm thinking you've played this more than a time or two."

"It could be beginner's luck."

"It could. Or you could be setting me up." He stepped up to the line and tossed, landing in the outer circle for a double.

He walked to the board and withdrew both darts before handing one to Marilee.

With a bow he said, "Looks like you get to go first."

He stood back, admiring her technique. She kept her eye firmly on the board while tossing the first dart. It landed with precision in the inner circle.

"Triple points."

Wyatt tossed and landed just beside hers.

She caught the smug look on his face. "Don't get cocky, rebel. You still have two darts to toss." She stepped up to the line and without hesitation tossed her second dart, which landed again in the triple area.

Wyatt was shaking his head. "Now I know I've been hustled. Nobody can do that twice. Except"—he wiggled his brows like a movie villain—"yours truly."

He stood at the line, assessed the distance, and tossed his dart. It landed directly beside Marilee's.

She was laughing. "If I hadn't seen it with my own eyes, I'd have never believed this." She took a moment to concentrate, then tossed her last dart. It landed squarely in the center. "Bull's-eye. See if you can match that."

"You don't make it easy, do you?" He studied the board, then tossed his last dart.

It landed beside hers in the center. Just as she was about to congratulate him, the dart slipped from the board and dropped to the floor.

They looked at each other and started laughing so hard they had to cling together for a moment.

"Oh, you should have seen your face," she said, still laughing.

"Are you sure you didn't have a magnet somewhere? I would have sworn that dart was a solid hit."

"Sorry about your bad luck, loser." Still laughing, she walked over to their table and picked up the bill Daffy had left there. "I believe this is yours."

He tucked it into his pocket and caught her hand. As they passed the dance floor he suddenly pulled back. Caught by surprise, she turned to look at him.

"They're playing my favorite song." He swept her into his arms and began to move with her around the floor.

The honky-tonk music was something low and bluesy.

Marilee looked up into his face. "I don't recognize this song. What is it?"

He gave her that soulful smile. "I don't know. But from now on it's going to be my favorite."

She felt her heart stutter.

He closed both arms around her, drawing her close.

She knew that everyone in the saloon was watching. At the moment, she didn't care. She couldn't think about anything except the press of his body to hers. The feel of those strong, muscled arms around her. The warmth of his thighs molded to hers. The touch of his mouth against her temple, his warm breath feathering her hair.

"This is nice." His voice vibrated through her, sending a series of delicious tingles along her spine.

"Yeah." She looked up into his eyes and could feel herself drowning in them.

She was melting all over him, with the entire town watching. She could actually feel her heart beginning to drum in her temples.

She knew she ought to draw back, but she couldn't. She didn't want the song to end. Or this night.

Oh, hell. Just look at her. She was falling for a foot-loose rebel with a smooth line who'd probably left a trail of broken hearts from Toledo to Timbuktu. The kind of guy she'd made a career of staying as far away from as possible. And here she was. Falling hard. Willingly. Right in front of the entire town. And loving every minute of it.

CHAPTER SIX

Y ou leaving?" Daffy paused, balancing a tray of drinks.

"Yeah. I left your money on the table, Daffy." Wyatt waved to her sister, Vi, sweating over the grill, who blew him a kiss. He returned his attention to Daffy. "You were right about those ribs. Be sure and tell Vi. They were the best ever."

"I told you so. You behave now, honey." She shot a knowing glance at Marilee. "Don't go doing anything I wouldn't do, girl."

She was still cackling over her joke as they walked out the door.

Wyatt kept his hand at the small of Marilee's back as they made their way to her truck.

She liked the way his big hand felt there. Not possessive. She would have resented that. But it definitely felt protective. She had the keen sense that he would be a fierce protector of anything or anyone he cared about. It was, she decided, just one more thing she liked about

Wyatt McCord. And this evening had revealed a treasure trove of good things about him.

He held her door and waited until she'd settled herself behind the wheel before circling around to the passenger side.

He fastened his seat belt. "You up for the long drive back to the ranch? Or would you rather save yourself the trip and just invite me to spend the night at your place?"

She saw the teasing laughter in his eyes. "Did I forget to tell you? I love long drives. They invigorate me."

"I was afraid of that." He was chuckling as they pulled out onto the street and headed through town.

"So." He turned toward her. "Seeing the way you tossed those darts, I think we can put to rest the lie that you've only played once or twice."

"Oh, did I forget to mention that I was the champion chucker in my dorm in college?"

"Yeah. You kept that a big, bad secret. At least the champion part. Judging by the way you aim, you're no chucker. You know exactly where your dart will land."

"Thank you, sir." She bowed her head. "What about you? This wasn't your first time. Not the way you matched me play for play."

"I may have played a time or two in a London pub during my rebellious days."

Marilee's laughter faded as a new thought dawned. "And that unfortunate loss? Was that really an accident, or did you lose deliberately so I wouldn't have to pay the bill?"

He shrugged. "My lips are sealed."

"I should have known."

Once on the open highway he turned on the radio, and

they both sang along with Garth as he lamented his papa being a rolling stone.

When the song ended, Marilee looked over. "I'll consider that a sermon. According to Garth, a woman would be a fool to lose her heart to a man who'd rather drive a truck than be home with her."

Wyatt winked, and in his best imitation of Daffy's smoky voice he said, "Honey, a man may love the open road, but any female with half a brain can figure out how to compete with a truck. Just bat those pretty little red-tipped lashes at any male over the age of twelve, and his brain turns to mush. Next thing you know, instead of revving up his engine, he's on his hands and knees, carrying a toddler on his back around a living room full of toys and baby gear."

Though the image was a surprisingly pretty one, Marilee had to wipe tears from her eyes, she was laughing so hard. When she caught her breath she managed to say, "You've got Daffy down so perfectly, you could probably answer the phone at the Fortune Saloon and no one would believe it wasn't her."

"She's easy." He chuckled. "I think she's the only female with a voice that's deeper than mine."

He looked out the window at the full moon above Treasure Chest Mountain in the distance. "It's a shame to waste such a pretty night. Maybe you ought to pull over and park. We can make out like teenagers."

"Not a bad idea." At his arched brow she added, "It would give me a chance to see if I could turn your brain to mush."

"Believe it."

Marilee felt the tingle of awareness as she turned

the truck into the long gravel lane that led to the ranch house. The truth was, she'd been half tempted to park and make out. She had no doubt that Wyatt would make it memorable.

She brought the vehicle to a halt and glanced at the darkened windows. "Looks like everybody's asleep. Don't they keep a light on for you?"

"They probably figured I wouldn't be needing it."

"Sorry to disappoint your cousins."

"Not to mention me. I'm gravely disappointed at the way this evening has ended. You're going to ruin my reputation as a lady-killer." He flashed her one of his famous smiles.

He opened the door and climbed down. When he rounded the front of the truck, he paused beside her open window. "Good night, Marilee. I appreciate the ride home. I just wish you didn't have to make that long drive back to town all alone."

"I'll be fine. I've got my radio to keep me company."

"You could always come inside and bunk in my room."

"What a generous offer. But once again, I'm afraid I'll have to decline, though I have to admit that I've had more fun in a few hours with you than I've had in years."

The minute the words were out of her mouth, she wanted to call them back. What was it about Wyatt that had her trusting him enough to reveal such a thing?

Though she barely knew him, she'd uncovered an inherent goodness in him that was rare and wonderful.

This had been one of the best nights of her life.

Still, he'd gone very quiet. As though digesting her words and searching for hidden meanings.

As he turned away she called boldly, "What? No kiss

good night? Just because I refused to spend the night with you?"

He turned back with a smile, but it wasn't his usual silly grin. Instead, she noted, there was a hint of danger in that smile.

He studied her intently before reaching out as though to touch her face. Then he seemed to think better of it and withdrew his hand as if he'd been burned.

His eyes locked on hers. "I've already decided that I'll never be able to just kiss you and walk away. So a word of warning, pretty little Marilee. When I kiss you, and I fully intend to kiss you breathless, be prepared to go the distance. There's a powerful storm building up inside me, and when it's unleashed, it's going to be one hell of an earth-shattering explosion. For both of us."

He walked away then and didn't look back until he'd reached the back door.

Startled by the unexpected intensity of his words, Marilee put the truck in gear and started along the gravel lane.

As her vehicle ate up the miles back to town, she couldn't put aside the look she'd seen in his eyes. The carefully banked passion he'd taken such pains to hide had left her more shaken than she cared to admit.

In truth, she was still trembling.

And he hadn't even touched her.

When Marilee climbed the stairs to her apartment, her cell phone rang. She was accustomed to getting emergency calls day and night.

She automatically flipped open her phone as she stepped inside and turned on the lights. "Emergency One. What's the problem?"

"It's my heart."

The familiar deep voice had her pausing mid-stride. "Wyatt?"

"Yeah. I meant to ask you to call me when you got home so I'd know you were safe. Now I've been having heart palpitations worrying about you all alone on that long stretch of highway."

"Pretty good timing, rebel. That highway is just a memory now. I'm already inside my apartment and heading toward the bedroom."

"I'm betting you set a new speed record."

She laughed. "And broke a few speeding laws along the way. But I'm home now, safe and sound. I hope this eases your worries about me."

"Yeah. I can sleep now. But I still wish you'd agreed to bunk out here with me. Good night, Marilee."

As she disconnected and set her cell phone on the night table, she paused to look out the window at the starry sky. Her hard-nosed father had treated her like a fresh recruit her entire life, undermining even the slightest hint of pride in her accomplishments. Her mother had been a clinging vine who couldn't make a single decision on her own. After her father's death her mother had spent years in a fog before discovering her own strengths. Marilee had fought long and hard to achieve any sort of independence. By design she'd been on her own for years. It had been a long time since anybody had worried about her.

She was oddly touched by Wyatt's concern.

"Oh, Amy." Marilee opened the door of her apartment and greeted her friend with a hug. "I'm so glad you could come by for a visit."

"Me, too." Amy stepped inside and sniffed the air. "Something smells yummy."

"Quiche. It's quick and easy." Marilee led the way to the kitchen.

Amy took a seat at the counter and watched as her friend removed a pan from the oven before putting the kettle on. Minutes later the two young women were enjoying salads and quiche, and steaming cups of tea.

Amy sipped her tea and looked over at her friend. "Okay, Lee, what's up?"

Marilee looked appropriately offended. "What's that supposed to mean? Can't a friend invite a friend to lunch?"

"We've been sharing lunch for years, Lee. As well as gossip. But something tells me there's something else going on here."

Marilee took her time setting aside her fork, avoiding Amy's eyes.

Finally she looked over. "Tell me about Wyatt."

Amy's smile bloomed. "I knew it. He's getting to you."

Marilee ducked her head. "I keep trying to write him off as just another charming bachelor looking to score. But every time I think I've got him pegged, he manages to surprise me. I know he's Jesse's cousin, and you probably feel an obligation to keep a few family secrets, but I really need to know more about him."

Amy sat back. "What would you like to know?"

"Whether he's the real deal or just a very good actor."

Amy hesitated. "Tell me how you see him."

"He's nice. Almost too nice. And sweet and funny and charming. He makes me laugh. And sometimes, when I least expect it, he makes my heart pound."

"Oh-oh." Amy chuckled. "This sounds serious."

"No. Really. You know me. I'm not interested in serious. No commitments. But . . ."

"But what?" Amy prodded.

"I can't stop thinking about him."

Amy caught her friend's hands. "Lee, it's like I said. He's getting to you."

"But is he just playing me? Is this all just a game with him? Does he see me as the latest conquest?"

"Hey." Amy studied her more closely. "This really matters to you, doesn't it?"

"I just don't want to be played for a fool." Marilee slid off the stool. Needing to be busy, she picked up their plates and walked to the sink. When she'd finished rinsing them, she looked up. "I've always been such a good judge of character, and all of a sudden, I'm not sure just what to make of Wyatt McCord."

Amy gave her friend a gentle smile. "Lee, in the short time that I've been in the family, I've found Wyatt to be everything you said. He's naturally charming, and that outrageous sense of humor is his most endearing quality. But I've never known Wyatt to be phony. He's the real thing. He's honest and up front with everyone he meets."

When Marilee remained silent she added, "For now, why not just enjoy his company. And if things start heating up, you're going to have to trust your instincts. Hey. You're a big girl now, playing in the big-girl league. I'm betting on you to make wise choices."

Wise choices.

By the time her best friend left, Marilee had decided to take her advice. For now she would relax and enjoy the ride. And if it got too bumpy, she'd simply bail.

* * *

"Hey, rebel."

At the sound of Marilee's voice on his cell phone, Wyatt was instantly awake.

"You free to go flying today?"

He thought about the crew heading up to the north range. He'd agreed to go along. He'd have to twist Zane's arm to be his substitute on such short notice. But there was no way he'd let this opportunity slip away. Especially since he'd just spent the past three days looking for an excuse to see Marilee again while working his tail off with Cal Randall and his wranglers.

"Free as a bird. What time are we leaving?"

"As soon as you get here."

"I'm on my way."

Marilee turned on the coffeemaker before stepping into the shower. By the time she was enjoying her second cup of coffee, she heard the roar of Wyatt's Harley, followed by the sound of his boots on the stairs.

She tore open the door. "'Morning, rebel."

"'Morning." A smile of pure pleasure lit his eyes. "Is this what the well-dressed pilots are wearing this year?"

She twirled, showing off a denim miniskirt and trim white shirt with the sleeves rolled to her elbows. "You like my uniform?"

"It beats the leather bomber jacket and flyboy hat with goggles that I was expecting." He inhaled. "Is that coffee I smell?"

"And here I thought you were about to compliment me on my perfume."

"I will. Right after my jolt of caffeine."

"Over there." She pointed to the mug on the countertop.

He filled the mug and drank it down in one long swallow.

Then he set down the empty mug and crossed to her, dipping his head to the column of her throat. "Great perfume, by the way."

She absorbed an unexpected sizzle of heat.

How did he always manage to catch her off-guard?

To cover her confusion, she grabbed her keys. "Come on. I've got a plane to fly."

Wyatt stood back watching as Marilee went through her routine at the airport, filling out a flight plan and conferring with Craig Matson, the mechanic, before doing a thorough physical check of her bright yellow, fixed-wing aircraft that bore the license MON342.

Satisfied, she opened the door of the plane and motioned for Wyatt to follow.

"Did I hear you mention Helena?"

She nodded as she fiddled with dials, adjusted her earphones, and slid on a pair of sunglasses. "Harding Jessup is paying me to deliver some plumbing supplies. So I promised Dr. Wheeler I'd pick up some medical supplies he'd ordered while I'm there. It will all be handled at the airport, so we can just do a quick turnaround."

"No overnighter?"

She arched a brow. "You sound disappointed."

"Not at all." He grinned. "But I was willing to sacrifice my time, not to mention my body, if you needed to stay over."

"Really decent of you, rebel. Maybe next time."

"That's what they all say." He glanced at the small, cramped space behind the pilot and copilot seats. "You think there's room for anything more than a postage stamp back there?"

She laughed. "That's why it's called a small craft."

"A mini, if you ask me."

He fell silent as the voice of the controller came over her earphones. She followed directions, steering her craft along the runway until she reached the turn. With the length of another runway ahead of them, the little plane picked up speed.

Wyatt adjusted his sunglasses and sucked in a breath, the only sign of nerves.

When the plane was airborne, he slowly exhaled.

Marilee glanced over. "You okay?"

"Fine. Now." And he was.

He understood his reaction to takeoff. From all accounts, something had gone very wrong with the plane his parents had chartered in the jungles of South America. It had barely made it off the makeshift runway of the small village when it had crashed into the trees and burst into flames.

How many times had he imagined their reaction? Had there been time for fear to set in? Panic? Had they had a moment to clasp hands? Whisper words of love? Had they thought about the son they might never see again? Felt a flash of regret? Or had it been over in an instant?

He hoped so. He fervently hoped there had been no time to suffer.

He touched a hand to his breast pocket. In it he carried the watch his grandfather Coot had given to his father when he'd graduated from college. It was the only thing of his father's that had been salvaged from the burning rubble. Along with that he had his mother's wedding ring, a simple band of platinum engraved with the word *Forever*. It currently resided in a small, velvet-lined box in his room.

He'd never had a chance to say good-bye. But then,

he thought, they weren't really gone. They'd just stepped into a place he couldn't see. That thought had given him a lot of comfort through the years.

"You're quiet." Marilee studied his profile as he stared out the window.

"I'm enjoying the view." He turned to her. "The one outside the window, as well as the one in here."

"Thanks." She smiled. "Just so you're not going to get sick on me."

"No need to worry. I can handle my nerves."

And a lot of other things, she figured. Aloud she merely said, "There's a thermos of coffee behind you. And a couple of bottles of water."

"What would you prefer?"

"I'll take a bottle of water. I've had enough caffeine."

He twisted off the cap before handing her the plastic bottle.

She took a long pull and set it in the cup-holder.

Wyatt watched as the small town of Gold Fever drifted out of his line of vision, to be replaced by acres and acres of grazing land and then, slowly, mile after mile of wilderness.

Marilee arched a brow. "What's with the smile?"

"I was just thinking how much I love this place. When I was traveling the world, all I wanted was to be here." He sighed. "Just here."

"Do you know how many kids growing up in small towns nurture the dream of leaving it all behind to explore the world?"

He shrugged. "Nothing wrong with that. We all have a right to our dreams. But it was never mine. It was the dream of my parents, and I was dragged kicking and screaming away from everything I loved."

"I'm sorry."

He glanced over. "Don't be. Everything in my wild youth was leading me back here. Even Coot's death. I felt so guilty, knowing I hadn't seen my own grandfather in years. But the minute I set foot on McCord land, I had the strangest feeling that I'd never leave again."

She reached over to lay a hand on his. "That's nice."

"So is this." He looked down at their hands. "You couldn't have picked a prettier day to fly."

"Yeah. That's why I called you. I figured since you'd admitted to being a nervous flier, I'd introduce you to my plane on a perfect day. No weather to worry about. No storms between here and Helena."

"Smart." He squeezed her hand. "And, by the way, I like your plane. Almost as much as its pilot."

"Thank you, sir." She removed her hand to fiddle with the controls. And noted that she could still feel the heat of his touch on her skin.

Their descent into Helena Regional Airport was as smooth as the entire flight had been.

Once again Wyatt stood back to watch Marilee at work. At the terminal she signed a stack of papers and supervised the unloading of plumbing supplies and the loading of the medical supplies.

Satisfied, she turned to him. "Are you up for lunch?"

At his nod she added, "The grill offers a hot dog or a burger."

"A dog. With chili if they have it."

"They do, and it's so hot your mouth will be on fire for hours."

"My kind of chili dog."

She was laughing. "I thought I'd order them to go. That way we can take our time eating while we enjoy the view on the ride home."

He caught her hand, linking his fingers with hers. "I like the way you think."

A short time later, after filing her return flight plan, she did a thorough examination of the plane before inviting Wyatt to join her in the cockpit.

Once they were airborne, she motioned toward the sack of food. "Think you can handle lunch, or do you need time to settle?"

"I'm fine. Let's eat." He opened the bag and unwrapped the chili dogs.

After his first bite he hissed through his teeth. "You weren't kidding." He reached for a bottle of water and took a long, deep drink. "These ought to come with a warning label."

"I told you so."

"Yeah." He grinned and took another bite.

Marilee arched a brow. "Getting used to it?"

"I guess so. By the time I dig into my second or third, I won't even notice the fire in my mouth."

He set a carton of chili fries between them.

Marilee adjusted her sunglasses and popped a fry into her mouth. "On a day like this, with the sky a perfect blue and the sun so bright it almost hurts, I always wonder what it would feel like to just keep on flying, with no end in sight."

"I've tried it. Believe me, it's exhilarating. For a while." Wyatt tipped up his water bottle and took another drink. His voice lowered with feeling. "But after a while, I realized that rebelling and flying aimlessly just isn't all that satisfying. I need to have a goal. These days, I like to know where I'm headed. And what I'm going to do when I get there."

Marilee shivered at the intensity of his tone, though she wasn't at all surprised by his admission. Wyatt McCord struck her as a man who set goals and met them. And despite all the years of aimless wandering in his misspent youth, he knew exactly who he was and where he was going at all times.

CHAPTER SEVEN

———◆———

The landing was as smooth as the entire flight had been. But Wyatt felt a rush of relief to be on the ground. As much as he trusted Marilee's competence, he couldn't completely shake the lingering dread of flying. Maybe he would have to fight these feelings for a lifetime. But at least he wasn't allowing them to control his life. That gave him a measure of satisfaction.

As they taxied to the small terminal and came to a stop, his cell phone vibrated.

He pulled it from his pocket. "Yeah?"

"Hey, cuz." Zane's voice sounded breathless. "Where've you been?"

"Helena. We just landed back in Gold Fever."

"Perfect timing. Stay in town. Jesse and Amy and I are headed there. We just got word that Delia Cowling is home."

"About time." Wyatt stepped into the sunlight and followed Marilee down the steps of the plane. "I'll wait for you at her place."

As he tucked his phone away, Marilee shot him a glance. "Delia?"

He nodded. "Back home."

"Her poor cousin probably couldn't take any more." Marilee paused. "I hope you and your cousins don't mind if I go along. I owe Delia an apology for taking those papers without her permission."

"And she owes us an even bigger apology for keeping them a secret from our family for all these years."

"I think I see a confrontation in our future." Marilee pulled a set of keys from her pocket. "If you wouldn't mind driving my truck across the tarmac, I'd like to unload the medical supplies and deliver them to the clinic on the way to Delia's."

"Good idea. Let's kill two birds."

Marilee shook her head. "Please. I'd rather not talk about killing any birds."

Wyatt paused and touched a hand to her cheek.

She felt the heat all the way to her toes.

He stared down into her eyes, and his lips curved into a killer smile that had those same toes curling with pleasure.

"My fearless, independent adventurer. You handle a plane like you were born with wings. I've watched you patch up battered, bloody cowboys without flinching. But you can't even think about harming a bird."

She couldn't say a word. Her throat was dry as dust.

With a thoughtful look he rubbed a thumb over her lower lip, then turned away and headed toward her truck.

Marilee remained where she was, absorbing the aftershock of his touch. She'd thought he would kiss her. Had wanted him to. Desperately. Instead, all he'd done was touch her. And that had been enough to reduce her to a weak, trembling mass of jelly.

She was going to have to do something about these jumbled hormones.

She sucked in a deep breath and got to work hauling the cases of medical supplies.

By the time Wyatt drove the truck close to the plane, she was in control and able to work alongside him without sighing like a girl with her first crush.

But just barely.

Wyatt and Marilee pulled up in her truck outside Delia Cowling's house within minutes of the ranch truck bearing Zane, Jesse, and Amy. They came together on the little walkway in front of her house to plan their strategy.

Jesse, always the hothead, was clearly in the mood for a fight. Being forced to wait these past few days had added to his temper.

"She'd better have a really good explanation for keeping these papers a secret." He held up the faded pages fisted in his hand.

Zane nodded. "I can't wait to hear what she has to say."

Marilee lifted a palm. "I hope you'll allow me to apologize to her first."

"For what?" Amy asked.

"For taking those papers from her home without her permission."

"They clearly weren't hers. You could see that they belonged to us," Jesse said reasonably.

"Which is why I brought them to you. But still, I had no right to take anything from her home without first asking. My job brings me into people's lives and into their homes. If Delia wanted, she could make trouble for me."

Jesse gave a snort of anger. "I'd like to see her try."

Wyatt decided to try to cool his cousin's heated temper. "We have a right to get some answers. But only after Marilee has had her chance to explain." He glanced around the circle. "Agreed?"

Jesse jammed his hands into his pockets and stared down at the ground.

Amy tucked her arm through his, knowing her touch would be enough to soften his attitude.

Zane nodded.

"All right then." Wyatt took the lead and walked up on the porch before knocking.

Minutes later the door was opened.

Delia Cowling peered at them in surprise. "What's this? A welcome committee?"

"Something like that." Marilee managed a smile. "How's your ankle?"

"Still sore. Most of the swelling's gone down. But since I can walk, and I'd had enough of my cousin and her grumbling, I figured it was time to come home. My cousin agreed with me."

That brought a round of silent glances and a few knowing smiles.

Delia stood in the doorway, looking distinctly unnerved by their presence. It was obvious that she wasn't accustomed to having visitors drop by unannounced.

After an uncomfortable pause, she reluctantly held open the door. "I suppose you'd like to come inside."

"Thank you." Marilee stepped in, followed by the

others. "Delia, I wanted you to know that when I returned to your basement to look for your mother's locket . . ."

"Oh." Delia put a hand to her mouth. "I never thanked you for that. I guess I was asleep when you came upstairs. But I found Mama's locket on my night table when I woke up and knew you'd been the one to put it there. I was so happy to have it back." She touched a hand to her throat. "My cousin had the chain repaired, and now it's back where it belongs, thanks to you, Marilee."

Marilee cleared her throat. "As I was saying, when I was searching for the locket, I had to wade through a pile of papers that had fallen from a cardboard box that you'd knocked over."

"Quite a mess, as I recall. I never expected you to clean it up."

Marilee shook her head. "I didn't mind. As I was returning the papers to their box, I came across these." She turned to Jesse, who handed the faded pages to the old woman.

Delia glanced at them, then looked from Marilee to Jesse. "You found these on the floor of my basement?"

"That's right."

The old woman peered at them more closely. "Does this say gold?"

Jesse started to answer but Wyatt cut him off, allowing Marilee to speak her piece.

"It does. As you can see, they're very old. And from things I'd heard over the years, I realized that they would be of special interest to the McCord family, since they've spent a lifetime searching for their ancestor's lost gold. I brought these upstairs to ask you about them, but since you were asleep, I decided to take them out to the ranch. I'm sorry that I did that without your permission."

The old woman shrugged. "These are nothing to me. I can't imagine what they would be doing in my basement." Hearing the whistle of her kettle, Delia frowned. "I was just making some tea." After a prolonged pause she said almost hesitantly, "Would you like some?"

Marilee spoke for the others. "That's not necessary. We don't want to make extra work for you."

"It's just tea." Delia started toward the back of the house, clearly favoring her sore ankle, while the others trailed behind.

Jesse spoke to Delia's back. "Are you saying you've never seen these papers before?"

Delia nodded. "That's what I'm saying. This is the first I've seen of them."

The three cousins exchanged a glance.

Jesse's anger had just been deflected. In its place was curiosity.

Wyatt spoke for all of them. "Would you allow us to go downstairs and look around?"

"Whatever for?" Delia crossed to the stove and removed a whistling teakettle.

"There could be more of these."

"More? Where?"

"Maybe in the box where Marilee found these. I'm sure she could show us which one it is."

Delia's tea was forgotten. "I believe I'd like to see that myself. I can't imagine where they've been all these years."

With Wyatt assisting the older woman down the stairs, the others followed.

"Careful," Delia cautioned. "This floor is old and damp and cracked. I wouldn't want any of you to fall the way I did." She winced, just thinking about that morning and the pain she'd been forced to endure. "I've paid a dear price for my carelessness."

In the glare of the single dangling lightbulb, Marilee looked over the row of boxes lined up on the metal shelving and lifted one down. "This is the box you upended when you fell, Delia."

As Marilee lifted aside the cover, Delia knelt down and began to sift through the papers inside. "Why, this is filled with nothing but faded papers. Most of them appear to be old college papers of Ledge's." She looked up. "Whatever would my brother be doing with your ancestor's papers?"

"That's what we came here to find out." Jesse's temper was back.

Delia didn't seem to notice. Distracted, she continued sifting through the box until she suddenly held up a scrap of yellowed paper. "Does this say murdered?"

Jesse, Zane, and Wyatt dropped down beside her and stared at the paper in her hand.

It bore the same scrawl as the other page taken from Nathanial's diary.

Jesse's voice grew thoughtful. "According to family lore, Coot's great-great-grandfather Jasper McCord was murdered. Most folks believe by a prospector named Grizzly Markham. Some of the pages recounting his son Nathanial's account of the incident were missing from his diary."

Delia nodded. "I'm aware of all that. But why is it here, in Ledge's papers?"

Wyatt's tone was sharp. "That's what we'd like to know. Would Ledge be at his bank right now?"

"Hmmm?" Delia glanced up. Seeing the looks being exchanged by the three cousins, she shook her head, as though slipping from a fog. Her tone sharpened. "Of course I couldn't say. I've only just returned to town today."

Wyatt helped the old woman to her feet. "Would you be willing to let us go through the rest of his papers? Just in case there could be something more?"

She gave a firm shake of her head. "It's not that I believe Ledge has anything to hide, you understand. But I would never give you permission to look through his personal papers without his consent."

They were so close. The three cousins could hardly contain their impatience to sift through the contents of the box.

"You're sure, Delia?" Marilee pressed.

"You'll have to get Ledge's permission." She placed the lid back on the box.

With a last reluctant look, Wyatt returned the box to the shelf before taking Delia's arm and walking alongside her as they climbed the stairs.

Once upstairs, he helped her to the kitchen. Without a word Marilee filled the old woman's cup with water from the kettle.

She turned. "What do you take in your tea, Delia?"

"Nothing. Thank you." She accepted the steaming cup and sipped.

As they turned to leave, her tone grew more stern. "I hope you believe me when I say that I never knew about those papers."

Wyatt paused in the doorway. "I believe you, Delia. Thank you for all your help."

He followed the others out of the house and to their trucks.

Jesse's voice was tight with anger. "I don't believe a word that old gossip said. She knows more about everything that goes on in this town than anybody else alive. I say we get to the bank and confront Ledge Cowling before his sister has a chance to warn him about what we've discovered."

Zane and Wyatt nodded in agreement.

Wyatt said aloud what they all were thinking. "I'm dying to know why the president of the town bank, knowing about our family's search, would keep something this important hidden for all these years."

It took them only minutes to drive from Delia's house to the bank, situated on the main street alongside the courthouse. It was a small, brick, one-story building with a row of windows overlooking the street.

As they stepped inside, they could see Ledge Cowling talking on the telephone and pacing behind the glass wall that separated his office from the rest of the business. When he spotted the McCord cousins, along with Amy and Marilee, he quickly returned the phone to its cradle and dropped into the chair behind his desk.

His secretary, Paula Henning, looked up with a smile. When she wasn't tending her small ranch and her son, Timmy, she worked at the bank to supplement her income. "Hey, Lee." When she spotted Jesse, Zane, and Wyatt, as well as Jesse's wife, Amy, her smile grew. "My goodness. I don't think I've ever had all of you here at one time. Is this something special?"

"Just business." Wyatt studied Ledge through the glass. "We'd like to talk to your boss."

"Of course. Let me tell him you're here." She stood and made her way to Ledge's office.

A minute later she returned. "Right this way."

She held the door until they were crowded inside his office. When Ledge lifted a hand in dismissal, she withdrew and closed the door before returning to her desk.

"Well. This is an honor." Ledge indicated the leather chairs in a half-circle facing his desk. When everyone was seated he settled himself in his big armchair and steepled his hands on the desktop. "Now what brings the McCord family to my humble bank? I know you aren't here for a loan. In all the years I've been in business, your family has never once asked for my help."

"It's comforting to know that you'd be here if we needed your help, Ledge." Without bothering to make further small talk, Jesse dropped the yellowed paper on his desk. "Do you recognize this?"

Ledge took his time studying it. When he looked up, he arched a brow. "I'm sorry. Should this mean something to me?"

Jesse frowned. "It was in your sister's basement. According to her, the box it was in contained old papers of yours."

Ledge gave a negligent shrug of his shoulder. "I have no idea what box that might be. Of course, Delia lives in our parents' old home, so there could be all sorts of things in that basement that neither of us could possibly identify. If you ever get down there, you'll notice that our parents saved everything from our childhood. Report cards, awards, trophies."

Wyatt picked up the page. "And you're saying you've never seen this before?"

"Afraid not." Ledge glanced around, allowing his gaze to linger on Amy, then on Marilee, favoring each with his best banker's smile. "Apparently this means a good deal more to you than it does to me. And for good reason. After all, everybody knows about your ancestor's lost treasure. I surely wish I could be more help to you."

He stood, indicating an end to the meeting. "If you're ever in the market for a loan, I hope you'll come see me. Now, if you don't mind, I have a meeting with Orley Peterson. He's thinking of adding to his feed and grain store and needs a bank loan. I always have time to do business with the folks who need me."

He offered his hand to each of them in turn, and they had no choice but to return the handshake.

As they made their way back to their trucks, Zane voiced what they'd all surmised.

"I'd bet any amount of money that the caller on his phone when we pulled up outside the bank was Delia. Ledge was way too cool to be caught by surprise."

"Yeah. Poor Aunt Cora. We told her where we were going and promised that we'd be coming back with some answers." Jesse's frustration was obvious. "And Ledge Cowling flicked us off like annoying flies."

"It doesn't matter." Wyatt's tone was low and even, a certain sign that he was fighting to control his temper. "He may have won the first round. But he'd better not mistake our departure for defeat. There are lots more rounds before the final bell. Ledge is going to find out that the McCords have the staying power to last as long as it takes to win it all."

As the others turned toward the ranch truck, Wyatt caught Marilee's hand. "I'm sorry the day has ended like this." He managed a quick smile. "And just when I'd planned a lovely evening of seduction. But I think I'd better go back with the others while they explain to Aunt Cora."

She felt her heart do a sudden flip and hoped she looked as cool as he did. "Well then, the seduction will just have to wait."

He squeezed her hand. "Not too long, I hope."

She watched him walk away and wondered at the way her pulse was pounding in her temples.

If she didn't soon get her hands on him, she might just have an explosion to match the one he'd promised.

The man definitely had a way about him.

Despite her best intentions to keep things light and impersonal, he'd managed to get under her skin the way no other man ever had.

Chapter Eight

———◆◆◆———

"Morning, Aunt Cora." Wyatt glanced around the kitchen, empty except for his aunt, busy loading supplies into an insulated box, and Dandy, stirring something over the stove.

"Good morning." Cora looked over with a smile. "You're up early."

"I might say the same for you." Wyatt didn't want to admit that his sleep had been disturbed by erotic dreams of Marilee. He was going to have to do something about her, and soon.

"Ever since this business with Ledge Cowling, I've been feeling uneasy." Cora finished what she'd been doing and picked up her coffee to sip. "I know it's irrational. Those papers could have been in Delia's basement for fifty years or more, when Ledge and Delia's parents were still alive. But now that we've found another piece of the puzzle, it's as though Coot is reaching out to us, urging us to move ahead with more purpose. I do so want to see my brother's dream to its conclusion."

He nodded. "I know what you mean. We've been making progress on tracking Coot's trail. But I think we need to start charting our own course. Ever since Jesse's wedding, we've been slacking off. But now, finding this latest clue . . ." He let his words die as Cal stepped into the kitchen.

The ranch foreman glanced toward the box of food, then over at Cora. "Another overnighter?"

She could tell, by the look on his face, that he disapproved. "I need to take advantage of the summer sunlight before it's gone, Cal. I need some alone time. I thought I'd camp out at Treasure Chest for a week or two and work on some of my canvases."

He accepted a cup of coffee from Dandy before pulling up a chair beside hers. "I wish you'd take somebody along. I don't like knowing you're out there all alone."

"Now, Cal." She laid a hand over his. "I've been doing this all my life."

"That doesn't mean I have to like it. It isn't safe for you to be alone in the wilderness."

She gave him a gentle smile. "I'll be on McCord land the entire time."

"There aren't any herds up there. And that means there are no wranglers, either."

She touched a hand to the pocket of her brother's old shirt, which she hadn't been able to discard. She still wore it for luck. "I have my cell phone. And you know I always carry a rifle in my Jeep and a handgun."

"Just the same . . ."

"You sound like a mother hen clucking at her chicks."

She set aside her empty cup and got to her feet. "Come on. You can help me carry my supplies out to the truck. I'm just too restless to stay here another minute."

The older man heaved to his feet and picked up the box of food, setting it on the wheeled cart he'd designed just for Cora's jaunts into the wilderness.

Cora kissed Wyatt's cheek. "I won't be gone more than a week or two. If you get any news, you can always call me."

Wyatt watched as she followed Cal through the mudroom.

He understood her need to cope with all that nervous energy and frustration. At least she had her art, which filled her hours from dawn to dusk. She often confessed to turning out some of her finest work when she was feeling stressed.

If only he had an outlet for his own frustrations.

Restless, he left the kitchen and walked to the great room, knowing the others would be downstairs shortly. On a ranch this size, chores started early. Dandy was up before dawn, preparing breakfast, and everyone was expected to eat a hearty meal before beginning a day that often didn't end until well past dark.

On the oversize coffee table lay a map of the area. It was dotted with sticky notes and pins that he and his cousins used to mark the places they believed their grandfather had already searched. From the various scraps of paper and doodles that Coot had left through the years, they'd mapped out a tentative trail.

Wyatt stood mulling the huge expanse of land between the last note they'd charted and the end of the McCord property, just beyond Treasure Chest Mountain. How many scraps of paper were lying around in waste bins all over Montana? Coot's absentmindedness was legendary. He'd been known to allow his drawings and maps to spill from his pockets along the trail, where they were often carried on the breeze for miles. Folks around these parts who recognized them returned them to their rightful owner. Others just tossed the papers away like so much litter.

He looked up when Jesse and Amy strolled down the stairs. "'Morning."

"'Morning." Jesse caught Amy's hand and the two paused beside Wyatt. "Something wrong?"

Jesse looked as sleek and happy as a mountain cat. Wyatt was betting it wasn't just his morning shower that put such a gleam in his eye. He was so much in love with his wife, he was practically glowing.

Wyatt thought of Marilee, fresh from her shower in her tidy little apartment, and felt a quick tug of desire.

"Nope. Just studying the map we made. I'm thinking we need to get more serious about searching for Coot's treasure."

Jesse grinned. "I've been thinking the same thing. Just knowing Ledge Cowling was sitting on something that could have been a clue has me champing at the bit."

Amy squeezed his hand. "We talked about it last night."

"What're we talking about?" Zane descended the stairs and joined them.

"Searching for Coot's treasure." Wyatt pointed to the map. "We had a plan. Then, in the afterglow of a certain wedding"—he shot a meaningful glance at Jesse and Amy—"we got lazy. I say it's time we get serious about this. As serious as Coot was."

"I agree." Zane lifted his latest camera from his pocket and took aim at his cousins. One day he planned to edit miles of film into a documentary that would end, hopefully, with the discovery of the lost fortune. It had been Coot's dream; now it was his. "Since this is being recorded for posterity, what do you say we make a pact to really bust our butts chasing Coot's dream."

"You mean our dream," Wyatt corrected.

He and Jesse sandwiched Amy between them and lifted their fists in a salute, mugging for the camera.

Wyatt spoke for all of them. "Let the record show that from this day forward, we intend to spend whatever time we can spare from ranch chores to continue our search for the lost fortune."

"And when it's found," Jesse added, "we'll just see who's crazy as a coot."

"Amen to that, cuz." Zane clicked off the recorder.

Wyatt's cell phone rang more than a dozen times before he managed to free it from his shirt pocket. "Hold on," he shouted before dropping it into the dirt.

After a very long pause he retrieved it. "Yeah. Hello."

"Hey, rebel." The sound of Marilee's voice on the phone had Wyatt's heart rate speeding up. "I hope I haven't caught you in the middle of driving a herd of cattle."

"Nothing quite so glamorous. I was trying to hold a heifer still so Jesse could inject her with a dose of antibiotic. Hold on again."

Marilee grinned at the sound of the bawling animal in the background.

"Okay." Wyatt rubbed his hand down his dusty jeans while retrieving the phone. "Job finished. What's up?"

"Orley Peterson hired me to fly up to Razorback Ridge to deliver some supplies. Want to tag along?"

He glanced at his watch. "I can be there in an hour."

"Why don't you drive directly to the airstrip? That'll give me time to do my preflight."

"I'll see you there." He tucked his cell phone into his pocket and turned to Jesse and Zane, who were grinning like fools. "What's so funny?"

"Another flying date with Marilee?" Zane exchanged a look with his cousin. "For a guy who's not fond of airplanes, I'd say this is getting serious."

Instead of the denial they'd been expecting, he shocked them both by tucking his hands in his back pockets before strolling away.

Jesse watched him, before turning to Zane. "Uh-oh. I think loverboy is hooked."

"Wyatt?" Zane started to grin, then frowned instead. "Oh, man." He dug out a bandanna and mopped at the sweat beading his forehead. "Before you know it, I'll be the only sensible one left."

"That was quick and easy." Wyatt felt the sudden rush of adrenaline as the plane lifted off the tiny airstrip at Razorback Ridge.

The flight from Gold Fever to the little town two hundred miles away had been smooth and uneventful, and now, with day turning into a golden, glorious evening, he was feeling mellow.

As they gained altitude, Marilee adjusted her sunglasses and glanced over. "You okay?"

"Fine." He waited for his heart to settle. Except for that

quick blip of his pulse when they became airborne, this had been an easy takeoff.

"Good. We should be landing in Gold Fever shortly after dark. Sorry there wasn't time for a leisurely dinner while we were at Razorback."

He pointed to the bag of burgers and fries he'd ordered from the little airport grill while Marilee filed her return flight plan. "This will fortify us. Want to eat now, or wait awhile?"

"I'll wait. But you go ahead."

He shook his head. "There's plenty of time."

"Okay. Then just sit back, relax, and enjoy the view before it gets too dark."

Wyatt found himself doing just that. It was one of those perfect, cloudless evenings, the sky a clear blue, the sun just beginning to set behind Treasure Chest Mountain, turning the peaks to an amazing purple and pink glow.

He uncapped a bottle of water and took a long pull. "So, you get these fly dates often enough to pay the bills?"

She nodded. "Some months are busier than others. And most are just a quick flight from home base to some of the smaller towns that have airstrips."

"Does each town maintain its own airport, or is this a state-run operation?"

She shook her head. "Neither. Most are privately owned. Our little airport in Gold Fever is owned by Orley Peterson, Stan Novak, and Ledge Cowling. The one we just left is owned by Orley and Ledge. In fact, they've invested in a number of small airports in the state." She paused. "Speaking of Ledge, Paula Henning told me that he's out of town. He left right after we met with him."

Wyatt capped the bottle and set it aside. "Did she say where he went?"

"He didn't tell her. Just said he had some business to take care of." She pointed. "If you look straight ahead, you'll see the beginning of your land."

Wyatt peered through the windshield. As far as the eye could see was the most breathtaking landscape imaginable.

"It's funny. In my travels, I was always looking for that perfect place, where I would be free of all the anger and baggage I was carrying. I did a lot of soul-searching while I meditated in Tibet. I tried to"—he shrugged—"I guess the word would be *atone*, for all the grief I gave my parents by taking on really thankless tasks in far-flung places like Africa and South America. And those things worked for a while. But then I'd have the urge to move on again, looking for some new freedom, some noble endeavor." There was a fierceness in his tone that had her looking at him as he studied the land below. "Then I came home for Coot's funeral and was persuaded to stay, and I discovered everything I was searching for right here. I've never felt freer or more genuinely myself than right here, doing all the filthy, backbreaking chores needed to keep this ranch going."

In silence they flew over vast herds of cattle dotting the lush hillsides. Wyatt pointed out the occasional ranches where wranglers lived with their families and tended the herds in the more isolated sections of McCord land.

"We'll be passing over Treasure Chest." Marilee had a firm grip on the controls as they caught the sudden downdrafts and air currents always present above the mountains.

Wyatt felt his stomach take a quick dip.

To distract himself from the turbulence, he peered down, searching vainly for a sign of Aunt Cora's Jeep, even though he knew that she could be hidden behind dozens of jagged ridges and outcroppings of rock.

As they crossed over the mountain range he spotted something puzzling. Craning his neck for a better look, he touched a hand to her arm.

"Is there time to circle back and make that run again?"

"Sure. What did you see?"

"I don't know." He scanned the ground below before pointing. "Does that look like a trail?"

Marilee studied the landscape below in the fading light. "Oh, yeah. Definitely a trail. A wide one. Looks like it might have been made by a horse and wagon." She pointed ahead. "Looks like it goes all the way from Treasure Chest to the river."

"That's odd."

"The trail? What's odd about a trail?"

"We don't have any herds in this area. In fact, we don't have any ranches or bunkhouses in this stretch of wilderness."

She shrugged. "Maybe it's an old prospector's trail."

"After more than a hundred years, wouldn't it have been covered over by vegetation?"

"You told me your aunt was painting somewhere out here. Could it have been made by her vehicle?"

"It appears to begin or end at the river. She would have been coming from our ranch"—he pointed—"in that direction."

"Yeah. Strange." Marilee's eyes widened as she suddenly tapped her instrument panel.

At her look of alarm, Wyatt tensed. "What's wrong?"

"This gauge. It should read full. It did in my preflight. Now it's showing no fuel and blinking an alarm."

"Didn't you refuel at Razorback?"

"Yes. And I have the receipt to prove it. This can't be right." She tapped the instrument panel again. "The gauge must be faulty. I saw one of the ground crew handling the refueling while our cargo was being unloaded."

"Could there be a leak in the fuel line?"

"I doubt . . ."

The engine sputtered, and Wyatt automatically clutched the armrests. "I don't like the sound of this. What can I do to help?"

The aircraft shuddered and did a sudden shift from side to side, dipping the wings.

Marilee's voice was calm and cool, as if she were declaring it a lovely day. "Make sure your seat belt is secure. Brace yourself for a rough landing. We're going down."

"How soon?"

"Now."

With absolute clarity Wyatt watched as Marilee calmly adjusted her earphones and spoke to the nameless, faceless entity at a control tower too far away to do more than listen and record.

There was an odd sound that Wyatt recognized in the dim recesses of his mind as wind, whistling past the plane as it hurtled toward the ground at a speed that seemed a hundred times faster than his thundering heart.

He thought about his parents, going down in a small jungle clearing, far from home and family.

He thought about Marilee, sitting beside him, calmly doing her job, as though it were a day in the park.

And then there was no time for thought.

Wyatt felt a strange sense of peace settle over him as the ground rushed up at them, blurring his vision.

CHAPTER NINE

The plane cleared the tree line, sailed over a swollen stream, and skimmed the ground before touching down with teeth-rattling force.

MON342 continued on, bumping over ruts and gullies with bone-jarring speed until at last it came to a wheezing stop. Just inches from the windshield loomed an enormous boulder.

Wyatt didn't permit himself to think what would have happened if they hadn't avoided that disastrous encounter.

After the whistle of air rushing past the little plane, the sudden silence was shocking.

Wyatt sat perfectly still, as though anticipating another crisis.

His first thought was Marilee. He looked over. Her hands were still tightly gripping the controls. Her eyes stared unblinking at the view outside her windshield.

At last she let out an audible sigh.

He touched a hand to her arm. "You all right?"

"Yeah." She relaxed her hands and let them drop to her lap before looking over at him. "You?"

"Not a scratch." He took her hand in his. "You sure you're okay?"

"I'm fine now." She let him continue to hold her hand. She needed the connection. It felt so good to know that he was here beside her.

"All right. No blood," she said with a sigh. "No broken bones. This is all good."

"How about the plane?" Wyatt looked around. "Since there aren't any flames coming from the engine, I'm guessing we're not in any immediate danger."

"Not from a fire. But I'd better check for structural damage before it gets too dark to see."

She released her seat belt, and he followed suit.

Her legs were none too steady as she stepped from the plane. Nerves were setting in now, big-time, and she could feel a weakness slowing her movements.

They circled the plane, noting the damage done to the tail and one wing as they'd scraped over rocks and low-growing brush and shrubs.

Wyatt leaned a hand against the wing to steady himself. "You think the plane is sound enough to take off?"

She shook her head. "I wouldn't risk it. I'll need a crew to go over every inch of it before I'll take it up again."

His mind began working overtime. They weren't going to simply lift off and fly home as he'd first imagined when he'd stepped outside the plane. Not that he was in any hurry to be airborne again, but if they were stuck here, he needed to readjust his thinking.

"How did this happen? What happened to the fuel?" Wyatt paused beside Marilee.

"There's no way to tell until I get the plane back to the hangar and have a crew check out the fuel line. There had to be a leak. I just don't understand how it was missed during refueling."

"Unless it happened after takeoff."

She nodded, deep in thought. "There was no collision. No jolt. No extreme wind or weather, or sign of any problem."

"Old age?"

She shrugged. "The plane isn't that old. And I have a maintenance contract with a really reliable crew to keep it in tip-top shape."

While she spoke, Wyatt dug out his cell phone and called Jesse to explain their situation. "Hold on." He turned to Marilee. "Jesse can get a crew out here in the morning. He'll try to locate a flatbed truck, too. Do you mind spending the night with the plane?"

She shook her head. "I don't see that we have any choice. There are no visible lights in the area. There's nothing out here but wilderness. It's only for one night. And we've got everything we need on board. Food. Water. There are emergency supplies I always carry."

Wyatt spoke into the phone. "Marilee's fine with it, and so am I. I'll hand the phone to her, and she can check the coordinates on the panel to let you know exactly where we are."

Marilee took his phone and climbed into the plane. A short time later she stepped out.

"I notified the control tower in Razorback about our situation. They'll contact Gold Fever's airport and alert them that we won't be returning tonight." She laughed. "Old Randy, who takes the evening shift, will be happy to know he doesn't have to miss a night with Vi and Daffy at the Fortune Saloon."

"Never let it be said that a plane crash kept good old Randy from happy hour."

The two shared a chuckle.

Wyatt rubbed his hands up and down her arms. "It's so good to be able to laugh."

"Yeah." She looked up at him, eyes shiny. "For a few minutes I wondered whether there'd be anything left to laugh about when this was over."

His eyes narrowed on her. "You were worried?"

"You bet."

"It didn't show."

She shrugged. "I had to stay focused on all the things I've learned through the years about how to handle the unexpected. And believe me, this was totally unexpected. Good thing I didn't have time to think about what was happening, or I'd have been scared to death."

He gave a quick shake of his head. "You had me fooled. You looked and sounded cool as a cucumber."

"You know what they say. Never let 'em see you sweat."

"I did enough sweating for both of us."

She lifted a hand to his cheek. "I hate that you had to go through this, Wyatt. Knowing what I do about your parents, I feel so guilty that you had to worry for even a few minutes. Thank heaven for happy endings."

Seeing the way his gaze intensified, she turned away, suddenly feeling the need to be busy. "There's a chill in the air. I'm going to gather up some wood for a fire."

Wyatt remained where he was, unable to shake the realization that, despite all the drama of a pending crash, Marilee had been worried about him.

When was the last time someone had done that? He couldn't recall. He'd been on his own for so long now, he'd grown accustomed to feeling alone in the universe. He'd even managed to convince himself that he didn't mind. But her simple admission touched him more deeply than anything else she could have said.

"Hey, rebel." Marilee's voice had his head coming up sharply. "You going to lend a hand, or just stand there watching the colorful sunset?"

With a thoughtful expression, he bent to the task of gathering wood.

"Oh, this is nice." Marilee sat with her back against a rock, nibbling the last of the cold hamburger Wyatt had bought at the airport grill. "I'm glad now that you stocked up on some dinner."

"Nothing like good food and a cozy campfire." Beside her he tipped back his head and took a long drink from the water bottle.

"I suppose, in your world travels, you've had your share of campfires."

He nodded.

"I'd like to hear about them."

He leaned back, remembering. "Some, like the ones in Nepal, were necessary for survival from the bitter cold."

"Why Nepal?"

"Why not? It sounded like a good idea at the time."

She gave a mock shiver. "Tell me about a warmer place."

"How about the jungles of South America? Those campfires were strictly for cooking the fish we caught in the rivers."

"And I suppose you had to avoid crocodiles while fishing?"

"A few."

"You've had some amazing adventures."

"Yeah. But I like this one best."

"In the middle of nowhere?" She glanced over. "Why?"

"I'm sharing it with you."

At his unexpected admission, her eyes widened. "Thank you. That's . . . nice to know. The funny thing is, I'm enjoying it, too."

"You seem surprised by that."

She tossed the paper bag into the fire and watched the flames consume it. "I guess I am. When I was fighting to bring down my plane, I was going over the rules of survival in my mind. Keep the nose up. Wings level. Stay focused. There isn't anything in the book about turning a crash landing into a cozy evening around a soothing campfire."

Because she was worrying the edges of her miniskirt, he caught her hand in his to still the movement. "You know what they say about rules."

When she looked over he was smiling, that dangerous, killer smile that had the power to make her heart stammer.

"They're meant to be broken."

"I don't think . . ."

He twined his fingers with hers and she felt a quick flare of heat race up her arm. "I do. Think," he added with a grin. "Probably way more than I should. And what I've been thinking is bound to affect both of us."

"Really? What have you been thinking about?"

"You and me. Where we're going. What we'll do when we get there."

When she opened her mouth he surprised her by pressing a finger to her lips to still her words.

At that simple touch she absorbed the most amazing collision of icy splinters along her spine.

"Earlier tonight, when we came through that crazy landing, you told me you'd been worried about me." He looked at their joined hands. "That's what I love about you, Marilee. No matter how much is going on in your life, you make room for everyone around you."

"This is getting way too serious." Nervous, she got to her feet.

He stood beside her, turning her to face him.

Her eyes, he noted, were misty.

He framed her face with his big hands. "What's wrong?"

"Nothing." She gave him a shaky smile.

He tipped up her face. "You're lying. I can tell. What's wrong? What did I say?"

"I'm just being foolish."

When she tried to pull away his fingers gripped the tops of her arms. "There's no place to run. No place to hide. We're about to spend the night alone out here in the middle of nowhere. So don't turn away from me. Tell me what's on your mind. Did I say something to hurt you?"

She lowered her head, refusing to meet his eyes. Her voice was little more than a whisper. "I'm giving you fair warning. It's silly." She swallowed. "You said that's what you love about me."

"Ah." He drew out the word as he studied her eyes. "And you're thinking I just tossed out some casual phrase that you've heard from dozens of guys? Or maybe one in particular, who mattered enough to turn you into a cynic?"

At the intensity of his tone she looked up. "Yeah. Something like that. After all, McCord, your reputation precedes you. You're not exactly shy with women. I'm sure you've used plenty of lines like that to get what you want."

His eyes, steady on hers, were hot and fierce.

His voice was equally fierce. "I'll admit that when I first saw you, my initial reaction was purely physical. A healthy combination of testosterone and lust. What guy could look at you and not feel what I felt? You're beautiful, and bright and independent. And did I mention beautiful?"

That brought a smile to her eyes.

"But the more I got to know you, the more I realized you weren't just a pretty package. I started learning that you were someone special. Someone I wanted to treat very carefully."

"And now?"

"I'm still battling lust."

There was that grin, sending an arrow straight through her heart.

"But there's more here. Much more." He stared at her mouth with naked hunger. "I've waited a long time for this, but now I'm going to have to kiss you. And when I do, I can't promise to stop."

She stood very still, heart pounding. "How do you know I'll ask you to?"

"Careful. Because unless you tell me to stop, you have to know where this is heading . . ."

In reply she stood on tiptoe to brush her mouth to his, stopping his words. Stopping his heart.

He drew in a deep breath and drew her a little away to stare into her eyes. "I hope you meant that."

"With all my heart."

"Thank God." He dragged her against him and covered her lips with his. Inside her mouth he whispered, "Because, baby, I mean this."

She'd waited so long. So long. And it was worth all the time she'd spent waiting and wondering. Here was a man who knew how to kiss a woman and make her feel like the only one in the universe.

This kiss was so hot, so hungry, she felt the rush of desire from the top of her head all the way to her toes. And still it spun on and on until she became lost in it.

He changed the angle of the kiss and took it deeper until Marilee could feel her flesh heating, her bones melting like hot wax.

She wanted to be sensible, to move slowly, but her mind refused to cooperate. With a single kiss her brain had been wiped clear of every thought but one. She wanted this man. Wanted him now. Desperately.

When at last they came up for air, she put a hand to his chest. "I need a minute to catch my breath."

"Okay." A second later he dragged her close. "Time's up."

Her laughter turned into a sigh as he ran nibbling kisses down her throat until the blood was drumming in her temples.

When his lips moved lower she gasped and clutched

his waist and gave herself up to the most amazing rush of heat that had the ground tilting beneath her feet.

Wyatt savored the taste of her, the feel of her flesh beneath his touch. Hadn't he known it would be like this? It was why he'd put off this moment. He'd sensed instinctively that the instant he kissed her, everything would change. Nothing less than everything she had to give would satisfy the need in him.

And what a need. It clawed at his insides, a beast fighting to be free.

His hands moved to the buttons of her shirt and he slid it from her shoulders before unfastening the wisp of lace that covered her breasts. The look in his eyes spoke volumes.

"Oh, baby." His words, whispered like a prayer, had her shivering. "You're even more beautiful than I'd thought. All this pale white flesh dotted with"—he trailed kisses across her shoulder to the sensitive hollow of her throat— "freckles. Have I told you how much I love freckles?"

In spite of the heat of his kisses, she managed a weak laugh. "That's good, because they're everywhere . . ."

"Shh. A very dangerous admission. Now you just know I'll have to count every single one." His hands slid beneath the denim miniskirt. "Ever since I saw you in this, I've thought of nothing but getting you out of it."

Her skirt drifted to the ground, followed by her lace bikini.

With his mouth feasting on hers, and his clever fingers working their magic, she gave herself up to all the pleasure he was offering.

Such exquisite pleasure. He knew exactly how to touch her. Where to touch her. How to please her. How to bring her to her knees with a desperate need that bordered on pain.

Wyatt drove her up and over. She was wonderful to watch. The way her eyes widened as she rode the first crest. The possessive way her arms circled his neck and drew his head down when he shifted his weight.

"Wyatt." Her sigh filled his mouth. "We need a moment."

"All I need is you," he growled. "Now."

"Not yet." And then her hands were at his shirt, tugging it over his head before reaching for the fasteners at his waist. When his clothes joined hers on the ground, she was finally free to touch him the way he was touching her. And to marvel at the beauty of his body, all corded muscles and sinew.

"Oh, yes, Wyatt." She ran hot, wet kisses down his throat while her hands moved over the flat planes of his stomach, and then lower, until his breathing was as ragged as hers.

His tongue traced the curve of her ear, nipping and tugging on the lobe before darting inside, sending shivers along her spine.

Against his chest he could feel the wild, erratic rhythm of her heartbeat, as ragged as his own. From deep in her throat her breath hitched on a sob.

Wyatt knew he could take her now. It was what she wanted. What they both wanted. They could be free of this terrible tension that was raging through them now like an unchained beast.

But he'd fantasized about this for so long now. From the first time he'd seen her, he'd known that one day he would have to have her. Now, finally, he was free to do all the things he'd only dreamed of. Now, at last, he would have it all.

But not just yet.

With sheer force of will, he banked his needs and ran butterfly kisses over her cheeks, her eyelids, the tip of her nose.

He felt her relax in his arms and brought his mouth to hers in a kiss so sweet, so tender, it brought a sigh from her lips.

"Here." He caught her hands and together they knelt in the grass, littered with their clothes.

With his eyes steady on hers he leaned close, touching her lips with his.

His arms came around her and he drew her down until they were lying together, flesh to flesh, heartbeat to heartbeat. He heard the purr of pleasure deep in her throat as he ran kisses down her neck, across her collarbone, over her breasts, then lower.

Her body convulsed when he moved lower still and another climax ripped through her. Stunned and reeling, she had no time to recover as, with lips and teeth and tongue, he took her on a wild roller-coaster ride that left her staggered and hungering for more.

He felt the madness taking over. A sense of desperation that had him driving her high, then higher still, until they were both beyond reason, beyond control.

"Marilee." Blinded by a hard, driving need, he knew he could wait no longer. His eyes steady on hers, he entered her.

She wrapped herself around him, opening to him, whispering his name like a prayer.

"Come with me, baby. Stay with me."

With hearts thundering, they began moving, climbing.

Lungs straining, bodies hot and wet, they reached the very crest of a high, sheer mountain.

For one heart-stopping moment they paused, taking in deep breaths.

On a shuddering sigh, they stepped off the edge.

And flew.

CHAPTER TEN

Marilee lay perfectly still, waiting for her world to settle. She had to fight the unreasonable urge to weep.

Wyatt's face was pressed to the hollow of her throat, his breathing rough, his damp body plastered to hers.

He nuzzled her neck. "Am I too heavy?"

"Umm." It was all she could manage.

"You all right?"

"Umm."

"Did anybody ever tell you that you talk too much?"

"Umm."

He brushed his mouth over hers. "If you hum a bit more, I might be able to name that tune."

That broke the spell of tears that had been threatening and caused her to laugh.

She wrapped her arms around his neck and kissed him back. "Have I told you how much I like your silly sense of humor?"

"No, you haven't." He rolled to his side and gathered

her into his arms, nuzzling her cheek, while his big hands moved over her hip, her back, her waist, as though measuring every inch of her. "What else do you like about me?"

"You fishing for compliments?"

"Of course I am."

"Glutton. Your sense of humor isn't enough?"

"Not nearly enough. How about my looks?"

"They're okay, for a footloose rebel."

"Stop. All these mushy remarks will inflate my ego." He gave a mock frown. "How about the way I kiss?"

"You're not bad."

"Not bad?" His hands stopped their movement. He drew a little away. "That's all you can say?"

"If you recall, tonight was the first time we've kissed. I haven't had nearly enough practice to be a really good judge of your talent."

"Then we'd better take care of that right now." He framed her face. With his eyes steady on hers, he lowered his mouth to claim her lips.

Marilee's eyelids fluttered and she felt an explosion of color behind them. As though the moon and stars had collided while she rocketed through space. It was the most amazing sensation, and, as his lips continued moving over hers, she found herself wishing it could go on forever.

When at last they came up for air, she took in a long, deep breath before opening her eyes. "Oh, yes, rebel. I have to say, I do like the way you kiss."

"That's good, because I intend to do a whole lot more of it." He lay back in the grass, one hand beneath his head. "Now it's my turn. Want to know all the things I like about you?"

"I'm afraid to hear it." Marilee lay on her side, her hand splayed across his chest.

"Besides your freckles, which I've already mentioned, the thing about you I like best is your take-charge attitude."

She chuckled. "A lot of guys feel intimidated by that."

"They're idiots. Don't they know there's something sexy about a woman who knows what to do and how to do it? I've watched you as a medic and as a pilot, and I haven't decided which one turns me on more."

"Really?" She sat up. "Want me to fetch my first-aid kit from the plane? I could always splint your arm or leg and really turn you on."

He dragged her down into his arms and growled against her mouth, "You don't need to do a single thing to turn me on. All I need to do is look at you and I want you."

"You mean now? Again? So soon?"

"Oh, yeah."

"Liar. I don't believe it's possible."

"You ought to know by now that I never say anything I can't back up with action."

"Prove it, rebel."

"My pleasure."

There was a wicked smile on his lips as he rolled over her and began to kiss her breathless, all the while taking her on a slow, delicious ride to paradise.

"Cold?"

Marilee's eyes opened and she found Wyatt watching her by the light of the moon. Nearby, the fire had burned to embers, occasionally sending up sparks that hissed and snapped in the darkness.

"You give off enough body heat for both of us." She drew her arms around his waist. "But your back's cold. I have blankets in the plane."

"I'll get them." He stood and slipped into his jeans, leaving the waist unsnapped as he made his way to the plane in that loose, lanky stride that had her mouth watering. She loved the look of him, like a cowboy in some Madison Avenue ad. Except that he was the real thing, with big, work-roughened hands and scuffed boots and a high-voltage smile that could reduce her to puddles when it was directed her way.

Minutes later he returned and shook out a quilt, which he spread out on the grass. Then he knelt beside her and draped a blanket around her shoulders before striding away to gather more wood for the fire.

A short time later, with the fire blazing, he dropped down beside Marilee, who had settled herself on the quilt.

She held out her arms and he moved in close before she wrapped herself and the blanket around him.

"Now this is what I call cozy and comfortable." He nibbled her lips and she sighed in contentment.

He offered her an apple he'd found amid the supplies. She took a bite before handing it back to him. Together they shared the fruit, then washed it down with a bottle of water.

He passed her the water. "What do you think about when you're flying?"

"Always happy thoughts. Sometimes I'm a kid again, riding on my father's shoulders. Sometimes I'm a pioneer, the first to fly to the moon or Mars. There's something freeing about being high above the ground and knowing I'm in control."

He glanced over. "How about when things go wrong and you have no control? How did you feel when you realized we had to land in the middle of nowhere?"

She shook her head. "It's hard to explain, Wyatt. I felt a flash of fear, but never any paralyzing panic. Even when we were heading toward rough terrain, I felt certain I could land without trashing the plane."

"What if you hadn't?"

She shrugged. "There wasn't time to play that game in my mind. I suppose it was the same for you when you decided to fall off that bull and land at my feet."

He chuckled. "Okay. I get it. Yeah. No time to worry. Just do the deed and live with the consequences. Looks like we're two of a kind."

"Exactly. Only you prefer to risk your life in the bull-ring, and I'd rather risk mine in the sky."

"I guess it proves we're a perfect fit. And both perfectly crazy."

She saw the way his eyes narrowed on her and recognized the same quick rush of desire that had suddenly come over her.

How was it possible that she could want him again?

There was no time to analyze her feelings as he gathered her close and kissed her until they were both trembling with need.

A spark from the fire shot into the air and blazed a fiery trail in the darkness. Neither of them took notice. They were too busy starting a blaze of their own.

"What are you thinking?" Marilee touched a finger to the smile that curved Wyatt's lips.

"That life doesn't get much better'n this." He stretched

out his long legs toward the blazing logs he'd added to the fire.

With one arm behind his head, he kept the other around Marilee, holding her close.

They'd spent the night alternately loving and sleeping. At times their lovemaking had been as soothing and gentle as a breeze blowing across a meadow, all soft kisses and easy sighs. At other times they'd been seized by a sort of madness that had taken them down, down into a deep abyss, where nothing had mattered except to feed the passion that drove them to the very edge of reason.

Now, as ribbons of dawn light began to streak the sky, they lay together, for the moment pleasantly sated, as cozy as old lovers.

"What took you so long?" Marilee played with the hair on his chest.

"So long?" He looked over.

"To make a move on me." She felt her cheeks grow hot at the way he was staring. "Most guys don't even give me time to learn their last name."

"I'm not most guys."

"I've noticed." It was one of the things that set him apart from every other man she'd ever known.

"You sorry we waited?"

"Oh, Wyatt." She lifted a hand to his cheek. "I'm not sorry about anything."

"Good." He leaned up on one elbow and kissed her. "It nearly killed me to walk away from you each time without so much as a kiss. But I knew the minute I tasted you, it was all over."

She laughed. "You make it sound like a death sentence."

"If so"—he gathered her close and kissed her until they were both sighing—"I can't think of a better way to die than this."

The need, sharp and swift, caught them both by surprise. With a blaze of passion they took each other into the very heart of their storm. A storm that, when finally spent, left them both shaking and craving more.

"Is that a plane?" Marilee awoke with a start, surprised to find the sun already high.

Wyatt shaded the sun from his eyes to scan the sky.

As the sound grew louder they both sat up at the same moment.

"A truck." Wyatt pointed. "Coming from that direction. Probably Jesse and Zane with that flatbed they promised."

"Oh, no. Look at me. What was I thinking?" With a cry Marilee grabbed up her discarded clothes and started dressing.

When she finished she tossed Wyatt's clothing at him. "Aren't you going to put these on?"

"Yeah. No rush."

"No rush?" She was already climbing into the cockpit of the plane to retrieve her gear.

Men, she thought. If they were standing naked in Grand Central Station, they would probably take their sweet time finding something with which to cover themselves.

While she ran a brush through her tangled hair, she watched as Wyatt calmly slipped into his clothes just as a ranch truck came into view over a hill. She let out a sigh of relief that at least they were both dressed.

As the truck roared to a halt and Jesse, Amy, and Zane

stepped out, Marilee rushed forward to greet them. "You made good time."

"We started at dawn." Jesse grinned at his wife. "If Amy had her way, we'd have started even earlier."

"I was worried sick." Amy grabbed her friend in a fierce embrace and held on. "Are you sure you're all right?"

"I'm fine." Marilee glanced over at Wyatt and the two exchanged a long, knowing look. "We're both fine."

"You look none the worse for it." Amy clutched her hand. "Lee, I was so relieved to hear that you two weren't hurt in the landing."

"Not as relieved as we were." Marilee gave her another quick, hard hug, and the two women clung for a moment before stepping apart.

"You had to be terrified."

Marilee managed a smile. "There was no time for terror, or any other emotion. But when it was over, I have to admit that my knees were quaking."

"Mine, too." Amy looked at her husband for confirmation. "When Jesse gave me the news, I thought for a moment I'd be sick. But then he said you were both fine, and I was so relieved."

Wyatt strolled closer to his cousins and indicated the ranch truck. "You promised a flatbed."

"It's on the way. Since it has to move at a snail's pace over this terrain, we decided to come ahead." Jesse gave him a slap on the arm. "How'd you two survive the night?"

"Fine." Wyatt smiled at Marilee, who returned his smile. "We had enough food and water and blankets. Since it didn't rain, we just made a fire and slept under the stars."

Zane glanced toward the ashes of the campfire, then at the bedroll beside it. "At least the plane's intact. If it had rained, you would have had shelter. Looks like you had all the comforts of home."

Wyatt crossed the distance to drop an arm around Marilee. "I don't think either of us would like to make a habit of this, unless we had all the provisions that Aunt Cora packs for her wilderness trips. And even then, I'm not sure it's something I'd do on a regular basis the way she does."

That had all of them laughing.

It was, Marilee thought, good to hear the sound of laughter.

Amy glanced toward the plane, noting the damage to the tail and wing. "That had to be some hard landing. You going to tell us all the details?"

"In time." Wyatt pointed to the cloud of dust coming up over the rise. "It looks like this is the flatbed truck."

Though they had dozens of questions, they managed to put them aside.

Within minutes the three cousins were working together, along with the crew from the ranch, to secure the plane for the long, tedious trip back to the airport.

CHAPTER ELEVEN

————◆◆◆————

As they crowded into the ranch truck, Amy passed a foil-wrapped container to Marilee, who'd climbed into the backseat with Wyatt.

She arched a brow. "What's this?"

"Breakfast. Dandy figured the two of you would be starving."

"Bless him." Marilee removed the foil wrapper and stared at the tray of deviled eggs, sliced ham and turkey, freshly baked rolls, and an array of fruit. Pineapple slices, grapes, strawberries, melon. "Was he planning on feeding an army?"

"Yeah. That's Dandy." Amy closed a hand over Jesse's. "That's why we all love him."

Marilee tasted the fruit, then offered a strawberry to Wyatt. As his lips closed around the tips of her fingers, she absorbed a jolt to the heart.

"After last night's cold burgers," she said, shooting a meaningful glance at Wyatt, "this is an absolute feast."

"Add this to the feast." Jesse handed Wyatt a thermos of coffee and some travel mugs. "There's nothing like really hot coffee to warm the soul."

While they bumped over rocky hills and dry washes, Marilee and Wyatt sat back enjoying Dandy's unexpected gift. And because they weren't able to eat everything, the others offered to help them out, since they'd eaten their own breakfast several hours earlier.

When they'd had their fill, Zane asked the question they all wanted answered. "Okay. Now that breakfast is out of the way, tell us. What happened to force a landing in the middle of the wilderness?"

"I'm not sure yet." Marilee set aside her mug. "The fuel gauge read empty. But I had the plane fueled in Razorback while Harding's supplies were being unloaded."

"Is it common to spring a leak?"

At Amy's question Marilee couldn't help laughing. "If it were common, you wouldn't find too many people willing to be pilots. We may like flying with the birds, but we're not willing to drop to earth like wounded elephants."

The others joined in the laughter.

Wyatt sat back, letting the laughter wash over him. It felt good to see Marilee interacting so easily with his cousins. Though he hadn't meant for it to happen, they'd become a family again. After their years of separation, Zane and Jesse meant a great deal to him, as did Amy. But this woman had begun to mean as much or more. It mattered to him that they were accepting of her. Though he hadn't planned on this happening, Marilee mattered.

He looked up to see Zane watching him in the rearview

mirror. It occurred to him that he was probably wearing a stupid grin. Not that it bothered him. Right now he didn't care if the whole world saw him grinning like a fool. He felt wildly, foolishly happy, and so glad to be returning to civilization, even though he'd thoroughly enjoyed his night in the wilderness. His time alone with Marilee had been like a special gift from the gods. One he would cherish for a long time to come. Now, he was more than ready to get back to reality.

Daylight had faded to dusk by the time the plane had been unloaded from the flatbed truck and towed to a hangar at the Gold Fever airport.

Jesse, Amy, and Zane had long ago returned to the ranch.

The airport's trusted mechanic, Craig Matson, was busy overseeing every step of the operation. By the time Marilee had filled out the necessary paperwork, Craig had already completed a preliminary check of the plane's exterior.

He looked up as she and Wyatt strolled toward the plane. "You really did a number on this wing." He ran a hand over the damage. "And the tail. Just how many boulders did you manage to crush in that landing?"

"I'm sure we left a trail of gravel." Marilee moved in beside him. "How long will it take to repair?"

He shrugged. "Not my area of expertise. That's up to the manufacturer. But I'd say you're out of commission for a couple of weeks, until the company can fly in the parts and put it all back together."

"What about the fuel line?"

He squinted in the artificial light of the hangar.

"Won't be able to give it a thorough going-over until morning, with the door open and enough sunlight to really see every little piece of it. Here's what I've checked so far." He pointed to an initial he'd scribbled with Magic Marker. "That's as far as I can see tonight. But I'll tell you this much: There was nothing wrong with the fuel line when you left yesterday."

Wyatt stepped up. "You're sure?"

The man met his look. "I make it my business to be sure. My pilots' lives are on the line every time."

"Thanks, Craig. This pilot is grateful for all you do." Marilee patted his arm. "I'll be here first thing in the morning."

"I'll add my thanks to hers." Wyatt shook Craig's hand before turning to follow her.

Craig picked up his cold coffee and made another turn around the plane before heading for his car. Marilee and Wyatt had already climbed into their vehicles. He watched their taillights as they sped off in the darkness. Then he turned his truck toward the Fortune Saloon. There was still time to join the sheriff, the mayor, and a few of his cronies for a beer before heading home.

On his Harley, Wyatt trailed Marilee's truck to her apartment and into the garage where she kept the emergency vehicle. By the time she turned off the ignition, he was holding her door.

"Thanks, rebel." She led the way up the stairs to her apartment. When she'd unlocked the door she paused, unsure of where the night was heading. "Want to come in?"

He stepped inside and closed the door before leaning against it.

Marilee walked around, turning on lights before heading toward the kitchen, where she filled the teakettle and placed it on a burner.

She could feel his dark gaze watching her every move.

"Want some tea? Or would you rather have a beer?"

"I'll take a beer."

He remained where he was as she removed a cold longneck from the refrigerator and twisted the top.

She glanced over with equal parts annoyance and fear. Annoyance that she couldn't read his emotions. His face was perfectly expressionless. Fear that he was about to live up to his playboy image and, having enjoyed his latest conquest, was getting ready to move on to someone new. He looked ready to bolt out the door the first chance he got.

There was a trace of anger in her voice. "Are you coming in, or do you intend to just stand there, guarding the door?"

He managed a half-smile. "I'm having a hell of an argument with myself."

"Want to let me in on it? Or is it a big, dark secret?"

"The truth?" He crossed the room and perched on a barstool before lifting the bottle to his mouth. After a long drink he set it down and met her questioning look. "I'm filthy. I haven't changed my clothes in twenty-four hours. And, except for Dandy's breakfast, I haven't had another thing to eat all day."

"If you'd like to go, I'll understand. Or, if you'd like, you could shower while I make . . ." She half turned before he sprang up and caught her arm, startling her. Her mouth went dry as dust. "I was just going to offer you the use of my shower while I fix some supper."

"It's not food I want. Or a shower. Or a change of clothes. All I want . . . all I can think about, is taking you to bed."

She let out a long, deep sigh as relief flooded through her. "Is that all? I thought maybe you were looking for an excuse to leave."

"An excuse?" He stared at her in disbelief. "After what we've shared, is that what you think?"

"I didn't know what to think. You were hovering over there by the door like someone who couldn't wait to run."

He drew her close and framed her face with his hands. "Marilee, the only place I want to run is here, into your arms." He lowered his face and captured her mouth with his.

She returned his kisses with such eagerness, they soon were both moaning with need.

In a rush they tore off each other's clothes before he backed her against the wall and lifted her. With hearts pounding and breathing labored, they took each other with all the fever of a raging wildfire.

Spent, he sank into her, heartbeat to heartbeat, and rested his forehead against hers.

He touched a hand to her cheek. "Sorry. I was rough. I didn't mean . . ."

"Wyatt." She placed a finger to his lips to still his words. "I'm not fragile."

"No. You're not." He stared deeply into her eyes. "You're amazing."

"You're not bad yourself, rebel."

He took a breath. "I guess I could use that shower now."

"We both could."

He smiled. "I like the way you think."

She returned his smile. "Good. Because I'm thinking that after we shower, I'll toss our clothes in the washer and you can make me some supper. I've always wanted my very own naked chef."

She caught his hand and led the way to the bathroom. As the door closed, they were still laughing. When the water began flowing, their laughter turned to muffled sighs.

"This is good." Marilee perched on a barstool, wearing a green silk knee-length kimono she'd snagged from the closet.

"You sound surprised." Beside her, Wyatt speared a broccoli floret.

With his clothes in the washer, he'd opted for a pair of discarded scrubs he'd salvaged from a box of hospital supplies.

"You continue to surprise me. But I have to admit, I like a man who can cook for himself." She took another bite of grilled chicken that topped their salads. "And cook for me, in the bargain."

"You want a cook, I'm your man."

She glanced over. "Yes, you are. And though you're not naked as I'd hoped, being shirtless is close enough."

"For now." He sent her one of those heart-stopping grins. "After I clean up the kitchen, I'd be happy to get naked for you, ma'am. After all, a personal chef has to please the boss."

She set aside her empty salad bowl and sipped her tea. "Are you thinking about spending the night?"

He met her questioning look. "I'd say that's up to you. I'd like to, but I don't want to get in the way of your routine."

"My routine is pretty undemanding. With my plane out of commission, I only have my emergency medical services to see to. What about your routine?"

He shrugged. "I'll have to drive out to the ranch. When Zane and I agreed to stay on, we also agreed to take on whatever chores are needed around the Lost Nugget. It could be tending a herd, minding a sick heifer, or tearing apart the engine of one of our fleet of trucks."

"A man of many talents, I see."

He chuckled. "Zane and I are finding out just what our talents are. I thought I'd done enough in my travels to prepare me for anything, but I'm constantly learning something new."

"And from the smile on your face, I'd say you're loving every minute of it."

"I am. And so is Zane. I really misjudged him. I figured, because he did his growing up in Hollywood, that he'd be lost on a ranch. But he dives into every chore with more energy than any of us."

"And you love him for it."

That had Wyatt going very still, mulling it over, before nodding his head. "I never thought about it before, but yeah. I do love him for it. When we were kids, he was always pedaling faster, running harder, just to keep up with Jesse and me. But now the years have evened things up. He's our equal. More than equal, in fact. There are a lot of things he can do better than the rest of us."

"Like what?"

"He has a way of mingling with the wranglers, like he's always been there. And Jimmy Eagle, who oversees all the herds and wranglers, has begun trusting Zane with more and more responsibility."

"And you?"

"I was born responsible." He said it so straight-faced, she found herself almost believing him before he sent her that famous grin.

"I should have known you were teasing me."

"Hey. How can you doubt the guy who just made you supper?"

"Why would I believe a guy who's wearing a pair of cast-off scrubs that don't even reach his ankles?"

He lifted his leg. "I thought they made me look like a surgeon."

"Or a comedian pretending to be a doctor."

He wiggled his brows. "You keep this up, woman, and I may have to forget about washing the dishes so I can operate on you."

"Only if you have a license."

"Baby, I don't need a license for what I want to do to you."

That had her laughing harder. "I can hardly wait to see what you have in mind. Could we hurry up in here, so you can show me everything?"

He brushed a kiss over her lips that had her toes curling. "All in good time. Now sit there and drink your tea while I finish what I started here. Any chef worth his salary cleans up his own messes."

She drained her cup and picked up a towel. At his arched look she said, "I thought I'd hurry you along."

"You're turning into a very greedy woman."

"Are you complaining?"

"Hardly." He laughed. "In fact, it's a real turn-on."

She joined in the laughter. "Oh, I think right about now, anything, including a sneeze, would be a turn-on."

"You got that right, woman." He lifted his hands from the soapy water to drag her close. "Let's leave the dishes to dry on the counter. I don't think I can wait another minute."

She tossed aside the towel and grabbed his hand.

Laughing, they ran to the bedroom. And lost themselves in pure bliss.

The ringing of a phone shattered the silence. Before the second ring Marilee sat up, shoving hair from her eyes, and snatched up the receiver.

"Emergency One. What's the problem?"

Beside her, Wyatt snapped on a light on a bedside table and noted the time. Almost four in the morning.

Marilee listened in silence before saying, "Okay. I'm on it." She replaced the receiver and looked over at Wyatt. "Lucas Sandler. His wife thinks it's his heart. Doc Wheeler's meeting me out at their ranch."

As she began dressing, Wyatt climbed out of bed and did the same.

She arched a brow. "I don't need help."

He merely smiled. "My cousins do. By the time I drive to the ranch, they'll be up and ready for morning chores. I wouldn't want to miss out on the work assignments."

"Not to mention Dandy's famous breakfast."

He upped the wattage on the smile. "Yeah. There's that, too."

Minutes later they both walked from her apartment down the stairs to the garage. With a quick kiss, Marilee headed out, sirens blaring, while Wyatt turned his motorcycle in the opposite direction toward the Lost Nugget Ranch.

Chapter Twelve

———◆◆◆———

Wyatt strolled into the kitchen just as Dandy was removing a pan from the oven. The entire room was perfumed with the fragrance of freshly baked cinnamon buns.

Wyatt snagged a glass of just-squeezed orange juice from a tray on the counter. "'Morning, Dandy. Marilee and I thank you for that care package you made us yesterday."

The ranch cook, sleeves of his crisp plaid shirt carefully rolled above the elbows, jeans looking like they'd just come from the store, sent him a warm smile. "Glad you enjoyed it. I figured after a night in the wilderness, you'd be ready for some real food."

He looked up as Cora stepped through the doorway. "'Morning, Miss Cora."

"Good morning, Dandy." She opened her arms wide to welcome her grandnephew. "Oh, Wyatt. I'm so happy to see you."

He gave her a warm hug. "It's good to be home."

Home. She felt a rush of pure joy at his easy use of the term. When he and Zane had first arrived at the ranch for Coot's funeral after years of separation, she'd feared that they would never be able to fully embrace their former home. But now, though there were still times when they butted heads with Jesse, who had never left, they had begun to bond like brothers.

She caught Wyatt's hand and led him toward the table. "I want to hear everything about the crash."

"Is that the reason for your early return?"

She nodded. "How could I stay away after such worrisome news? Even when Cal assured me that both you and Marilee weren't hurt, I had to come home and see for myself."

While Dandy poured her a fresh cup of coffee, Wyatt sat beside her. "It wasn't really a crash. I mean, we were forced to land in the wilderness, but except for some exterior damage to the plane, we weren't hurt."

"Thank heavens." She touched a hand to her heart. "When I heard, I was so afraid for you both. Considering the way you lost your parents, this had to be especially hard for you to endure. You're sure you're all right?"

He patted her hand. "Not a scratch."

"Maybe not on the outside." Jesse and Amy came in together and overheard the last of Wyatt's remarks. "But I think if you check his heart, Aunt Cora, you may find it changed."

Cora glanced from Jesse to Wyatt. "Your heart?"

Zane walked in and picked up a glass of orange juice. "Yeah, his heart. We're thinking it'll never be the same. Our world-traveler, old love-'em-and-leave-'em, man-of-the-world Wyatt may have finally met his match."

As she caught on to their little joke, Cora chuckled. "Ah. I see. You and Marilee?"

"Careful, Aunt Cora." Jesse devoured a cinnamon bun in three bites. "The mere mention of Wyatt and Lee in the same breath will probably jinx any chance they have for a real relationship. It's bound to tarnish his playboy image."

She looked over. "I really like Lee Trainor. I'm glad to learn that you like her, too."

"Thanks, Aunt Cora. That makes two of us." Wyatt sat back with a smile of pure contentment that had Jesse and Zane looking at each other with confusion.

"Uh-oh." Jesse squeezed Amy's hand and winked. "I'd say our cousin has fallen hard."

"Either that or he hit his head in that rough landing, and we ought to get him to the hospital for some tests."

"Are you guys through having fun yet?" Wyatt calmly picked up an empty plate and walked to the stove, where bacon sizzled and light-as-air flapjacks were stacked on a platter.

Filling his plate, he returned to the table and began to eat.

"It's even worse than I'd thought." Jesse kissed Amy's cheek before helping himself to a similar breakfast. "Our man's down for the count, and he's about to be declared out."

"You won't hear me complaining." Zane was grinning as he filled his plate. "That just leaves more unattached females for me."

"There are plenty of females looking your way, but they're all afraid of those damned cameras you carry with you everywhere." Jesse looked over. "If you want my advice, you should ditch the Hollywood filmmaker routine and concentrate on looking like a cowboy. That's what the ladies really like."

Amy playfully smacked his arm. "A lot you know about women."

"Hey. I married the prettiest girl in town. That makes me something of an expert."

"Well, Mr. Expert, consider this." Amy winked at Zane. "All women love to think they're just one step away from being discovered as the next big movie star."

Jesse roared with laughter. "Yeah, that's why they duck and run whenever they see our cousin walking toward them with his camera in hand."

"Well," she admitted, "only if they don't have any makeup on, or it's a bad-hair day."

Wyatt set down his cup. "Some women look gorgeous even without makeup and never have bad-hair days."

"I assume you're thinking about a certain drop-dead gorgeous redhead." Zane exchanged a grin with Jesse.

Instead of the expected defensive outburst, Wyatt merely shrugged. "I'm only speaking the truth. The woman doesn't have a flaw."

That had all of them, including Cora, laughing.

Dandy, busy at the stove, kept his face averted. But the shaking of his shoulders was a dead giveaway that he was enjoying this as much as the others.

All day, as he tended ranch chores, Wyatt was forced to endure the jokes about his time spent in the wilderness with Marilee. It had become the favorite topic of conversation.

At some other time he might have grown weary of the

teasing, and would have resorted to his temper to stop some of the wranglers from their endless comments, but this day, it all rolled off his back like rain off the ducks in the ranch ponds. He simply wasn't capable of anger on this perfect day.

By dinnertime, his family and fellow wranglers had given up ribbing him, recognizing that he was far too mellow to rise to the bait.

He emerged from his room freshly showered and wearing clean clothes, his dark hair still sporting droplets of water.

"Looking good, cuz. Off to see your lady?" Jesse looked up from the map, where he and Amy, Zane, and Cora were gathered around, checking their latest route.

New flags marked the trail they'd begun charting, along with sticky notes. The sight of the map jolted Wyatt's memory.

"In the excitement of the crash I almost forgot something I spotted from the air." He walked over to the map and drew a finger along the trail they'd been mapping for the past months. His eyes narrowed. "I only caught a glimpse of it, but I'd swear I saw this same path as we flew over. It appeared to be the width of a crude horse-drawn wagon trail, and it stretched from the river to Treasure Chest Mountain."

"You're sure?" Jesse walked up beside him and moved his finger along the flag-marked trail. "From Grasshopper Creek to Treasure Chest?"

"Yeah." Wyatt glanced around. "Do you think Coot left a trail?"

They all turned to Cora.

She shook her head. "It's hard to say. Coot searched

alone. And spent a lifetime looking for the gold. But he rarely ever went out on horseback. These past few years he always used a truck or an all-terrain vehicle, especially if he was traveling through the more rugged stretches of our land."

"So how do we explain the trail I spotted?" Wyatt continued studying the map.

"I don't know." Jesse's mind was awhirl with ideas. "But I think we ought to take another flyover and see if we can pin it down more accurately."

Zane and Wyatt nodded in agreement.

"Let's see how soon Marilee's plane can be airborne." Wyatt pulled his cell phone from his shirt pocket and dialed Marilee's number. Instead of her voice he got her voice mail and left her a message. Knowing the others were listening, he kept it short: "Hey, I bet you're out on another emergency. Give me a call when you get this. I thought I'd head into town and treat you to one of the Fortune Saloon's famous greasy burgers."

He dropped the phone into his pocket and glanced around. "Anybody feel like tagging along to town?"

Jesse and Amy were the first to refuse. "Sorry. We're bringing supper to Amy's father."

"How is Otis feeling?" Cora asked.

"Dad claims, now that the treatments are finished, he's as good as new." Amy gave a sigh of relief. She had returned to Gold Fever to nurse her father through a serious illness. Now in remission, Otis Parrish had been transformed from an angry, grudge-holding man to a kindly, grateful neighbor who looked forward to visits with his daughter and her new husband. "He's been handling all his own ranch chores lately without outside help, so that's a very good sign."

"Indeed it is." Cora turned to Wyatt. "I'm off to my studio for at least another hour. Then I promised Cal I'd have dinner with him here at the ranch. We have a lot of business to catch up on."

Zane gave a quick shake of his head. "I can't go either, cuz. I'm joining Jimmy Eagle and some of the crew in the bunkhouse for an evening of Texas Hold 'em."

"Drinking. Gambling. Next thing you know," Wyatt said with a grin, "you'll be chewing tobacco and looking for loose women."

"It can't be soon enough for me," Zane added with a laugh.

That had the others laughing, as well.

Wyatt kissed his aunt's cheek before heading out the door.

All the way to town his heart was light. It wasn't the thought of Violet's burgers, or Daffy's bawdy jokes. He was feeling like a randy high school boy with his first crush.

And truth be told, he didn't care if the whole world knew it.

"Hey, rebel." Marilee yanked open the door of her apartment before Wyatt had a chance to knock.

"Ahhh." He breathed the word while he studied the way she looked in her faded jeans and tee that showed every line and curve of that fabulous body. "Now this is what I call perfection."

She felt the heat stain her cheeks and was surprised by it. How could she be blushing after all they'd shared?

She shot him a dimpled smile. "You're not bad yourself."

"Not bad? I bet you can do better'n that." He dragged her close and kissed her until she clutched at his shirt-front.

When he lifted his head she sucked in a breath. "I meant to say you look so good to me I could drink you up in one big gulp."

He chuckled. "Much better. And I have to say, I feel the same way about you. Ready for some of Vi and Daffy's beer and burgers?"

"As long as I don't have to cook, I'm ready for anything."

He caught her hand and led her down the stairs. In her garage he paused. "My Harley or your truck?"

She shrugged. "I think I like the idea of having the wind in my hair."

He climbed on his motorcycle and she settled in behind him.

While he revved the engine and started forward she rested her cheek on his back, loving the strong, solid feel of him.

They rode in silence, unable to carry on a conversation over the roar of the engine. He pulled up outside the saloon.

In the sudden silence he pocketed the keys and caught her hand. "Long day?"

"Yeah." She sighed.

Hearing it he paused. "Is Lucas Sandler okay?"

"He's fine. Doc said it was heartburn. Wrote him a prescription for acid-reflux medication and we were on our way."

"Were you out on another emergency run this afternoon?"

She shook her head.

"I tried calling you and got your voice mail."

"Yeah. I turned off my phone after meeting with Craig. I wanted some time to absorb the news."

"News?" He was suddenly alert. "About the fuel line?"

She nodded.

"Did he find something?"

"He did. But not what we were expecting." She took a breath. "Do you remember how Craig explained that he'd examined part of the line, but that he would have to wait until today for a thorough examination?"

"I remember."

"He initialed the portion that he'd already examined, so he could begin from there." She looked over. Met Wyatt's steady gaze. "Today he couldn't find his initials."

Wyatt's brow furrowed. "I don't get it."

"Neither did Craig for a while. Then he figured it out. Overnight, somebody must have switched fuel lines."

When he realized the implication, Wyatt's eyes narrowed. "Somebody would have to be really worried about what Craig would find. Especially if the fuel line had been tampered with. The only way to get rid of the evidence of their crime would be to replace the entire fuel line with a new one before morning."

"Exactly. And whoever did it had no idea that Craig had left his mark on the existing one."

"Did Craig report this to Sheriff Wycliff?"

"He called and left word that we wanted to meet with him. Deputy Atkins took the message and said he'd get back with him."

"Good. It's time to bring the law into this." Wyatt

squeezed her hand. "We need to know who has access to the hangar after hours. And who Craig might have talked to last night. Where can we find him?"

She nodded toward a rusty old truck parked outside the saloon. "That's Craig's. I'd say the odds are pretty good that he's inside right now."

Keeping her hand firmly in his, Wyatt made his way into the Fortune Saloon with blood in his eyes.

Daffy was the first to spot the couple stepping through the door. With a tray full of drinks she swooped down on them.

"Aren't you the pair? The whole town's talking about the fact that you survived a plane crash and spent a romantic night out in the wilderness."

She managed to balance the heavy tray in one hand while patting Wyatt's cheek with the other. "Leave it to a McCord to come through it all smelling like a rose."

She turned to Marilee and dropped a hand to her shoulder. "Girlfriend, I hope you realize that the minute you become romantically involved with a McCord, the whole town considers you fair game to suffer the curse of the lost fortune."

"You know better than to believe in urban legends, Daffy."

"Hey, tell it to all these folks. I'm just the messenger." She leaned close. "I expect to hear every yummy little detail of your hot new romance the next time you come in here"—she stared pointedly at Wyatt—"without your copilot."

By the time she'd turned away and strolled over to a nearby table to deliver drinks, it seemed as though half the patrons had paused to watch as Wyatt and Marilee made their way to an empty table in the corner.

Once they were seated, the buzz of conversation resumed.

Wyatt leaned his face close to Marilee's ear. "So much for having a private conversation with Craig. By now, half the town knows our business, or thinks they do. And the other half wants to."

Marilee nodded. "We both know that there are no secrets in Gold Fever."

"Unless you're a bad guy." Wyatt held up two fingers, and minutes later Daffy brought them two frosty longnecks.

"You two want the special?" She stood, pad and pencil in hand.

"What is it?" Wyatt asked.

"Vi calls it Bull on a Bun. Ground Angus, grilled onions, tomato, cheese, and Vi's secret hot sauce that gives it a kick."

Marilee couldn't help grinning.

"We'll have two of those. And some of Vi's fried potatoes." Wyatt lowered his voice. "I'd like to buy Craig a beer. When you deliver it, ask him if he'd mind coming over to join us."

"Sorry, honey." Daffy finished making notes on her pad before looking up. "He got a phone call about a minute ago and said he had to go."

Wyatt looked over to the empty stool where Craig had been seated just minutes earlier. "Did he say where?"

She shook her head. "Just bolted out of here like he had a bee in his britches." She shrugged. "He'll be back tomorrow. Old Craig hasn't missed a night at our place since we opened."

She maneuvered her way through the smoky room and

shouted her order to her sister, who was sweating over the grill.

Seeing Wyatt's thoughtful look, Marilee touched a hand to his. "What are you thinking?"

He took her hand between both of his. "I don't like it. We walk in and Craig takes off."

"It isn't as though he's ducking us. Craig has been a fixture out at the airport for as long as I've been flying. Every time I go up in my plane, I trust that Craig has gone over every inch of it with a critical eye. I put my life in his capable hands."

"I get that. And I appreciate what he does. But . . ."

She shook her head. "You heard Daffy. He'll be here again tomorrow. Besides, talking here isn't such a good idea. Too many ears. Tomorrow we can catch him alone in the hangar, where we can have some privacy. And hopefully, Sheriff Wycliff will be there, too."

He willed himself to relax. When Marilee picked up her bottle and took a long drink, he did the same.

By the time Daffy returned with their order, Wyatt was able to put aside his concern and concentrate all his energy on the strong, funny, vibrant woman seated across from him.

But in the deep, dark recesses of his mind, a nagging little fear remained. Somebody knew something important about Marilee's plane. Something important and perhaps critical. Something they didn't want anybody else to learn.

And he wouldn't be satisfied until he had a chance to quiz Craig Matson and be assured that the sheriff was on the case, because there were pieces of the puzzle that didn't fit.

Chapter Thirteen

W ell?" Daffy paused beside their table. "What'd you two think of Vi's bull on a bun?"

Wyatt drained his beer. "Tell Vi we give it two thumbs-up."

"Want another round?" Daffy slid their empty plates onto her tray.

Wyatt glanced across the table at Marilee before shaking his head. "I think we'll head home now. Thanks, Daffy."

"Sure, honey. Anytime." In an aside to Marilee she added in her smoke-fogged voice, "If I had a cowboy who looked like this, I'd be in a hurry to get him back to my place, too."

With a loud cackle that caused heads to turn, she strolled away.

Wyatt caught Marilee's hand and the two walked out of the saloon after waving good-bye to Vi, still at her post at the grill.

Outside it had begun to rain. A soft, misty rain, which, after the heat of the day, felt as soothing as a shower.

They rode in silence, enjoying the mist on their faces. They had just pulled into Marilee's garage when her cell phone rang.

She answered it, listened in silence, then gave her usual response. "Thanks. I'm on it."

She looked up. "Got an emergency run to Highway Six. Accident and injuries."

Wyatt helped her from the back of his Harley before walking with her to her emergency vehicle.

She arched a brow. "Thinking of going somewhere?"

"Yeah. With you. I figure you might need an extra pair of hands."

"Suit yourself." She grinned as she fastened her seat belt and put the vehicle in gear. With lights flashing she headed out of town.

Once they hit Highway Six she gunned the engine. "You're a sly one, rebel. Tell me the truth. You just didn't want to be cheated out of a good-night kiss."

Laughing, he held up both hands. "Guilty. In fact, I'm hoping, if I play my cards right and prove to be really helpful, I may even be invited to spend the night again."

"I think I could be persuad . . ."

They heard the sound of a blowout at the same instant the vehicle fishtailed.

Gripping the wheel, Marilee struggled for control as they swerved from one side of the rain-slicked highway to the other. As the wheels encountered the gravel shoulder, they stuck, and the ambulance gave a sudden lurch before tumbling end-over-end, finally landing in a field alongside the highway.

The passenger-side air bag had exploded, cushioning Wyatt. When he managed to release his seat belt he turned to Marilee, slumped over the wheel.

"Oh, baby. Hang on." He released her seat belt, noting idly that it had almost torn free and was holding on by a thread. He helped her lean back.

There was a gash on her forehead where she'd come in contact with the steering wheel. Heart racing, he pressed a handkerchief to the spot while he looked for other injuries.

With a moan, she opened her eyes. "You all right?"

"Fine. It's you I'm worried about. Thank heaven your seat belt held. You'd've been really tossed around without it, because your air bag didn't inflate."

"Umm." She struggled to clear her head, but there were butterflies fluttering and bees droning. Not to mention pain radiating from her head to her neck and across her shoulders. "Just had the safety inspection last month."

"They did a lousy job." He reached for his cell phone and pressed Zane's number.

"Hold on," came Zane's excited voice. "Four aces. I win it all."

"Collect later." Nerves had Wyatt's tone sharpening. "There's been an accident. Highway Six, a couple miles out of Gold Fever. I need you, cuz. Now."

"I'm there." The line went dead.

Wyatt drew Marilee into his arms and leaned back, willing his nerves to steady.

"Hold on, baby. The cavalry's on its way."

A fleet of ranch trucks formed a convoy of lights looming out of the darkness. From the number of headlights,

Wyatt decided that Zane must have alerted the entire bunkhouse about the news of the accident.

Arriving on their heels was a police car, siren wailing, lights flashing.

Zane, Jesse, and Amy were the first to race up to the emergency vehicle, where Wyatt sat holding Marilee.

"What happened?" Jesse demanded.

"Blowout." Marilee's tone was still dazed. "Lost control."

"What's the damage?" Zane demanded. "Can you two stand?"

"Yeah." Wyatt lowered the driver's-side window. "Marilee hit the wheel pretty hard. I'm pretty sure she'll need stitches."

Blood oozed through the gauze dressing Wyatt had found among the supplies. He was pressing it firmly to the wound on her forehead.

Deputy Harrison Atkins hurried over.

Zane seemed surprised to see him. "How'd you make it here so soon?"

The lawman shrugged. "I was in the area. Checking out an accident on Highway Six. No serious injuries, so when I got your call, I sent them on their way and raced over here." Seeing Marilee's injury he pointed to his car. "I'll take you to Doc."

"We'll drive." Zane took hold of the door. "Let's get you out of there."

The door didn't budge. It took both Zane and Jesse working together to pry the badly damaged door open.

They helped Marilee from the wrecked vehicle and walked on either side of her as they made their way to their waiting truck.

Wyatt held back. Turning to the deputy, he kept his voice low. "You'll want to have this vehicle towed and looked at by a mechanic you trust. Maybe you ought to use one from the state police."

The lawman shot him a startled look. "And just what'll he be looking for?"

"Any sign of deliberate damage to either the tire or the air bag."

"You mind telling me what's going on here, McCord?"

Wyatt could feel the deputy's obvious annoyance. "Look, Harrison, most nights, Marilee would have been making this run alone. It was an accident that I happened to be along. All I'm saying is that it bothers me that the passenger side air bag worked perfectly, and the driver's-side air bag didn't."

"Okay." The lawman looked from the battered vehicle to Marilee's pale face as she climbed into the ranch truck. "I know you two have a thing going on. Hell, the whole town knows it. I'll get somebody on it. But I think you're seeing bad guys where none exist."

"I hope you're right." Wyatt shook the deputy's hand before walking to the truck.

In the backseat he drew Marilee close, needing to assure himself that she was all right.

They rode the entire distance back to town in silence.

"That's a nasty cut," Dr. Wheeler said as he tied off the last stitch. "But it could have been a whole lot worse."

"Yeah. Thanks, Doc." Marilee sat up and waited until her head cleared. She was grateful for Wyatt's strong arm around her shoulders.

"Take this." The doctor handed her a pill and a glass of water and waited until she'd swallowed. "Just a mild sedative to help you sleep. You probably shouldn't be alone tonight."

Wyatt's voice was firm. "She won't be."

Dr. Wheeler smiled. "Good. It's just a precaution. If she complains of a severe headache, I want you to call me."

"Thanks, Doc, for everything." Wyatt eased Marilee off the examining table and kept his arm firmly around her as he led her out the door of the clinic.

In the waiting room, Amy, Jesse, and Zane stopped their pacing to look up. Though Wyatt knew they probably had a million questions, they remained silent out of respect for the pale young woman who appeared absolutely drained.

"You can drop us both at Marilee's place."

"I'll get the truck." Zane raced out the door while the others stepped out into the rainy night and waited.

Within minutes Zane drove right up over the sidewalk to the door of the clinic.

Wyatt helped Marilee into the backseat, while Amy and Jesse climbed in beside Zane.

Once again they drove in silence.

When they arrived at her apartment, Zane called over his shoulder, "You'll call us in the morning?"

"Yeah. Thanks. For everything."

"Hey, that's what family's for." Jesse jumped down and raced ahead to hold open the door of her apartment.

Wyatt helped Marilee up the stairs. "Thanks, cuz."

When the truck backed away, Wyatt closed the door and led her into the bedroom.

As she sat down on the edge of her bed, she looked up

with a weak smile. "It's a cut, Wyatt. It'll heal. I'm not an invalid."

"I know. But I want to take care of you, so humor me." He rummaged through her closet until he found a night-shirt. He slipped off her shoes, then ever-so-gently slid the blood-spattered T-shirt over her head, careful not to disturb the dressing that covered her stitches. When he'd helped her remove her jeans, she pulled on the nightshirt. Even that simple task left her drained.

Noting her pallor, he pulled back the bed linens and tucked her in as gently as possible.

"Want some tea?"

"Mmm. That would be nice."

He made his way to the kitchen and filled the kettle. A short time later he returned to the bedroom. Marilee was fast asleep.

He set the tea on a night table and kicked off his boots. Crawling into bed beside her, he propped up some pillows and sipped the tea, all the while watching the gentle rise and fall of her chest.

He knew he was too wired to sleep for several more hours. But right now, this moment, it was enough just to sit here by her side, content in the knowledge that she was safe.

In her dream, Marilee was flying above Treasure Chest. The sky was a clear, cloudless blue. Her father, frowning, was seated beside her, wearing a parachute. She didn't think it odd because, after all, he was always angry, and always flying in and out of her life. Before she could speak he was gone, and in his place was Wyatt McCord, smiling at her with that magical, heart-stopping smile. He started to tell her something very important, but just then the plane was diving, falling, spinning. And then the plane turned into her rescue vehicle, and it was swerving back and forth across a rain-slicked highway and she realized she couldn't control it. There was a sickening sound, like breaking glass, and the vehicle suddenly broke apart and she was flying, falling . . .

She woke with a start, thrashing about, sweating, disoriented.

"It's okay, baby. I'm here." Wyatt's deep, soothing voice in the darkness, and his lips pressed to her cheek as he gathered her close, helped her settle.

"I . . ." She moistened her dry lips. "Bad dream."

"Yeah. I've had a few of those. Hold on."

And she did. She clung to him like a lifeline, loving the strength of him. His strong, steady heartbeat soothed her own rapidly beating tattoo until it began to slow, keeping time to his. Her breathing slowed, as well, until she was no longer sucking air into starved lungs.

"Did you sleep at all?" She whispered the words against his throat, causing a rush of heat that had him sweating.

"Some."

"You need to sleep."

"I will. Right now, I'm more concerned with what you need."

She touched a hand to his cheek. Just a touch, but it brought a smile to his lips. "I'm so glad you're here, Wyatt."

He pressed his lips to her forehead. "Me, too."

"You were going to bring me some tea."

"I did. You were asleep, so I drank it."

She chuckled.

"I could make you some more if you'd . . ." He looked down.

Her eyes were closed, her breathing soft and rhythmic.

He kept his arms around her and lay perfectly still, listening to the sound of her breathing, loving the fact that her fears were gone. At least for the moment. And if the demons should return, he would be here to help her fight them.

To keep her safe. It was all that mattered.

To keep her safe. It became a litany in his mind.

He would do whatever it took, pay whatever price necessary, to keep her safe.

How had it happened that this woman in his arms had begun to mean so very much to him?

He hadn't meant for this to happen. But now that it had, there was no denying the truth.

He loved her. Loved her so much, he'd willingly lay down his life to keep her safe.

CHAPTER FOURTEEN

$\mathbf{A}$rchie." Wyatt stood in the shadows of Marilee's garage, speaking softly into his cell phone to the mysterious man he'd met in his world travels who was not only a private detective, but also a bounty hunter. Archie had spent a lifetime learning things about elusive figures who managed to stay below the radar of police agencies. "I'm in need of your special services."

The Cockney voice on the other end had him smiling. "In trouble with the law, are you, boyo?"

"Not that kind of trouble. But there have been some strange things happening that have me concerned. First there was a leak in the fuel line of a friend's plane, forcing us to make an unexpected landing in a wilderness area. The airport mechanic who examined the fuel line has suddenly gone missing. When I tried phoning him this morning, I got his message machine. And when I phoned the airport, I was told that he had to leave town suddenly to help with an emergency at his sister's place in Wyoming. Nobody knows when he'll be back."

"Emergencies happen, my friend. This doesn't sound ominous to me."

Wyatt added, "Yeah. That in itself doesn't sound ominous. I'm hoping by tomorrow the mechanic will be calling with news of when he'll be able to return to work. But now, on the heels of the forced landing, this same friend and I had a blowout on the tire of her emergency vehicle, and when it flipped, the driver's air bag didn't inflate, even though the vehicle had just passed its annual safety inspection."

"*Her* emergency vehicle. Why am I not surprised that there's a female involved? I take it she's worth all this concern on your part?"

Archie's words had him chuckling. "I guess I should have mentioned that up front. As you guessed, she's a gorgeous female, and she's special to me."

"I hope you haven't withheld your suspicions from the local constabulary."

"I already told the local deputy my concerns. But he's a lawman, Archie. His job is to deal with facts. Right now, he knows only that the plane ran out of fuel, even though it had just been refueled before takeoff, and that an air bag didn't inflate, even though the vehicle had recently passed a safety inspection. None of which, he insists, has him considering them to be anything more than a series of accidents."

Archie's voice grew louder. "You know I don't believe in that many coincidences."

Wyatt paused before adding, "My thoughts exactly. Now this is what I'd like you to do."

For several minutes more they talked, while Wyatt gave Archie the information he wanted checked out.

"Thanks, my friend. If anybody can untangle this mess, it's you. I leave it in your capable hands."

After ringing off he stood a moment, staring at the peaks of Treasure Chest in the distance. He'd been willing to write off one incident as an accident. But two dangerous incidents happening in such a short time felt like much more than mere coincidence.

And there was one other thing that tugged on his conscience. He'd had a lot of time to think during his long, sleepless night. And he was feeling guilty.

What if these things that had begun happening were aimed at Marilee because of her association with him and his search for the treasure? It had happened to his cousin Jesse and his wife, Amy. Even though the one responsible for those attacks was now dead, there could be others who had more than a passing interest in the fabled lost fortune. Money, or the desire for it, often caused people to do strange and desperate things.

This was why he'd phoned Archie.

Now that Archie was on the case, Wyatt felt a whole lot better. If he had to put his money on Archie or the sheriff, it wasn't even a contest. Ernie Wycliff was bound by the rules of fair play. Archie played by his own rules.

Satisfied, Wyatt climbed the stairs to Marilee's apartment above the garage.

"Hey." He found Marilee in the kitchen, whipping up some scrambled eggs. "Aren't you supposed to be resting?"

"I can't just stay in bed all day." She fed bread into the toaster and turned bacon sizzling in a pan.

He caught her hand and led her toward the barstools. "Sit. I'll finish this."

Grateful for his quiet strength, she sipped her tea and watched as he smoothly slid the eggs onto a plate, drained the bacon, and popped up two slices of perfect toast. "When I found you gone, I figured you were headed back to your ranch. You must have dozens of chores piling up while you're here playing nursemaid."

"Don't worry about my chores. They'll keep. The most important thing in my life right now is seeing that you rest and recover."

"Wyatt . . ."

He touched a finger to her lips. "Eat. I'll clean up the mess you made. You really are a messy cook."

She laughed as he moved about the tiny kitchen, scrubbing the skillets, wiping the stove and countertops until they gleamed.

He wasn't fooling her. She recognized that underneath his charming pose, he was as concerned as she was about these troubling accidents. She understood his need to do something, anything, while he worked through his thoughts. She'd been dealing with similar thoughts, until, too agitated to rest, she'd been forced to get up and get moving.

She had to admit that the thing she found most troubling of all was the sudden disappearance of Craig Matson. In all the years she'd been here, Craig had been a fixture at the airport. Never once had he ever spoken about family. Now he was gone, claiming a family emergency.

Still, she wanted to believe that there was a reasonable explanation.

Wyatt picked up her empty plate and helped her to her feet. "Come on. You're going back to bed."

"Wyatt, I'm fine."

"Yes, you are. But you're going to do what the doctor ordered."

"And if I don't?"

He gave her one of those dangerous, heart-stopping grins. "I'm thinking, if I really apply myself, I can probably find several clever ways to keep you in bed all day, Ms. Trainor."

She was laughing as she allowed him to lead her to her bed. But as he lay beside her and drew her into his arms, her laughter faded, replaced by a series of soft, gentle sighs.

"All right. I'll let you persuade me. But only because the doctor ordered it."

Her words were followed by muffled laughter as they found the perfect way to leave the cares of the world behind.

"Well, my friend." Archie's voice on the cell phone had Wyatt stepping out of Marilee's bedroom and closing the door behind him. "You've got quite a cast of characters in that charming little town you currently call home."

"What's that supposed to mean?"

"Let me begin with the Cowling family."

"Ledge and Delia?"

"Brother and sister." The Cockney accent thickened. "Did you know that there was an . . . interesting connection between the sister, Delia, and your grandfather?"

Wyatt stopped in mid-stride. "What?"

"I see that got your attention." Archie's booming laughter carried over the cell phone. "It seems that once upon a time, in their younger days, they had a hot little romance. Rumors are that it was Delia's bully of a brother, Ledge, who caused their breakup."

"Ledge? Ledge Cowling?" Wyatt had an image of the prissy, suit-and-tie banker balking at getting his hands dirty. "What did he do to break them up?"

"There are several versions of the story. Nobody knows the truth except those intimately involved. But the bottom line is, after a knock-down, drag-out fight with Ledge Cowling, Coot took off on his horse for parts unknown. He was gone for quite some time. When he returned, he was accompanied by a brand-new wife, pretty little Annie Moffitt."

Wyatt chuckled. "Thank heavens for sweet little Annie. She and my grandfather were devoted to one another for more than thirty-five years."

"According to my information, Delia Cowling never married. It would seem she carried the torch for your grandfather until the day he died."

"Who knew?" Wyatt gave a mock shudder. "I'm trying to imagine life on the ranch with the town grouch Delia as my grandmother." By way of explanation he added, "I'm sure you wouldn't understand, Archie, but I can assure you that Coot was one lucky man to have dodged that bullet."

The two men shared a laugh until Archie said, "Just a thought, since you know the parties involved more than I do. Could Delia be holding a grudge against Coot's family for all these years?"

Wyatt was reminded of a long-forgotten incident from his childhood. He was seven years old and had gone into town with his father. He'd been standing outside the feed and grain store when Delia Cowling had walked past. She'd paused, looked back, then retraced her steps until she stood towering over him. "Aren't you Benjamin McCord's boy?"

"Yes'm." He'd given the woman his best smile.

Instead of the charmed reaction he usually got for such efforts, she merely glowered at him. "Are you chewing gum?"

He blinked. "No, ma'am."

"But you were. And you spit it out, didn't you?"

Before he could deny the accusation, she rounded on his father as he stepped through the doorway. "Benjamin McCord, your boy has the manners of a sow. His chewing gum is now stuck to the bottom of my shoe."

Ben glanced at his son, then back at the furious scowl on Delia's face. "Sorry about that, Miss Cowling. I'll have a talk with my boy."

"See that you do. And see that this never happens again." She turned the full volume of her temper on the boy. "Do you understand me?"

Wide-eyed, he stammered, "Ye . . . yes'm."

As she walked away, his father got eye-level with him. "Was it your gum, son?"

"No, sir."

"I didn't think so." Ben grinned as he watched the older woman's progress. "She surely blows like a Texas norther, doesn't she?" He laughed. "That's Delia Cowling. Got the meanest mouth in town. Though I don't understand it, she seems to have a special grudge against the McCords. Remember to steer clear of her, Wyatt."

"Yes, sir."

Hearing Archie's voice on the other end of the phone, Wyatt sobered. "If she carried a torch for Coot, that would explain why she might hold a grudge against our family. But to think that one old woman could cause the incidents I described to you is just too much of a stretch. I can't picture Delia Cowling going so far as to cause real physical harm to anyone. Most of her damage is inflicted by that mean mouth."

"You'd know better than I." Archie paused for emphasis. "But what about her brother, Ledge?"

What about Ledge?

The question worried the edges of Wyatt's mind days later as he and Marilee pulled up on his motorcycle outside Delia's tidy little house.

Marilee shot him a quick glance. "You sure we're doing the right thing?"

"No." He took a deep breath and slid off his helmet before taking her hand. "But I think the time for misunderstandings and unanswered questions is over. Now it's time for some straight talk."

Marilee paused beside him on the little front porch as he lifted a hand to knock. "She could order us to leave."

"She could. She certainly has the right to."

The door opened and Delia peered at the two of them in surprise. "Marilee. Wyatt. What can I do for you?"

Wyatt offered his most charming smile. "We have some questions, if you don't mind."

"I don't know. I'm not in the mood for company." She started to close the door.

"Please." Wyatt lifted a hand to the door to halt its motion. "Just for a moment."

Grudgingly the old woman stood aside and held the door as they walked past her into the neat little parlor.

She looked around as though searching for an escape. "Why don't we go to the kitchen?"

Marilee shot Wyatt a guilty look. "We don't want you to go to any trouble, Delia."

"It's no trouble. Really." She led the way. "I don't know about you, but I always prefer a nice cup of tea whenever visitors come calling."

She indicated two chairs at the table before she busied herself filling the teakettle and setting it on the stove.

Watching her, Wyatt and Marilee could see that she was actually relieved to have something to do. It was obvious that she entertained few visitors.

While the kettle heated she placed tea bags in a floral pot and set out dainty cups and napkins.

She smiled at Marilee. "I'm grateful for the professional way you handled my fall, Lee. I was feeling really frightened, and more than a little embarrassed. And I know my neighbor, Frances, was feeling helpless until you came along."

When the kettle began whistling she filled the teapot and set it on a tray with cream and sugar and some raspberry-filled cookies before settling herself at the table.

"I'll let you pour, Lee." The old woman held out her cup.

Marilee filled it, then filled Wyatt's cup and her own.

"Oh. My." Delia stared at the stitches on Marilee's forehead, and the bruise that spread down to her cheek. "I heard about your accident. I had no idea you'd been so badly injured."

Marilee flushed. "It looks worse than it feels. Really."

"That's a relief to hear." Delia passed around the plate of cookies before helping herself to one and nibbling. "I'm afraid I'm not very good at entertaining company, especially young people. I so rarely have any visitors. Oh, not that I'm complaining. I keep myself busy. But this is rather . . . pleasant." She studied Wyatt and the words tumbled out before she could stop herself. "You're the image of your grandfather, you know."

"Speaking of my grandfather . . ." Wyatt found himself sweating. He'd come here hoping to bully a meddling old gossip into telling him the truth about what she knew. Now she'd turned into some lonely, neglected old woman who looked like everybody's sweet grandmother, complete with tea and cookies. He didn't know how to handle the situation.

"Yes?" Delia sipped her tea. "I believe you said you had some questions."

Wyatt shifted, avoiding Marilee's eyes. "I wondered . . . That is, I heard that you and my grandfather were once close."

The old woman went very still, but a look crossed her face that had Wyatt mentally cursing himself.

Delia chose her words carefully. "My brother and I were once friendly with Coot. That was a long time ago, when we were all young and carefree."

"Did something happen to end the friendship?"

"Did I say it ended?"

He shook his head. "You said you were once friendly. That suggests it didn't last."

She looked away. "As you know, Coot's strange behavior made it difficult for anyone to be his friend."

"In what way?"

She picked up her cup. Sipped. Set it down. "He was a tortured soul. Obsessed with his family's lost fortune. Those of us who . . . cared for him realized that he was slipping further and further into some sort of dangerous fantasy."

"Did you point that out to him?"

She nodded. "Many times. But he was beyond listening."

"Did my grandmother share that view?"

Delia shrugged. "I couldn't say. Annie Moffitt and I were never close."

"But you knew her?"

She avoided Wyatt's eyes. "I knew of her." She lifted her chin. "Once Coot married, he stopped seeing old friends." She glanced pointedly at her kitchen clock. "I suppose I should be thinking about fixing something for supper. Is there anything else?"

Wyatt drained his tea. "I know you once said that you wouldn't be comfortable allowing us to look at your brother's old keepsakes without his permission. But since we're here, and we're still missing a lot of my grandfather's papers, I was hoping that you might have had a change of heart."

"I'm afraid that's not possible." She looked up with an odd little smile. "As soon as Ledge returned home from his latest business trip, he stopped over and retrieved all his belongings."

"He emptied the basement?"

"Completely. He knew the clutter bothered me. It's such a relief to have all those old boxes and plastic bins gone. I was able to find my mother's recipe box, and even managed to locate some of our old family albums." She got to her feet. "Would you like to see them?"

Wyatt glanced at Marilee, who gave a slight shake of her head.

"I'm sorry. There's no time. But maybe we could stop by another day."

"Of course." Her smile faded and she became once again stiff and formal. "Another time."

They made their way to the front door.

Marilee took Delia's hand in hers. "Thank you for the tea and cookies."

"You're welcome."

"Thank you." Wyatt surprised himself by pressing a kiss to her cheek. "I enjoyed it, too."

Delia was completely caught off-guard.

She was still standing stiffly at the front door watching as they climbed aboard Wyatt's motorcycle and took their leave.

Marilee wrapped her arms around Wyatt's waist and pressed her cheek to his back. She'd made this trip half fearing a confrontation with the feisty old woman. She was leaving with the realization that Delia Cowling was much more than the nosy old biddy she showed the town.

What would it be like, Marilee wondered, to be Delia's age and look back on a life with very few family and friends?

Did she also live with regrets?

Marilee had a flash of her own future. With her mother gone, she now had no family.

Regrets? She could probably list hundreds.

She decided not to dwell on the past.

For now, for today, she felt perfectly content.

She would worry about her future tomorrow.

CHAPTER FIFTEEN

Wyatt broke the news of Delia's empty basement the following morning over breakfast. Jesse and Zane were both frowning.

"I say we go to Ledge and demand to see anything that may have belonged to Coot." Jesse, too pumped to sit, paced the kitchen.

"I'm with you, Jess." Zane nervously tapped his fork against the edge of the plate, Dandy's perfect French toast forgotten. "He knew we wanted to look through those papers. That's got to be the reason he took them away."

"I agree." Wyatt glanced at their aunt, who had remained silent throughout his narrative. "Did you know about Coot and Delia?"

She nodded. "It wasn't a secret. We all knew that they were sweet on each other. Delia's family wasn't happy about it. They considered my brother beneath them." She sighed. "When Coot came home with a bride, Delia's family was relieved. I was a bit puzzled by how quickly it all happened, but I was soon completely convinced that Coot and Annie were a perfect fit. Annie was content to raise her family. In all the years they were married, I never heard her complain about the time he spent on his all-consuming search for the family treasure. In fact, she believed in the lost treasure as deeply as Coot."

Cora looked down at her hands. "But I've always felt sorry for Delia. I believe she really loved Coot. I saw the gradual change in her. She went from being a sweet, sunny young woman to a lonely, bitter gossip who seemed to take joy in learning anything unpleasant about anybody around her."

Wyatt gave Cora's hand a squeeze. "She may have been caught by surprise when Marilee and I came calling, but after her initial shock, she was more than civil. She even made us tea."

Cora gave him a gentle smile. "And why not? Look at you." She glanced around the table at her nephews. "There's no denying that the three of you carry Coot's blood. The look of him is there in your faces." She lifted a hand to Wyatt's cheek. "Maybe, for just a little while, Delia felt the way she had when she was young and happy and wildly in love with your grandfather."

Her words had the three of them falling silent.

Later, when Cora headed to her studio, the three walked to the fleet of trucks in the main barn.

Wyatt tossed the keys to Jesse. "I say we follow your suggestion and pay a call on Ledge Cowling."

"Good. If you hadn't said that, I was planning on paying a visit alone." Jesse yanked open the truck door, only too happy to oblige.

Zane and Wyatt quickly crowded into the front seat, eager for the challenge.

"Ledge will see you now." Paula Henning held open the door to Ledge's office at the bank, closing it behind the three McCord cousins after they'd stepped inside.

"Well." Ledge gave them his best professional smile and handshake before inviting them to sit. "You three in need of a loan? Or maybe, in your case, you're here to see if I need one."

They smiled pleasantly at his joke.

He sat back, looking pleased and relaxed. "Tell me what I can do for you."

Wyatt spoke for them. "Your sister told me that you'd picked up all your belongings from her basement."

"Did she happen to mention how happy that made her?" He chuckled. "She's been after me for years to clean up that mess. Our parents were pack rats. I think they saved everything, from our nursery rhymes to my college awards. I've finally given Delia the space she wanted."

"My cousins and I were hoping you would give us a chance to look through the boxes in case there were more of Coot's notes or scraps."

Because Wyatt was bracing for a vague rejection, or even an outright refusal, he was surprised when Ledge's smile grew.

"Well now. I wish you'd come to me sooner. I would have been happy to let you rummage through that old junk. Unfortunately, it's not possible now."

"Why is that?" Wyatt's uneasiness grew in direct proportion to Ledge's easy affability.

"I shredded everything." Ledge tipped his chair back, lacing his fingers over his substantial middle. "Ten boxes in all."

"Shredded everything?" Wyatt glanced at Zane, who looked thunderstruck, and then at Jesse, who wore a look of disbelief. "Must have taken you hours."

"Yes, indeed. Kept me here long after everyone else had gone home for the night. But I considered it my patriotic duty." He was positively beaming. "I certainly didn't want all those old papers and documents to clog a landfill."

"That lying . . ." Jesse turned the key in the ignition before exploding. "Destroying papers that don't belong to him and acting as though he was doing his sister a favor."

"And having a good laugh at our expense." Zane swore under his breath.

"With that smile in place, he completely transformed himself from Scrooge to jovial Old Saint Nick." Wyatt grew thoughtful. "You have to admit that he made a smart move. We'll never know how many pages of Nathanial's journal or how many of Coot's notes and maps were in those boxes."

Jesse drove the truck along the main street. "Now what?"

Wyatt shrugged. "Ledge won this round. We'll just have to come up with another way to entice him back into the ring."

Zane stared at the sunlight glinting off the peaks of Treasure Chest in the distance. "Maybe he's already won the fight and we just don't know it." When Jesse and Wyatt turned to him he added, "Who's to say he didn't shred important papers that could lead him right to the treasure? He could be waiting for us to lose interest in the search, and then he'll step in and quietly claim the prize."

"Just as Vernon McVicker had hoped." Wyatt digested his words before nodding. "All right. And maybe all these things that have been happening were designed to distract us from our original goal. If so, my pal Archie will fill me in with whatever details he can learn. And since there's nothing we can do until we have more facts, I say it's time for us to get serious and step up our game."

As the others turned to him he mused aloud, "It's time to put down everything we know, from the trail we've drawn of Coot's wanderings, from the places he searched and discarded, to the places we believe are unlikely to be good hiding places. And then, taking it all into account, I say we chart our own course. And that means using modern technology to aid in our search." He turned to Jesse, then to Zane. "Do you agree?"

Jesse nodded.

Zane shrugged. "Why not? I say we go for it full-steam ahead."

The three solemnly shook hands.

Wyatt suddenly burst into gales of laughter.

At their matching looks of concern he explained, "I was thinking about the time we took a solemn vow to not let anybody know about where we found that nugget."

Jesse thought a moment. "The one that turned out to be fool's gold?"

"That's the one. You realize, of course, that it's our duty to continue the family tradition of looking like crazy coots to everyone in this town?"

The other two joined him in laughter.

It was, Wyatt realized, good to find something to laugh about. And good to have a common goal with his two cousins.

Cora, Jesse, Amy, and Zane, seated in the great room enjoying the evening sunset, looked up as the roar of a motorcycle broke the calm that had settled over the land. Minutes later Wyatt and Marilee entered through the kitchen, greeting Dandy as they passed him. Entering the great room, they hurried over to greet the family.

"Miss Cora." Marilee brushed a kiss over the older woman's cheek.

"I'm so glad you're here, Lee. Did you and Wyatt have dinner?"

"Vi's burgers and fries."

As Marilee and Amy hugged, Cora thought how young and pretty they both looked. Amy, with her fair hair in a ponytail; Marilee wind-tossed and casual in denims and a gauzy shirt, her cheeks bright pink from the long ride on the back of Wyatt's bike.

Cora returned Wyatt's hug. "Dandy made apple cobbler."

Wyatt nodded. "He was just filling a tray with desserts and coffee. Our timing is perfect."

Within minutes Dandy entered and set the tray on a side table. Seeing that they had everything they needed, he walked away, eager to tidy the kitchen before retiring for the night.

Amy passed around the plates of cobbler while Marilee handed out cups of coffee.

While they enjoyed their dessert the three cousins

walked around the map with its parade of pins and sticky notes, examining it from every direction. By the time they'd set aside their empty plates and cups, they were ready to tackle the problem at hand.

"We can easily see where Coot was headed." Jesse ran a finger along the trail of red pins they'd used to indicate the land Coot had already studied and discarded as a possible hiding place for the treasure.

Zane pointed to the accumulation of paper scraps they'd pieced together. "And from his notes and drawings, we know that he continued moving toward Treasure Chest."

"What's more, Vernon McVicker admitted following Coot for years, hoping to take up the hunt if Coot should ever die or grow tired. When Vernon realized that Coot might outlive him, he decided to"—Wyatt glanced over at his aunt, knowing how painful it was for her to hear, even now—"get rid of Coot so that he could search by himself, without interruption." Wyatt sighed. "Gold has a way of bringing out the worst in some people."

"And bringing out the best in others." Cora set aside her coffee and glanced around at her grandnephews. "I know how much you yearn to find our family's treasure. But I want each of you to promise me that you'll never allow this search for the gold to tear apart the bond that we've been building here. No treasure is worth that."

Hearing the passion that caused her voice to tremble, they were quick to assure her.

"I give you my word, Aunt Cora." Jesse crossed the room to place a hand on her shoulder.

"You have my word, too." Zane nodded his head for emphasis.

"And mine." Wyatt met her steady look. "We've all been witnesses to just how fragile this bond is, and how easily it can unravel. That makes us more determined than ever to see that it doesn't happen again."

She gave a long, deep sigh before the smile returned to her eyes, and to her voice. "Now. Let's get down to the business of determining just where we want to take up the search." She closed a hand over Jesse's. "Why don't you begin?"

As he pointed out the place on Treasure Chest where his grandfather had been found after his fall, the others became animated and jumped in with their own suggestions.

Cora studied their faces and found herself once again thinking about how deeply ingrained her brother's influence had been in the lives of these three young men. In their boyhood he'd been their rock. It was Coot they had gone to with their questions and concerns, knowing he would always have time for them, unlike their fathers, who were often too busy with ranch chores. And even though Wyatt and Zane had been absent for much of their growing-up years, it was Coot who had continued to color their lives. Now they were here, taking up the cause that had consumed him, and making it their own.

"It's agreed then?" Jesse's voice broke through Cora's reverie. "We'll concentrate on the foothills around Treasure Chest?"

"It's the most sensible place to start." Zane, busy setting up his camera, brought Jesse and Wyatt into focus before joining them for the picture.

"Right." Wyatt stuck out his hand.

With Jesse on one side of him and Zane on the other, the three cousins clasped hands and smiled at the camera as the moment was recorded.

Then they drew Amy and Marilee over with them as they gathered around the map and added a red flag to the exact spot in the foothills where they intended to begin their search the following day.

Hours later, as the logs on the fire burned low, they shared a round of longnecks and reminisced about their childhood spent roaming free on the thousands of acres of ranchland that had been their playground.

Cora found herself laughing aloud as they revealed some of the adventures they'd shared and the trouble they'd gotten into.

"Do you remember the time we tied a lasso to a tree limb and decided to swing across the creek like Tarzan?" Wyatt tipped up his frosty bottle and took a long pull.

"Yeah." Zane was already laughing. "As usual, you two decided that I'd be the one to try it out first. That way, if it broke, I'd be the one tossed into the creek."

"It stands to reason." Jesse chuckled. "You were the youngest. That's just the price you had to pay to hang out with us."

"And," Wyatt added, "you were always willing to go along with whatever we decided."

"What choice did I have?" Zane set down his beer. "The few times I refused to try one of your crazy schemes, I was sent back to the ranch and had to hang out with the wranglers for the rest of the day, which usually meant that they'd dream up some chores for me to do, just to get me out of their hair."

"So?" Amy demanded. "Did the rope break?"

Zane shook his head. "Not when I used it to fly across the creek."

"And not when I followed him," Wyatt said with a laugh. "But Jesse, assured that it was safe, grabbed hold and was flying through the air when the branch snapped."

Amy looked over at her husband. "You landed in the creek?"

"Yeah. On the day after one of our biggest storms, with the water spilling over its banks and rushing so fast it carried me downstream half a mile or more."

She put a hand to her mouth to cover her shock and saw Cora do the same.

Wyatt laughed. "He was lucky Zane and I had our horses tethered nearby. We chased along the banks of the creek until we could get far enough ahead to toss him a tree branch to catch. By the time we hauled him out, he looked like a drowned rat and was spitting mad."

"I had a right to be. I swallowed half the creek."

Zane laughed. "But think how lucky we were that it happened to you instead of me. At least you could swim."

Marilee's eyes rounded. "They had you test the rope when they knew you couldn't swim?"

Wyatt was laughing even harder. "We figured it was one way for him to learn."

"How old were you?"

They thought a minute before Wyatt answered. "I was eight, so that would make Jesse ten and Zane seven."

"You could have all drowned."

"Yeah. Looking back, we were lucky to have survived so many foolish adventures. But," Wyatt added, "I wouldn't have missed a single one of them."

An hour later, as Cora made her way to her room, she listened to the roar of Wyatt's motorcycle fade into the distance. Zane had retired to his suite, where he routinely stayed awake until the wee hours of the morning reviewing film for his documentary project. The sound of muffled laughter drifted from Jesse and Amy as they made their way to their suite of rooms on the far side of the house.

Too wired to settle down, Cora stepped into her studio and cast a critical eye on her latest canvas. It was an extreme close-up of a bitterroot in full bloom. The pink blossom with its yellow center filled the entire canvas and seemed to explode with vibrant color.

She couldn't help smiling. Her creations always had that effect on her. But it was especially easy to feel joy tonight.

She'd spent such pleasant hours watching her nephews reliving their childhood pranks and reestablishing that invisible thread that held all of them together.

Oh, Coot. Did you see them? Did you hear the laughter? Did you feel the love?

She paused beside a window and stared at the full moon resting at the very tip of Treasure Chest, casting a pale glow over the entire mountain range. As though, she thought, in benediction.

She was still smiling as she made her way to her bedroom and prepared for bed.

Her nephews had confided their concerns about Ledge Cowling, and the papers he'd destroyed. But now, this night, she couldn't work up any emotion except happiness.

Her nephews had taken up Coot's lifelong odyssey. They were on the right course. She was convinced of it.

And at least for tonight, she was filled with a quiet sense of peace.

On this very special night, nothing could possibly go wrong.

All was right with the world.

CHAPTER SIXTEEN

Chief Wycliff was beaming as he handed Marilee the keys to her restored emergency vehicle.

"Deputy Atkins made the round-trip to the state police post and back just to pick up this report. Their lab gave it a clean bill of health. They found a glitch in the driver's-side air bag, but they assure me it's been corrected."

"Thanks, Ernie." She opened the door and breathed deeply. "I wonder how they got that new-car smell in this old thing."

"Probably a combination of disinfectant and wax." He looked over her shoulder. "Clean as a whistle."

"Yeah." Her spirits lifted considerably. She couldn't wait to fill it with supplies and get on with her job.

Get on with her life.

"How about you, Lee?" The police chief studied the faded bruise on her forehead. "You nervous about getting that first call?"

She shook her head. "You know me, Ernie. I just want to get past this."

"Fearless. Good for you. When do you expect to get your plane ready to fly?"

"The manufacturer sent a crew with the parts. They're planning a test flight in the next day or so."

"Any word from Craig Matson?"

She shook her head.

The chief glanced past her to where Wyatt stood, watching and listening. And frowning. "I want you to know I'm looking into his sudden departure. I talked to Harding and Ledge to see if they knew anything. After all, they're the ones who pay his salary. They don't seem to know any more than we do. He left to see about a family emergency, and nobody's heard from him since. But I've got a couple of leads, and when I know more, I'll get back to you both."

"Thanks, Ernie. I'll let you worry about all that." Marilee ran a hand over the gleaming door of her vehicle. "Right now, I'm just happy to get back to work."

"Then I'll leave you to it." He turned away and climbed into his four-wheel-drive truck decked out with the town logo and sporting every bell and whistle the town could afford.

By the time Wyatt was headed toward the ranch for a day of chores, Marilee was happily loading medical supplies into the back of her vehicle before making a run to the clinic.

The ringing of her phone dragged Marilee out of a sound sleep. She reached for the receiver in the same instant that she glanced at the clock. Why did so many accidents occur at two in the morning?

"Emergency One. What's the problem?"

She listened in silence, aware of Wyatt sitting up in bed beside her.

"The Turner place? It'll take me half an hour at least."

She slipped out of bed and reached for a shirt, trying not to think about the long, dark ride ahead of her. But though she was outwardly calm and controlled, her heart was working overtime. This would be her first run since the accident. Her first real test of nerves. Though she was determined to be the victor in the battle for control, so far, nerves were winning.

She was still snapping the waist of her jeans when she walked from the bedroom. All her concentration was on the need to banish these fears that had come sneaking up on her like a thief in the night.

Wyatt fell into step beside her.

Surprised, she swiveled her head. "What are you doing?"

"Going with you."

A part of her felt a quick rush of relief. She wouldn't be alone. Another part of her deeply resented her reaction. She needed to be strong, not weak at a time like this.

She crossed her arms over her chest, determined to hold herself together. "Don't be silly. This is my job, not . . ."

He cut off her argument by opening the door of her apartment and stepping aside, forcing her to precede him.

Stiff-backed, she descended the stairs. She heard his footsteps behind her and knew that he was following. The knowledge was both a comfort and an annoyance.

She didn't want comfort. She wanted to stand up against her fear and conquer it. Alone.

She paused, hand on the waiting vehicle, and turned to him. "Go back to bed."

"Too late." He tried for a smile, but it lacked the warmth or humor that had become his trademark. Instead he appeared . . . watchful. Wary. "I'm wide awake. I'd never fall back asleep now."

Her tone lowered in direct contrast to her rising anger. "I don't care, Wyatt. I don't need you here."

"I know you don't. But I need to be with you."

"You know I work alone."

"Not tonight."

She heard the finality in his tone and realized that it was useless to argue this any further, especially since she needed to be on the road as quickly as possible.

Without a word she climbed into the driver's side and turned the key in the ignition.

He climbed into the passenger side and fastened his seat belt. "Where are we headed?"

She sighed before turning on the flashing lights. "Turner ranch. Ken's moaning in pain. Laura doesn't have a clue what's ailing him. Doc will drive to the clinic and wait for my report."

As they headed out of town, Marilee was grateful for the hot, dry weather. Would rain have spooked her? She hoped not, but she couldn't be certain.

When a truck's headlights crossed the median, appearing to be headed right toward her vehicle, she turned on the siren and swerved.

"Damned drunk." Her heart was thundering in her chest, and though she hated to admit it, she was suddenly glad for Wyatt's company. That thought had her frowning.

When she glanced over at him, he smiled and closed a hand over hers.

She drew her hand away and returned her attention to the road, waiting for her heart rate to return to normal.

She was so glad he was here beside her, and so frustrated with herself because of it. What the hell was happening to her? She needed to get a grip.

"We're heading into town, Doc." Marilee spoke quietly into her cell phone. "Ken's in the back, in a lot of pain. High fever. Lower abdomen and side very tender. My best guess is a ruptured appendix. Laura will stay home, since the little ones are asleep, and wait for your call."

She listened, before adding, "Right. I have the lights flashing, but will kill the siren. No sense waking half the town. I should have Ken there in less than half an hour. Do you have Elly there to assist you?"

His voice broke through the static. "She will be by the time you get Ken here."

Marilee tucked her cell phone into her pocket and pressed down on the accelerator. With no traffic at this hour, she would be back to town in record time.

It was, she thought, a relief to be busy once more. Though she'd enjoyed some time to herself, and loved being pampered by Wyatt, she'd missed this more than she cared to admit.

Now if she could just shake off the last of her nerves, her life could return to normal.

Marilee was feeling sluggish after a very long night. Instead of collapsing into sleep when she'd returned to her apartment, she'd tossed and turned, too wired to relax and turn off her brain. When she finally did sleep, it had been interrupted with strange, dark dreams.

Knowing that Wyatt was asleep beside her gave her no consolation. In fact, seeing him so completely relaxed only added to her discomfort. How had he adjusted so easily to sharing her bed? And why couldn't she do the same? Why did she have this prickly feeling along her scalp, as though everything she'd been building in her life was slowly unraveling?

Now, seeing the bed empty, she walked to the shower and stood under a steamy spray for long minutes, hoping it would revive her.

Once dry she dressed in a pair of cuffed shorts and a denim shirt tied at her midriff. Before she could slip into a pair of sandals the phone rang and she picked it up, talking as she made her way to the kitchen.

"Oh, Laura, thanks for the update. I'm so glad Doc has it all under control. How long will Ken have to stay at the clinic?"

While she listened, she was distracted by the wonderful fragrance of cinnamon French toast wafting from the griddle.

"I'm glad it wasn't anything more than his appendix. Tell him he'll be much happier without it."

She rang off and watched as Wyatt set a plate on the bar counter. "Something smells wonderful."

"Dandy's secret recipe for French toast stuffed with apples and drizzled with syrup and cinnamon."

"If it's a secret recipe, how did you get it?"

He wiggled his brows like a villain. "I could tell you,

but then I'd have to kill you. Now eat, woman. You need your strength."

"Yes, sir." She dug in and watched as he sat beside her and did the same.

At last she sat back, sipping strong, hot coffee. "Oh, that was wonderful. I didn't realize just how hungry I was. Thank you."

"You're welcome. But don't tell Dandy. This must remain our little secret."

Wyatt saw the smile that touched her lips and was grateful that he'd been able to lift her spirits, at least for the moment. She'd been so tense last night. So coldly, carefully controlled, as though holding herself together by sheer force of will.

It was natural enough to have to deal with nerves, especially so soon after the accident. Still, he was worried about her reaction. It seemed a bit extreme.

He shot her a sideways glance. "You were having quite a dream this morning."

"A dream?" She went very still, as bits and pieces of the bad dream began flashing through her mind. "Did I say anything?"

"You were saying lots of things, but nothing that made sense. My impression is that you were mad as hell, and somebody was going to feel the sting of Marilee's mighty temper."

"Is that all?" She started toward the sink with her empty plate.

Wyatt held out his hand. "I'll take that."

She held back. "You cooked. I'll clean up."

"I don't mind. You're still recovering from . . ."

She poked a finger at his chest. "You have to stop this."

He jerked back. "Stop what?"

"Coddling me."

"I'll coddle if I want . . ."

"Wyatt. I'm serious." She stepped around him and set her plate in the sink before taking his empty plate from his hands. "I'm warning you to stop. You're not only coddling me, you're crowding me."

"Crowding . . . ?"

"Suffocating me, in fact."

She saw the look in his eyes. As though she'd slapped him. And though it pained her to hurt him this way, she couldn't seem to stop. All the feelings that she'd kept bottled up now began to bubble to the surface. All her old fears erupted.

"Like you, I've been on my own for a long time now. I'm used to making my own decisions. Making my own mistakes. I had to fight long and hard to overcome the feeling that I'd never be smart enough, good enough, to please my father. I'd never be the son he wanted. And then there was my mother, who couldn't make a simple decision without first consulting him. I swear, she couldn't even decide which dress to wear without first getting his approval. I made myself a promise that I'd never let that happen. I'm my own person. I answer to nobody. I don't want anybody else directing my life."

"Directing . . . ?

"So as much as I love having you here, I can't allow this to continue. You can't keep up with your ranch chores during the day and then race all over the countryside at night every time I have an emergency run. Before long, you'll hate me for making such a mess of your life."

"That's nonsense. I could never hate you, Marilee. I love being with you. Taking care of you. Don't you think this should be my decision?"

Her voice rose a fraction. "What about me? What about what I want?"

"You have to know that I care about you and what you want."

"If that's so, then you'll listen to what I'm saying."

He went very still. "Are you saying you don't want me here?"

"It isn't about that. I love having you here." Frustrated, she could feel her temperature rising along with the tone of her voice. "Wyatt, you need to get your life back." She took a quick, steadying breath. "And so do I."

"You want your life back." He studied her, eyes narrowed in thought. "And so, for that reason, you're ordering me to leave?"

"Not to leave. Just to step back. You have to trust me . . ."

"Of course I trust you."

"You have to trust that I can take care of myself. Trust that I can decide what's best for me." Her voice trembled. "Do you know how wonderful it is to have someone care this much about me? Wyatt, I've waited a lifetime for someone like you. But you've started to make me your responsibility. Your . . . job. And I'm afraid that very soon your job will become your . . . burden."

He took a step back, studying her with eyes that had gone flat and cold. "I can't believe what I'm hearing. You can't be serious."

Not trusting her voice, she merely nodded.

At first, all he could see was the way she kept her spine rigid, her head high in that haughty, take-charge stance he so admired. Wasn't it the first thing he'd noticed, right after that lush body, that flaming hair, those kiss-me-until-my-heart-stops lips?

Now he saw more. He saw that she was stubborn and intractable and completely unreasonable. Every cliché he'd ever heard flew into his mind. She wasn't just take-charge, but bossy. Not just capable, but demanding. Not just independent, but selfish.

She blinked, and he could see the sudden trace of sorrow in her eyes. Could see the way her lower lip was trembling. Now she was going all female on him. God, he didn't think he could bear it if she started crying.

Though he could think of a dozen things he wanted to say, he turned away, needing to escape as much as she needed her privacy.

He retrieved the keys to his motorcycle and let himself out of her apartment without a word.

He gunned the engine and took off without a backward glance.

As his bike ate up the miles back to the Lost Nugget, he found himself fuming over all the things she'd said.

How could she believe that he'd been crowding her? Suffocating her? He swore. All he'd wanted was to keep her safe.

He'd never before felt the need to so completely take over someone else's life. But this was his beautiful, talented Marilee, and all he wanted was to keep her out of harm's way. Couldn't she see that?

When he arrived at the ranch he avoided the big house, choosing instead to storm into the barn and work alongside a couple of the wranglers who were mucking stalls. If they were surprised by his presence, they gave no indication.

By the time Jesse and Zane had finished breakfast and saw Wyatt's bike parked beside the barn, he had worked up a sweat, doing the job of three men, forking enough straw and dung to completely fill a wagon.

"Hey." Jesse leaned on a rail to watch as Wyatt bent to his task. "When did you get back?"

Wyatt barely paused. "Not sure. Time passes, you know?"

"Yeah." Jesse arched a brow. "Something eating you, cuz?"

"I'm fine."

"Yeah. I can see that." Jesse turned to Zane and rolled his eyes. "We're heading up to the north range. Want to ride along?"

"I'm fine here."

"Well, yeah, you're doing a great job on that stall. But when you're through shoveling manure, what're you planning on doing the rest of the day?"

Instead of the laugh he was expecting, Wyatt swore. Loudly. Fiercely.

"I guess that means you'd like to be alone." Jesse shoved his hands into his back pockets. "Speaking from experience as an old married man, I'd say this also means that you and the lovely Lee have had a lovers' spat."

In response Wyatt dug the pitchfork into a pile of dung and tossed it Jesse's way.

Jesse ducked, avoiding most of the mess, except for a few bits of straw that clung to his hair.

From a safe distance Zane gave a roar of laughter. "I think that means he isn't seeking your sage advice, O Ancient One."

"Your loss, cuz. I could have told you that what women really want is for you to admire their minds. Even when they don't make any sense at all." Jesse picked out the pieces of straw and tossed them aside before turning to Zane. "Come on. We've got a herd to deal with. Let's leave Mr. Happy to work out his problems in this pile of . . . horse manure."

Laughing, the two strolled out of the barn.

Wyatt swore again and continued shoveling until every stall sparkled. Then he moved on to the cow barns, working his way through a mountain of frustration.

CHAPTER SEVENTEEN

H ello, handsome." Daffy managed to press a kiss to Wyatt's cheek while balancing a tray filled with longnecks. "You want a table, or are you sitting at the bar?"

His gaze roamed the entire room and back before he shrugged away the quick wave of disappointment at not seeing the familiar flaming hair. "Guess I'll just sit at the bar."

"Zane is there, right next to Jimmy Eagle."

"Yeah. I see them. Thanks." Before he could turn away Daffy added, "You just missed Lee."

He paused, hating the way his heart stopped for the moment. He hoped Daffy would say more without forcing him to ask.

Daffy patted his hand. "She was here with Amy. It was good to see those two best friends making time for one another."

"Yeah." He forced a smile.

She gave him a long look. "You been busy up in the high country?"

At his arched brow she explained. "Delia Cowling was hovering over their table, and I overheard Lee saying something to that effect." She gave one of her throaty laughs. "The old busybody is never happy unless she knows everything about everybody. And that includes why two of the town's hottest couples aren't together every minute." There was another long look, followed by an even longer pause, before she walked away.

Frowning, Wyatt threaded his way between tables and made his way to the bar. So much for keeping this under wraps. Not in Gold Fever.

As soon as he was seated beside Zane, Vi slid a frosty bottle down the bar. Wyatt caught it and tipped it up, draining half the bottle in one long swallow.

Zane swiveled his barstool to study his cousin. "Didn't expect to see you here tonight."

"Didn't expect to be here."

"Did your date stand you up?"

"Didn't have a date."

"Too bad. There was quite the hot-looking babe in here just a few minutes ago."

Wyatt gave a sigh of disgust. "Okay, you're the second one to tell me that breaking news."

Zane winked at Jimmy Eagle. "My cousin's a little edgy these days. He's taken a real liking to mucking stalls, though, so the wranglers in the barn are mighty grateful for his new attitude."

Seeing Wyatt's scowl deepen, Jimmy bit back his grin. "Hard work's good for a troubled soul."

"Then I say more power to you, cuz." Zane touched his beer to Wyatt's. "I'll gladly leave the manure removal in your very capable hands."

He and Jimmy were still chuckling when Wyatt picked up his beer, slid from the barstool, and joined a table of wranglers in the rear of the saloon.

The afternoon sky was as dreary as Marilee's mood as she drove the rescue vehicle around to the rear of the medical clinic and parked in the designated space. Opening the back door, she began hauling fresh supplies from the clinic storeroom to the ambulance. When it was neatly stocked she made her way inside, where Elly Carson and Dr. Wheeler were talking quietly.

Elly looked over. "Hi, Lee. You just missed Wyatt. He was here on an emergency run and walked out the front door to his truck not five minutes ago."

Marilee's heart slammed against her ribs. "Was he hurt?"

"Not Wyatt. One of the wranglers. Got careless mending a fence and had a really nasty gash from the barbed wire. Wyatt drove him in for stitches."

"Oh." Marilee felt almost giddy with relief.

"I'm surprised he didn't tell you." Elly turned away to remove the disposable covering from the gurney. "He could have called you and saved himself that long drive from the ranch."

Doc peeled away his sterile gloves. "Just as well he didn't wait around for an ambulance. That wound was deep. Len had already lost a lot of blood. Wyatt did the right thing bringing him in immediately."

He handed Marilee a slip of paper. "Next time you're making a run to Helena, we'll be needing these supplies."

"Thanks." She pocketed the list and turned away. "See you soon."

Once in the emergency vehicle, she leaned her head back and closed her eyes for a moment.

Minutes sooner and she would have come face-to-face with Wyatt. Maybe he would have smiled, or talked, and she could have done the same. Maybe then they could break through this terrible wall that they'd built.

That she'd built.

Or maybe, she thought, struggling to ignore the stab of guilt, they would have merely added another layer of pain and deepened the wound.

She opened her eyes, lifted her head, and turned the ignition, determined to get on with the day.

To get on with her life.

She absorbed a fresh stab of pain. A life without Wyatt.

"Hey, Wyatt." Amy sat astride her mare and watched as Wyatt and a crew handled the backbreaking job of setting new fence posts.

He looked up, then, lifting his hat to wipe at the sweat, ambled over. "Hi, Amy. What brings you out this far?"

"Jesse and I are going to drive up in the hills tonight to look at the piece of land we've chosen for our home site. We thought you and Lee might like to come along."

Except for a slight narrowing of his eyes, he managed to keep a tight lid on his emotions. "Thanks for the offer, but by the time we finish here, I'm betting I'll be ready to fall into my bunk and zone out until morning."

"Okay." She bit her lip. "Maybe another time."

"Yeah." He replaced his hat while walking back to join the crew.

When Amy rode away he turned with a thoughtful expression. Was she trying to play matchmaker on her own, or had she and Jesse hatched this plan together, hoping to meddle?

For one quick moment he wondered whether Marilee had had a hand in it. Then he berated himself for wishful thinking. Marilee had made herself perfectly clear.

Whatever game Amy was playing, he had no intention of setting himself up for any more heartache.

Wyatt stood under the shower, hands braced on either side of the tiled wall, face lifted to the spray of hot water.

It had been the longest week of his life. And though he'd waited and wondered, and even picked up the phone a dozen or more times, in the end he'd decided that Marilee would have to make the first move. He wasn't going to call her. He wasn't even going to allow himself to think about her. She needed her space? Fine. He'd give it to her. In spades.

He'd made a good life for himself. Alone. He didn't need anybody calling the shots. Especially some female who blew hot and cold, loving his pampering one day and feeling crowded the next.

Crowded. The very thought had him frowning.

By the time he'd toweled himself dry and was pulling on a clean shirt, he was toying with the idea of driving into town. He was sick and tired of the looks he was getting from his aunt and cousins. This ranch may consist of thousands of acres of land and a hundred or more wranglers, but there was nowhere to hide from the rumors and gossip that floated around.

Everyone on the Lost Nugget Ranch, it seemed, knew that he and Marilee were no longer together.

Together. What a strange word that was. There were probably plenty of married couples who thought of themselves as more alone than together. And plenty of his friends who thought of themselves as so together they would never need a partner to add anything to their lives.

He paused. Marilee had added so much to his life. Everything had been more fun with her. Laughter had been more spontaneous with her. With Marilee, work had become play. And play had become pure joy.

He wadded the damp towel into a ball and slammed it into the corner of his room, determined to put her out of his mind once and for all.

Maybe he'd stop at the saloon and have a beer with the wranglers. Listen to Daffy's throaty laughs telling one of her stale jokes, and enjoy one of Vi's greasy burgers.

He stepped into clean denims and boots.

Maybe *she'd* be there. He'd be civil. Cool and civil. Let her make the first move. If there was a first move. Or not. It didn't matter to him. She didn't matter to him. Nothing mattered to him.

When he descended the stairs and walked past his aunt's studio, he was relieved to see the door closed. That meant she was still working on her latest canvas. He could leave without suffering the need to pause and make small talk. Doing that lately had begun to stick in his throat.

He made his way through the kitchen, where Dandy was chopping vegetables at the counter.

The cook looked over. "You staying for supper?"

"No thanks. Heading into town." He hurried out to his Harley and climbed aboard, eager for the wind to take his hair. And hopefully his dark thoughts.

Marilee finished polishing the last of her living room shelves and returned the baskets and masks to their former positions. She stepped back and looked around her apartment. In the past week, between ambulance runs, her floors had been scrubbed and waxed to a high shine. The kitchen tiles gleamed, looking as new as the day they'd been installed. The windows sparkled in the sunlight. The bed had been freshened with new linens. Her laundry was folded and put away. She'd even cleaned out her closets and drawers, and had filled a garbage bag with discarded clothing, which she would drop off at a local charity.

She set the kettle on the stove and sank down on a barstool to wait for the familiar whistle. She'd needed this time to work. Hard work had always been her refuge when she was troubled. But now, after scrubbing, polishing, and waxing, she ought to be feeling a sense of accomplishment. Instead, she felt only a vague sense of dread at the days and weeks and months looming ahead of her.

She'd hurt Wyatt. Had seen it in his eyes. Heard it in his voice. And even though she had no doubt that she'd needed to say what she was feeling, it didn't make it any easier. Being right didn't help much when it meant hurting the one you loved.

The one you loved.

Shocked, stunned, she put a hand to her heart to ease the sudden spear of pain.

She did love him. In a way she'd never loved anyone else. She loved his silly humor, his quick, sharp mind, his sense of fair play. She loved his interaction with his large, loud family. She especially loved his fierce independence.

Her beloved rebel.

What would she do if the tables were turned? What if she believed Wyatt was in some kind of danger? Wouldn't she move heaven and earth to keep him safe? And yet she'd asked him . . . no, she'd ordered him away. Had told him that he was suffocating her. Smothering her with his care and concern. She'd sent him away, angry and hurting, and all because of her damnable need to take care of herself.

What had she done? Oh, what had she done?

She grabbed up the bag of discarded clothing and went in search of her keys.

She had to get out of here. She had to escape her dark thoughts, her perfectly appointed apartment, her uncluttered life that was suddenly making her feel horribly, miserably alone.

As Wyatt's Harley danced along the open highway he mulled the things Marilee had said, playing them this way and that through his mind, turning them over and over, struggling to make some sense of them, as he had a hundred times in the past week.

She needed the freedom to live her life on her terms. To make her own mistakes. Well, wasn't that the same thing he'd wanted all these years? Hadn't he been the original rebel, letting his family know in no uncertain terms that he would live by his own code?

Didn't everybody have the right to that?

He slowed the bike. Stared around as though coming out of a fog. Had he been holding her too tightly? Afraid to let go, not only out of love, but also out of fear for her safety? If someone did that to him, no matter how noble the reasons, he'd clench his fists and fight until only one of them was still standing.

What had she said about her father? That she'd never been the son he'd wanted. And so she'd rebelled and fought and clawed her way to a life that satisfied her needs.

She had her own demons to fight. A distant father and a clinging mother, and Marilee struggling to find out where she fit into that equation. A classic contest of wills, and one that she had to fight every day for the sake of her battered self-esteem.

Maybe, Wyatt thought, the only way to keep from losing her would be to learn to let her go. Even if it meant knowing that she could be putting herself in harm's way.

Dear God, was he strong enough?

It went against everything he'd ever believed about love and family. Didn't a man have a duty to keep his loved ones safe, by any means possible?

The mere thought of stepping back, of letting go, of abdicating what he considered his right, had him shuddering. It would be harder than anything he'd ever done before, and he wasn't at all certain he was up to the task.

But, if it was really a test, not just of moral strength but a test of love, how could he do otherwise?

Suddenly, this was all too much to take in. It was too deep, too threatening.

He gunned the engine, taking the curves and slopes of

the highway with breathtaking speed. And all the while he was wishing the wind blowing past him could blow away every dark, daunting thought swirling through his mind. Thoughts that were making him question every truth he'd ever held sacred.

CHAPTER EIGHTEEN

———◆———

Wyatt slowed to make the turn into town, then thought better of it and continued on along the highway until the pavement ended. He followed a dirt track through scrub and gnarled trees until he came to an outcropping of rock that ended in a sheer drop-off overlooking a stretch of rangeland.

Dismounting, he left his Harley and walked to the very edge of the rocky promontory. He sat with his back to a boulder and listened to the sudden, shocking silence. Tipping back his head, he studied the path of a shooting star and found himself making a wish.

"Old habits," he muttered aloud when he realized what he'd done.

That had him grinning, remembering nights under the stars with his cousins. As boys, they had scrupulously shared every myth and legend they had ever heard. And believed, as only kids could believe. They'd believed that if they wished on a shooting star, it would be granted.

They'd believed with all their hearts that they would remain best friends forever. They'd believed that their grandfather had the strength of a superhero, and the laser vision, as well, and that he would find the treasure of his ancestors. They'd believed in keeping promises, in always telling the truth, in love that would last forever.

And yet, scant years later, many of those beliefs had been shattered, often by people they trusted.

Now that he had allowed his senses to become attuned to the night, Wyatt became aware of a symphony of sound. Instead of silence, he heard the buzzing and chirping of insects. A night bird cried, and in the distance, its mate answered. Somewhere on the range a coyote howled to the moon, and others picked up the song until their voices echoed across the hills.

He studied the stars, looking close enough to touch, and felt his heart swell with sudden understanding. Wasn't it the same with people? Sometimes it was necessary to listen, not just to the words they said, but to the words they left unspoken.

Sometimes he needed to just sit and be in the darkness until he allowed his mind to hear the little sounds that he'd originally missed.

As a boy, he'd blamed others for taking him away from all that he loved. But here he was, back where it all started. Not because of others, but because of the choices he'd made. He had spent endless years mourning the loss of his beloved ranch, without taking the steps necessary to return. But now he had returned, and because of that choice, his life was richer, fuller.

Despite all that had happened in his life, he still believed.

He and his cousins were rebuilding the friendship they'd thought lost forever. They had vowed to continue Coot's search for the lost treasure. And though the last week had been a trial by fire, he was slowly beginning to believe that it was still possible, with honesty and discipline and sweat, to cut through the layers of words to the core of truth and find love.

Love.

It wasn't enough to just feel love for someone. Real love, honest love, meant putting the well-being of the other ahead of self. Giving a partner the things that were needed, even if it cost him dearly.

But could he do that, and still remain true to himself?

He stretched out his long legs and tipped his head back, letting the healing power of the night wrap itself around his mind and heart.

Here in the moonlight, with a million stars twinkling above, he had some heavy-duty thinking to do.

Marilee dropped off her discarded clothing at the local charity and drove her truck past the Fortune Saloon. The smell of grilled onions wafting through her open window, usually so tempting, held no appeal this night. She didn't think she could bear another knowing look from Daffy and Vi, or an encounter with Delia Cowling or any of the other folks in town, so determined to make her business theirs.

She drove back to her apartment and climbed the stairs. She had forgotten to eat today, but it didn't matter. She had no appetite. In fact, she'd noticed that her jeans were getting too big for her. The thought gave her no pleasure. She wasn't interested in a misery diet. But there it was.

She let herself into her apartment and put the kettle on for tea before dropping onto one of the stools at the counter.

Why in the world did she have to be so abrasive with people who cared about her? Why couldn't she learn to overlook the things that irritated her and just move on? *Because,* a small voice in her mind whispered, *you're terrified of becoming your mother.* She'd constantly needed her husband's approval, in even the smallest things. But, Marilee wondered, had she, in her determination to avoid becoming her mother, begun to emulate her overbearing father?

No, she thought with a vehemence that surprised her. She could never let that sort of anger take over her life. But she had to admit that she'd been strident. Her unexpected outburst had caught Wyatt by surprise. And for that she was deeply sorry, and unable to think of any way to atone. If she apologized, he would think she hadn't meant what she'd said. But unless she apologized, they were at an impasse.

She was locked so deeply in her disturbing thoughts, it took several moments before the whistling of the teakettle broke through enough to jar her.

Just as she started toward it, there was a knock on her door.

Ignoring the kettle, she crossed the room and peered through the peephole on her door.

"Wyatt." She tore it open and stood there, drinking him in. Just the sight of him had her heart doing a happy dance in her chest.

"Don't throw me out." He lifted a hand. "I come in peace. With food."

When she didn't say a word he added, "Pizza. With all your favorite toppings. Sausage, mushrooms, green . . ."

"Well, then." To hide the unexpected tears that sprang to her eyes, she turned away quickly. "Since you went to so much trouble, you may as well come in."

"It was no trouble. I just rode a hundred miles on my Harley, fought my way through the smoke screen at the Fortune Saloon, had to fend off Daffy's attempts to have her way with me, and discovered that I'd left my wallet back at the ranch, which meant I had to sign away my life before Vi would turn over this pizza, wine, and dessert. But hey, no trouble at all. It's the sort of thing I do nearly every day."

He followed her to the kitchen, where he set down the pizza box and a brown bag.

He glanced over at the stove. "Are you going to lift that kettle, or did I interrupt you making a recording of you whistling along with it in harmony?"

Despite her tears, she found herself laughing hysterically at his silly banter.

Oh, how she'd missed it.

He set the kettle aside. The sudden silence was shocking.

Because she had her back to him, he fought the urge to touch her. Instead he studied the way her shoulders were shaking. Troubled, he realized he'd made her cry.

"Sorry." Deflated, his tone lowered. "I guess this was a bad idea."

"Wyatt."

He paused.

"It was a good idea. A very good idea."

She turned, and he saw the tears coursing down her cheeks.

"Oh, God. Marilee, I'm sorry. I didn't mean to make you . . ."

"I'm not crying." She brushed furiously at the tears. "I mean I was, but then you made me laugh and . . ."

"This is how you laugh?" He caught her by the shoulders and held her a little away. "Woman, I didn't realize just how weird you are. Wait a minute. Do you think being weird might be contagious? Maybe I ought to get out of here before I turn weird, too."

The more she laughed, the harder the tears fell.

Through a torrent of tears she wrapped her arms around his waist and held on, burying her face in his neck. "You can't leave. I won't let you."

He tipped up her face, wiping her tears with his thumbs. "You mean that? You really don't want me to go?"

"I don't. I really want you to stay, Wyatt."

"For dinner?"

"And more."

"Dessert?"

"And more."

His smile was quick and dangerous. "I'm beginning to like the 'and more.'"

She smiled through her tears. "Me, too."

"Maybe we could have the 'and more' as an appetizer, before the pizza."

Her laughter bubbled up and over, wrapping itself around his heart. "Oh, how I've missed your silly sense of humor."

"You have?"

"I have. I've missed everything about you."

"Everything?" He leaned close to nibble her ear, sending a series of delicious shivers along her spine.

"Everything."

Catching his hand, she led him to the bedroom. "I worked very hard today making up the bed with fresh linens. Want to be the first to mess it up?"

He looked from the bed to her and then back again. "Oh, yeah."

He drew her close and brushed her mouth with his. Just a soft, butterfly kiss, but she felt it all the way to her toes. "I mean I want to really, really mess it up."

"Me, t . . ."

And then there was no need for words.

"I missed you. Even though it was only for a week, I missed you." Marilee sat back against a mound of pillows, sipping wine.

"Not as much as I missed you." Wyatt nibbled a slice of pizza before offering some to her.

She took a bite and passed it back. "I cleaned the entire apartment while I missed you."

"I can top that. I mucked out an entire barn. Not one, in fact, but two. Horse manure, and then cow manure."

She ran a hand down his biceps. "That was a pretty good workout."

He smiled at her. "So was this. And I enjoyed this a whole lot more. You smell so much better than the cows and horses."

They both laughed as he reached for another slice.

"Try not to get crumbs on the clean sheets."

"Yes, ma'am." He reached for a napkin.

She closed a hand over his. "I'm sorry, Wyatt."

She didn't need to explain. They both knew what she was talking about.

"You had a right to vent. I was behaving like a mother hen."

"A very sweet mother hen with too many chicks."

"I promise to back off." He offered her another bite of pizza. "But I can't promise not to worry."

"Fair enough." She kept her hand on his. "It's natural to worry. But you have to trust, too."

"You know what I've decided?" He plumped up a pillow and stretched out beside her. "You're even more of a rebel than I am."

"You think so?"

"Yeah."

"Next you'll be loaning me your Harley."

"I could be persuaded." He linked his fingers with hers.

She stared at their joined hands and sighed. "This is nice."

"Yeah. I was just thinking the same thing." He leaned his head back and began chuckling.

"What's so funny?"

"I've been a bear for the past week. I'd have happily snapped off anybody's head who dared to cross me."

"I know what you mean. Fortunately, there was nobody around for me to snap at. I had to content myself with yelling at the talking heads on TV." She paused. "How're you feeling now?"

He looked over at her. "What a difference a week makes. The thunderstorm's gone. The cloudy skies. The nasty rain. I'm all sunshine and blue skies and sweet-smelling flowers, thanks to you."

"Me, too." She set her wine on the nightstand and leaned over to brush a kiss over his mouth. "I'm so glad you're here, Wyatt. This has been the longest week of my life."

His arms came around her, gathering her close. Against her lips he whispered, "Speaking of which, you make me weak."

"And you make me . . ."

His kiss cut off her words.

As they rolled together, one word played over and over in her mind.

Content.

Wyatt McCord made her feel content. And safe. And absolutely, completely, thoroughly loved.

The ringing of the phone shattered their sleep.

Marilee untangled herself from Wyatt's arms and legs and sat up, shoving hair from her eyes. As she picked up the receiver she glanced at the clock on her night table. Almost six o'clock. Not only had she and Wyatt put in a very enjoyable night, but they'd been able to sleep uninterrupted for hours. For once the two-in-the-morning rule hadn't applied.

"Emergency One. What's the problem?"

She listened, then said, "I'm on it. I can be there in ten minutes or less."

She stumbled out of bed and pulled on her clothes. When she turned, Wyatt had followed suit and was walking toward the door.

She went very still while memories of their separation filled her mind and sent her heart tumbling to her toes. "Where are you going?"

He picked up his keys. Met her eyes. Gave her one of those cocky, heart-stopping smiles. "I figure, by the time I get to the ranch, Dandy will have breakfast ready, and I can get a head start on my chores."

She exhaled slowly, feeling her heart rate return to normal.

She grabbed up the keys to the emergency vehicle.

In the garage Wyatt hauled her up against him and gave her a long, slow, delicious kiss that had her head spinning. "Stay safe."

Did he know what that did to her? A part of her wanted to take him by the hand and drag him back to her room, lock the door, and hold the world at bay. The other part of her, the sensible part, knew what she had to do.

She gave a long, slow sigh. "You, too."

As she drove out of the garage, Marilee watched the Harley in her rearview mirror. It gave her such comfort to see Wyatt there.

At the intersection, he lifted his hand in a salute as the motorcycle veered right, heading toward the long ribbon of highway that would lead to the Lost Nugget Ranch. Marilee waved before heading in the opposite direction, keeping an eye open for the stretch of unmarked dirt road that would take her to a ranch not far from town.

She wondered just how much it was costing Wyatt to set aside his fears for her safety and live up to his promise to give her some room and get on with his own life.

He would never know how grateful she was that he'd been able to work through his frustrations and accept her as she was. In just seven long, dismal days she'd had a glimpse into her life without him, and it hadn't been a pretty sight. But as lonely and bleak as the time had been, she hadn't been ready to sacrifice her independence just to get him back into her life.

How was it possible that, in the space of a few weeks, someone could tumble off the back of a crazed bull and so completely change her world? Before she had met Wyatt McCord she'd had an existence that was both challenging and fulfilling. She certainly hadn't needed a man to complete her. In fact, she'd considered most men a complication. Or at the very least, a pleasant diversion.

Now a single day without Wyatt seemed flat and colorless. He'd begun to mean more to her than she was comfortable admitting to.

"Damn you, McCord." She was laughing as she said it. "I don't know what kind of magic potion you slipped into that pizza, but it certainly has done the trick. I don't ever want to live another day without your magic potion. Or another night without you, rebel."

CHAPTER NINETEEN

———◆———

This gadget's going crazy." Zane paused, holding a metal detector over a mound of earth.

Wyatt backtracked and studied the gauge. "Okay. Looks like we get to dig in the dirt again, cuz."

He and Zane took turns digging up the rock and sand. They had long ago shed their shirts and had tied bandannas around their heads to mop the sweat. Despite the fierce summer heat, they were in high spirits. Chasing the gold seemed to have that effect on all of them.

Wyatt bent to retrieve something from the hole they'd dug.

"Looks like an old tobacco pouch."

"Anything in it?"

When he tried to open it, the fragile fabric began to shred. "Empty." He stowed it in a sack before he and Zane moved on.

The three cousins had begun taking turns as often as possible, walking a prescribed area in the foothills of Treasure Chest Mountain, which they carefully mapped, and using the latest high-tech detectors and global-positioning tracking systems.

Everything they uncovered, whether it turned out to be ore-laden rock or foil gum wrappers, was cataloged and stored for reference. They had already discovered half a dozen of Coot's handwritten notes and doodles buried in the sand, along with artifacts from the 1862 gold-rush days. Miner's picks, mismatched boots, and broken tools. Lanterns. Even bits of furniture. Though they seemed useless, Jesse, Wyatt, and Zane recognized them as bits and pieces of men's dreams. Men had left the comfort of home and family to search for the elusive gold. Many had died, alone and desperate. And some had even killed. Those facts made this land, as Coot had taught them, sacred ground. They felt that they had a solemn duty to treat each discovery with respect.

Wyatt and Zane hiked for another hour without locating a thing.

"Time to head back." Zane tipped up a bottle of water and drained it.

"Yeah. I'm ready for a long, cool shower."

Hearing the drone of an airplane, both men looked up.

As soon as Zane recognized it, he glanced over at Wyatt, who was staring transfixed at the sky.

He grinned. "I see Marilee's plane is repaired."

"Yeah." With a look of naked hunger, Wyatt continued to track it as it drew closer.

"I'm surprised you're not up there with her."

Wyatt's gaze never wavered. He stared transfixed. "Today's a test run. If she's happy with the way it handles, she'll be back in business tomorrow."

As the plane passed overhead it dropped low enough for them to see Marilee at the controls. She waved before dipping the wings, first one way, then the other.

Both Wyatt and Zane pulled off their wide-brimmed hats and waved them wildly.

They could see Marilee's bright smile as she waved once more before pulling up and away.

When the little plane was just a streak of yellow disappearing over the mountain peaks, Zane shouldered the metal detector and led the way back to their truck in the distance. "What happened, cuz? You lose your taste for flying?"

Wyatt caught up with him, carrying the picks and shovels. "Marilee wanted to go it alone."

"You're okay with that?"

Wyatt shrugged. "Flying's her business. That means she gets to call the shots." After they'd climbed yet another hill, he met Zane's frown with a grin. "Hey. It's not a problem. I'm okay with it."

"Even after that crash landing?"

Wyatt winced. "If I secretly worry about her, I'll just have to live with it and deal with it in my own way."

At least he was working on it, he told himself as they began loading their equipment into the back of the truck before heading toward the ranch. And maybe one day it would actually get easier.

The roar of Wyatt's motorcycle had heads turning as he arrived at the airport. Marilee and several representatives from the airplane manufacturer were huddled around her aircraft.

When he strolled over she gave him a smile and took

his hand while handling the introductions, before returning her attention to one of the men who'd been speaking.

"As I was saying, we haven't had a single complaint about trouble with our fuel line. Despite your claim, we didn't find anything out of place. Naturally, we'll want to know if you should spot a problem."

"Oh, you'll hear me hollering loud and clear," she said with a laugh. "But today I gave it every test I could think of, and it passed with flying colors."

The company's chief mechanic strolled over. "I've checked and double-checked everything. It all appears to be in perfect shape. Is there anything more you'd like us to look at?"

Marilee shook her head. "Can't think of a thing."

The mechanic handed her a checklist, which she carefully read and signed.

They shook hands all around before the representatives climbed into their own aircraft.

Marilee and Wyatt watched as the sleek plane taxied down the single runway and turned. The engines revved and it gained speed before lifting and becoming airborne.

As soon as the sound faded Wyatt turned to her. "You're looking pretty pleased with yourself. I take it you had a good flight."

She nodded. "Not a single hitch. It couldn't have gone any smoother."

"I'm glad. You looked really happy when you did the flyover."

"I was. Happy to be flying again, and happy to see you and Zane. Find anything interesting? Like a pot of gold?"

"Not today." He grinned. "Hungry?"

"Starving."

He caught her hand. "Let's see what Vi has on the grill tonight."

"You realize she's becoming our own personal chef." With a laugh Marilee climbed aboard the Harley and wrapped her arms around his waist.

"I thought that was my title."

"You're my naked chef. But that has to remain our secret."

Her laughter bubbled on the breeze.

She'd loved the fact that she could fly again. Being up above the clouds had restored her sense of freedom. But having Wyatt here, she thought, was the perfect ending to a perfect day.

"Marilee." Ledge Cowling stood blocking the entrance of the Fortune Saloon as he waited for several of his friends to make their way to the table Daffy was indicating. "I hear you took your plane up for a test run. How'd everything go?"

"Just fine, thanks." Marilee stepped aside, revealing Wyatt behind her.

"McCord." Ledge's smile thinned. "You and your cousins have tongues wagging here in town."

"I'd say that's nothing new." Wyatt held up two fingers to indicate to Daffy how many were in his party.

"You know how folks love to talk." Ledge planted himself directly in front of Wyatt. "I hear you had some pretty impressive equipment shipped out to the ranch."

"I guess Joe Morris does more than deliver." Wyatt glanced at the owner of the delivery service, seated at the bar and surrounded by half a dozen ranchers who were hanging on his every word. "Do folks here in town pay him to report on what we order, or does he just do it for free drinks?"

Ledge refused to be sidetracked. "They're saying you've been seen digging in the foothills of Treasure Chest."

"Is that so?" Wyatt merely smiled and neatly stepped around Ledge before taking Marilee's arm. "Daffy has a table for us. Way back in the corner, far from the maddening crowd."

As they walked away, they could hear the buzz of conversation.

". . . following in crazy old Coot's footsteps."

". . . ought to know better than to ignore the family curse."

". . . won't be surprised if I hear about them meeting the same fate as their ancestors. They're all loony."

By the time they were seated in a far corner booth, Marilee was fuming. "Did you hear all that garbage?"

"Yep." He was wearing a silly grin.

"Doesn't it bother you?"

"No. And you can't let it bother you, either."

"I'm furious. They have no right to discuss you and your cousins as though you're a pack of idiots. Can't they see that they're the ones who are idiots?"

Wyatt leaned over and kissed her.

She gaped at him. "What was that for?"

"For getting mad on my behalf. And may I add"—he took her hand in his—"you're absolutely adorable when you're mad. You should do this more often. Your cheeks are so flushed they're almost as red as your hair."

For just an instant she looked as though she might explode with temper. Then, just as quickly, her little frown turned into a laugh of pure delight.

She touched a hand to his cheek. "You really know how to play me, don't you?"

"Do I?"

She gave a little shake of her head. "You're good, McCord. Really good."

"Why, thank you. Though I don't have a clue what you're talking about."

"And pigs fly."

They were still laughing together when Daffy walked up to take their order and, as usual, set a couple of frosty longnecks in front of them before dropping down on the opposite side of the booth and slipping off her shoes with a weary sigh.

"You realize, Wyatt, that you and your cousins are the object of some very heated discussions."

Wyatt grinned. "We heard bits and pieces of some of those discussions."

"You ought to hear as much as I have."

"Care to share?" He smiled at Marilee, whose look had sharpened.

"There's lots of talk that all the McCords are fated to chase their dream into the grave."

Wyatt chuckled. "Does that make us different from everybody else? Do they figure they'll avoid the grave?"

"You know what they mean." Daffy glanced around before lowering her voice. "That McCord curse. All the McCord men died chasing after that fortune."

Wyatt arched a brow. "You sound as though you're

going over to the dark side, Daffy. Are you beginning to believe them?"

She stared pointedly at her feet and wiggled her toes before sliding them back into her shoes. "You know how it is. When you get that many people harping on the same subject, it starts to make sense."

"If gossip about the so-called McCord curse is starting to turn you into a believer, I'd say it's time to call their bluff." Wyatt's smile widened. "For now, let's just talk about food. I'm going to have whatever Vi has on the grill that smells so wonderful."

Marilee nodded. "Me, too."

"Would that be the prime rib, or the liver and onions?"

Marilee and Wyatt both said in the same breath, "Prime rib."

"That pretty much makes it unanimous. I haven't had one taker for Vi's liver and onions yet." Giving another exaggerated sigh, Daffy stood.

As she walked away, Wyatt and Marilee fell into each other's arms laughing.

As they moved apart and sipped their beer, Wyatt gave a slight shake of his head. "I can't believe that damned curse is making the rounds again."

"Do you really think anybody believes it?"

"You heard Daffy."

"Yeah. Repeat a lie often enough, people mistake it for truth."

"But not sensible people." He glanced around the saloon, pausing to study the townspeople and cowboys who clustered around the bar and several tables, faces close, voices a low drone. "I don't believe anybody actually believes what they're saying. It may stave off boredom, or spice up a weekly bingo game, but I'm betting that most people in Gold Fever know better than to pay any attention to such garbage."

Daffy walked up with a tray and set two plates in front of them. "Enjoy your prime rib. Especially since yours is the last of it. Vi says anybody who comes in now will have to settle for liver and onions."

"Thanks for the warning." Wyatt picked up a fork. "I guess I won't be asking for seconds."

He winked at Marilee, who choked back her laughter until Daffy had turned away.

They took their time enjoying their meals, sipping their beers, and greeting old friends.

At last Marilee pushed aside her plate. "Perfect. Now I wonder what Vi has for dessert."

"I don't know about Vi, but I was hoping we could enjoy our dessert back at your place."

"I don't think I have a thing in the cupboards."

He caught her hand and gave her one of his best smiles. "I'm betting we can come up with something sweet."

Her sudden knowing smile matched his. "I'm sure we can."

They strolled hand in hand from the saloon, completely oblivious of the whispered comments from the crowd.

Wyatt roared up to the ranch just as Cal Randall began loading Cora's Jeep with supplies.

"'Morning, Cal. Aunt Cora." Wyatt kissed his aunt's cheek. "Looks like you're heading out for another artistic marathon."

Cora nodded. "I have to take advantage of the sunlight while I can. Summer never lasts long enough here in Montana."

Cal stood shaking his head and looking absolutely miserable. "I just wish you had someone going along. I don't like you all alone out in that wilderness."

"Now, Cal. We've been down this road a hundred times or more." She patted his hand. "I have my cell phone, my rifle, and my trusty handgun."

"So did Coot." Cal finished loading the last of the supplies and closed the door. He gave her a long, steady look. "But it wasn't enough."

"I don't intend to do anything foolish. I won't be climbing the foothills or even scrambling over rocks. I'll just find a nice sheltered spot to set up camp and then get to work on my canvas."

Choosing to ignore Cal's protest, she settled herself in the driver's side and fastened her seat belt. Through the open window she blew Cal and Wyatt a kiss. "I'll check in every evening. And I'll be back as soon as I'm satisfied with my work."

"No more than a week, Cora, or I swear I'll send out the troops."

She merely smiled at the weathered ranch foreman and put the vehicle in gear.

Cal watched until she rounded a corner of the long driveway before, grumbling, he made his way to the barn.

Wyatt headed in the opposite direction, hoping Dandy had made scrambled eggs. He didn't need pancakes or French toast this morning. He'd had enough sweetness last night to tide him over for the day.

* * *

Wyatt was whistling as he worked alongside Jesse and Zane and a handful of wranglers in the north pasture, mending fences.

When his cell phone rang he saw Archie's number and answered it before the second ring.

"Yeah, Archie. What've you learned?"

The distinctive Cockney voice broke through the static. "I've found your missing airport mechanic, in, of all places, a little one-horse town in Wyoming."

Wyatt's smile faded. "You're sure it's him?"

"It's him."

"Did he say why he went missing?"

At his tone of voice Jesse and Zane glanced up sharply and moved closer.

"I don't have all the details yet. I'll tell you what little I know. When I confronted him, and let him know you'd sent me, he reluctantly admitted that he was Craig Matson. He said he didn't even take the time to go back to his place and collect his things. He just hightailed it out of town, using cash for fear that a credit card would leave a paper trail. He found a job bartending in a place so secluded, he figured he'd never be found."

"Why, Archie? What's this all about?"

"I'll tell you as soon as I know. For now, he says he stumbled into a conspiracy."

"A conspiracy?"

"That's the word he used. And he added that somebody big was calling the shots. When he realized what was happening, and that his initials on that sabotaged fuel line would lead them right to his doorstep, he had no choice but to run. He said to tell you he fears for his life and Marilee's."

"Marilee's?" Wyatt swore. "Get me all you can on this. I'm hanging up now. I need to let her know right away."

He disconnected before dialing Marilee's number. When she answered he could hear the drone of an engine in the background. His heart started hammering. "Where are you?"

"Heading back from Razorback."

"Razorback?"

"I got a surprise request from Ledge Cowling to handle some of his messenger service for the bank. Talk about timing. The pay is enough for me to cover all the debt on my latest repair work." Her tone was so cheerful, it tore at his heart. "I should be home in time for dinner. What's up?"

"Where are you right now?"

He could hear the smile in her voice. "Flying over the prettiest landscape ever created. I'm about halfway between Razorback and Gold Fever with nothing but wilderness below."

"Wilderness. Do you see anything flat enough to attempt a landing?"

She laughed. "Get it through your head, rebel, I only land in the wilderness with you along as my copilot. Can you imagine me down there alone?"

It was too painful to contemplate. He pondered the wisdom of telling her what he'd learned from Archie. What was the point, when she was in no position to do a thing about it? If he were to tell her, she would carry the burden of fear all the way back to the Gold Fever airport. The fear that was weighing him down at the moment would be enough for both of them.

He struggled to keep his voice calm and reasoned. "I'll

tell you all about it over dinner tonight. I'll be waiting at the airport when you land."

"Wonderful." She gave a long, deep sigh. "I can't think of anything I'd rather see when I land than you waiting for me."

He swore again, loudly, fiercely, as he tucked his cell phone into his pocket and beckoned his cousins to follow him to their ranch truck. They had to run to keep up with his hurried strides.

"Okay." Jesse caught up with him and grabbed his shoulder, spinning him around. "Let us in on this."

Tight-lipped, he handed the keys to Jesse. "I'll tell you on the way. You drive. I'm too tense."

Alarmed, they climbed inside. And as Jesse headed back to the ranch, Wyatt filled them in on all that Archie had told him.

The two cousins listened in silence before hitting him with a barrage of questions.

Zane's eyes narrowed. "So he's saying that Marilee's forced landing wasn't an accident, despite what the manufacturer's representatives found?"

"That's how I read it." Wyatt's tone was low, controlled, to hide the fear that bubbled just below the surface.

Jesse spoke the words that they were all thinking. "And right now Marilee is returning from the very airport where that first fuel-line incident occurred."

"I just hope it was also the last."

Zane shot him a look. "You don't think lightning could strike twice, do you?"

At that Jesse floored the accelerator, sending the truck bouncing over ruts and rocks as they drew near the ranch.

Minutes later, while Wyatt sped off toward town on his

Harley, Jesse phoned the sheriff's office with details of what they had learned so far.

When he rang off he looked as worried as Wyatt had been. "Deputy Atkins left no doubt that he thought I was crazy, talking about a damned conspiracy. But I made him promise to give Ernie the information as soon as he gets back to town. The sheriff's out investigating an accident at the Fitzgerald ranch." He shared a look with Zane. "You thinking what I'm thinking?"

"Yeah. Wyatt needs us. I say we head into town now."

The two dashed to one of the ranch trucks. But though they broke every speed limit, they couldn't catch up with Wyatt's motorcycle, burning rubber with every mile as he sped to the airport, hoping against hope that Marilee would defy the odds and arrive safely.

CHAPTER TWENTY

———◆———

Marilee pocketed her cell phone. Up ahead were the peaks of Treasure Chest Mountain, bathed in sunlight and sparkling like the spires of ancient cathedrals.

How she loved this land. Every hill and rock and gully. Though she loved it in every change of season, she loved it best in summer, the sunbaked sand glistening like gold far below, feathery clouds above.

She was deliriously happy to be flying once more. She'd missed it terribly. It wasn't something she could explain to others. Flying, to her, was an expression of freedom. Without her plane, she'd felt like a bird with its wings clipped. Now she'd been given back her wings, her freedom.

When the plane cleared the mountaintops she reached for a bottle of water. As she drank she studied the scene spread out below. The foothills, some of them already in shadows, were a mixture of pink and mauve and purple.

She spotted a glint of sunlight off glass and realized

it was a vehicle parked near an outcropping of rock. She lowered the altitude of the plane enough to make out the Jeep. Though she couldn't see Miss Cora, she smiled at the thought of the older woman standing in the shadow of the mountain, lost in her work.

Marilee could understand Miss Cora's passion for her art. Didn't she have a similar passion for flying?

Some distance ahead she saw the path carved into the soil, resembling the marks made by wagon wheels, which she and Wyatt had first spotted on that fateful flight.

The thought of that flight had her glancing at her fuel gauge with a smile, knowing she'd gone to great pains to oversee the refueling at Razorback before climbing into the cockpit.

She stared in absolute disbelief.

The fuel gauge registered empty.

For the space of a heartbeat she couldn't process the information. It simply wasn't possible. How could this be happening again?

"No!" The word was torn from her lips, though she wasn't even aware that she'd spoken it aloud.

At almost the same instant an alarm sounded, and then the flashing light on the instrument panel, announcing the dangerous lack of fuel.

There was no time to think. No time to permit fear to paralyze her. Acting on pure instinct, she took a firm grasp of the controls, determined to take charge of the landing as much as possible, considering the fact that the little plane was already speeding on a course toward disaster.

The last time she was forced to make such a landing, she'd been blessed with relatively smooth ground. This time, so near the foothills, there was nothing but rocks and hills and deeply carved gorges that would surely rip her little plane to shreds.

With all her senses heightened, and a litany of survival tips playing through her mind, she braced herself for whatever was to come.

"Hey, Randy." Wyatt leaned on the counter that served as the nerve center for the tiny Gold Fever airport.

The grizzled old former pilot was able to listen to chatter from any aircraft in the vicinity while mopping the floor or servicing the occasional planes that came and went.

In a month's time, they would rarely have more than two or three aircraft pay a call. The rest of the time was spent keeping up with the backlog of paperwork demanded by the county, state, and federal government agencies.

"How're you managing without Craig Matson?"

The old man shrugged. "Not the same without Craig. He was better at most of this stuff than me. And these damnable documents." He held up a fistful. "They drive a man half crazy."

The two were sharing a laugh when there was a blast of static from the speakers, and then a voice calling, "Gold Fever. You there, Gold Fever?"

Old Randy limped over to a chair and sat, adjusting several dials before saying, "Gold Fever here."

"This is the control tower at Razorback. I've lost contact with MON342. Have you been in contact?"

"No, sir. No contact here." Out of the corner of his eye the old man saw Wyatt come charging around the counter to stand directly behind him. "Where was she when you lost contact?"

The voice gave specific information before saying, "One minute I had MON342 on radar, the next it was gone. No visual, no voice exchange, nothing. Just disappeared. I thought I'd check with you to see if she may have contacted you on another frequency." There was a pause. "I'll continue trying to reach her. I'd advise you to do the same. She was last tracked flying over some pretty rough terrain."

Jesse and Zane raced into the room just in time to hear the last words he'd said.

One look at Wyatt's face told them all they needed to know.

Marilee was in mortal danger. Hundreds of miles from civilization, in some of the roughest Montana wilderness.

And they were helpless to do more than wait and hope and worry.

As for Wyatt, his mind filled instantly with shattering images of his beautiful beloved Marilee, bruised and battered, all alone and fighting for her life. The thought of her suffering, mentally, emotionally, physically, was almost more than he could bear. But the alternative, that her wounds could be fatal, was simply beyond comprehension. He wouldn't allow himself to go there in his mind.

She had to be alive. Had to. He would cling to that thought, and that alone, for he knew, with absolute certainty, that he couldn't continue to live if he lost her now.

While Wyatt paced, his cousins did what they could to offer a measure of comfort.

"Marilee would be the first to tell you that she's a tough, independent woman, Wyatt." Jesse laid a hand on Wyatt's shoulder. "She'll come through this. You'll see."

In the background they could hear Randy contacting every airport within range, asking if they'd seen anything on their radar, or heard a distress call from an unknown aircraft. Their negative responses, broadcast at earsplitting level over the speaker, added to the dramatic sense of urgency.

They all looked up when a shiny black car pulled up to the door and Ledge Cowling hurried inside.

Seeing Wyatt, he stopped mid-stride and blinked before recovering. "McCord. I thought . . ." He glanced toward the old pilot who sat at the controls. "When Randy said Marilee Trainor's plane was down, I just assumed you were with her."

When Wyatt said nothing he cleared his throat and continued. "I feel totally responsible for this."

"You?" Zane stepped close, his gaze narrowed on the banker. "Why?"

"I was the one who hired Lee for this job. I should have never allowed a girl to do something so dangerous."

"Too dangerous for a girl?" Wyatt's hands balled into fists at his sides, causing Ledge to take a step back. There was a dark, dangerous look in his eyes. Eyes glazed with both pain and fury. "Marilee Trainor is the most competent, capable *pilot*," he said, emphasizing the word, "that the people of this town have ever known. She's been flying for years. Why should today be any different?"

"You know what I mean. It's too soon since her accident. Like having to get back up on a horse after a nasty spill. After that crash landing, you can hardly blame her for losing her edge. Just the thought of what almost happened probably caused her to get careless." Ledge shook his head. "Pilot error or not, as I said, I blame myself."

"Pilot error . . ." Wyatt's hand was halfway to the banker's throat before he brought his temper under control.

Completely ignoring Ledge, Wyatt turned toward the old pilot. "Randy, is there a plane for hire?"

"Sorry. There's nothing here. The best I could do is issue a request for a plane from a nearby airport. I could probably get one here tomorrow."

"Tomorrow." Wyatt spun away, his simmering frustration reaching the boiling point.

"Come on, cuz." Jesse dropped an arm around Wyatt's shoulder and began herding him toward the door. "We'll load your Harley in the back of our truck and drive to the sheriff's office. We need to file a report with Ernie."

On the drive across town Wyatt stared morosely out the window, lost in thought. Images of Marilee, alone and hurt, played through his mind, tormenting him.

At the sheriff's office Deputy Harrison Atkins wrote out a report and asked them to wait while he contacted the state police.

Half an hour later he brought them word that the state police would begin an air search in the morning.

When Wyatt started to protest, Jesse stepped in front of him. "Thanks, Harrison. We appreciate that. You'll see that the sheriff is told about this?"

"You bet." The deputy watched Wyatt begin his pacing and said softly, "If I were you, I'd see that he got something for those nerves before he explodes."

"Yeah. Will do." Jesse once again steered Wyatt toward the door and herded him into the truck.

"Morning." It was the first word Wyatt had spoken

since he'd left the airport. "Harrison says the state police won't even begin to search for the plane until morning. What if she's bleeding? Unconscious? Worse?" He ran a hand through his hair. "I should have been with her."

"That's what Ledge thought." Jesse stared over Wyatt's bowed head and caught Zane's eye.

The two exchanged a meaningful look that said they were both on the same wavelength.

Ledge Cowling had looked not only startled, but annoyed, when he'd caught sight of Wyatt at the airport.

Was there more to this? And if so, how much more?

Neither of them dared to put their thoughts into words for fear of sending Wyatt over the edge. He was already near the breaking point. There was no sense adding to his distress until they could prove their theory.

"I think," Jesse began, choosing his words carefully, "you may need to contact your friend Archie again, and see if he can use his influence to get a pilot willing to begin an air search tonight."

His words had the desired effect, giving Wyatt something on which to focus all that smoldering energy. With a look of gratitude he dug his cell phone out of his pocket and dialed the familiar number.

While Wyatt filled his friend Archie in on the latest developments, Jesse's cell phone rang.

"Hey, Aunt Cora. How're you surviving in the wilderness?"

He listened, then said, "Wait. I want you to tell Wyatt all that you just told me."

He handed the phone to Wyatt, who had just finished talking to Archie.

Puzzled, Wyatt shot his cousin a look. "The last thing I need at a time like this is to make small talk with Aunt Cora."

"Trust me. Talk to her."

With a sigh of frustration Wyatt said, "Hey, Aunt Cora."

It was all he managed to say before the voice on the other end, high-pitched with excitement, brought a gasp of pleasure.

"Say that again, Aunt Cora." He held the phone away and pressed the speaker button so the others could hear every word.

"At first, I was so caught up in my work, I wasn't even aware of the sound of an airplane. But when it dipped low overhead, I looked up and realized that it was Marilee's little yellow plane. She must have spotted my campsite. I returned to my work until a few minutes later, when I heard the sound of a crash, and my poor heart nearly stopped. I jumped into my Jeep and drove toward the sound. I'm here now, and though Marilee has some injuries, and, I suspect, some broken bones, nothing appears to be life-threatening . . ."

"Can I talk to her?" Wyatt held his breath until he heard Marilee's voice.

"Wyatt." Her tone was so soft and weak, he could barely recognize it.

"Oh, baby. I'm so glad my aunt found you."

"She saved my life. I was certain I'd be burned alive, but with my injuries, I couldn't work myself free. Wyatt, she got me out of the plane minutes before it exploded."

The three cousins gave a collective gasp when they realized the seriousness of the crash.

"Wyatt . . ."

He could hear her struggling for breath and interrupted her. "Save your strength now, Marilee. We'll talk when you're stronger."

"No. I need you to know. It was just like before. I refueled in Razorback." She paused, fighting for every breath. "My instruments gave no indication, and then all of a sudden everything went crazy and I was diving straight for the ground." She was silent for so long he thought she had passed the phone back to his aunt, but then her voice came back, each word an effort. "I . . . don't believe . . . was an accident."

"Neither do I. But for now I just want you to . . ."

Cora's voice came on the line. "That's enough, dear. I need to tend to Marilee's wounds. I'm afraid she's too shaken, and in too much pain, to speak coherently anymore. I'm going to get her as comfortable as I can tonight, and let her rest before we head home at first light. I wish I didn't have to make her wait until tomorrow for expert medical assistance, but I'm just not comfortable driving her alone in this darkness."

"I understand, Aunt Cora. Do what you have to."

For long minutes after he rang off Wyatt held the phone in both hands, his head bent low, eyes closed, as though unwilling to let go of the only connection he had with Marilee.

Finally he looked at his cousins and shook his head in wonder. "She's alive."

"That's the best news of all. For now, cuz, her safety is all that matters." Zane clapped a hand on his shoulder. "I guess you ought to file a report with the sheriff's office."

"Yeah."

He retrieved his cell from his pocket, but before he could make the call, it signaled an incoming call.

Seeing Archie's number, he snapped it open. "Archie, sorry, I forgot you were on the phone. I just got the best news of all. Marilee's alive."

"That's fantastic. Now you'll want to have the law take a close look at one of the owners of the airports at Gold Fever and Razorback."

"One of the owners? You mean Ledge Cowling?"

At Wyatt's question, the voice on the other end paused. "I see we're on the same page."

"I knew it." Wyatt's voice lowered with feeling. "All along he seemed to have more than a passing interest in our business. He had a stash of Coot's papers hidden in his sister's basement storage. And from what you uncovered earlier, he's probably been harboring an old grudge against the family because of Coot. Would you care to add to the list?"

Archie chose his words carefully. "Craig Matson has said he would only return to Gold Fever if he were promised protection. He fears reprisals if he makes public what he knows."

"You tell him the McCord family will guarantee his safety."

"Not good enough, Wyatt." Archie's voice was tinged with humor. "You may be strong and fearless, but you're not the law. Craig wants to hear it from the sheriff himself."

"He'll get it."

"There's more." Archie paused before adding, "I bought Tim Moody, the regular maintenance worker at the Razorback airport, a couple of beers and learned something interesting. On the day of your first forced landing, he'd been unexpectedly given the day off by one of the owners."

"Ledge?"

"That's right. Again today, with no notice, he was told to take a paid vacation day. Again, by the owner, Ledge Cowling."

"You're sure of this?"

"I don't see any reason why Tim would lie. But I intend to have him sign a document to that effect."

"Thanks, Archie. For everything. You'll stay on this?"

"Oh, be assured, I'm on it. Your family leads a . . . most interesting life." His deep rumble of laughter could be heard as he disconnected.

After hanging up, Wyatt turned to Jesse. "I don't know if you heard all that, but Archie confirmed our suspicion that Ledge had a hand in this." His voice was tinged with bitterness. "This time Ledge Cowling's gone too far. He very nearly succeeded in killing Marilee. I say we turn around and ask Ernie Wycliff to issue a warrant for Ledge's arrest."

Jesse shot a glance at Zane, seated on the other side of Wyatt.

Zane nodded. "I agree. But not just because of what he did to Marilee."

At Wyatt's arched brow he added, "You were probably too worried about Marilee to notice, but Ledge seemed genuinely surprised to see you at the airport. Jesse and I think he expected you to be on that plane with Marilee. Now that he knows you're still around, you never know what he might do to try to finish the job."

"Oh, I wish he'd try." Wyatt's hands balled into fists. "What I wouldn't give to face off against that bastard in a down and dirty fight."

"While it might be satisfying," Jesse said with a chuckle, "I think the best thing we can do is report our suspicions to the sheriff and let him do his job."

He hit the brakes and turned the truck around on the darkened highway, heading back toward town.

CHAPTER TWENTY-ONE

———◆◆◆———

As the three cousins strode into the sheriff's office, Harrison Atkins and Ledge Cowling were bent close in earnest conversation.

Their heads came up sharply, and Deputy Atkins shifted his attention to his visitors.

"I was just helping Ledge file a report with the Federal Aviation Administration. I figured you boys would be home by now. What brings you back to town?"

"Police business." Wyatt glanced around. "Where's the sheriff?"

"Still out on the Fitzgerald ranch. Old Fitz got thrown from his horse, and it's looking bad. Doc Wheeler and Elly Carson are with him until the medevac team arrives. It could take all night. What can I do for you?"

Wyatt glanced at his cousins for confirmation before saying, "As a matter of fact, we were hoping to have the sheriff question Ledge about his involvement in Marilee's accident. It seems the regular maintenance worker at the

Razorback airport said Ledge gave him an unexpected day off."

"Why, you lying . . ." Ledge leaped to his feet, nearly knocking over his chair.

The deputy put a hand on his arm. "Calm down now, Ledge." He turned to Wyatt. "Are you suggesting that it's a crime to give an employee a day off?"

"I'm saying it's strange that on the same day Marilee paid to have her plane refueled, the regular employee was absent, and a stranger was working in his place. The same stranger, I might add, who replaced that employee just weeks ago, on the same day Marilee was forced to land in the wilderness because of a leak in the fuel line. What are the odds that a regular employee was replaced twice, and twice a certain plane was forced to make an unplanned landing?"

Ledge, his face a mottled shade of red, stood glowering at the McCord cousins, who looked equally furious and ready to do battle.

The deputy looked from one to the other.

"We can't afford to have a fistfight right here in the sheriff's office, boys. Now," Harrison Atkins said reasonably, "I think the safest thing to do is ask you, Ledge, for the sake of fairness, to go quietly home while these boys file a report."

Wyatt stepped closer. "If you're smart, you'll keep him here."

"Is that so?" The deputy smirked. "Why is that?"

Wyatt watched Ledge's eyes as he replied, "Because Craig Matson is willing to testify that the fuel line on Marilee's plane isn't the one he'd checked the previous day."

"Craig Matson? You've found him?" When Wyatt

nodded, Harrison Atkins turned to Ledge. "Maybe, until all this can be straightened out one way or the other, you ought to just step into a cell."

"What?" Ledge's face grew several shades darker. "Just like that? With no proof? Are you planning on taking their word over mine?"

Deputy Atkins looked distinctly uncomfortable. "I don't like this any more than you do, Ledge. How will it look when the good folks of Gold Fever hear that their bank president spent a night in jail?" He opened a desk drawer and removed a set of keys. "That's why, as soon as you're locked up, I'll grant you one phone call to your lawyer. With any luck you ought to be home and in your own bed within a couple of hours. And with the cooperation of Wyatt here, we can get all this straightened out."

Wyatt raised a fist to Ledge's face. "It'll be straightened out, all right . . ."

His angry tirade was interrupted when the deputy stood and took hold of Ledge's arm.

Keeping a hold on him, Harrison walked Ledge to the back of the room and unlocked a door leading to the cells. All the while, Ledge swore a blue streak and gave every indication of putting up a fight.

As they stepped through the open doorway, the deputy unlocked one of the two cells in the jail section and waited until Ledge stepped inside before slamming it shut.

He glanced toward the McCord cousins, who were watching and listening. "There's fresh bed linens, and plenty of soap and water while you wait, Ledge. I'll bring that phone in just a minute, as soon as I have Wyatt sign some papers."

From a desk drawer he produced a legal document

and handed it to Wyatt with orders to read, sign, and date it. "This says you're swearing out a warrant for the arrest of Ledge Cowling, with proof to be forthcoming of a commission of a crime. You'd better be certain of your facts, son, or Ledge could sue you for defamation of character."

Wyatt barely read a word before scratching his name and the date and shoving the document across the desk.

Deputy Atkins set the document aside. "I'll sign a request for that state police plane first thing in the morning."

Wyatt blinked. In the excitement, he'd forgotten the most important fact. "Sorry. There's no need now."

"No need?" The deputy's jaw dropped.

"Marilee crashed not far from where our aunt was camped out at Treasure Chest Mountain."

"Miss Cora was on the mountain?" Harrison lifted a brow.

Wyatt nodded. "The foothills. She managed to pull Marilee from her burning plane, and though she's injured, it isn't life-threatening. She plans on bringing her home at first light."

"Well . . ." Harrison shook his head in disbelief. "You're one lucky man, McCord."

"Yeah." Wyatt started toward the door. Over his shoulder he called, "Tell Ernie Wycliff I'll want to talk to him first thing tomorrow."

"You bet."

As they walked to the door Charity Atkins, the deputy's daughter, was just stepping from her car to handle the night shift.

Seeing her, Harrison called, "No need to come in, Charity. You can head on home."

"You don't need me? Who'll tend the phone?"

Her father put his hands on her shoulders and turned her toward her car. "I have someone in the holding cell, and since I have to be here anyway, no sense in you giving up a night's sleep, too. I'll see you tomorrow."

"I won't argue with a night off. Thanks, Dad." She gave him a quick peck on the cheek and hurried back to her car, waving to the McCord men as she passed them.

When Wyatt, Jesse, and Zane climbed into the ranch truck they could see the deputy still standing in the doorway, watching as they started toward home.

Wyatt pulled his cell from his pocket and dialed his aunt's phone. When he heard her voice he asked the question that was uppermost in his mind: "How's Marilee?"

"Dozing on and off. But she's in pain, dear. And the medical supplies she always carries in her plane were destroyed in the explosion."

Holding a hand over the phone he asked Jesse, "Mind dropping me at Marilee's place?"

"Not at all. You planning on staying the night?"

He shook his head. "I'm going to pick up the emergency vehicle."

Seeing where this was leading, Jesse gunned the engine. "We can be there in five minutes."

Wyatt spoke into the phone. "Aunt Cora, Doc Wheeler is on an emergency run, but I'm going to bring the ambulance to your campsite."

"Tell her we'll all be there," Zane added.

Wyatt glanced over at him, and then at Jesse. Both cousins were nodding.

"All three of us are coming, Aunt Cora. Once we're on the road, you can give us directions."

Relief sounded in Cora's voice. "I'm so glad you're coming, dear. I'll feel a lot better when you get here. I'm feeling just a bit overwhelmed at the moment."

"Hang tough, Aunt Cora. We're on our way."

He disconnected, then dialed Cal Randall. Hearing the ranch foreman's voice, he explained what had happened before adding, "I know how you worry about Aunt Cora. I thought you might want to ride along."

"Thanks, Wyatt. I appreciate that. I'll do you one better. While you boys are fetching that emergency ambulance, I'll take a couple of the wranglers and head on out to Treasure Chest right now."

"I know Aunt Cora will be glad for the company."

"She's not the only one. I should have been there with her."

Wyatt tucked his cell phone into his pocket and fell silent, his mind in turmoil over so many conflicting thoughts.

Craig Matson had spoken of a conspiracy. Someone big. It had to be Ledge, and the substitute mechanic he'd hired to sabotage Marilee's plane.

His cousins believed that he had been the actual target, and that Ledge had looked surprised and unhappy to see him at the airport.

Would a man like Ledge, successful and respected in the community, risk everything for an old family feud? Or did this go deeper? Was it all about Coot's fortune? Or were the two reasons so deeply intertwined, Ledge had simply gone over the edge of reason?

Wyatt's hands fisted at his sides. Ledge may have planned this incident, but that didn't make Wyatt feel less guilty. It was he who had brought danger to Marilee's doorstep.

The McCord curse. Though he knew it was nothing more than a stupid legend, and had no basis in fact, there was no denying that the search for the gold had brought real danger to Marilee.

My fault. My fault.

The words played through his mind.

The thought that he had put the woman he loved in harm's way was like a dagger through his heart.

Wyatt got behind the wheel of the ambulance. "You two catch some sleep. I'll drive. I'm too wired to even close my eyes."

"Not me." Zane pulled out his ever-present video camera and began filming his cousins, narrating the events that had them driving into the wilderness in the middle of the night.

Jesse gave a shake of his head. "Hearing all that, cuz, I'm beginning to think that if you actually get your documentary released one day, nobody will ever believe one family could have so many wild adventures."

Checking the vehicle's Global Positioning System, he turned to Wyatt. "I'm afraid I'll miss some of the excitement if I sleep. I'll be your backup."

As they raced across miles of rangeland, Jesse kept in almost constant contact with their aunt. When at last they'd left civilization far behind, they were grateful for both the GPS and Cora's directions. The ambulance swerved over dirt roads and rocky trails as they made their way unerringly toward her campsite, despite the cover of darkness.

"Oh, my dears, what a lovely sight I see." Cora's voice grew warm with pleasure.

Wyatt held the phone away from his ear and pressed the speaker phone so the other two could hear.

"Cal has just arrived, and I'm so glad to see him."

They could hear Cal's growl, a mixture of relief and recrimination, and could only guess that he was gathering their aunt into his arms for a fierce hug.

A little breathlessly, Cora said, "Cal brought several of the wranglers, along with our dear Amy, and they're already busy gathering up my supplies for the trip back to the ranch."

"That's great, Aunt Cora." In an aside to Jesse, Wyatt said, "Your wife went along with Cal and the crew."

Jesse nodded. "I heard. I'm glad she's there."

To his aunt Wyatt added, "They made good time. How's Marilee?"

"Marilee is . . ."

Suddenly Cora was heard giving a shrill cry, followed by the sound of masculine shouting and then shots ringing out.

"Aunt Cora . . . Aunt Cora!"

Wyatt's shouts went unanswered.

He felt his heart nearly stop as he floored the accelerator. Though it took them only minutes more to arrive at the campsite, it felt like hours. Wyatt's pulse rate was speeding out of control.

"Aunt Cora." He lurched from the vehicle, followed by Jesse and Zane.

For a minute they were surrounded by complete chaos.

Cora and Amy were kneeling beside Marilee, who was lying in a bedroll near a fire. One of the wranglers took aim with his rifle as the three cousins approached, until they stepped into the circle of firelight and identified themselves to him.

"What's this about?" Wyatt's voice was strangled with fear and fury.

Just then Cal Randall came running up, looking like a wild man. "He got away."

"Who? What's going on here?" Wyatt demanded.

Cal swore. "We spotted somebody sneaking into this campsite, and when he saw us and realized Cora wasn't alone he took off in a beat-up old truck. I fired off a couple of shots and managed to hit the rear of his truck, but missed hitting his tire."

"You think it was just a drifter?"

Cal swore again. "Could be. Or it could be something more sinister. I'm just glad we were here. I hate to think what might have happened to Cora and Marilee if they'd been alone."

While Jesse and Amy embraced, and Zane hugged their aunt, Wyatt hurried over to kneel beside the bedroll. With as much gentleness as he could manage he touched a hand to Marilee's fevered brow. "Hey, baby. How're you doing?"

At the sound of his voice her lashes fluttered and she looked up at him with a trembling smile. "Oh, Wyatt, I'm so glad to see you."

He closed a hand over hers. "Not nearly as glad as I am to see you."

For long minutes he gathered her close and held her in his arms, breathing her in while he waited for his heart to settle.

There'd been a time, back at the airport, that he'd feared he might never again get this chance to hold her. All the images of her, shattered and broken, remained in his mind, making this moment so much sweeter.

At last he brushed a kiss over her mouth. "Think you're up to the ride home?"

"Now that you're here, I'm ready for anything."

"That's my girl." He kept her hands firmly in his as the others quickly began dismantling Cora's campsite and loading her art supplies into the back of her Jeep. When that was done Cal and the wranglers took her keys and started the engine, prepared to form a caravan.

When all was in readiness, Wyatt lifted Marilee in her bedroll and carried her to the back of the ambulance, securing her on a gurney. Cora and Amy took seats beside her to tend her on the drive, keeping cloths pressed to her most serious cuts to stem the flow of blood.

Wyatt took the wheel, with Jesse and Zane up front beside him, and, with a phone call to alert Dr. Wheeler, they began the long trek back across miles of rocky wilderness to civilization.

CHAPTER TWENTY-TWO

In the sudden silence Marilee opened her eyes. Throughout the painful jostling on the long ride back, she'd managed to escape several times into mindless sleep. "Are we home?"

In the background could be heard the slam of truck doors and the low drone of men's voices.

"Yeah, baby. We're at the clinic." Wyatt tucked the ring of keys in his shirt pocket before walking around to the rear of the ambulance and lifting her in his arms.

She attempted a feeble protest. "The gurney has wheels."

His voice, muttered against her temple, vibrated through her. "I'd rather have you here in my arms."

She buried her face in his neck. "I'm glad. I feel a lot better with your arms around me."

"Me, too."

With Jesse holding open the doors and Amy rushing ahead to alert the staff, Wyatt carried Marilee into the clinic and looked around at the gleaming, silent room.

One of the cleaning crew poked a head around an open doorway.

"Where's Doc?" Wyatt demanded. "I phoned him and said we were on our way."

"He said to tell you he was sorry to leave, but he had an emergency."

"This is an emergency." Wyatt's tone was sharper than he intended. "How about Elly Carson?"

"She's assisting Doc." The young woman paused, holding a mop and bucket. "Doc said if you got here before him, you should put the patient in one of the examining rooms, and he'd be here as soon as possible."

Wyatt nodded toward an open door. "Are you finished cleaning in there?"

At the young woman's nod he started toward it, with Jesse going ahead to switch on the lights. The rest of the family remained in the waiting area.

While Wyatt deposited Marilee on an examining table, Amy located a supply of blankets and tucked one around the patient.

Wyatt saw the way Marilee winced, and took a blow to his heart. He couldn't bear to see her suffering. "I know you're in pain, baby."

"Some. I've been a medic long enough to know that these cuts need stitches to heal. My left arm may be broken, or badly fractured. Too much pain to know what else is wrong. But I don't mind now that I'm safe. Oh, Wyatt." She wrapped her good right arm around his neck and held on, loving the feel of his calm, steady heartbeat. "I was so scared. This was even worse than before. I wasn't sure I'd ever see you again."

Her words sent another burst of pain stabbing through his heart.

"Shh." He softly kissed her lips. "No more talking. I want you to rest until I get Doc and Elly here to tend you." He turned to Amy. "Will you stay with her while I call the doc and see what's holding him up?"

Amy took up a position beside the examining table.

Before Wyatt reached the door Marilee's eyes were closed, her breathing soft and easy as she slipped into blessed sleep.

"Thanks, Zane." Wyatt accepted a coffee from the vending machine as he dialed the doctor's cell phone.

His frustration grew when he was forced to leave a message. "I should have followed my first instinct and gone directly to the ranch."

"The clinic is the best place for Marilee to be," his aunt reminded him.

"It's cold and sterile and empty." He dialed the emergency number once again and let out a breath when he heard the familiar voice of Dr. Frank Wheeler.

"Hey, Doc. Wyatt McCord. Where the hell are you?"

"Wyatt." The doctor's voice was barely above a whisper. "Sorry to keep you waiting. Are you at the clinic?"

"Yeah. Marilee's in a lot of pain. Deep cuts, lots of blood, and she thinks her left arm may be broken. Except for trying to keep her warm, I haven't even taken the time to look her over carefully. The windshield shattered on impact, so there could be glass fragments embedded in some of the cuts. I just know we need you here now."

"Tell you what. I'll send Elly on ahead. She can make Lee comfortable until I get there. As for me, it'll be awhile yet, Wyatt. I'll have to sign some documents and finish up here before I can head to the clinic."

"Finish up what? Where are you?"

"I'm over at the jail."

"What are you doing there?"

"I'm here in my capacity as coroner."

"Coroner?" Wyatt couldn't seem to take it all in as his family suddenly looked up with interest. "Why does Ernie need a coroner?"

Doc's words had everyone gathering around Wyatt, wearing matching looks of shock and disbelief.

"Ledge Cowling was found dead in his cell. It appears that he hanged himself."

Wyatt and the others greeted Elly Carson in the waiting room and peppered her with questions as soon as she stepped inside the door. As she explained, they stared at her in openmouthed surprise.

"Deputy Atkins said he fell asleep shortly after allowing Ledge to make a call to his lawyer. When the lawyer arrived at the jail, he woke the deputy and the two of them walked to Ledge's cell, where they found him hanging by a rope made of bedsheets. They both worked on him, but it was too late. They couldn't revive him. By the time we arrived back in town with the sheriff, there was nothing to do but determine the approximate time of death and sign the official documents."

With that too-brief explanation she hurried into the examination room to see to Marilee's needs.

Cora sat with her hands to her hot cheeks, trying to take it all in. "I just can't imagine Ledge taking his own life. Not for any reason." The exhaustion of the past hours was evident in her eyes, red-rimmed from lack of sleep. "Poor Delia. Except for a distant cousin, Ledge was all the family she had. She must be devastated."

Cal dropped an arm around the old woman's shoulders. "Leave it to you to think about Ledge's sister at a time like this."

"Will you call her for me, please, Cal?"

He nodded and stepped out of the room.

Jesse passed around more cups of coffee from the vending machine. "Looks like Ledge took all his secrets to the grave."

"What secrets?" Cora looked up.

"It was Ledge who arranged to have Lee's plane tampered with. An employee of his at Razorback admitted that he'd been given the day off on both occasions, so that someone Ledge trusted could do the actual refueling." Jesse glanced at Wyatt, who had turned to stare morosely out the window.

He and Zane exchanged a look before Zane walked over to touch a hand to Wyatt's shoulder. "There's something more. What's eating you, cuz?"

Wyatt gave a shake of his head. "I don't know. It all just seems . . ." He shrugged. "I know I'm not making any sense. But I wanted answers. I wanted to know the why and how of it all." He shrugged again. "There are just too many unanswered questions."

Jesse dropped an arm around his wife. "I'd take unanswered questions anytime over facing two crazed gunmen who thought they knew everything."

"Sorry. I know you two had to go through hell and back with Rafe Spindler and Vernon McVicker." Wyatt thought about the danger his cousin and wife had faced at the hands of their grandfather's jealous lawyer and a ranch employee, who had plotted to kill them over the lost fortune.

Cal returned and spoke quietly to Cora, who looked stricken.

Seeing the way his great-aunt was clinging fiercely to Cal's hand, Wyatt asked, "You all right, Aunt Cora?"

She shook her head. "Cal tried phoning Delia and got her voice mail. He even tried her neighbor, Frances, who said Delia was too depressed to talk to anybody. I'm worried about her." She lifted pleading eyes to Wyatt. "I haven't spoken to Delia in years, and I don't want to add to her pain now. But you've had some contact with her recently, and she may be more receptive to you. Promise me that you'll see Delia when you have some time. She needs to know that any old issues between our families have been wiped away. Will you tell her, Wyatt?"

He set aside his coffee and crossed to her. "I'll see to it, Aunt Cora. I promise." He wrapped his arms around her and held her close, feeling her deep sigh of relief before she reached for Cal's hand.

Wyatt turned and headed toward the examining room. "Send Doc in as soon as he gets here."

He would mull everything later. For now, he just desperately needed to be with Marilee.

"You're one lucky lady, Lee." Dr. Wheeler watched as Elly Carson administered a sedative into an IV line in their patient's arm.

Marilee had been transferred to one of the rooms used for overnight patients. The family had been sent back to the ranch to rest and recover from their ordeal. Only

Wyatt remained with Marilee, unwilling to leave her for even a few minutes.

The doctor walked to her bedside. "Not too many pilots get to walk away from a crash like the one you described, with only a few cuts and no broken bones."

"Without Miss Cora, I wouldn't be here at all." Marilee could feel herself sinking into sleep. "There's nothing left of my plane but some ash and crumpled steel."

"Then Miss Cora's your angel."

"And your angel," Wyatt added, "is worried about Delia's state of mind now that she's lost her brother."

Doc nodded. "She took the news hard. When I can find time in my crazy schedule, I intend to call her and ask her to come in for a checkup." He glanced at Wyatt. "Isn't it just like your aunt to worry about everybody, even the town busybody?" He turned back to Marilee. "And thanks to Miss Cora, you're just fine. That fractured arm will heal cleanly. No fragments, nothing shattered. A good thing you won't need pins or surgery. There's no reason you shouldn't heal without complications. Still, for your peace of mind, I'd be happy to order a medevac to take you to the hospital in Helena."

"It's not going to happen." Marilee looked pleadingly at Wyatt to agree with her. "No planes just yet. I'd rather stay on solid ground."

"She needs some time. We all do." Wyatt stood on the other side of the bed and closed a hand over hers. "When can she be moved? I'd like to take Marilee back to the ranch for some pampering."

Dr. Wheeler looked at his patient, reading the pain and exhaustion in her eyes, before turning to Wyatt with a quick shake of the head. "I don't think she's up for that long ride just yet. Why don't you stay here at the clinic and keep an eye on her? There's a bed in the other room, if you want to sleep. Once Elly and I have a few hours of rest, we'll be back to take a look at our patient and I'll decide if she can be released."

Elly set a syringe on the bedside cart. "You'll be dealing with some big-time pain for a little while. There's a full dose of Dilaudid here. When the pain gets to be too much to handle, show Wyatt how to add it to your IV."

"I can do it. . . . Not sure Wyatt's got the stomach to handle big-time drugs." Marilee could feel her eyes closing.

As they started out of the examining room, Wyatt followed, still eager for answers.

"Did Ledge leave a note behind?"

Dr. Wheeler shook his head. "I wish he had. I hate loose ends. A note would have answered all our questions. But I suppose a proud man like Ledge would choose death over being forced to face the contempt of the townspeople when they learned what he'd done."

Wyatt walked with them as far as the door of the clinic. "Ledge didn't seem suicidal to me. In fact, I'd describe him as smug and arrogant and believing himself above the law. He seemed to think that Harrison had no business locking him up, and that his lawyer would have him out of jail in no time."

Doc shook his head. "There's just no way of predicting how people will react when caught in a trap of their own making." As he turned away he added, "My phone is always on. If I'm tied up, leave me a message and I'll get back to you. Call me with any questions."

Questions were all he had, Wyatt thought. As he made

his way back to Marilee's room, his mind was filled with too many troubling questions. He hoped a long, hot shower and some sleep would bring him a measure of relief.

Loose ends. Like Doc, he didn't like them. And there were just too many. Messy bits and pieces. And all of them dangling just out of reach.

Or maybe he was just too weary to fit them all together now.

The clinic was deathly silent.

Wyatt chose to ignore the inviting bed in the room next to Marilee's, stretching out instead in the visitor's chair he'd pulled alongside her bed. He couldn't bear to leave her side for even a few hours. He had a terrible need to assure himself that she was really alive and safe and here with him.

He wasn't certain he would ever be able to completely dispel the fear and horror he'd experienced when he'd heard about the crash. Those images would stay with him for a very long time.

But there was something else keeping him too wired to think about sleep.

For the life of him, he couldn't figure out this vague uneasiness that had settled over him like a fog. He should be relieved that the threat posed by Ledge was now resolved. Knowing Archie, he would continue to pursue all the angles until the witnesses had signed documents attesting to what they knew and when they knew it. Then, hopefully, they could put this thing to rest.

Still, something didn't fit, and he couldn't put his finger on it.

He struggled to settle down and rest, but his mind refused to cooperate.

When the door opened he looked over, expecting to see Doc or Elly. Seeing Deputy Atkins walking toward him, he struggled to his feet.

"What're you doing here, Harrison?"

"Just hoping to clear up a few things." The lawman saw Marilee stir.

He shifted his attention back to Wyatt. "Sit down, son. This won't take long."

Wyatt sank back into the chair while the deputy remained standing at the foot of the bed. "You said that Craig Matson was willing to testify against Ledge. But you didn't bother to say where Craig is."

"I don't see that it's important."

"I'll decide what is and isn't important." The deputy's eyes grew flinty. "He's considered a witness to an alleged crime. I need to know where to find him."

Wyatt glanced at Marilee, who had come fully awake and was struggling to sit. He was at her side at once, lifting her to a sitting position and fluffing extra pillows behind her back to support her.

She gave him a grateful smile before reaching for his hand.

Wyatt looked over at the deputy. "I'm afraid I can't answer your question."

"Can't? Or won't?"

Something in Harrison's tone had Wyatt straightening. He released Marilee's hand and stood a little taller. "I'll give that information to Sheriff Wycliff when I go in to see him and make out my report."

"You'll give it to me now."

Wyatt felt a chill, and then a sudden rush of adrenaline. Bits and pieces were beginning to fall into place, though, as yet, they didn't make any more sense than Ledge's suicide. "Just as we arrived at Aunt Cora's campsite, she had a surprise intruder. Cal and some of the wranglers were already there and managed to fire off a couple of shots, but they couldn't stop him." He watched Harrison's eyes narrow. "At the time, we thought it might have been a random attack. But my aunt was in the middle of the wilderness. That suggests to me that she had been deliberately targeted for the attack."

The deputy calmly, deliberately pulled his handgun from its holster.

Wyatt watched the movement, feeling a quick jitter of nerves. "Something didn't quite fit in that attack, and now I know why. Beyond our family, nobody knew the exact location of Aunt Cora's camp in the wilderness, or the fact that Marilee had survived the crash, except you and Ledge. And Ledge was in no position to contact anybody without your knowledge."

Harrison's tone was grim. "I knew that sooner or later you'd figure that out. That's why I'm here. You and your lady love will have to be eliminated, of course. You know too much. But first you're going to tell me where I can find Craig Matson."

Wyatt shook his head. "You don't really think I'd tell you."

"I know you will." Harrison Atkins walked to the side of the bed, keeping it between himself and Wyatt.

He aimed the pistol at Marilee's head. "You'll tell me what I want to know, or this pretty little lady will pay the price."

Wyatt's tone hardened. "Keep her out of this."

"She's in it, and has been since the two of you became . . . close. And now that you've made it clear to everyone in town how much she means to you, I doubt you'll be willing to sacrifice her life for Craig Matson's."

"Why are you doing this?" Wyatt gauged the distance across the bed, wondering how he could possibly reach the gun before it would discharge. If he was killed in the attempt, it wouldn't matter. His life didn't matter. But Marilee . . .

Could he leap far enough, fast enough, to save her life? He knew only that he had to try.

"I figure, with the two of you out of the picture, the rest of your family will be too distracted, or too devastated, to continue searching for the treasure."

"All of this just for some gold that could remain lost forever?"

"Why does that surprise you?" The deputy sneered. "I suppose, growing up in a fine, fancy ranch house built like a palace, the hunt for a lost fortune is merely an amusing way for you to spend your summer vacation." His tone lowered. Hardened. "For some of us, it's a chance to change our lives forever."

"You'd actually kill for it?"

"I'd kill for a whole lot less." He brought the gun close enough to Marilee's temple to make her flinch. "Now you'll tell me where Craig Matson is, or I'll blow her head off and you'll get to watch."

Hearing the note of finality in the deputy's voice, and seeing the gun so close to Marilee, caused the rebel inside Wyatt to snap.

Without a thought for his own safety he lunged across the bed, arms outstretched toward the man's throat. "You won't get away with this."

Harrison Atkins whirled and fired. An explosion of sound bounced off the walls and ceiling as the two men came together and fell to the floor in a wild tangle of arms and legs.

CHAPTER TWENTY-THREE

Marilee heard her own voice, high-pitched in horror, as she watched a thin line of blood slowly stain the front of Wyatt's shirt.

The two men were pummeling each other over and over. Desperation had them fighting with all the force and fury of mad dogs, teeth bared, guttural sounds coming from their throats as they battered and punched and bloodied one another.

For a moment Marilee thrilled to the fact that Wyatt had the upper hand as he landed a fist in the deputy's face that had Atkins falling backward, sending blood gushing from a nasty cut above his eye.

But when she saw Wyatt's face turn ashen, she knew that the bullet had taken its toll.

She looked at the night table, hoping for something, anything that she could toss at the deputy as a distraction. It was bare except for the syringe. But as she reached for it, it slipped from her fingers and was buried in the folds of the bed linens.

Before Wyatt could attempt another blow, Harrison's hand closed around the pistol. He scrambled to his feet, keeping the gun pointed directly at Wyatt's chest.

Through clenched teeth he hissed, "Now, McCord, you'll tell me what I want to know."

Wyatt was forced to struggle for every breath, fighting a heaviness in his chest that made his breathing labored. "Never. I gave my word."

"Is your word more important than the woman's life?"

Wyatt lifted a hand as if to protect her.

When he refused to speak, Harrison gave a hiss of impatience. "Your precious word just sealed your lover's fate."

As the deputy stepped to the bed and placed the gun against Marilee's temple, she struggled against the drug that left her feeling so weak she could barely lift her head from the pillow.

The drug.

She latched onto that thought. The same Dilaudid that had deadened her pain could render this monster helpless if administered in one sudden dose. But only if she could find the strength within herself to catch him by surprise and do what was necessary.

Her fingers fumbled under the covers for the syringe she'd managed to snag from the night table. In her half-conscious state she'd dropped it in the bedding, and now she could feel her last chance slipping away.

Her fingers were still slightly numb from the sedative. She flexed them beneath the blanket until she was certain she could make them work.

So close. So close, but she could feel herself losing the last bit of strength.

She breathed deeply, filling her lungs for the task ahead.

"Say good-bye to your lover, McCord."

In the tangled sheet Marilee's hand closed around the cold syringe and she prayed that she could hold on to it without giving away her intentions.

"I . . . know where Craig is." The words, barely above a whisper, had the deputy going very still.

His eyes narrowed as he leaned close to catch every word. "Tell me."

Marilee waited, gathering her courage, forcing herself to meet his narrowed gaze without flinching. If he had even a trace of suspicion, she would lose her only chance.

"He's . . ." She deliberately kept her whisper so soft, Harrison was forced to lean even closer.

Again she waited, though her heart was now pounding. Adrenaline began pumping through her veins, a certain sign that she would have but one chance to make this work. Once the adrenaline rush was over, she would be rendered as helpless as a newborn.

"Wyatt told me he was . . ."

When the deputy was so close she could feel his breath on her cheek, she freed her hand from the cover of the blankets and jammed the needle against his arm with all the strength she could muster.

For a moment her heart stopped when she felt the slight resistance as needle met tough skin.

Had her hand been stronger, her aim truer, she thought, she might have succeeded.

But just as fear of failure began to surface, she felt the syringe bite deep, penetrating his flesh.

"What the hell . . . ?" Caught by surprise, he jerked back. The gun discharged, firing wildly into the ceiling.

For a moment Atkins merely stared at the syringe that protruded from his flesh. Then, as he tore it loose and tossed it aside, he tried to take aim. His arm, already numb, refused to obey. While he watched in disbelief his legs began to tremble, no longer able to support his weight. The string of oaths he was trying to mutter became unintelligible babble as he dropped weakly to the floor.

The gun clattered from his grasp and Wyatt scrambled to retrieve it. While he dialed for help he kept a wary watch on the deputy, who lay as quiet as death on the hard wooden floor. Then he dropped to one knee beside the bed and gathered Marilee close.

"You were amazing," he whispered against her temple.

"You didn't give me any choice. I thought he'd killed you." She looked at his stained shirt. "You're bleeding."

"I am?" Wyatt looked down at himself in surprise. In the excitement, he hadn't even been aware that he'd been shot. Now, as he saw the blood, he gradually became aware of a heaviness radiating from his chest area.

He pulled the ring of ambulance keys from his breast pocket, and a bullet pinged on the floor.

He and Marilee stared at it with solemn looks as they realized the enormity of what had just happened.

"Saved by a key." Wyatt sank down on the edge of the bed and caught Marilee's hands in his. With a shake of his head he muttered, "I guess Harrison's aim was

better than I realized. Thank heaven for you. The key
to my heart."

As he pressed his lips to hers, Marilee felt again the
quick jitter of adrenaline. Wyatt's kiss? She wondered. Or
the knowledge that she'd succeeded in saving his life?

Both, she decided.

Then, as the last vestiges of energy drained away
and the drug once more took over her reflexes, she lay
back, eyes closed, breathing slow and labored, as chaos
ensued.

The once-quiet clinic was suddenly alive with humanity.

A caravan of trucks from the Lost Nugget Ranch
chose that time to pull up to the clinic, bearing food from
Dandy and clean clothes from Wyatt's closet. Jesse and
Amy were the first to come running into the room, followed by Zane.

"I thought I heard gunshots . . ." Jesse skidded to a halt,
with Zane on his heels.

Zane peered at the figure on the floor. "Is that Harrison
Atkins?"

"Yeah."

Before Wyatt could say more, Cora and Cal hurried
inside and stepped gingerly around the unconscious man.

"What . . . ?" Cal stared around in disbelief at the signs
of a deadly struggle. Bloodstains smeared the walls and
floor, as well as the front of Wyatt's shirt.

They all looked up as Sheriff Wycliff stormed into the
room. "I was afraid I wouldn't get here in time." He pointed
to his deputy. "What did you hit him with, Wyatt?"

"Not me. Marilee. I think he'll be out for a couple
of hours."

"Lee?" Ernie Wycliff looked skeptical. "Doc said you had some pretty painful injuries. How could someone so badly injured manage to subdue my two-hundred-pound deputy?"

Marilee pointed to the syringe lying on the floor beside Harrison Atkins. "Just doing what I know best."

The sheriff gave her a look of admiration. "However you managed it, you did just fine."

"Thanks." She was grateful for Wyatt's hand on hers. She was feeling oddly out of focus and knew it was the drug. For someone so accustomed to being in charge, this was an uncomfortable feeling.

She roused herself enough to say, "Wyatt came close to being killed. Even though the bullet didn't penetrate, Doc needs to take a look at him."

"Hey, baby, didn't you know that Superman never gets hurt?"

While the others joined in a chorus of nervous laughter, the sheriff pushed a speed-dial button on his phone and spoke tersely. "No rest for the weary, Doc. You're needed back at the clinic." He paused. "No. It's not Lee this time. It's Wyatt McCord. He's been shot, but like Superman, he claims the bullet bounced off his chest."

They heard the note of excitement in the voice on the other end, followed by a sudden disconnect.

"How did you happen to be here, Ernie? I tried phoning you and got no answer."

At Wyatt's question the sheriff bent and cuffed his unconscious deputy before getting to his feet. "I was busy taking a call from a man named Archie"—he stared pointedly at Wyatt—"a bit of a shady character, who claimed to be a friend of yours."

"He is. And has been for years. What did Archie say?"

"He wanted me to know that the substitute employee who'd been hired by Ledge Cowling disappeared before he could be deposed. Archie figured Ledge had warned the man off. But since Ledge was in a cell, and only made one call to his lawyer, it meant that someone else had warned the man to take a hike. The phone company confirmed that Harrison had made a number of calls last night, which would disprove his claim of having fallen asleep right after you left. Harrison was, in fact, very busy, phoning not only the substitute mechanic at Razorback to warn him to get lost, but also an ex-convict who owed him a favor. The state police picked up the ex-con an hour ago. His vehicle bore several bullet holes. I'm sure when they get time to compare them to the ones from Cal's rifle used to ward off that late-night robbery attempt at Miss Cora's campsite, they'll prove to be a perfect match."

"So it wasn't a random thief?" Cora sank down into the chair vacated by Wyatt. "What was this all about, Sheriff?"

"I've asked the state police investigators to handle this. I'm sure in time we'll be able to piece it all together."

Wyatt glanced around at the family. "Harrison admitted that he did it for the lost fortune. He thought by getting rid of us"—he glanced at Marilee and tightened his grasp on her hand—"the rest of the family would be too devastated to continue the search."

"Oh, dear heaven. First there was the danger to Jesse and Amy. And now the two of you." Cora lifted a trembling hand to her lips. "I know this wasn't what Coot wanted for any of you when he enticed you to stay and continue his search."

Jesse hurried over to kneel in front of her. "Don't dwell on it, Aunt Cora. We're not responsible for every crazy person who wants to steal the gold."

"But don't you see? Everyone believes there's a curse connected to the gold. Maybe the true curse is that history will keep repeating itself." She touched a hand to her great-nephew's cheek. "This all began when a madman coveted what our ancestor had found. Grizzly Markham slit Jasper McCord's throat in the night and stole the sack of nuggets. And now there are others willing to do violence, and all for the lure of a fortune that may never be found."

"I know." He took her hands in his and kissed her cheek gently. "But history doesn't have to repeat itself. We're forewarned now. We'll know better than to let down our guard again."

Dr. Wheeler came bustling into the room. When he saw the crowd he paused. Then, seeing the weariness etched on the faces of Wyatt and Marilee, he took charge.

"Sorry. You folks will have to wait in the outer room. Now I have two patients to look after."

Amy and Jesse led Cora away while the sheriff and Cal hauled the unconscious deputy from the room.

Zane stood back, filming everything, until Doc ordered him out, too.

The doctor paused beside Wyatt. "You strong enough to stand?"

"Yeah. The bullet hit a ring of keys in my pocket, and I guess one of the keys cut me. It's nothing. Except that I feel like there's an elephant sitting on my chest."

"From the force of that bullet hitting you at a hundred miles an hour. Come with me." With his hand under

Wyatt's arm, the doctor led him from the room and helped him onto an examination table.

A short time later Wyatt returned to Marilee's room, trailed by Elly Carson in her crisp white uniform.

The doctor looked up from Marilee's bedside.

"It seems all we do is disturb your sleep." Wyatt's discomfort had lessened considerably after Elly had administered a shot to numb the pain.

Dr. Wheeler chuckled. "No problem. I'll catch up on sleep later."

"Are you done with us, Doc?"

"You can go." Dr. Wheeler nodded. "I just hope you know how lucky you are, Wyatt."

"Yeah. I know." Wyatt paused. "How about Marilee? Can she leave with me?"

The doctor gave her a cool, assessing look. "Are you feeling up to leaving?"

"Oh, yes." Marilee felt her spirits lift as she turned to Elly Carson. "Can you help me dress?"

"All I have is a spare set of scrubs."

"They'll do nicely."

Doc herded Wyatt through the doorway and into the waiting room, where the entire family had gathered.

Wyatt turned to Jesse. "If you want to head back to the ranch, Marilee and I will join you there later."

"You don't have to stay for observation or anything?"

Wyatt shook his head.

As the others began filing out the door, his great-aunt paused and returned to his side.

"Cal and I tried to see Delia, but she didn't answer our knock. I'm worried about her, Wyatt. She has to be feeling so alone in her grief. I know you have so much to do already, but in the next day or so, if you could just pay a call. Would you mind . . . ?"

Seeing Marilee standing in the doorway, Wyatt cut off his aunt with a quick kiss to the cheek. "I'll stop by. And I won't leave until she agrees to talk to me."

"Thank you, dear." With that assurance, Cora took her leave.

Wyatt hurried over to wrap an arm around Marilee's shoulders, and the two made their way to the ambulance.

When Marilee was comfortably seated in the passenger side, Wyatt turned the key in the ignition. "I thought I'd take you back to your apartment first, so you can change into your own clothes."

Marilee leaned her head back and smiled. "Oh, it feels so good to be out of the clinic. I don't mind bringing other people there, but it's not my favorite place to stay."

"I know what you mean." Across town he guided the emergency vehicle into her garage, then carried her up the stairs to her apartment.

"Wyatt, I'm perfectly capable of walking."

"Relax and enjoy the ride." He brushed his mouth over hers before setting her down in the middle of her bed. With great care he slid the top over her head. "Tell me what clothes you want and I'll find them."

She gave a firm shake of her head. "You're going to the other room. When I'm dressed, I'll let you know."

"You've decided to get overly modest on me now?"

She laughed. "I've decided to take back my power. Now get out."

He shot her a wicked grin before strolling from the room.

* * *

Wyatt paced the length of Marilee's apartment and back, mulling all that had happened. The plane crash. The late-night gunman in his aunt's camp. The endless ride to the wilderness and back with Marilee wounded and in pain. And now they'd been given a second chance. He wasn't about to blow it this time.

Marilee walked from her bedroom wearing a gauzy mint-green sundress and strappy sandals, her hair long and loose spilling down her shoulders.

At the sight of her Wyatt sucked in a breath. "Now that's a big improvement over faded scrubs. Have I told you how beautiful you are?"

"Not lately."

"Sorry. I've been a little preoccupied. You're so beautiful you take my breath away."

"Thank you." She gave an exaggerated flutter of her lashes.

She was still laughing as Wyatt dropped to one knee in front of her.

Her smile faded. "What are you doing?"

"Isn't this what a guy is supposed to do when asking—"

She clapped a hand over his mouth to halt his words. Sudden, unexpected tears filled her eyes and she brushed at them. She could feel herself hyperventilating. "Wyatt, don't do this to me."

"Don't do this to you?" He looked puzzled, and then, as he came slowly to his feet, it dawned. "You're afraid."

"I am not. I'm just feeling ... too emotional." She scrubbed at the tears that had trickled down her cheeks. "Maybe it's the accident. Everything's happening so fast. There hasn't been time to let it all sink in, I guess. Oh, don't you see? I've worked so hard to be free. To be independent. I vowed I would never let someone have power over me."

"Power? Is that what you think this is about? Marilee . . ."

"No. Of course not. You're the kindest, most amazing man I've ever known. But I've . . ." She was blubbering, but she couldn't seem to stop herself. "I've spent years fighting to live on my own terms. And now, right now, I don't want to think beyond today. I'm not ready to face the future and make a lifetime commitment. Not today. Not now. Don't you see?"

"I guess I have no choice but to hear what you're saying. I shouldn't have sprung this on you." His tone went flat. "You've been through way too much. You need time. Maybe I'll head back to the ranch and give you some space."

Marilee knew that once again she'd hurt him deeply. If she let him go, how could she ever make things right between them? But she was simply too overwhelmed at this moment to think of how she could ever make amends.

As she watched him walk through the door and pull it closed behind him, she experienced a moment of absolute panic, aware that this time she'd stepped way over the line. How many times could a proud man like Wyatt McCord accept rejection before he simply walked away forever?

Why did she always have to hurt the ones she loved? Was it pride, or was it, as he'd said, fear?

Whatever the cause of her obstinate nature, she was about to pay a terrible price.

She absorbed an almost crippling pain around her heart.

This time, she knew, as she heard the sound of his Harley roaring away, she'd gone too far.

And she was too exhausted, too overcome with emotion, to do a thing about it.

CHAPTER TWENTY-FOUR

———◆———

Jesse and Zane strolled into the barn, where Wyatt was mucking out a stall. The back of his work shirt was stained with sweat, his boots caked with mud and dung, attesting to the hours he'd been working.

Jesse leaned on the rail to watch. "Did Doc say you could do this so soon after that gunshot?"

"I wasn't hit by the bullet." Wyatt kept his back to his cousins.

"I know." Jesse exchanged a look with Zane. "But Doc said you should take it easy for a few days."

When there was no response he tried again. "We noticed that you skipped dinner last night, and Dandy said you didn't bother with breakfast this morning before heading out here. You planning on driving into town later to check on Lee?"

"I'm sure she's just fine." Wyatt barely paused in his work.

"Amy talked to her a little while ago and got a bit worried."

That had Wyatt's movements going still, though he didn't turn around.

"Amy said Lee was awfully quiet. Just said she was mending, and would probably see Doc later today."

"Good." Wyatt forked dung into the wagon with more force than necessary.

"Word from town is that Delia took Ledge's body to Helena for burial. Her neighbor said she was hoping to avoid a public display."

"I don't blame her." Wyatt continued shoveling. "Small towns just can't resist enjoying gossip. The uglier the better."

"Well." Jesse and Zane exchanged another look before Jesse said, "We thought we'd head on over to the saloon tonight. Want to join us?"

"No thanks."

"If you change your mind, just let me know." Jesse dug his hands into his pockets and sauntered out of the barn, with Zane trailing behind.

When they were gone Wyatt stood for long, silent moments staring into space. He'd played so many scenes over and over in his mind. The helplessness he'd experienced when Harrison held a gun to Marilee's head. The desperation that had him leaping into the path of a bullet rather than risk losing her. The pride and awe at her courage in overcoming the effects of the drugs in order to end the gunman's madness. And the wave of pure relief when he'd finally been allowed to take her home.

Marilee had made it perfectly clear how she felt about losing her independence. And still he'd foolishly forced the issue. He'd allowed his own selfish needs to drive her away. Again.

Maybe they weren't meant to be together. Maybe they had very different goals. But being with her made him happy. Being apart was killing him. And he had no one to blame but himself and his foolish heart. He had convinced himself that, having come so close to death, she would fall into his arms and beg him to keep her safe for the rest of her life.

When would he learn that the woman who owned his heart wasn't like other women? She didn't need a hero, or a warrior. She needed her freedom, her independence. And she saw him as a threat to both.

He swore and bent to his task.

Cora stepped into the barn and peered around until her eyes adjusted to the gloom. After the sunlight of her studio, this place was like a cave.

When she spotted her nephew at one of the benches, oiling a leather harness, she walked over and took a seat beside him.

"Jesse said you've been spending your time out here."

He glanced over. "Making up for all those years when I couldn't be here."

"Yes. It must have been hard, leaving your only home." She placed a hand on his, stilling his movements. "I've heard that you and Marilee have had a spat."

When he said nothing she went on. "I don't believe in giving advice. Each of us must come to terms with life in our own way. And I know you're wise enough to figure things out. But I would think, Gold Fever being so small, that sooner or later the two of you will have to meet. I hope, when you do, that you can at least be friendly."

He looked over, and she was startled by the sadness in his eyes. She'd expected anger. Or perhaps cool disdain. But this was almost more than she could bear.

"I don't think I'd know how to be just her friend. But I won't embarrass you, Aunt Cora. I can be civil."

Getting quickly to her feet she cradled his face in her hands and bent to press a kiss to his cheek. "I'm sorry, Wyatt. I wish I knew how to make things better." She stepped back and took a deep breath. "I spoke with Frances Tucker. She said Delia is home now and refuses to see anyone. I know she'd never agree to see me, but I was hoping that, since she's had contact with you, she might allow you a brief visit. That is, if you're willing."

Wyatt gave a slight nod of his head. "I'll try, Aunt Cora. But I doubt that she'll want to see any of the McCord family."

"All you can do is try, dear. Sometimes in life, that's all any of us can do."

When she walked away, Wyatt set aside the harness, the cleaner, and the rag and got heavily to his feet. The last thing he wanted to do was go to town. But there was no way he could ever refuse his great-aunt.

All you can do is try, dear.

Wasn't that what he was doing each morning? Getting out of bed, just to try to get through another day?

Wyatt parked the ranch truck in front of the neat white house and walked determinedly up the steps.

When the door opened, Delia took one look at him and turned pale before she started to close the door.

"Wait." Wyatt's hand shot out to keep her from shutting the door in his face.

Delia's eyes filled. "I know why you're here. I can't tell you how sorry I am about . . . everything."

"I'm here," Wyatt said softly, "because I know my neighbor is hurting from the loss of her only brother, and my family and I want to know how we can help."

Delia's eyes went wide with stunned surprise. Then, remembering her manners, she moved stiffly aside. "Please. Come in."

He stepped inside and stood awkwardly in the little front parlor. Both Wyatt and Delia seemed at a loss for words.

Wyatt decided to take charge. "I don't know about you, but I could use some tea."

The old woman was too shocked to react.

With his hand beneath her elbow, Wyatt steered her toward the kitchen.

While Wyatt held a chair, Delia sat numbly. He put the kettle on the stove and, after a brief search of her cupboards, located some dainty cups.

Though Delia remained frozen at the table, a lifetime of good manners had her rising to the occasion. "There are some cookies in that cupboard."

Wyatt filled a plate and set it on the table while Delia sat stiffly.

When the kettle boiled, he made tea and filled two cups.

Delia stared, transfixed, at the tabletop, unable to meet his eyes.

Wyatt leaned toward her and took her hand in his. It was cold as ice.

"I'm sorry about Ledge."

"How can you be sorry?" She took a breath and forced herself to say the things she was thinking. "The sheriff told me he found pages from your ancestor's diary in Ledge's things. And dozens of Coot's maps and drawings, even though he'd told me he had all those old papers shredded." Her lower lip trembled. "I swear to you I didn't know."

"Of course you didn't."

Her head came up. She looked at him. Really looked. And saw the compassion in his eyes. "You believe me?"

He nodded.

Before he could say more there was a knock on the door.

When Delia started to get up he held out a hand. "Would you like me to get that?"

"Yes, please. And send whoever it is away."

He left the kitchen and walked to the front parlor. When he opened the door and saw Marilee standing there, he felt as if he'd just taken a blow to the midsection. All the air left his lungs, and for a moment he couldn't find his voice.

She looked equally stunned. "Sorry." She put a hand on the opened door to steady herself. "I saw the ranch truck and thought it was Amy." She was babbling, she knew, but she was so startled to see Wyatt standing here, she couldn't seem to stop. "She phoned me to ask if I'd look in on Delia. It seems your aunt is very worried about her."

"Yeah. That's why I'm here." He stepped stiffly aside. "She's in the kitchen."

As Marilee made her way through the parlor, Wyatt followed behind, feeling an empty ache at the sway of her hips, the drift of fiery hair around her shoulders. He could hardly bear to look at her. And yet he couldn't look away. He felt like a drowning man reaching out for a safety net, only to have it snatched away each time he got close.

"Marilee." Delia looked up. "I suppose you're here with Wyatt."

"I'm here alone." The word hung in the air as Marilee and Wyatt stared at each other with naked hunger.

Seeing it, Delia said softly, "I'd know a good deal about being alone. I've decided to sell my place here and move to Shelbyville to be closer to my cousin. She's my last living relative."

"But you won't know anybody there. Won't you miss your friends and neighbors?"

"I will." Her voice grew sad. "But I doubt they'll miss me." She quickly changed the subject. "We're having tea. Will you join us?"

At Marilee's nod, Wyatt reached for another cup and saucer and proceeded to pour tea before setting it on the table.

"I was just telling Wyatt how sorry I am. I wasn't aware of the fact that Ledge had many of Coot's old papers hidden among his things." Delia folded her arms over her chest, as though the mere mention of such things left her chilled. "Bless him, Wyatt says he believes me."

Marilee rubbed a hand over the older woman's arm. "I believe you, too, Delia."

"That's more than kind of you. Of both of you. Thank you. It gives me comfort to know this."

When Marilee took the seat beside hers, Delia surprised her by touching a finger to her cheek. "Are those tears?"

"I'm just"—Marilee struggled to stem the flow— "feeling emotional."

"Of course you are. So much has happened. It's the way of things, I suppose. Life deals us blows, and some of us remain standing, while others fall." Delia fell silent for a moment before giving out a long, deep sigh and turning to Wyatt. "I thought I was so strong because I remained standing in the face of life's pain. Now, I realize that standing isn't enough." She took a deep breath before saying, "I once hurt your grandfather. Hurt him deeply."

"I know."

At Wyatt's response she shook her head. "But you don't know the whole story. No one knows." She paused, going back in her mind. "I loved Coot McCord. Loved that man with all my heart. But my family felt he was beneath them. At that time his ranch was little more than a hardscrabble patch of forest and prairie. Everyone in town knew how he used to go off for weeks at a time, all alone in the wilderness, searching for his ancestor's lost treasure. My parents warned me that I'd live to regret a life of loneliness married to such a crazy man." She shook her head. "I wouldn't listen. We used to meet on horseback at our secret place, in the foothills of Treasure Chest. And when Coot asked me to marry him, I agreed. We made plans to run away and marry without my family's knowledge. I was so wildly in love, and so happy. But I made the mistake of sharing my good news with Ledge." She withdrew her hands and folded them in her lap. "Ledge agreed with our parents that I was nothing more than a foolish girl."

She paused a moment. "On one of Coot's forays into the wilderness he got caught in a nasty blizzard, miles from home, and spent a couple of weeks on a ranch the other side of Treasure Chest Mountain. Ledge learned that the rancher, Ben Moffitt, had a pretty daughter, and, knowing I had a jealous streak a mile wide, he made sure that I heard about her, too. Coot tried to convince me that he'd merely taken shelter from the storm, but I wouldn't believe him. We had a terrible argument. When Ledge learned of it he inserted himself into our business, making thing even worse. Ledge called Coot a liar and a fool if he thought he could ever win my family's trust. That pushed Coot over the limit of his patience. Blows were exchanged, and when it was over, Ledge had a broken nose and enough bruises that he needed weeks to mend. He threatened to have Coot arrested for assault."

"And I . . . I told Coot that I never wanted to see him again. Of course I didn't mean it. I just spoke out of fear and anger. If I'd taken the time to cool down, I would have let Coot know that I didn't mean any of the things I'd screamed at him. But he gave me no chance to set things right. Coot was so hurt and so furious that he took off on his horse for parts unknown. He was gone for months. I kept thinking that he'd come back and we'd make up. Instead, when he finally returned, he was accompanied by his brand-new wife, pretty little Annie Moffitt."

Tears filled Marilee's eyes. "I'm sorry, Delia. Is this why you never married?"

"How could I, when I still loved . . ." Delia paused, too overcome to speak.

After several long moments of silence she found her voice. "The first time I saw Coot in town with his Annie, I thought my heart would break and I would surely die right there on the spot. But in time I learned that people don't die of a broken heart. They just die a little at a time. I learned that living was even harder than dying. Every time

I saw Coot and Annie, another piece of my heart broke, until, in time, I felt as though I had no heart at all. But I held my head high, and I pretended not to care about anyone or anything."

Her voice trembled. "When Annie died, I actually entertained the thought that maybe Coot would pay a call, but he never did. Why should he? By then I was a dried-up old spinster with a mean, spiteful tongue. The laughing-stock of the town. When Coot died, I thought maybe the pain would end, but it hasn't." She turned toward Wyatt and swallowed. "That day you and Marilee came to visit, I looked at you and saw your grandfather. The same hand-some face. The same charming smile. The same laughing blue eyes. You were so kind to me. So sweet and funny. And for the first time in fifty years I felt a little bit of my heart start to beat again." Hot tears spilled down her cheeks. "And then Ledge tried to kill even that tiny piece with his spiteful behavior."

Unable to bear the old woman's sorrow, Marilee pushed away from the table and wrapped her arms around her. "Don't dwell on it now, Delia. Don't let the bitterness eat at your soul again. It's time to let go and start to live again, before it's too late."

Delia bowed her head and sobbed. "Don't you see? It is too late. I've spent a lifetime without the only man I ever loved, because of my foolish pride. And all I have left are the bitter memories of an old maid."

At her words of anguish Marilee glanced over her head and met Wyatt's gaze.

She had to struggle to swallow the lump in her throat. "Thank you for sharing your story, Delia. I needed to be reminded how rare and fragile love can be. Sometimes, by holding on too tightly to old . . . complications, we fail to see how simple the path before us can be."

Delia glanced from Marilee to Wyatt, who were staring at each other with matching looks, as though they'd both been struck by a bolt from heaven.

Wyatt pulled himself together first and leaned over to kiss Delia's cheek. "Thank you."

She touched a hand to the spot. "For what?"

"As Marilee said, for sharing your story." He shoved away from the table. "I'll leave the two of you to visit."

In a hurry to escape he let himself out of the house and walked to the truck. Before he could climb inside Marilee raced down the steps.

Breathless, she came to a sudden halt in front of him.

At the dark look in his eyes she swallowed. "Please don't go, Wyatt. I've been such a fool."

"You aren't the only one." He studied her with a look that had her heart stuttering. A look so intense, she couldn't look away. "I've been beating myself up for days, because I wanted things to go my way or no way."

"There's no need. You're not the only one." Her voice was soft, throaty. "You've always respected my need to be independent. But I guess I fought the battle so long, I forgot how to stop fighting even after I'd won the war."

"You can fight me all you want. You know Superman is indestructible." Again that long, speculative look. "I know I caught you off guard with that proposal. It won't happen again. Even when I understood your fear of commitment, I had to push to have things my way. And even though I still want more, I'm willing to settle for what you're willing to give, as long as we can be together."

She gave a deep sigh. "You mean it?"

"I do."

"Oh, Wyatt. I was so afraid I'd driven you away forever."

He continued studying her. "Does this mean you're suffering another change of heart?"

"My heart doesn't need to change. In my heart, I've always known how very special you are. It's my head that can't seem to catch up." She gave a shake of her head, as though to clear it. "I'm so glad you understand me. I've spent so many years fighting to be my own person, it seems I can't bear to give up the battle."

A slow smile spread across his face, changing it from darkness to light. "Marilee, if it's a sparring partner you want, I'm happy to sign on. And if, in time, you ever decide you want more, I'm your man."

He framed her face with his hands and lowered his head, kissing her long and slow and deep until they were both sighing with pleasure.

Her tears started again, but this time they were tears of joy.

Wyatt brushed them away with his thumbs and traced the tracks with his lips. Marilee sighed at the tenderness. It was one of the things she most loved about this man.

Loved.

Why did she find it so hard to say what she was feeling? Because, her heart whispered, love meant commitment and promises and forever after, and that was more than she was willing to consider. At least for now.

After a moment he caught her hand.

"Where are we going?"

"Your place. It's closer than the ranch, and we've wasted too much time already."

"I can't leave the ambulance . . ."

"All right." He turned away from the ranch truck and led her toward her vehicle. "See how easy I am?"

At her little laugh he added, "I'm desperate for some time alone with you."

Alone.

She thought about that word. She'd been alone for so long. What he was offering had her heart working overtime. He was willing to compromise in order to be with her.

She was laughing through her tears as she turned the key in the ignition. The key that had saved his life.

"Wyatt McCord, I can't think of anything I'd rather be than alone with you."

CHAPTER TWENTY-FIVE

M arilee glanced at her bedside clock. "When I left, I told Delia that I'd be right back."

Beside her, Wyatt chuckled. "Two hours went by like two minutes."

"It may feel that way to us. But poor Delia must be wondering what in the world we were thinking, rushing away like that. Come on." She caught Wyatt's hand and together they made their way down the stairs.

They were across town within minutes.

When they walked up the steps to Delia's house, the older woman greeted them with a rare smile. "If I didn't know better, I'd say the two of you managed to find something good to share on this strange day."

"We have." Marilee touched a hand to Wyatt's. "And after hearing your story, I have to agree with you, Delia. Wyatt is just like his grandfather."

The old woman led them inside. "That he is, dear."

Wyatt leaned down to kiss Delia's cheek. "I guess

now it's your turn to make some choices. You spoke about leaving Gold Fever and going to live with your cousin. Maybe you should consider another choice. You can continue to live with regrets as before, or you can take what's left of your life and make it all you'd hoped it could be."

Delia was shaking her head. "With the town knowing about Ledge's crimes, I'll just be fodder for gossip."

"They won't blame you for the sins of your brother. This town is better than that."

The old woman gave a long, deep sigh. "I've wasted so many years, I wouldn't even know where to begin."

Marilee touched a hand to Delia's shoulder. "I'd know a thing or two about fighting old battles. Sometimes, they go on for so long, nobody can remember how they started, or just what they were fighting for. All that anger and resentment, and all that wasted energy, could be put to better use. You've made friends with your neighbor, Frances, haven't you?"

The old woman shrugged. "She refused to be put off when she first moved here and I tried to ignore her. After a while, she just wore me down. And frankly, I'm so glad to have a good friend like Frances."

"You see? There are lots more neighbors in Gold Fever who would like to be your friend, Delia. Sometimes you just have to reach out and let them know."

The older woman gave a shake of her head. "I've held everyone at arm's length for such a long time, I wouldn't even know how to begin."

Wyatt surprised her and himself by saying, "You can start by accepting our invitation to come out to the ranch with us for dinner."

"Oh, I couldn't. Your aunt Cora and I haven't spoken in . . ."

She stopped herself. Swiped at her eyes with the backs of her hands. And tried again. "Sorry. That was the old Delia talking." Her lips trembled as she struggled to smile. "The new Delia would . . ." She took a breath then tried again, a bit more forcefully. "The new Delia would love to go with you."

Marilee looked at Wyatt, his arm around this trembling old woman, and felt her heart fill to the brim.

His generosity was another thing she admired about him. There was so much goodness in him.

They made their way to the ambulance parked at the curb. With Delia seated between them, they started toward the Lost Nugget.

Wyatt spoke into his cell phone. "Dandy. Tell my aunt and cousins that we'll be home for dinner. We're bringing a guest. Delia Cowling."

He slipped the phone into his shirt pocket, and that had him thinking about the bullet that had nearly taken him away from all this. He had the ambulance, and a ring of keys to thank for this moment. And the kindness of the Fates.

"I think, to add to the festive occasion, we ought to turn on the lights and siren." He turned to Delia. "What do you say?"

"Oh, heavens no." She covered her mouth with her hand before giving it a second thought. "Sorry. That was the old Delia. The new Delia says yes. That would be so exciting."

Beside her, Marilee said sternly, "The old Marilee says you'll be breaking the law."

Wyatt winked. "This old rebel says he doesn't care. A celebration requires some noise."

The two exchanged a long look, then broke out into peals of laughter.

As they sped along the open highway, lights flashing, siren blasting, Delia found herself laughing along with them in absolute delight. Despite all the heartache, and all the turmoil, she was sharing a ride with Coot's grandson, heading out to Coot's ranch for the first time in over fifty years, and having the time of her life.

"Sheriff Wycliff." Cora greeted him warmly and led him into the great room, where the entire family, as well as Delia and Cal Randall, had gathered after supper. "If you had let us know that you were coming by, we'd have delayed dinner."

"Thanks, Miss Cora. I ate at the Fortune Saloon. The place was crawling with people, and all of them speculating about what happened."

He glanced at Delia, seated on the big sofa beside Cora. Would wonders never cease? How had the town gossip managed to end a lifetime feud with the McCord family?

That had him wondering just how much he could say without causing her pain.

He glanced at Wyatt and Marilee, close together in front of the fireplace. "Good to see you two looking as good as new."

Marilee laughed. "I wish someone would tell my body. Every time I try to do the least little thing, I ache all over."

"As Dr. Wheeler told you, dear, you just have to give it time." Cora was still reeling with delight at the sight of

Wyatt and Marilee together again. Apparently they had mended their latest tiff. They both looked relaxed and happy.

She indicated a tray on which rested steaming cups of coffee. "Will you have some, Sheriff?"

"Thank you. I will." He sipped, then explained why he was there.

"The state police have been conducting their investigation. As near as they can piece together, they've learned that Ledge . . ." He turned to Delia. "Begging your pardon, ma'am. Your brother was investing heavily with Harrison in some land ventures for future airports, and gave in to the temptation to use bank funds. In order to cover it up, Harrison coerced him into sharing what information he'd acquired regarding the lost fortune."

He sipped his coffee again, then settled onto a nearby chair. "Their plan was to scare away the family so they could be free to hunt without intruders finding out about them. Because trucks make too much noise, they'd been hauling heavy equipment using a team of horses to avoid being detected by any wranglers in the area. But they figured it was a good bet their tracks could be spotted from the air. Which is why you became a double threat to them, Lee. You fly often enough to notice anything out of the ordinary. And once you and Wyatt became more than friends, Harrison figured it was only a matter of time until you conveyed your thoughts to the McCord family."

Cora set down her cup. "Did Ledge agree to this?"

The sheriff shrugged. "Near as the state police can tell, Ledge was a very reluctant partner. He had, in fact, gone so far as to notify a bank examiner about the money, and was hoping to cut a deal. Harrison was actually plotting each step and calling the shots. It was Harrison who disabled the air bag in the ambulance. Now that I've seen the state police report, I realize that he changed that to hide his deed. And when Ledge learned that Harrison had once again sabotaged Marilee's plane with the hope of silencing forever both Lee and Wyatt, Ledge rushed out to the airport, only to find Wyatt alive. By then, we suspect, he feared for his own life and was too afraid to tell anyone."

The sheriff turned to Wyatt. "When your friend Archie gets signed testimony from Craig Matson and the young mechanic at Razorback, we'll know more. Right now we're going on the assumption that Harrison made most of these vile plans on his own, and he kept Ledge in the dark until it was too late for him to stop the momentum."

He turned to the others. "The state police have uncovered excavating equipment and precious metal detectors that were apparently delivered under cover of darkness and hauled out to Treasure Chest and hidden in several caves. Harrison figured he could work undetected as long as Lee's plane was grounded."

The sheriff set aside his empty cup. "It will be months before the state police wrap up their investigation." He shook his head. "I'm sorry about Ledge and Harrison, but I'm glad you two were spared. Sometimes, the Fates are cruel. And sometimes they give us a second chance."

That had Marilee and Wyatt turning toward each other. Though they spoke not a word, the look they shared spoke volumes.

"See you all later."

As the others were distracted bidding the sheriff good night, Wyatt caught Marilee's hand and led her from the room and up the stairs to his suite. Once inside he closed the door and watched as she looked around.

"So this is where you grew up."

"This is it." He continued to lean against the door, wanting to touch her, but knowing if he did, he wouldn't be able to stop. He still couldn't believe his good fortune.

"It's a lot bigger here than I'd imagined. Didn't it seem strange having so many generations under one roof?"

"That was my normal." He chuckled. "Didn't it seem strange having no family but your parents as you moved all over the world?"

She laughed. "Good point. It was my normal."

"Do you think there's any way your normal and mine could ever coexist?"

She looked over and felt her heart take a slow dip. "Are you thinking about proposing again?"

"That depends. Are you thinking of accepting?"

She couldn't quite meet his eye. "I'm not sure. Not that it matters. I don't think you're serious. After all, last time you proposed, you were on one knee. Isn't that traditional?"

"Last time, you weren't very receptive to my proposal. I've decided that you and I aren't meant to be traditional. I'm hoping you like this proposal better."

"And just what are you proposing?"

He walked to a cabinet and removed a tiny box. He opened it to reveal a simple platinum band.

"This was my mother's. I'm proposing that, if you accept this, it means we throw caution to the wind and just take the leap."

"Oh, Wyatt." She stared at the ring for long minutes. "What if we take the leap and fall?"

"People fall, Marilee. And when they do, they pick themselves up and try again." He gave a wry smile. "I'd be an expert on that."

Without warning, she held out her hand.

He shot her a questioning look before she wriggled her fingers and extended the third finger of her left hand. "Why are you looking at me like that?"

He hesitated. "Like what?"

"Like I've just dropped down from another planet."

"I'm just wondering who you are and what you've done with Marilee?"

"It's still me, Wyatt." She stretched out her finger. "Why don't you try it on?"

He did as she asked.

As the ring slid onto her finger she surprised herself and him by bursting into tears.

At once he opened his arms to comfort her. "Hey now, I didn't mean to make you cry."

She flung herself into his arms. And clung. And wept. And blubbered, "Here I am, sobbing like some weak, silly teen."

All the while he held her, Wyatt's heart plummeted. This had been a mistake. Another terrible misstep that she was already regretting.

Finally, she pushed a little away.

Before she could say a word he whispered, "Look, I know you don't want to be tied down. I would never do that to you. You don't have to wear my mother's ring, or make any promises that smother you. I'll understand. I know this is all new to you, and that you're feeling a little overwhelmed by so much family. I promise you, they'll back off and give you all the space you need. And best of all, if you give them a chance, they'll love you just the way I do, and accept that you need your freedom."

When she opened her mouth he went on a little too quickly, "Don't say a thing. I know marriage isn't for everyone. And I won't press you. But I don't want to settle for a few nightly visits and a lot of good-byes for the rest of our lives. I want it all, Marilee. When you're ready, I want love, marriage, forever after. As the sheriff said, we got another chance. I don't want to squander it. I want to spend the rest of my life with you. I'll do whatever it takes . . ."

She put a hand to his mouth. "Wyatt, you don't have to convince me. If I didn't know before, I certainly know now just how foolish I'd be to throw away what we have. I want what you want. Love, marriage, forever."

He stared at her in astonishment. "You're not just saying that because it's what I want?"

"It's what I want, too."

He stared deeply into her eyes. "Oh, Marilee, you've just made me the happiest man in the world."

"And I'm the luckiest girl."

"Not girl. Woman," he growled against her mouth. "A thoroughly independent woman. And all I'll ever want in this life."

He could wait no longer to kiss her. With a sigh he dragged her close and slowly, reverently nibbled her lips, tasting the salt of her tears.

But, he thought with a soaring heart, these, at last, were happy tears.

"Aunt Cora." Holding firmly to Marilee's hand, Wyatt watched as Dandy brought in a tray of champagne glasses, as he'd requested, and began passing them around to the family members gathered there.

Everyone looked up in silence.

"Marilee and I have an announcement." He turned to Marilee, and the two of them shared a smile so radiant, it seemed to light up the entire room. "She's agreed to make me the happiest man in the . . ."

Before he could say more his cousins were slapping him on the back, and Amy was hugging Marilee like a long-lost sister.

Then it was Cal's turn to shake Wyatt's hand, while Cora embraced the young woman.

Suddenly everyone was talking at once.

The love reflected in the eyes of these two was almost blinding as their family raised their glasses in a toast to their bright, happy future.

Delia Cowling studied them and turned to Cora. "It's funny. I had the strangest feeling, when these two came to visit me, that the tears I spotted on Lee's cheeks may have been caused by more than the events of the past few days."

Cora nodded. "We were all so worried about them. We were aware that they'd quarreled, of course, but they didn't seem able to resolve it. Then Amy and I decided to have them 'meet' at your place."

Delia's eyes sparkled. "And here I thought I'd had a hand in all this." She lowered her voice. "I told them that it had been my foolish pride that had cost me the love of your brother."

Cora closed a hand over Delia's and felt a warm glow as she sipped her champagne.

Oh, Coot. Will wonders never cease? Despite her heartache, Delia seems almost the lovely young girl who owned your heart all those years ago. As for Wyatt and Marilee, I can read the happiness in their eyes. You've not only brought our family together, but you're bringing so much joy to each of us. Thank you, darling Coot. I miss you. I will always miss you. But I see your hand in all of this and I feel you here, enjoying this moment right along with me.

EPILOGUE

———◆———

Oh, just look at what you've done to this place." Amy and Cora stepped into Wyatt's suite of rooms where Marilee was arranging the last of her personal belongings.

Cora ran a hand over the baskets and masks adorning a wall of shelves in the living room.

"I think they look good there, don't you?" Marilee stood back for a better view.

"Lee, you have a real eye for decorating." Amy nodded toward the rich silk framed in black hanging on one wall.

"Thanks." Marilee gave a laugh. "I could fit my entire apartment into one of these bedrooms. This place is huge."

The three women shared a laugh.

"Speaking of your old apartment, is there a new tenant?"

Marilee nodded. "A retired Army medic. He answered

the town's ad for an ambulance driver, and he was thrilled to get a place to live in the bargain."

"Will you miss the emergency runs?" Cora asked.

"I'm sure I will at first. But living way out here, it's impossible to keep the job. Of course, on the plus side, I won't miss those calls at two in the morning."

"And what of your plane?" Amy saw a quick flash of sorrow in Marilee's eyes before she blinked it away, and she wished she'd left the question unasked.

"The insurance wasn't enough to cover buying a new one. I think I'll just keep the money in the bank and forget about flying. It doesn't seem fair, since Wyatt's such a nervous flier." She turned toward the elegant, private kitchen. "Shall I make tea?"

"There's no time. We're going to leave you to shower and get ready. Reverend Carson will be here soon." Amy turned in the doorway. "After I'm dressed, I'll come by to see if you need any help."

"Thanks." Marilee waited until the door closed before circling the rooms for a final look. Satisfied, she made her way to the master bathroom and couldn't help pausing to take in all the grand expanse of marble and glass. Wyatt's parents had definitely had a taste for the best.

As she showered and dressed, she thought about the girl who had been all over the world, always yearning for roots, for a place to call home. This was so much more than she'd ever dreamed. Not the place, though it was grand. Much more important to her was the thought of belonging to this big, raucous family. With each day they were becoming more and more dear to her.

When her hair was dry she pinned it behind one ear with a jeweled comb, leaving the soft curls to fall over the other shoulder. Her ivory gown was a simple column of silk that fell to the ankles.

Simple. That was what she'd requested when she and Wyatt made their wedding plans. Because she had no family, she was eager to embrace his. But the thought of inviting the entire town was too much to contemplate. They had agreed on hosting a dinner at holiday time that would include all their friends. But for now, Marilee was content to keep the ceremony small and intimate, with just his family, as well as Cal Randall and Delia Cowling.

Marilee had thought she could manage her nerves, but as she worked the zipper of her gown, her fingers trembled.

Maybe, she thought, some people just weren't meant to give up independence for togetherness.

This wasn't about loving Wyatt. She did love him. With all her heart.

So why this sudden flutter in the pit of her stomach? She placed a hand over the spot and prayed she wouldn't be sick.

Would she ever be able to completely give up the battle she'd fought for so long?

The fireplace of the great room was banked with masses of white hydrangeas, Marilee's favorite flowers. In the late summer heat, there was no need of a fire.

Dandy was busy preparing a wedding supper for the entire family. Wyatt had requested prime rib, and Marilee's only request was for Dandy's special carrot cake with creamy frosting. He'd baked three tiers, and instead of the traditional bride and groom on top, he'd crafted the bridal couple on a motorcycle. He smiled as he added the finishing touches. There was nothing traditional about Wyatt and Marilee. They added the perfect spice to this family.

Jesse, wearing fresh denims and shirt, poked his head in the kitchen. "Have you seen Wyatt and Zane?"

"They said they'd meet you at your special spot."

"Thanks, Dandy."

Jesse hurried out the door and across a patch of lawn until he came to the fenced-in area dotted with several headstones.

"I thought maybe you'd forgotten." Wyatt, dressed in a dark suit and tie, looked up and grinned as he began filling glasses with Irish whiskey. "Hey, cuz, you got all duded up just for me?"

Jesse laughed. "You did say this was to be a casual affair."

"I did. But I'm thinking your wife will make you change before the preacher gets here."

"You bet. And after a tug-of-war, I'm sure I'll do exactly as she asks and put on a shirt and tie."

Zane had removed his jacket in the heat and draped it over the fence before lifting his camera and motioning for the two to move closer. "Let's record this for posterity."

"Set it on a tripod and get yourself in the picture." Jesse looked over. "Is that jacket cashmere?"

Zane grinned. "A holdover from my Hollywood days."

Jesse nudged Wyatt. "You can take the boy out of Hollywood, but you can't take Hollywood out of the boy."

"Hey, it got me plenty of women. Chicks dig cashmere."

That had the three laughing as the camera recorded them holding their glasses aloft.

They looked up as Cal arrived.

"Well." He handed around cigars and held a match to the tips before snagging a tumbler of whiskey. "Here we are again, gathered for yet another wedding celebration."

They emitted rings of smoke and waited for his toast.

"Wyatt, here's to you and your bride. You've found yourself a fine woman. May the two of you have a long and happy life together."

They drank.

"And here's to Coot." Cal's voice thickened, and he paused to clear his throat. "You three have stayed the course, and kept your promise to continue his search. I'd say you've done your grandfather proud."

"To Coot." In unison the three intoned the words before taking another drink.

"And to his sister, the finest woman in the world."

At Cal's words, the three shared knowing smiles before draining their glasses.

Did he have any idea how his voice gentled whenever he spoke Cora's name? Probably not. But the others had begun to take note of it, especially since Amy and Marilee had pointed it out.

"Now," Cal said, again clearing his throat, "you three had better get up to the house. The preacher's waiting."

As they walked away Cal remained, taking a drag on the cigar, emitting a wreath of smoke, and staring at the gravesite before turning away. With a thoughtful look he trailed slowly behind.

Reverend Carson stood before the fireplace, watching as Wyatt and Marilee walked past the line of family to stand before him.

Reading from the paper he'd been given, he looked at those assembled. "Wyatt and Marilee have prepared their own vows, and ask only that we give witness." He turned to the bride. "Lee, would you like to be first?"

She faced Wyatt and wondered at the way her poor heart was hammering. But when he gave her one of those heart-stopping smiles, all the butterflies disappeared. In their place was a feeling of calm.

"Wyatt, I've spent a lifetime fighting for my independence. For my place in the universe. I didn't want to fall in love. It wasn't part of my plan. But there you were, making me laugh, making me question everything I'd worked so hard to achieve, and making me love you when I wasn't ready. I guess that's what I needed to learn. Love isn't convenient. It doesn't happen when we want it, but when we need it. And I realize now that I need you in my life. Even when I don't necessarily want you there." She took his hands. Her tone lowered to an intimate purr. "So be patient with me. It may take me a while to learn how to be part of a team. But I'm a fast learner. And I have one thing in my favor. I love you more than anyone in this world."

Delia let out a loud sigh, causing the others to smile.

Wyatt kept hold of Marilee's hands as he said solemnly, "Marilee, I've been all over the world. I told myself I was searching for adventure. What I was really

looking for was my life. I had to come back to Montana
to find myself, my roots, my home. Best of all, I found
you. You're not just my love, you're the other half of my
heart. I love you. And I give you this pledge: Even if I
smother you with love, I will honor you and your need
for independence every day of my life."

While Delia openly wept, and Cora squeezed Cal's
hand so hard he cringed, Reverend Carson spoke the
words pronouncing them husband and wife.

After a long, lingering kiss, Wyatt accepted the hand-
shakes and backslaps of his cousins, while Marilee was
hugged and kissed by the women.

A short time later they were enjoying Dandy's excellent dinner while being relentlessly teased by Jesse and
Zane, who kept the entire company laughing.

"Here's the cake you requested." Dandy rolled a
serving cart into the room, and they gathered around to
exclaim over his clever artistry.

"I think the groom looks like me." Wyatt placed
his hand over Marilee's, and together they cut the first
slice.

Soon they were enjoying the wonderful dessert while
toasting the happy couple with champagne.

"I have something I'd like to say." Marilee got to
her feet, staring around the table. "As an only child,
I often felt so alone. No brothers or sisters, no aunts
or uncles or cousins. And now, I have a sister." She
walked to Amy and the two embraced. "And brothers." She hugged Jesse and Zane, and the two kissed
her on each cheek, making the others smile. "I've even
acquired an aunt." She paused to kiss Cora's cheek.
"And good friends I know I can count on." She kissed

Cal, and then Delia. "And all of this because of you, Wyatt."

The two kissed, bringing a round of cheers from the others.

Jesse stood and lifted his glass of champagne. "I'd like to say something to my cousin and his bride . . ." He paused at the roar of a plane's engine flying directly overhead.

Marilee shot a questioning glance at Wyatt.

In reply, he gave her a mysterious smile and caught her hand. "It's about time your wedding gift made an appearance."

With the others following, he led her outside and to a waiting convoy of trucks.

"Wyatt, what on earth . . . ?"

He put a finger to her lips to silence her questions. "All in good time."

Their party drove across a meadow and paused at a newly constructed hangar and a private airstrip. Sitting on the tarmac was a bright yellow plane, the pilot standing beside it.

Seeing it, Marilee felt her eyes begin to fill while the others gathered around.

So many tears, she thought. She'd shed more in the past few days than she'd shed in a lifetime.

Wyatt kept his tone casual. "We all agreed that it was time for the Lost Nugget to step into the twenty-first century. And that meant a private airstrip and plane, to keep us up to date on our vast holdings. Who better to handle this than you, Mrs. McCord?"

"Wyatt, I know how you feel about flying. Besides, I told you I was through with it forever."

"Yes, you did. But I know your heart said otherwise. Marilee, I want you to share my life, not my fears. You love flying. It gives you a sense of freedom. I don't ever want to take that away from you."

"Oh, Wyatt." With a sob she wrapped her arms around his neck and buried her face in his throat, too overcome to find her voice.

"There's no sense fighting it any longer. You're stuck with me for a lifetime. Now . . ." He turned to the others with a grin. "If you don't mind, I think it's time my wife took me for a spin in her new plane."

"When will you be back?" Cora asked.

"An hour or two. Or until Marilee gets tired of her newfound freedom."

She looked up at him. "Are you sure you want to do this? It's your wedding day, too."

"I've never been so sure of anything in my life." Wyatt drew Marilee close. "If you ever start to worry that you're losing your independence, just kiss me and you'll see how much power you wield."

She drew back to stare at him.

At her arched brow he grinned. "If I'm Superman, then baby, you're my kryptonite. I promise you, one kiss from you and I'm so weak, you'd have to scoop me up with a spoon. So be very careful with such awesome power."

They climbed into the plane and, with their family watching and cheering, rolled down the new runway and lifted into the air, waving to those on the ground.

She turned to him. "You all right?"

"I'm fine. In fact, I'm better than fine."

This, Wyatt thought as his heart did a flip and began to settle, was exactly where he wanted to be. As the ground dropped away, and the blue sky swallowed them up, he felt a rare sense of peace. He would continue the search for the elusive treasure. It was his promise to his grandfather.

But if he never found the McCord gold, at least he'd already found, in this woman's love, the rarest treasure of all.

ABOUT THE AUTHOR

*N*ew York Times bestselling author R.C. Ryan has written more than a hundred novels, both contemporary and historical. Quite an accomplishment for someone who, after her fifth child started school, gave herself the gift of an hour a day to follow her dream to become a writer.

In a career spanning more than thirty years, Ms. Ryan has given dozens of radio, television, and print interviews across the country and Canada, and has been quoted in such diverse publications as the *Wall Street Journal* and *Cosmopolitan*. She has also appeared on CNN and ABC-TV's *Good Morning America*.

You can learn more about R.C. Ryan—and her alter ego Ruth Ryan Langan—at:

RyanLangan.com
Twitter @RuthRyanLangan
Facebook.com/RuthRyanLangan

Enjoy the best of the West with these handsome, rugged cowboys!

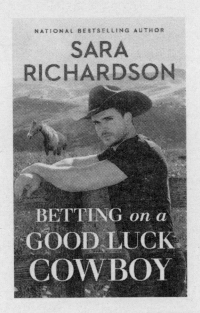

NATIONAL BESTSELLING AUTHOR
SARA RICHARDSON

BETTING *on a*
GOOD LUCK
COWBOY

BETTING ON A GOOD LUCK COWBOY
by Sara Richardson

Single mom Tess Valdez is determined to honor the memory of her late husband—so when she hears the wild horses he loved will be culled, she swears to protect them. She'll need the help of Navy SEAL Silas Beck, but Silas is leaving. He may have started working for Tess to honor his fallen friend, but now he's fallen for her, hard. He vows to finish one last mission, then go…but can Tess say goodbye to the man who opened up her heart?

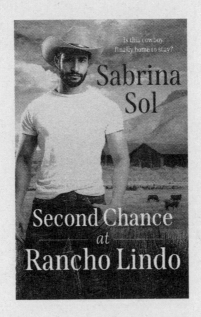

SECOND CHANCE AT RANCHO LINDO
by Sabrina Sol

After being wounded in the military, Gabe Ortega has returned home to Rancho Lindo. But he plans to leave as soon as possible—despite his family's wishes—until he runs into a childhood friend. The beautiful Nora Torres is now a horticulturist in charge of the ranch's greenhouse. She's usually a ray of sunshine, so why has she been giving him the cold shoulder? As they work together and he breaks down her walls, he starts to wonder if everything he'd been looking for has been here all along.

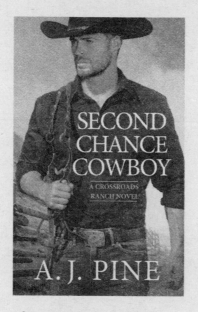

SECOND CHANCE COWBOY
by A. J. Pine

Ten years ago, Jack Everett left his family's ranch without a backward glance. Now what was supposed to be a quick trip home for his father's funeral has suddenly become more complicated. The ranch Jack can handle—he might be a lawyer, but he still remembers how to work with his hands. But turning around the failing vineyard he's also inherited? That requires working with the one woman he never expected to see again.